THE
OAQL SEED

— *Book One of the Treeboat Series* —

Z.A. ISPHARAZI

—for the denizens of the rainforest—

Like the fruit that tastes exquisite in a mouth long unfed, the heart upon tasting Presence yearns to be fed again.

—The Encyclopedia Cyanica

Prologue:

THE WANDERING LOVERS

One afternoon, bright reflections of the sun gleamed unnaturally from in between thin gaps in the dense purple-hued foliage of a forest called a *City Garden*. These places were treacherous. Footholds couldn't be trusted, the air was poisonous, and the creatures that *could* breathe the air were noxious in most ways themselves. The title given to this wilderness was a misnomer, imposed by those who wished to undermine the truth, that what they called "Gardens" were in fact utter ruins of towering cities that humanity once inhabited with great pride. That is why the presence of two human people there—in the latter half of their lifespans—was particularly odd.

Maya had long red hair, red like a ripe tomato. Her renown referenced in heroic tales often began with her hair—for redheads were a rarity in this time—but at the age of sixty-two years, it was her history of courageous deeds that really defined who she was.

Her husband, Jöshi, had defining characteristics too. He sported a long white beard and a perfectly bald head. Now, there was nothing uncommon about a beard and baldness, but the pairing of Maya and

Jöshi's striking qualities, and an air of mystery about them, all wound together into the legend of *the Wandering Lovers, Madam Red, and Mr. Snow*, in many communities around the world.

More history was being made in the remote City Garden, as these two intrepid souls made their way up the corpses of buildings, which formed squarish hills and a profusion of sheer cliffs under a shroud of soil, plants, a network of thick vines, and trees that grew in defiance of their unnatural foundation. Trudging up one of these hills at an angle of nearly seventy degrees Maya and Jöshi finally had to stop and take some deep, labored breaths through their respiration masks.

"Please dear, keep your mask on," said Jöshi noticing that Maya had impatiently released the pressure of her mask.

"I can't use my nose under this thing," Maya replied like a child caught playing with fire.

"We agreed that we'd rely on tech for this expedition," said Jöshi as he raised his thin eyebrows and the lines along his scalp deepened. "Remember, we have people waiting for us back home."

"Oh, don't get sentimental now."

Maya re-pressurized the mask and started walking again, keeping her eyes fixed on a handheld device that shot out a green light that slowly undulated as it scanned the ground. It was only after a few minutes that they arrived upon a plateau that she stopped, put her scanner away in a brown satchel across her chest, and crouched down over something silver gleaming through the soil and roots of the vegetation of the jungle. "This seems to be it," she said, looking up at him. "Are you ready?"

"Months of investigation brought us to this point, and yet my knees shake when I consider that our hunch might be correct," Jöshi replied.

He pulled up his sleeves and sank down to his knees beside her, pulling out a sharp hunting knife and crowbar from his own satchel. They began digging into the earth, cutting through tough roots, soon revealing that what had seemed to be a shiny object was only a portion of a larger underground structure.

"We could be digging for years," Jöshi said loudly, wiping the sweat from around the corners of his mask. The chiming of insects seemed to grow out of the humidity of the air itself.

"We've nothing left but to trust our sources," Maya replied. "The map indicated that this was the south-central entrance to the laboratory in this city."

"And how many generations ago was the map made? We don't know if it was the most recently updated version either."

"But it's all we have."

"We're not as young as we'd like to think we are, Maya. It'll be hard to keep this up, let alone survive in this forsaken place for much longer."

Maya wiped the sweat from around her own mask and chuckled, "Always the optimist, aren't you, honey? I need some water."

"Use the tube to drink, and don't take off your mask!" Jöshi called out after her.

She raised her hand dismissively as she rose and stood for a moment, analyzing the trees nearby. She chose one with a girthy trunk, coiling branches, thin needle-shaped leaves, and finally a sign, which made Maya smile and say, "A little blessing for our task." She was speaking of an almost imperceptible powdery golden glow that eminated in instants from different parts of the tree. At times it was high above the ground amidst the leaves before appearing closer to the earth where the tree's serpentine roots rose high out of the ground. She took off her satchel and placed it down on the ground, and then taking a larger travel pack off her back, she detached a coil of rope from it. Pacing around, looking at the branches above, she finally chose a sturdy looking one to throw some of the rope coil over. Where the rope landed, she walked over and gathered it up, tying it to her travel pack, which she then proceeded to hoist up high and out of reach.

From Jöshi's vantage point, Maya had her hands on her hips, her back toward him, and it looked like she was admiring her work. He shook his head and smiled. *How could someone change so little?* He thought to himself, admiring how her lean frame was virtually unchanged from the first time he saw her forty-three years ago. When she disappeared behind the tree, Jöshi got back to digging.

And she, as soon as she was sure Jöshi couldn't see her, sank down to her knees and sat still for a time, clutching at her chest and breathing with difficulty. Frustrated, she pulled the mask off her face. Though she could take in more air now, the quality of the air made her take breaths with discomfort anyway. Acridity filled her mouth, reminding her of the taste of rusty metal and battery cylinders when she worked at a tech shop for salvaged materials years ago, often using her mouth as a third hand.

After a few minutes, Jöshi called out to her, "Bring me the laser-knife. I think I've found a spot where I can cut into it."

"One moment," Maya replied, getting to her feet, fixing the mask over her face again. "You better be sure because firing it up once more will drain the rest of its charge."

Jöshi demonstrated his certainty by stomping on a part of the uncovered surface. Loud, hollow echoes filled the air.

"You hear that?" he shouted.

"That I do!" she replied. She turned back to the tree and lowered the pack down and extracted something from a side pocket covered in a tattered gray cloth, about the length of her forearm.

A minute later, she returned to the dig site. She handed Jöshi the tool still covered in the cloth. As he took it, he did a double take of her. Though most of her face was concealed by her oxygen mask, the strain in her eyes and her unusually crouched posture made his mouth sink into a frown.

"This is it," he said. "If this doesn't work, we're leaving."

He unwrapped the laser-knife from its sheath. It looked like a large butcher's knife from a distance, but upon closer inspection, the blade was much wider, and where its sharp edge would have been, there was a minute gap with a green light glowing in it. Taking hold of it with a firmer grip now, Jöshi flipped a switch at the butt of the handle, and the green light along the edge of the blade turned bright red.

He didn't waste another second, plunging the laser-knife into the unnaturally silver surface smeared in the remnants of the moist earth they had dug through. Soon the blade's whole length was in up to the hilt. Ignoring the sizzling sounds, the smell of burning, and a chalky taste, he cut horizontally until he had carved out a large imperfect circle.

"That was easy enough," he said just as the laser-knife began blinking red. "That's it; it's about to die." Then, it was blinking green, and finally it switched off completely.

The little suction pads Maya provided him were attached to the surface of the metal, and they pulled the freshly cut trap door open with surprising strength—as compared to most people their age. Looking down into it at first revealed nothing but darkness, but when they leaned down closer, heads poking into the hole, they saw dim white lights flickering below like stars in a clear night sky. This gave them a sense of reverse vertigo, as if they found a hole in the earth that led out straight to the vastness of the universe.

"Alright; let's set up the cable and lower me down," Maya said resolutely. They both made their way over to the tree she had selected and Jöshi attached his own pack to the rope hoist, but before raising them out of reach, they unpacked an array of travel-size gadgets and carefully organized materials like color-coordinated cords, little light emitting glowterns that could be worn like necklaces, and two sets of detachable cleats for their boots.

Within a few minutes, they were ready. One end of a thin but extremely durable cable-rope was tied around the trunk of a girthy tree near the hole, while Jöshi wound some of the slack of the cable around his waist through a friction and ratchet device attached to his belt. The other end was attached to Maya around her leg, torso, and right shoulder. She was wearing her brown satchel again, her cargo-pants pockets were full, and she zipped up her vest that she wore over spandex material that clung to her muscular body.

She tied her hair up into a tall bun and positioned herself at different distances, progressively getting farther away from Jöshi, testing the integrity of the connection by pulling the rope with all her weight by squatting down to the ground initiated by sudden leaps backward. Each time the rope tightened, Jöshi braced himself, never letting her bottom touch the ground.

"Seems sturdy," Maya said. "I'm going in."

"You sure you don't want me to go?" Jöshi asked, in a soft voice he used only when he spoke to her. He walked up to her and stroked his hands over her head to push back a few stray red hairs that drifted free of her hair tie.

"It would be more difficult for me to pull you up," she replied. Her tone would sound cold to many who weren't familiar with her, but she spoke the same way to everyone, including her grandchild, who she would give up her life for in an instant and who she missed dearly.

They walked over to the hole they had cut, positioned themselves, and with a final nod Maya pushed herself off the edge without hesitation. Jöshi gave her some slack, and so the rappelling process began.

Maya noticed that the air was cooler below. Initially, it was distinctly silent as the jungle sounds above were drowned out by the immense chamber she was in, but as she got to about seven meters below the surface, she became aware of a faint hum. Around her neck, was her dimmed spherical glowtern; she turned up its brightness by swiping her hand across it, revealing towers of silver and white all around her. They lined glistening walls that stretched out of sight, forming long shadowy corridors.

"The Old World still lives," she whispered to herself. "Amazing. None of the roots of the forest were able to penetrate the dome."

At about fifteen meters, she became aware of the floor, a shiny, reflective surface. She looked up and could no longer see the dome above, just an inky darkness. She was about thirty meters below when she unfastened herself from the cord just above the ground and dropped only a few centimeters. Her cleated boots clicked against the floor uncomfortably. She immediately decided she'd be taking them off. Then she gave the cable three firm tugs and waited. Three opposite pulls came in reply.

With one last tug of the cord, she turned and stood for a moment and gazed at the work of her distant ancestors with quiet deliberation as any sound she made felt compressed and unnaturally contained within the massive and yet somehow limited atmosphere. She recognized the engineering and materials used in the cityforts around the world—like Citadelia and Atlantia—but those constructions, impressive as they were, paled in comparison to what she was seeing now, hidden below the City Garden ruins. She felt as though she had stumbled into a tomb that had remained untouched for millennia, a bit of the past miraculously left intact.

She took out her little scanner device from her trusty satchel again, this time pressing a triangular button upon its surface. A small holographic projection of a map shimmered into being above the device. According to her research, these ancient laboratories were part of a family of architectural design replicated across many sites thousands of years ago. The map showed a concentric ring structure of corridors, with entrances to chambers at the center. Even if her map wasn't an exact blueprint for this particular lab, the idea, or the hope, was that it would prove accurate enough to guide her through any related facilities.

Maya turned left. Walking briskly, she could see her blurry reflection along the shiny walls. The sound of her hard rubber soles clomping along the floor echoed through the halls. A little farther along, she was relieved to see that nature had in fact penetrated this human-made world. Bulbous, brown-and-bruise-purple fungi had created a superficial ecosystem along the floors and walls, wherever it was able to take hold on the smooth, artificial surfaces.

After about twenty more minutes of walking slowly as she referenced her map, she came to large, partially transparent doors. She could see the orange glow of lights behind them, but the material was cloudy, so she couldn't see much else.

She went up to the doors and tried looking for a handle or keypad, but there was nothing. She found where the two doors met, but they were touching so tightly that she could barely wedge her fingernails into the seam. She stood pensive for a time, becoming aware of the humming sound of machinery again that sounded too clear and too uncluttered, compared to the salvaged motors she used to bring back to life. She took a deep breath and was about to give up trying to get through when a familiar sensation tickled at the back of her head.

Reaching out until her hand was just a few centimeters from the doors, she grew still, let her vision blur, and extended her awareness to the tingling sensation that had now spread to her fingertips. *Open*, she commanded with her mind. Coming into focus again, she saw the cloudiness of the doors clearing, leaving them completely transparent within seconds. Then, the doors slid open as if along slick ice. Maya's heart sank at this, but she moved forward resolutely, her jaw muscles clenched tight.

What she saw next made her stomach clench. In a large tank, made of the same transparent glass-like material as the entrance doors, floated a large humanoid figure with disproportionate arm to leg length in white neon liquid. Maya couldn't make out any details, for the material was cloudy and the bright white light of the tank silhouetted the form, but the shape of the head was round—too round—the arms were very long, reaching past its hips, and the mid-torso and legs were very thin. And something else was also clear. From the bubbles filling the tanks, the glowing lights of the machinery, and the occasional twitching of the body, it was evident that everything in the room was functional.

The creature was alive.

As soon as this realization dawned upon Maya, the tingling sensation at the back of her head returned, and suddenly there was a great pull of appetency for awareness coming from the creature; the transparent material of the tank began clearing just as the doors into the lab had done in response to Maya's command. As if hit by a gale of wind from behind, Maya staggered in place as her leg muscles contracted against some unseen force moving her toward the glowing cylinder. The naked form of the creature slowly became more visible as the white light of the tank began to dim and the clouded glass began to clear. It had a gray skin tone and lack of key human features in terms of glandular tissue at the chest and reproductive glands between the legs. Maya desperately withheld her consciousness from the psychically ravenous organism and refused to issue the command *OPEN* that kept trying to sneak into her mind.

Back at the noisy and humid surface of the City Garden, Jöshi was sitting cross legged by the opening of the hole. His eyes were closed, but he was extraordinarily alert to his surroundings and to Maya somewhere below him. He could sense that she had traveled some three kilometers away to the west and that she was suddenly struggling against something minacious. It had been nearly an hour since he had lowered her down and all had been tranquil up until then. With a swelling chest, a stern frown, and nostrils flaring with the intake of oxygen through his mask, Jöshi bent his awareness full tilt toward Maya.

Below, Maya's heart fluttered with a sensation that she had first felt when Jöshi told her he loved her back when Madam Red and Mr. Snow didn't exist, back when she was just Maya Airgialla of the Enané, and he was naive Jöshi Halla of Halla Manor. Following a deep, trembling breath, Maya was promptly bolstered in such a way that she felt the tension loosen in her body. The nonphysical tug from within the tank lingered, but now it felt like an infirm solicitation. Her eyes still closed, she could feel Jöshi's presence withdrawing gently, but she was back in control now.

State your identity and purpose, Maya telepathically commanded the creature. The response was faint in her mind, as if it was having difficulty tuning into her, but finally a message came through with programmed cadence.

Identity: Eldeshian of the West Atlantic Sector. Purpose: to serve you, Master.

Maya's brow tensed and she shook her head. *I am not your master,* she said.

You are human. Therefore, you are my master.

And what are you?

Eldeshian: a humanoid intelligence.

What were you created to do?

Purpose: to serve you, Master.

Maya pursed her lips. *What is the current era of the earth?*

Era, date: Disconnect from the NTN—Neural Time Network—makes this question impossible to answer. Last connectivity date registers as the Aquarian Era by reckoning of constellation mapping within the 3rd millennium, 22nd century, 2105 December 31ST 23:59.

At this, Maya opened her eyes in surprise. What the Eldeshian had just communicated meant that this lab beneath the City Garden, the ruins above, and the Eldeshian itself were more ancient than she had ever conceived. By her reckoning, she was standing in a chamber that was some 14,600 years old.

Maya closed her eyes and reconnected with the Eldeshian within the tank.

Tell me all that you know about our world, she said.

Eldeshian of the West Atlantic Sector has never left incubation and disconnect from Neural Network renders this impossible.

How do you know I'm human?

Your biosignature confirms this.

Can you override my commands as your master?

There was a pause—only a measly extra second—that Maya distinctly noticed.

Then the reply came, *Only when it is in your best interest.*

That was all Maya needed to hear. She opened her eyes and looked at the twitching gray figure within the tank for a moment. Then, when she moved to turn toward the rest of the lab where glowing controls and screens lay embedded in shiny adamantine surfaces; the pull from within the tank suddenly grew in intensity again.

Then came the voice of the Eldeshian, it was louder in her head this time, *OPEN.*

Maya replied, *As your master, I say no.*

Overridden: Release from incubation is in the best interest for you and your species.

I disagree!

Maya overwhelmed the force emanating from inside the tank, but this was not an act of pushing away; it was a counter pull, a taking away of the vital force that pulled at her own. A burst of energy filled her mind and body. Her mind was clear now; she was not at all engaged with the creature in any tangible sense anymore. The fog of the transparent material of the tank slowly become opaquer and the lights grew brighter again.

She now made her way toward the control panels that glowed with an eerie respiratory rhythm. She quickly removed her face mask as it had fogged up and she didn't want to waste any time. She was relieved to find that the acridity that filled the air out in the City Garden was not present here.

Above, at the snap of a twig from somewhere not too far away behind him, Jöshi opened his eyes and, with the most steady and intentional of movements, took his time to reposition the lid onto the hole and walked to the tree where their travel packs were left hanging. He climbed up, giving the cord around his waist some extra slack as it trailed down the tree, along the grass, and into the hole that led into the underground lab. Then he waited in silence, taking a moment now and then to become of aware of Maya, who seemed to be back in control.

Minutes later, a medium-sized doglike creature came sniffing along the ground. It had unassuming brown fur and boney legs but glinting at its mouth were two protruding fangs. It was a scout for its pack, and though Jöshi could have terminated it with ease, with either his crowbar or hunter's knife, a single howl or bark would have their location crawling with its companions.

The creature sniffed the air and then the ground, exactly where Jöshi had been on the ground. Then, it sniffed at the edges of the metal dome and the hole Jöshi had cut into it. At this, it lowered its ears and quickly scampered away.

A few moments later, a squirming sensation in Jöshi's gut told him that Maya had completed her mission and was heading back toward the entry point. Jöshi waited an extra couple of minutes and then quickly climbed down the tree and ran to the hole, prying the lid open again. The tug from below came after thirty minutes or so. He set up his ratchet mechanism and began pulling Maya up, using a crank that utilized the tension of the cord wrapped around the tree. With each click of the ratchet, Jöshi hoped that the dog-creature wouldn't return with its pack too soon.

After he lifted Maya out of the hole, they embraced for a few seconds.

Then she pulled her head back and looked into his eyes. "It's all older than we thought, but we were right correct in assuming that the technological societies of Dooña-Proto created things they couldn't control—*beings* they couldn't control."

At this, Jöshi lowered his gaze solemnly.

She continued, "I've shut down the power to everything I could find, but imagine, each City Garden must have a laboratory like this one below it. There's no way you and I could visit each one alone."

"And who knows if we're doing the right thing? Should we even be shutting these things down at all?"

"I don't know. I erred on the side of caution because if these beings, these Eldeshians, are somehow related to Revalo's plan, then we have to do everything we can to stop him. Besides, the one that I encountered below is dangerous, especially to those who have no prowess in the faculties of the mind—"

Jöshi picked up on her train of thought and added, "The kind of people Revalo gathers—those within the cityforts."

Maya nodded in confirmation.

Jöshi sighed deeply, fogging his mask. "I hope that Delamina, Jiji, and their team find some answers soon. I don't know where they are anymore, but that young man Iloy—who divulged Revalo's intentions—is safe with her at least.

"Anyway, tell me more later. We have to get out of here. We've had a visit from a wolfcoon that looked pretty hungry to me."

Maya was still lost in her thoughts though, and she spoke them aloud, "It looks like we don't have time to take the voyage back to Lindum. We're not going home yet."

Jöshi bit his lip and nodded. "It's not completely unexpected, and at least we didn't make any promises."

Maya shook her head and stepped away from Jöshi, her hands on her hips. "But that's just it. I wish we had told Navis and the children everything about us before we left. It was a mistake to leave them ignorant of everything. We really do think of ourselves as younger than we are."

"Hey, that's my job," Jöshi said, his eyes smiling from behind his mask, trying to cheer her up. "You just lead on as you do, love. I don't know what I'd do if we *both* became cynical grumps."

This made Maya let out a single breathy chuckle that fogged her mask. They stopped talking then, moving quickly to wrap up their cords, lowered their pack from the tree, and shut the lid they had made to the laboratory below.

As the sun sank and grew golden, the shadows of the City Garden deepened, and the yips, howls, and gurgles of the forest teeming with hungry creatures grew in intensity. Maya kept up with Jöshi, following close behind him, as they made their way downhill under the canopy of the gnarled, violet shaded trees, but her expression was grim, and her breaths were labored again.

Chapter 1

ARRIVAL AND TAKEOFF
AT SEA WILLOW AISLE

The sky was dark, with a touch of deep purple. The little bayside town of Lindum lay still. Only the sounds of water lapping against the docks and a few scattered chirps from the leafy trees along the brick-lined avenues disturbed the silence. A cobblestone road ran from the gates of the town toward the hills and the wilderness of pines beyond, tapering into a dirt trail at its border. This path was well trodden, and the grassy knolls to either side were well inhabited by those folks who chose to live on the outskirts of town in little cabins, away from gossip and politics.

On the farthest inhabited hillock stood a worn but well-tended cabin surrounded by a field of tall grass woven through with purple and white morning-glory vines and the occasional pine tree. The cabin seemed tiny under the majesty of the colossal Lindarious Mountains, coming to light not too far in the distance.

At the bottom of this hillock, a rocky, muddy passage descended west toward uninhabited shores where a complex of inlets and streams connected Miner's Bay to the sea. The necessary precautions were to be taken here, mostly peppermint oil and salvia smoke to ward off insects and, at times, a machete in case a wildcat was to feel plucky on a particular prey-scarce night. Still, the forests sprinkled around the bay and along the Lindarious valley, and the streams that ran through them had their regular visitors: fishermen, hunters, mushroom foragers, woodsmen, and even children who pursued secretive adventures against the wishes of their parents.

Before the sun had begun to warm the world, one such regular visitor was running under the perpetual shade of the pine forest canopy, her bright red hair trailing wildly behind her and eyes puffy from a long, restless night. That morning, she wore the distinguishing smirk that had contributed to her reputation among parents of other adolescents her age as "trouble."

Some distance behind her came another child, three years her junior at nine years old, who evidently was not pleased to be up so early. Every so often, he stopped to lean on a tree, scratch his sweaty scalp through his brown curls, catch his breath, and call out, "Ari! Can't you slow down at least?"

"Just there—you see them, Lemay?" she called back excitedly, pointing toward the water where a subtle golden glimmer flashed in and out of perception just over the surface.

At first, he squinted with curiosity but when the undulating golden dust and the multicolored insects that he had seen so many times came into focus he sighed and said, "Those are just pond-sprites and insects Ari."

At this boring logic, Arionella only rolled her eyes and continued to run at top speed toward the Aisle, a tributary lined by bushy sea willows.

The waters of Miner's Bay and its feeders in these parts were always a translucent algae-green due to the weedy beds that grew in their depths. The bay had received its name from the endless stores of pink-salt the locals mined from the great Lindarious Mountains and then shipped to various ports across the Cyan Sea where merchants paid happily for the reputed seasoning.

Lemay arrived at the Aisle a good minute or so after Arionella, who had longer legs than he did, which made it all the harder for him to keep her out of trouble. Arionella waved him over silently while, with her other hand, she pressed a finger to her lips.

There were only plush beds of moss underfoot, but Lemay tiptoed in his sandals anyway.

"Is the boat here yet?" he whispered when he got close enough to the decaying log she was crouching behind.

"Shh. No, not yet."

Dawn had finally arrived. The few glowing bands of sunlight accented the ripples of the green water with orange highlights, while dragonflies zipped over its surface. A cool breeze came from the north, making the sea willows rustle and dance. Their long, thin branches floated far across the surface of the water.

The erratic flight of the dragonflies continued. They hovered in the breeze at times, riding its currents like sea birds floating on choppy waters. Whether by the light of the sun or their own inner fluorescence, the dragonflies began to twinkle in varying shades of neon blues, golds, reds, and yellows that flashed in bright, colorful instants. The shady avenue of willows was now a show of motion and pretty lights as the great trees came to life by the glow of the rising sun and fresh breezes that came with it.

Arionella tensed and craned her neck, looking for any sign of movement down the glimmering path of water that stretched away down and around jutting pieces of land. "Shouldn't be long now," she whispered.

Lemay sank lower behind their precarious rampart. "Ari, what's going to happen?"

"I told you not to come!" she hissed. "I told you that you'd be scared."

"I'm not scared." He didn't sound too convincing, but his brow was furrowed, and his fists were clenched. "I just think that you don't know what you're doing."

She didn't reply this time; her eyes were fixed on something ahead of her. A figure, at the far end of the winding tributary, loomed forward out of the mist rising up over the water. The children's bodies tightened into goose pimples as its presence reminded them of a bear they had accidently startled on a mountain trail some weeks ago. Its great silhouette looked as if a *tree* had broken off the shore and—still upright—had been carried off on the current. Lemay shut his eyes tight and crouched even lower behind the log, while Arionella looked like she was waiting for the opportune moment to pounce out from behind it.

As the floating mass easily followed a bend in the tributary, a square glow appeared through the shimmers of the mist. The dim light revealed the outline of a white wooded boat gliding along the water.

"Look!" said Arionella. "It's a tree. A tree in the middle of a boat!"

Lemay poked his head out from behind the log. "That's strange. I don't see anyone on the boat." He was all caution.

"Look!" Arionella repeated. "There's a cabin onboard. I think someone's inside!" The source of the light was revealed, for at the far end of the boat stood a small cabin with a square window with a candle glowing behind it.

"What?" Lemay asked as he craned his head out farther. The tree and the boat—or, rather, the treeboat—was close now. As it pulled up to the shore, the water and plant matter of the shallows made thudding sounds on its hull, and the sound of gentle waltz music crackled through the otherwise hushed morning air.

"Do you hear that?" Lemay asked. "There's music playing."

"I hear it too. Didn't I tell you something was going to happen?"

"How did you know?"

"I already told you—I had a dream."

"I thought you were making something up to 'go on an adventure,' as usual."

"Well, now you know I wasn't—Look! Someone's come out of the cabin!"

A woman with long black hair in a white button-down shirt and light-blue linen pants rolled up just above her ankles was twirling around the boat barefooted. Arionella and Lemay watched in mute wonder as she did a figurative dance to a waltz that was increasingly becoming more dramatic. Right on cue with a crescendo, she tossed one end of a rope to the shore and, with a flick of her head, whipped her hair over her shoulder. Her hidden spectators found themselves moved to giggles at her antics. She reminded them of Uncle Navis when he was in a good mood. And so, they found themselves wondering if all youngish adults behaved like this when they thought no one was watching. Then the lady on the boat sprang lightly into the water, pulled the boat a bit closer to land by its long brown rope, and tied it to a tree on the shore. Her feet were still bare, and her figure was draped by clothes a few sizes too large for her—though to Arionella the woman looked and moved as she imagined a princess would, each movement accented with an extra flourish, as if there were invisible harp strings to be plucked all around.

The woman of the treeboat climbed back aboard, disappearing behind the door of the cabin for a minute. She reemerged with worn brown boots on and a knitted cloth sack strung across her chest. She hopped off the boat again, looked to her right and left—straight past her audience of two—and then strode off into the shadows of the bushy sea willows, whose branches closed behind her like a curtain.

"Looks like she's gone," Arionella said.

"What if there's someone else on the boat?" Lemay asked in reply.

They looked at the treeboat as it bobbed gently on the water. The tree definitely wasn't one of the sea willows along the shore. Though it did have many dangling vines attached to its crown, its leaves and branches were arranged more like a plump broccoli.

"You keep watch," Arionella said to Lemay. I'm going to check it out."

"No, don't!" he said and grasped her arm.

"Let go, you scaredy cat."

"Ari, no!"

"You saw her—she seemed nice. I saw you laughing when she danced."

"So? That doesn't mean anything! What if she's a witch looking for kids like us to steal away?"

"Don't be ridiculous. My grandmother's practically a witch and she's the nicest, most special person you could ever meet."

"Doesn't mean they're all that way, silly. Besides, she could be back any moment."

"Just a quick look then," and with that, Arionella twisted her arm out of Lemay's grasp and jumped over the log. She ran ahead for the first few steps but slowed herself to a crawl as she approached the water. The music from the boat had now turned into a mysterious arrangement of violins playing minor notes, as if providing soundtrack to the sneaking child moving like a fox on an evening hunt.

The edge of the boat stood a full arm's length above her head. Standing on tiptoe, she reached up and got a firm grip. She looked back and saw Lemay's little reprimanding head, shaking vigorously at her above the log. Then, with a grin, she jumped and—with legs scrabbling on the hull—pulled herself aboard.

The moment she landed on the boat, a tingling sensation trailed through her sandals from the base of her feet, up her shoulders, and lingered for a moment like static in her hair. Shaking it off, she rebalanced herself and tried to breathe her adrenaline down. The interior of the wooden boat was white like the exterior, a creamy shade that was natural to the timber. There was nothing onboard except for a few more coils of the brown, manila-hemp rope the dancing lady had used to tie the boat to shore.

Arionella moved toward the tree at the center, shuddering with excitement as the baseboards groaned beneath her feet. In the cracks and corners of the timber, little flowers, grasses, and what appeared to be the roots of the tree itself were sprouting from and embedded in the frame of the boat. Farther ahead, around the base of the tree, large roots rose up in lumps, with a covering of a circular carpet of moss and plants growing all over them. The warm light of the cabin behind the tree spilled through its leaves, vines, and branches, making it glow eerily like the dusty windows of Madam Shagufta's old cottage at the east edge of town. Arionella had convinced the majority of children in Lindum that Madam Shagufta was a bad witch, one that captured children for use in stews that she would then serve at the market in Lindum. This should make it clearer where Lemay's fears about witches came from.

She skirted the tree with a skip, as goose pimples erupted all over her skin again, and walked toward the cabin, which was made of the same white wood as the rest of the boat. The window nearest to her was situated above her head. Standing on tiptoe, she was able to see inside. There was an elaborate display of brass instruments, figurines, and all sorts of paints, brushes, pencils, and stacks of curled, water-stained paper.

She went up to the door, turned the ovular doorknob, and went inside.

Back on shore, Lemay rubbed his eyes and blinked a few times. He was standing now and leaning forward over the log. With a cool breeze came the sound of the music from the boat—a distant, joyful waltz again. More wind swept in from all directions. The dragonflies and pond sprites were gone. The thin branches of the sea willows whipped around, the surface of the water bristled and spat, the treeboat lurched, and Lemay's curly brown hair was tossed about. With a final gust of wind against his face, and a loud cracking sound, his eyes seemed to clear of some subtle veil.

Lemay let out a shout of wide-eyed terror. "Ari!!"

He leapt over the rotten trunk and ran to the edge of the water. To his horror, the treeboat was farther from shore than he'd thought—and it was picking up speed.

"Ari! The boat's come loose! Arionella!" But his voice was lost in the sweeping winds. He plunged into the churning waters, and though he never was adept off dry land, he swam toward the large and receding silhouette of the treeboat. The water was freezing cold. His arms and legs progressively stiffened, and soon he was under the surface of the salty water more than he was above it.

The light of the treeboat faded as it drifted around a bend. Lemay cried out, struggling as his legs cramped. Then a small yet ferocious wave plunged him underwater. Though he clawed skyward with all his strength, he sank farther and farther into the deep. In a stretch of timeless agony, his mind and body were lit with fires of suffocation and despair. But just as he was about to lose his breath, his feet met something hard that he was able to push off of and, as his head breached the water's surface and he gulped for air, the tide receded briefly.

Lemay swam and then crawled desperately toward shore, sputtering and coughing all the way. When he was safely away from the reach of the waves, he collapsed on the ground, puking up water and losing consciousness for momentary spells. Finally, at the thought of Arionella, he regained a firm hold of his awareness. He willed himself to stand.

Then, with heavy steps, he rushed back home, knowing that with every passing minute Arionella was drifting farther and farther away.

About twenty minutes later, the dancing woman of the treeboat returned. At first, she thought she had gotten lost because there was no sign of the vessel she had arrived on. She stood and blinked for a few moments and then walked away before returning and stepping a few feet into the water. She hurried over to where she remembered tying the boat, but to her dismay, she found that the tree she had tied it to along the shore had snapped.

"Argh, termites! I shouldn't have let that damn boat out of my sight!"

She plodded back to dry land and began pacing back and forth with her hands on her hips. "Think, Taola, think!" she said aloud in frustration. She paused and looked out over the tributary, tapping her finger on a large oval locket that hung from a silver chain around her neck.

At least I've collected some salt and had a few licks, she thought to herself. *I can think a little clearer now—otherwise, I never would've tied it down to such a precarious hold. That Oaql tree always has plans of its own. I mean, how long has it been—only thirty minutes since I left it?*

Without a captain it's surely going to make its way to the nearest Haelin Island. So maybe it's time I activate this seed after all. She lowered her arms to her side and balled her hands into fists. *First, I'll need a proper boat.*

With that, the dancing woman of the treeboat hastened to find the town of Lindum, which she'd seen on her map initially, and had avoided on purpose.

Arionella at Sea
I. "I'm on an Adventure."

Inside the cabin on the treeboat, Arionella was fiddling with a carved figurine of a horse made from more of the same white wood of the boat.

Earlier, peeking through the window of the cabin hadn't revealed the corridor, and a small staircase that led up to a loft. Also, there were levels of shelves built into the walls containing books, instruments, tinctures, and a milieu of artifacts.

"This is great!" Arionella said aloud, her voice blending with the music that issued from a piece of technology, the likes of which she had never seen before. It was composed of a black disk spinning around slowly and a little shiny stylus with a needle tip that was dragging along its surface. When she touched it, a loud scratching sound made her jerk back and completely disrupt the music. Outside, the music had sounded distant and tinny; inside it had been rich and heavy—now only a compressed silence remained. Arionella turned away from the device, left to lopsidedly spin the strange disk. She marveled at the mobiles that hung all around. Some were little wooden carvings of treeboats hung on stick and string, revolving around elaborate carvings of little islands, and others were of birds, four legged creatures, and even humans. Arionella looked through a brass telescope, wound a music box that cut the silence with a tinny lullaby, and she sniffed at various jars of perfume. "No one will believe me." Arionella gazed around for a few moments and then gasped, "Lemay has to see this!"

As Arionella burst through the door, the warm September wind rushed through her red hair. She ran to the edge of the boat. As her eyes adjusted to the light of day, she was appalled to find that she was out on the Cyan Sea, already far from land. A sense of desperation followed a sinking feeling in her chest as she tried to recognize the mess of vegetation along the shore.

"Oh gawd!" Arionella cried out suddenly. "This is worse than when I melted Mrs. Botson's clay sink! Even worse than when I left Mr. Pierson's goat pen open!" Arionella was pacing relentlessly. Thoughts ran through her mind: *Uncle Navis will be mad, but I know how to deal with him. Lemay is the one who will never let up—I'll be an old hag someday and he won't let me forget it. And what about the lady whose boat this is? What if she really is a witch like Lemay thought, and not a nice one?* Arionella looked around nervously from one end of the boat to the other. There was no sign of a wheel to steer with, only two oars, which were giant in size relative to Arionella, on each side. *Surely, I can't row the whole boat.* Arionella tried to remember if she had seen a steering wheel inside the cabin. She went back to look.

There was the workstation by the window to the left of the entrance. To the right was a dimly candle lit corridor that led to a kitchen, and another door opening to a bathroom tiled with aqua-green stone, a large clay sink and a toilet that smelled of sawdust.

Arionella nipped at her fingernails, bewildered by the seeming absence of a control room—*unlike every damn boat in the harbor!* And yet, as her eyes caught sight of the carvings and mobiles hanging from the ceiling, bathed in the warm light of the room, her heart fluttered with something beyond fear.

I'm on an adventure. The words soundlessly formed on her lips, and then her hand fell away from her mouth and she repeated aloud with delight, "I'm on a *real* adventure!"

Chapter 2

STARTLING NEWS

Though the cabin was still out of sight, a familiar sound came to Lemay's ears. Like a trombone, the sound of a table being pushed, and a din of children's laughter echoed across the rolling hills.

A few seconds more and Lemay appeared over a shadowy knoll. The sunlight had fallen upon the stable beside the cabin, the random bales of hay had a dusty glow, and the morning larks fluttered about collecting their breakfast. He made his way toward the garden in the backyard—he didn't notice the little head poking through the back doorway of the cabin. Exhausted, he finally made it to the veranda door and stepped into the dark and dusty end of the cabin, where boxes full of junk were stored. He could hear the radio in the far room playing the merry folk music of Lindum.

Suddenly, a voice rose up in a shout, amidst lights and noise, "Halt thief! The noble troop of the Bay will bring you to justi—"

The theatrical cry choked off. Two children, on the cusp of growing out of toddlerhood, were brandishing spatulas, wooden spoons, and pans, and a tall young man wearing an iron cooking pot on his head, stood frozen at the sight of Lemay, drenched and looking ghostly pale before them. A pan slipped out of someone's hand and landed with a crash—which startled everyone out of the spell of silence.

"Are you alright, buddy?" the young man asked, taking the pot off his head awkwardly to reveal a puff of curly, golden-brown hair. He knelt before Lemay and put a hand on Lemay's shoulder. "Myli told us you were home, and we thought we'd surprise you."

"Uncle Navis," Lemay said through chattering teeth. "I told Ari not to get on the boat at the Aisle. Then I was trying to save her from the boat. But, but . . . now it's gone!"

"Wait, where's Arionella?" Navis's voice dropped.

"She's on a boat that has sailed away!" Lemay said and broke into tears.

"What boat?"

"The dancing lady's boat!" he sobbed out. The two small children glanced through their long blond bangs from Lemay to Navis, as they had many times before when Lemay would come home and tattle on Arionella. This time, however, even they could feel that the energy in the room was different—and that Lemay's tears were copious and sincere.

Navis sprang into action. He fetched a towel from a closet, wrapped Lemay up in its folds, and then carried him to a chair near the wood-burning stove. Hastening into the kitchen, he grabbed a glowtern, stringing it around his neck. The little boy and girl had been running after him the whole time, creating a bedlam of clattering kitchenware and voices shouting at once. Navis himself was saying aloud to everyone and no one, "*Always* getting into trouble, that one! She's got to be leashed!"

At one point, Navis was at the front door, but the little girl Myli, had wrapped herself around his leg, insisting that she wanted to go find "Ari" with him.

"Yes, yes. I was just going to saddle up Gretch and Gomer," said Navis as he lifted Myli up, walked across the shaky porch down the two wide steps, and took her over to a hitch that had hay in it. "Now sit here and wait until I get your brothers."

After getting Lemay changed into dry clothes, Navis shepherded him and his little brother Tumy to the wagon, which he attached to Gretch and Gomer, his—currently very sleepy—mules. Navis settled himself at the front, gave the reins a shake, and set out for Lindum with as much speed as he could coax from the recalcitrant animals.

Arionella at Sea
II. The moving ecosystem

Arionella stepped out of the cabin on the treeboat and looked around. The land she had known her whole life was now starting to look like a green blur. She had never been out this far on the open Cyan Sea. Fishing in Miner's Bay with Navis, Lemay, and her grandparents had always been fun. The bay always seemed huge to her, but now she was truly overwhelmed. The ocean stretched as far as she could see, save for a thin band at the horizon that she took to be the last sign of land. Otherwise, she could look in all directions and see nothing but water. Dizzied, she turned to gaze at the tree in the center of the boat, whose greens, browns, and general earthiness gave her eyes something to hold on to, as if it were an emissary of the land accompanying her on this adventure. She realized that there were birds in the branches. Their chirps cut through the monotony of the water lapping against the hull of the boat. It all made her feel like she was on a little island, which in fact was somewhat true, for she was on a moving ecosystem.

She took shaky steps toward the tree, noticing that the boat was swaying more here. As soon as she walked onto the carpet of moss that surrounded the base of the trunk, her skin tightened with goose pimples, and when she touched the tree with one hand, something like a static shock sparked at the contact, except the surge ran through her whole body. She took a few steps back, flexing and shaking her hand as if to throw off the unsettling tingles still running up and down her spine.

It wasn't until she stepped off the moss that the tingles finally subsided.

Chapter 3

A COURSE OF ACTION

It was well into the morning when Navis and the children arrived in Lindum. The problem arose when Navis tried to put them into the care of an old shopkeeper, Rudsa, who was a friend of his. Well aware of the long hours of sitting on moth-ball-scented carpets and stale cream of wheat meals, Myli and Tumi both grasped Navis's legs when he tried to exit the shop.

"Could you take them and tend to them, please?" Navis shouted, turning to look at Rudsa who looked dull behind his bushy gray eyebrows and then at Lemay who opposingly looked impassioned like he was ready to walk out the door himself.

"No, you all are staying here!" Navis shouted again.

In response to this, Lemay stepped forward with clenched fists. Whether he was going to help peel Myli and Tumi off Navis's legs or fight with Navis to allow him to go was never determined because just then Lemay caught sight of a woman he recognized. He sprang forward and slipped past Navis, Myli, and Tumi.

"Lemay, no!" Navis shouted after him, dragging the children at his feet outside onto the dirt road. Naturally, attention from the townsfolk was immediately upon them. Just a moment before, it had been the tall, gray-eyed, raven-haired woman who drew the nosy gazes of the people. She, however, hadn't noticed the attention. Her bright eyes were fiercely searching the docks, sizing up the mariners and craftsmen going about their day.

"Uncle Navis!" Lemay exclaimed. "She's the one who came on the boat at the Aisle!"

The woman heard this and spun on her heel toward him. The townsfolk were now really invested in the unfolding show. Those who sat on benches along the dock, moved to the edge of their seats, and those that stood, balanced themselves on the tips of their toes.

Rushing toward him and then kneeling down, a brown locket made of a fibrous seed pod attached to a long hemp necklace swung forward, which she caught and tossed behind her shirt. Then she took Lemay's little hands into her long slender ones and asked, "Did you see my boat this morning?"

"Yes, I did," Lemay replied, blinking rapidly. "You were dancing, and there was a tree onboard, and—"

"Okay, okay," the woman quickly cut him off, suddenly aware of all the eyes and craned ears upon them. She let go of Lemay's hands and dropped her voice, her tone hushed but still urgent. "Did you see what happened to the boat? Was anyone else there with you?"

"It was just me and Ari."

"Ari?"

"Arionella, my sister. She's on your boat. It somehow floated away, and I couldn't save her," Lemay said, as his voice choked off and tears welled up in his eyes.

Navis hobbled over with the twins still attached to his legs.

"I'm sorry about your boat, miss," Navis said. "That Arionella of ours is always up to something. She's twelve, and I'm afraid I'm a terrible disciplinarian."

"I see," the woman replied as she stood up slowly, looking thoughtful again. "It's fortunate we ran into each other though," Navis continued. "I was just looking to set out on a motorized dinghy. The word around town is that nobody has seen any boats enter or exit through the bay, so there still may be hope."

She shook her head. "That's because I came in through a tributary."

"Oh, right. Lemay said you were at the Aisle. Why did you do that? It's a maze over there."

She leaned forward and whispered, "Well, you can't expect me to parade a *treeboat* across the town. That would be dangerous."

"A tree . . . boat? As in *the* treeboats sailors tell tales about? Are you being serious?"

"Shh, not so loud! Come with me." Her eyes fell upon the two children wrapped around each of Navis's legs, both with wispy blond hair and fat little arms, and a striking resemblance to each other. "But first, I'll help you with this ankle biter." She bent over and scooped Myli off Navis's leg. Myli's cheeks were already flushed from wrestling Navis, and now she was turning even more red, her chin tucked down and her eyebrows high, gawking at the woman's face so close to her own.

"Follow me," the woman said with a smile. She strode ahead past the town center and the stone clock tower that poked out just above the single-story shops and homes. Navis lifted Tumi, who had loosened his grip because he was interested in the quirky, beautiful woman who was carrying his twin sister away.

The woman turned toward a less populated end of the dock, went up some steps, and halted abruptly to face Navis, Tumi, and Lemay. She put Myli down, who ran back over to Navis, hid behind his leg, and peeked out from behind it.

"Captain Taola Lonwë of the Oaql boat, at your service," Taola said with her pointy nose high in the air. "Now to pick up where we left off. Of course, I am serious—serious that I came here on a treeboat, that is. Why wouldn't I be?"

Taola looked sincere, but Navis was examining her more closely, mostly to assess whether she was crazy or not. He reflected upon whether someone so charming could be . . . well, mentally ill—her clothes *were* tattered and baggy, her hair was sea kissed and wild, and there was something feral about her demeanor in general. "Look," he said at last. "I don't know who you are or what you are about, but I don't have time for this. I need to get on one of these boats." He pointed at the vessels along the dock.

"None of them will do," Taola replied matter-of-factly.

"I have to find Arionella," Navis insisted. "What do you expect me to do? Swim?"

"Look, I know how to trace my treeboat," Taola said. "If you want to ease your worries, then come along. Believe me, you won't find your friend without me. The treeboat is gone, and where it will end up is a place where no regular boat would be able to go."

Navis tried to ignore Taola's cryptic words. "Arionella isn't my friend," he said. "She's my—"

Taola eyed him inquisitively. "Were you going to say parent?"

"The point is, as her *guardian*, I am fully responsible for her behavior. I'm sorry she took your boat, but I will handle this situation myself. "

"I wouldn't say she took it," Taola replied, sounding like she was telling a scary story now. "Rather, *the treeboat took her.*"

"I thought treeboats were a myth," Navis said.

"Yes. However, some myths come from realities, usually hidden ones. Also, the image you have in your mind of a little girl forlorn on a little boat, lost on the great big ocean, should be discarded. She is probably having an excellent time, has plenty to eat and drink, and should be safe . . . for a while." The last part Taola added under her breath as an afterthought.

Lemay cleared his throat. "How do you know she won't get caught in a storm, or a wave won't flip the boat over?"

Taola bowed down to look at him directly in his light brown eyes. "Treeboats *know*," she said. "They can sense bad weather well before any human can and propel themselves to safety using chosen currents and channels. In fact, your Arionella will probably get to run around on land soon."

Navis raised an eyebrow. "How's that?"

"Well, treeboats dock on mainland like this only rarely. Their most frequent stops are at the Haelan Islands."

Navis scratched his head. "The Haelan Isles. . . treeboats . . . I don't mean to be disrespectful, but all of this talk inclines me to think you're a little loopy, Miss."

"Why do you say that?" Taola asked, containing her anger with gritted teeth as she refolded the sleeves of her large button-up shirt, which were slipping over her elbows.

Lemay spoke up again. "I saw it, Uncle Navis! I saw a big ol' tree sticking out of the boat. There was a cabin too! And it was strange the way it left, like it was alive."

Navis regarded him with a skeptical eye. "Lemay, don't get caught up in stories now. Just because a plant is growing on a boat doesn't mean that all this manooga is true."

Taola wasn't listening anymore. She had walked on ahead, assessing the boats along the dock. "A craftsman is what we need," she said. "One who can or has constructed a boat from aged trees."

"Wait!" Navis called out. His mind was full of doubt, yet a side of him wondered if the strange lady was telling the truth after all. Taola turned, her arms crossed, brows raised, gray eyes fixed unmoving on his deep brown ones. Navis paused, a little intimidated, but he found his voice again. "I'm not sure what you mean by 'needing a craftsman.' We don't have time for a whole new boat to be made for you. However, in the meantime, while you look for whatever it is you are looking for, I'm going to scour the bay and inlets. If I don't find anything, and if you really know what you're doing, and if there really is a way to track this magical treeboat of yours, then I'll go with you."

Taola was looking at him with narrowed eyes, but her gaze softened when Navis continued, his voice shaking now, "All I know is that Arionella is a child, alone at sea, and therefore in danger. In the end, it's my fault that I didn't do my job properly and protect her." Navis looked away, turning to collect the children.

Taola smiled and said, "I understand. You get going. I will search for the boat I want, and if I can't find one by noon, we will leave on any boat of your choosing."

Navis nodded and began to walk away.

"Oh, and should I call you Uncle Navis?" she called out to him jestingly.

"Just Navis is fine."

Taola nodded and locked eyes with him. "I hope that I'm wrong, Navis, and that you do find her. If you see the treeboat, hook it somehow, and please don't parade it into town."

Navis nodded in return. Then he and the children walked away. However, a few minutes later, their raised voices came echoing along the dock. The children were arguing with Navis again because he was insisting they stay with the old shopkeeper Rudsa again while he went to look for Arionella. Taola watched as Navis finally freed himself from the clutches of the twins, successfully foisting them off on Lemay. Navis hurried to board a small dinghy that was ready to set off.

Taola was about to walk away, but a thought occurred to her. She walked over to the shop where Lemay was staring forlornly out the front window. He saw her coming and immediately perked up.

She opened the door and walked in. "Navis just told me that Lemay knows the town quite well and can help me navigate it," she stated to the shopkeeper.

Lemay looked from Taola to old Rudsa, who was struggling to calm the twins with an empty cookie jar. Lemay didn't waste another second. He took Taola by the elbow and steered her back out the door.

Time passed, and the sun climbed higher into the sky while Taola and Lemay went from boat to boat, sailor to sailor, fisherman to fisherman, and some who in Lemay's opinion had the look of pirates, though Taola didn't hesitate to speak to—and argue with—them. At one point, Lemay got especially nervous when a gaggle of them lumbered so close that he could smell their ocean crusted stench and could see their hunter's knives attached to their thick leather belts.

"You must be loaded missy, asking for a whole boat," said a grizzly, tattooed woman chewing on a long cinnamon stick.

"Locked and loaded, if you know what I mean," Taola added boldly. The tattooed woman blinked in surprise, and then spat out her cinnamon stick in a fit of laughter as her companions joined in, slapping their knees. Taola took Lemay's hand and walked away without a second glance at them. Lemay, however, kept nervously glancing back at the leather covered thugs that continued to hoot with laughter and call out breathlessly after them. This and other interactions, all to no avail. Nothing Taola saw or heard kindled her interest.

Finally, there was only an hour and a half left till noon. Discouraged, they settled on a bench next to an antique shop that stood at the edge of a little canal that cut through the inner market of Lindum.

"What was wrong with all those boats?" Lemay asked. "Why didn't you pick any of them?"

"To be honest," Taola replied, "we could take any wooden boat and plant the Oaql seed I have within its hull somewhere." Her left hand came to rest on the locket upon her chest.

"What's an O-ko seed?"

"The Oak-kul seed is the seed from an Oaql tree from Oaql Island. This seed will create another treeboat someday.

"Anyway, the boats here are all carelessly assembled and wouldn't last long with a tree growing onto and *into* the hull. Once the seed is activated, it quickly starts sprouting and laying out its roots. It cannot be carried around for too long, or removed from the initial location it was planted, without serious risk of killing it. The seeds are so precious and rare that it would be a great loss to set it in such an impermanent environment. What I'm looking for, Lemay, is its home."

"Why do you need to plant the seed now though?" Lemay asked, thinking it was a simple question, and was surprised to see Taola looking disgruntled.

"Well, Lemay, here's a confession, while we're at it. One thing I never fully figured out was how to sense or completely control that boat that has taken your sister—especially when I am off it. I became captain of it about six months ago, but it's been a difficult one to subdue. It was already fully grown when I took over.

"Anyway, I'm still trying to figure things out. By activating this seed, resonance between it, its parent tree, and its sibling tree on that boat will be created—hopefully making it easy for me to track it. Besides, in addition to the Oaql boat, we would have great difficulty in finding and entering a Haelin island without the seed being activated."

By now, Taola was gazing out across the town, talking more to herself than to Lemay. "What we need is a boat made from the naturally resistant wood of a seyba tree, or a kiro, or a caaspi, or any of a dozen others. We need trees that yield hardwood that is extremely durable, and whose core is of a spongy material that allows the wood to bow and flex without splintering and breaking. The living tendrils of the seed I have will eventually spread through the structure of the boat and reinforce it for ages. That is, if the material is of the kind I have spoken of."

"Well, there's a nice boat," said Lemay.

Taola turned to look at Lemay and found him gazing into the window of the antique shop behind the bench. She pressed her face against the glass, hands cupped around her eyes. A shop full of old furniture and trinkets came into focus; the lighting predominantly came from candle lamps, creating a dim orange glow and deep shadows.

In a glass case was displayed a detailed model of a boat of rose-brown wood. Its body was engraved in fine, meticulous detail. From the rear began a geometrical pattern, bold at first, which gently tapered into an echo of ripples throughout the rest of the hull. The next distinct shape that grew out of the geometrical design was a plant with drooping trumpet-shaped flowers. The third design was of a bird with a long beak and wings raised in frozen motion. The fourth was a fox with a pointed nose and a bushy tail that blended into the figure of a young maiden who was leaning against a tree. The carving of the tree bulged out of the boat's upper deck, creating a bubbled texture that leveled out into the point of the bow. A plaque of copper just below the glass encasing read, *Miniature of the Masterpiece: the Maradona.*

"This is it!" Taola exclaimed. "The craftsmanship, the materials, the carving—what a worthy vessel!" She ran to the door before Lemay knew what was happening. Lemay followed as she rushed to the service counter where a man was tinkering with the pieces of an artifact of. "This miniature has a full-scale counterpart, does it not?" Taola asked abruptly, pointing at the model boat.

"Yes, um, hold on a moment; I will get Ms. Niniola." The man went into the back of the shop through a double-hinged door. Minutes passed. Finally, a graying woman with salt and pepper cornrowed hair came out wearing a peach-colored apron over a forest green turtleneck sweater and beige khaki pants.

"Where can I find the life-size version of this vessel?" Taola asked, barely containing her enthusiasm. The lady didn't say anything. She and Taola looked at each other for a moment. One with a keen, appraising gaze and the other with eyes glistening with excitement.

"You've been traveling." The old lady's voice was surprisingly youthful. "And you're ready to embark again. Why do you want this boat?"

Taola spun around and walked over to the replica. "If this is an accurate model of the boat, then the caaspi-hardwood and the non-segmented build of its body is perfect, perfect for what I need."

"I am impressed by your attention to detail," the woman said, "but many have come asking for my boat, and I have turned away every one of them. You are no exception."

The old lady walked through the flap doors to the back of the shop again. Taola looked more enthusiastic than ever.

"Lemay, did you hear her? It's her boat!"

Lemay just shrugged with eyes wide.

"Please, Ms. Niniola!" Taola shouted with her hands cupped around her mouth. "Are you the craftswoman of this boat too? Please let me at least see the original. Please, please!"

The man appeared from behind the doors, awkwardly looking down at the floor. "Um, I'm going to have to ask you to leave, please," he said, his face flushed.

Taola didn't budge. Instead, she put her hands on her hips and tapped her foot. She felt she was a step away from finding a home for the Oaql seed, and yet she was running out of time because of the deal she had made with Navis. She began considering letting him go off, so she could stay behind until she could secure her find.

Meanwhile, Lemay looked around, feeling uncomfortable at the fact they were staying beyond their welcome. He started to move toward the door, but in his periphery, he thought he saw a golden shimmer from a shelf standing in dusty corner of the shop. When he looked closer, he didn't see what he'd thought he had seen, but instead his eyes fell upon another little wooden carving that caught his attention.

"Taola, look!" He ran over and picked up the little figurine. Taola came to him and took it into her hands. Her eyes grew wide with surprise.

It was a wooden sculpture of a treeboat.

She held it up to the light of a candle, marveling at the attention to detail of the living form of the tree. It was quite different from her Oaql boat but definitely a treeboat nonetheless. She turned to look at the timid man behind the counter.

"Is this one of her carvings too?" Taola asked fervently. He nodded with obvious reluctance. "Take this with you and tell her that I am the captain of an *actual* treeboat."

He looked perplexed but silently took the carving and disappeared behind the doors once again. Minutes passed again. Taola paced back and forth along the counter. Lemay took to biting his nails as he stared at a wall clock in a shadowy section of the rear end of the shop and began to imagine Arionella lost at sea. The shadows of the trinkets looked like spiky sea waves and the light of the candles that wavered now and then from a draft through the cracks in the doorway, brought the scene in Lemay's mind to life.

Finally, Niniola reappeared. Without any niceties or transition, she said, "If it is my boat you want to set on the Cyan Sea then I must come with you."

Lemay looked up at the lady, shocked. She was already taking off her apron as if getting ready to leave. Without skipping a beat, Taola raised her hand in a salute.

"Captain Taola Lonwë at your service!" With a stamp of her foot, she swept her arm down and bowed a little bow.

"Niniola Maradona at yours," the lady of the shop replied. "And what about this child?"

"He is one of my little companions on this expedition."

"One of?" Niniola glanced at Lemay, and their eyes met for a moment. They had seen each other several times around town before. Niniola curled her nose and looked away.

Taola didn't seem to note their exchange at all. "Well, there are twins younger than Lemay here, who are with their father by the dock at the moment."

"Twins?" Niniola raised her brows. "Interesting. And you aren't making arrangements for their care?"

"They are coming with us to find their sister, who was swept away by my boat."

"Your *tree*-boat?" Niniola emphasized the word "tree."

"Yes," Taola replied, looking straight into Niniola's eyes.

Lines of age seemed to disappear off Niniola's strong dark face. "Well, you seem to be in a rush, and I'm not one for wasting time, especially not at my age. Come behind the counter and into the back."

"Lemay, you go stall Navis!" Taola said urgently. "I'll make sure to meet you all at the harbor as fast as humanly possible!"

"What should I say or do?"

"Whatever you can to stop him! Go!"

Lemay ran out of Niniola's store and toward the harbor. Pushing through the bustling morning crowds, he finally caught sight of Navis, Myli, and Tumi standing on one of the docks and talking to a man with a showy captain's hat and a big mustache that blended into a large dark beard. At the center plaza the town's clock tower read thirty minutes to noon. Lemay reached the dock just as Navis was handing money over to the rather piratical-looking man.

"Wait!" Lemay shouted. "She's found one!"

———◆———

Navis didn't know what to think when Lemay said that based on a model boat in an antiques store, Taola had found the actual boat she wanted, and that the boat maker was joining them.

Surely it can't be Niniola and her boat, Navis thought to himself.

Listening to Lemay, the man Navis had handed the money to, looked a little disgruntled and started trying to move things along. "Are these your things?" he said with a heavy East Cyanian accent, pointing to a pile of sacks and a small crate full of fruits and nuts. "I take them for you, sir, don't worry!"

"Yes, but wait one moment," Navis replied, glancing around at the heads turning toward the commotion.

"No, no! It's no problem! Here is boat—I put it in here, and off we go."

"Hold on a moment. We may have a change of plans."

"Deal is deal! You have paid me, and you say it is emergency!"

"We have someone else with us who wants a very particular boat and—"

"Deal is deal!"

Navis and the foreign boatman began arguing. Arguments weren't uncommon in the town, but people still looked and settled in to enjoy the show. Lemay glanced anxiously in the direction of the antiques store. Though he wanted to set out after Arionella, he had taken a liking to Taola, and furthermore, the thought of being trapped on a boat with the hot-tempered boatman was unsettling.

"Oy! Look 'ore there!" A voice rose up out of the crowd. A purple flag was seen poking out over the roofs of the shops and houses along the bay. From the canal inlet, along where the antiques store stood, and now, to the surprise and delight of the gawkers, a fine boat drifted out toward the main dock area where Navis and the man, oblivious to the new arrival, were arguing.

"Is that Niniola's boat?" another anonymous voice cried out.

"There she is!" Lemay cried. He tugged at Navis's sleeve and pointed. Taola stood proudly with arms crossed at the bow of the beautifully carved vessel. Her oversized shirt flapped in the wind, yet to the transfixed onlookers the simple garment seemed like some majestic gown worn by an enchantress.

"I'm on time, Navis!" Taola called out as the boat approached the dock.

Navis still hadn't formulated words. He was familiar with the boat and Niniola—in fact everyone was. She, and it, had become a part of the town's history in a way, but few save Navis had actually seen the Maradona, which Niniola always kept covered under large tarp cloths.

As the Maradona pulled up, Lemay ran over to help tie it to the dock. Taola tossed him a rope, and he wound it around an anvil.

"Well, let's get going!" Taola said.

Clearing his throat, the boatman stepped forward. "You see, madam, Mr. Navis has already made deal with me."

Taola looked at the man in surprise and then turned to Navis. "You didn't have faith in me, did you?" She leaned forward with her hands on her hips. "Even before my time was up? I hope you understand that if we are to be successful in finding Arionella, we are going to have to trust each other." She turned back to the boatman and said something in a foreign language.

Cocking his head to one side, in disbelief that she knew his language, he replied with a bow. "Captain Abdenbi Marsai of *Bartholomew the Unsinkable*."

"Captain Taola Lonwë at your service," Taola replied with a deep bow of her own.

The two continued to speak to each other in a tongue Navis couldn't understand. Soon, Abdenbi was smiling widely, and his laughter came as an inward suction of breath, like happy hiccups. Finally, he walked over to Navis and patted him on the shoulder.

"Good luck finding your little one, my friend," Abdenbi said sincerely and handed Navis back his money. "Don't be afraid to ask Captain Abdenbi Marsai if you need help setting out on sea another time."

"Uh . . . well, thank you, sir," Navis replied, surprised at the change in his demeanor.

The bearded man gave another bow and went on his way. Lemay had already clambered aboard, and now, as Navis lifted Myli and Tumi in turn, he reached down to swing the twins up onto the deck, much to their delight. After collecting the few supplies he had purchased from the markets, and giving Gretch and Gomer into the care of Rudsa, Navis took Taola's hand and boarded the Maradona.

Arionella at Sea
III. Feeding the Birds

Arionella needed a bathroom and food, so she ventured back inside the cabin. The washroom contained everything she needed, including a composting toilet—with sacks of sawdust next to it to toss in behind the stinky contents—and a special filter for converting the saltwater from the ocean into freshwater for drinking and bathing. However, there was no heating mechanism that Arionella could find, so she skipped what would have been a cold shower. For food, she sifted through the pantry in the kitchen. It was a closet filled with shelving and containers of various sizes and shapes. She found an abundance of dehydrated snacks that included all different kinds of berries, strips of mango, apricot, and many others that she couldn't recognize. She also found a few pieces of dried bread that was quite flavorless, as well as a dwindling supply of nuts and seeds like walnuts, cashews, almonds, pumpkin seeds, peanuts, anise, fennel, and cardamom.

Arionella made herself a bowl of oatmeal by mixing some oats she found with cold water. She looked everywhere for some sort of seasoning, particularly salt or sugar, but found none. She made do with mixing anise seeds and dried fruit into her oatmeal. Then, she brought her breakfast outside on the deck in a sturdy wicker basket. This time she forced herself to push through what could only be described as an electrical field around the tree so that she could sit leaning against it and have a proper picnic.

As soon as Arionella opened the basket, she heard shuffling sounds up in branches of the tree, and in the next moment, in a flash of color, several birds flew down and surrounded her. The larger ones looked like white doves, except that they had thin, stringy plumes of royal blue that grew out of their head. The smaller birds were an assortment of finches in all the colors of the rainbow, including purple, orange, olive green, and some multicolored in patches of yellow, red, blue, and shades of black. These little birds landed on Arionella's head, shoulders, and legs without hesitation.

"Wow, you aren't afraid of me one bit!" Arionella exclaimed, delighted at the dreamlike scene. The birds ate out of her hand and settled comfortably either on or next to her when breakfast was over. There Arionella sat, in the throne of birds with her chin held high, overlooking the ocean with a big smile on her face.

Chapter 4

ACTIVATING THE OAQL SEED

It was soon after the group boarded that Niniola emerged from her cabin. Her hair was tied up tight in cornrows, her lips pursed slightly, and her jaw clenched.

"Let me introduce—" Taola began, but Niniola raised a hand.

"Yes, I know. Greetings, Navis," she said with a nod.

"Hello, ma'am," Navis replied with a slight bow.

"That's great, you know each other!" Taola said happily.

"Lindum's a small town," Niniola said matter-of-factly. "Now then, I'd like to reiterate some rules that I've shared with Taola already." She glanced at the twins, who had already begun to run around the deck, exploring their surroundings. "And add some new ones," she said under her breath before continuing in a louder voice. "You all may call me Captain while we are on this boat. To maintain order, and therefore safety at sea, I will need you all to adhere to a chain of command. Myself as chief, Taola as second-in-command—though her experience of the seas is yet to be seen—and Navis to maintain order of the children.

"Food is to be rationed, and therefore, a log will be kept whenever any is consumed. The same goes for drink. The captain's cabin is off limits, as well as poking around in other parts of the boat that are not included in the tour I'm about to give you."

Lemay glanced at Navis, and their eyes met for a second. Lemay suddenly thought that Captain Abdendi didn't seem so bad after all, and Navis looked like he shared that opinion—even Taola's expression appeared to indicate second thoughts.

The captain's cabin was on an elevated section at the stern of the boat overlooking the deck. Behind the steps that led up to the captain's cabin were drums of fresh water and a door that led to the larder. At the center of the boat were three steps that led down into a thin room with two bunk beds on opposite sides. Then, back outside, Niniola walked the group over to two canoes that were shelved on a rack and finally toward the bow of the boat, where there was a square impression built into the deck for a seating area with large cushions.

"Truly is a beautiful ship, just how I remember it," Navis said to Niniola. "With any luck, this trip will be a quick one, so you won't have to worry too much about wear and tear."

Niniola cleared her throat and said, "Regardless, I hope to keep it in top shape and free of any tampering."

Lemay and Navis nodded, but Niniola shot a glance at Taola, who quickly looked away at the water and began whistling a random melody.

The tour was finally over and Niniola climbed off the boat to gather a few items she needed from the market. Seeing the stern expression upon her face, the crowd that had gathered to admire the boat, began clearing up as she walked toward them.

As soon as she was out of sight, Taola clapped her hands. "Time to inoculate this boat! We will not be able to approach the Haelin Isles if we do not activate this seed by animating it with fresh water." Taola took her necklace off as she spoke. "I'm going to do this right away so that within a few hours the seed can start resonating with the Oaql boat or the Islands and we can catch up with Arionella." Taola opened the locket and took out a small coil-shaped seed that glistened deep-red in the sunlight. "This is an important moment. Whoever thought my first Planting would be so unceremonious?" She ladled some fresh water out of the water drums into a small tin bucket. Next, she held the seed in her palm and took a breath and then lowered her hand into the bucket and held it there.

"Is Niniola aware of . . . ," Navis began, but Taola, still bent over the water, regarded him with a look that plainly said *Of course not*. Navis glanced nervously toward the town as the resounding pounds of the twins' feet along the deck made him anxious. "She's not the kind of person you mess with, Taola," he said in a low voice. "It is known around the town."

"I find it easier to ask for forgiveness after than permission first," Taola said feigning innocence through a big toothy smile.

Navis's eyes narrowed as he was distinctly reminded of Arionella. He then glanced at Lemay—who was listening intently—to see if he noticed the same thing. "So, you want to transform this boat?" Navis continued.

"That is what will happen . . . only not overnight. For weeks, you won't even notice a difference. Nobody will except me. But years down the line . . . it will be . . . well, apparent."

"I don't know," Navis said. "This prank will be a permanent one."

"Prank?" Taola sounded insulted. "This boat is about to become one of the rarest, most precious organisms on the planet! Niniola came on this expedition for one reason and one reason only. Not to rescue Arionella but to see and document the Oaql boat—apparently she started writing a book about the history of our world and its wonders but was never able to finish it. It seems the missing chapters will have to do with treeboats. But when I told her that her own boat could *be* a treeboat, she didn't see the grand opportunity!" Taola gestured angrily, reliving the frustration of the conversation she had with Niniola. Then she turned back to the bucket of water and lowered the seed into it again. "I mean, she could document the life cycle of the seedling growing into an adolescent plant and maybe even into an adult someday!"

Navis wasn't convinced. "This is setting the tone for a tense voyage, Taola. I don't want to lose any more time if Niniola decides to kick us off the boat."

Taola pulled her hand out of the drum and opened it palm up. The seed glistened, looking softer. "What do you want me to do, Navis? This is the only way to find Arionella."

"The only way? Humph. Maybe the only way you know."

"And that's your best bet right now."

"I'm still trying to figure out how you lost your own boat, *Captain*," Navis said with an edge of accusation.

Fire flickered in Taola's eyes. Navis was turning red. Lemay looked at them both and screwed his face up with resolve. "We have to find Arionella; that's what's important. I'm a kid, but even I know we should work as a team." Lemay said this forcefully with his hands on his hips. Taola took one look at him and began to smile. Navis, still frustrated, walked away briskly to contain the twins.

"Alright, Lemay, we don't have much time. Feel this—it's already coming to life." She passed the seed to Lemay, who took it in hand carefully. At first he felt nothing, but after a moment, the seed twitched gently in his palm, reminding him of jumping beans that he and Arionella often played with.

Soon Niniola returned, and the Maradona was untied from the dock and set off across Miner's Bay toward the Cyan Sea.

Taola and Lemay spent the rest of the day trying to appear nonchalant while trying to find a spot for the seed to grow. Niniola spent most of her time in her cabin, instructing Taola to keep watch and only disturb her for "important nautical reasons."

There wasn't a loose baseboard on the whole boat, and the larder was stocked neatly to the brim and would see too much human activity anyway. There were a couple of closets and storage areas for life vests and tools, but again Taola determined that the seed would be unsafe (and surely be discovered prematurely by Niniola). What she really wanted was a location just below the surface of the deck where it would be dark and yet central enough so that the roots could connect themselves throughout the boat with ease.

Soon it was night. The seed, in a little box full of earth and wood chips that Taola had collected outside Niniola's workshop before they set sail, was tucked underneath her floor-level bunk. "Might just have to have it grow under here," she said with a sigh. Navis was lying across the room on the upper bunk above the twins, and Lemay was on the bunk above Taola. The twins were already asleep, but the other three were restless. A few minutes passed, and all was quiet. Then shuffling sounds came from Navis's bunk, followed by the creaking of his ladder. The baseboards groaned as he quietly walked over to Lemay and Taola.

He whispered, "Come with me, and bring the seed with you." He then walked up and out of the bunk room. Taola and Lemay quickly followed. It was a cloudy night and hard to cross the boat in the darkness. When Taola suggested getting a glowtern, Navis said he already had one but didn't want to use it yet. They reached the pantry door behind the steps that led up to the control door and the captain's chambers where Niniola was. With great caution, Navis tried to turn the doorknob, but it did not move.

"What is it?" Lemay asked in a whisper.

"The damn door is locked. She's really a piece of work," he replied, sounding frustrated.

"Navis, we checked this pantry anyway," Taola said. "It wouldn't work."

"There's an opening to a hidden chamber in there," he said matter-of-factly.

"WHAT? Why didn't you tell me before?"

"Shh! It would've been too risky with Niniola awake, and I thought you might find a spot you were content with. Then we wouldn't have to invade the Room."

"The room?" Lemay asked.

"Yes, the Room, at the heart of the Maradona."

"How do you know all this?" Taola asked.

"Now is not the time for a conversation. We have to figure out how to open this door." Just then, a dim orange light shone from above the steps. Niniola was still awake and was checking the controls and coordinates of the boat. The three froze and pressed themselves against the wall. They listened intently as the thuds of Niniola's footsteps crossed the threshold of her cabin and onto the control deck and then faded as she went back to her quarters.

"She has the key," Navis said finally.

"Let me see the lock," Taola said. "Maybe I can spring it."

Navis shook his head and said, "There's no way I'm going to turn this glowtern on now. We'll come back later tonight."

The three crept back to their bunk room and waited. Navis sat on the floor, leaning against the bunk where the twins slept. Taola sat on the edge of her bed, next to Lemay, who didn't want to climb back to the top bunk because he wanted to quickly get into action when the time came. Time passed, and every so often he would ask "How about now?"

"Not yet," came Navis's reply each time.

Soon, Lemay fell into a dream-filled sleep where he thought he was still awake and was still asking when it was time to go. He tossed and turned as the time to go find the hidden room never came in his dream world.

Meanwhile, in the waking world, Navis and Taola were back by the pantry door. Taola was bent over the lock, and Navis was holding the spherical glowtern under his jacket on its lowest setting, letting a little light shine through a gap.

"Can you hold it still, please? Here, here . . . No, just . . . ," Taola's efforts to pick the lock with a hair pin were complicated by the swaying of the boat that repositioned Navis and the light every few seconds.

"What's taking so long?" Navis hissed impatiently.

"I'm not a crook. I'm a seafaring captain. I haven't done this since I was a child."

"Back when you *were* a crook?"

Taola didn't reply to that. She just sat down with her back against the door and sighed. "It's not working."

"What kind of bolt mechanism did she install?" Navis reached for the doorknob without any intention of opening it, but it turned with ease. "Oof!" Navis fell forward over Taola as the door opened. He tried to leap over her, and it was a good thing she ducked, for he did make it over her instead of stomping on her—but it cost them a loud thud on the wooden floor as he landed.

"Oh my! I guess I'm better than I thought," Taola said in a jolly whisper, soundlessly clapping her hands together in celebration.

Navis, on the other hand, stood frozen with his fingers on his lips, looking at her with his brows raised. Finally, he brushed off his agitation and fear, and got to work.

"Alright, let's shut that door and lock it while we're in here. I wouldn't be surprised if Niniola was awakened by all the noise. Ready? We have to move these crates together. There's a trap door on the floor just under there," he said as he uncovered the glowtern and its light spread over surfaces and darkened shadowy corners. The trap door was in the rear section to the left, where there was no shelving but instead a stack of crates with dried fruit and a few kinds of tubers in them.

"So, can you tell me now how you know about this trap door?" Taola asked.

"Is knowing that consequential to anything?"

"No, I'm just nosy."

"At least you're honest." Navis lifted a crate, and the seam of the door in the floor appeared. "Almost there!"

"Oh, Navis, do tell me!"

"Gawd, Taola, don't be such a child."

"Why not?"

"Because it's annoying, alright?"

Finally they revealed the trapdoor. It was circular and had little handles. Just before opening it, Navis paused and said, "When I was a lad, I used to help Ms. Niniola and her husband, Mr. Aldarwin, with chores. I was an assistant of sorts. This boat was one of the things I helped out with."

"Wow! Then you should be credited to this masterpiece as well!"

"No, no. I was eight or nine when I began working with them. I would hold things, pass over a hammer or wrench, and make the afternoon tea."

"Still," Taola insisted.

Navis lifted the trap door, and woody aromas rose up; a mixture of pine spice and maple sweetness.

"You all used different wood under here," Taola said.

"Taola, watch your language. Don't be saying 'you all' around Niniola."

"Why not?" Taola asked.

"This is why I didn't want to tell you. It's uncomfortable, okay? Mr. Aldarwin's passing was hard on us—." Navis cut himself off on "us" and instead said, "Hard on Ms. Niniola." He lowered himself down onto the narrow steps, which led down past the trapdoor entrance, his round, yo-yo shaped glowtern lighting the way down a narrow corridor.

There was only one way to go. There was plenty of space for children; Myli and Tumi could've walked upright. But for Navis and Taola, it was a cramped single file crawl. Aldarwin and Niniola had clearly put a lot of heart into the Heart of the Maradona. All along the walls were etchings like ones on the exterior of the boat. One sequence of etchings followed the progression of a young girl with two human legs that fused together image by image until, halfway through the tunnel, she transformed into a mermaid, but by the end had two legs again. Taola strained her neck to look up at the ceiling where another pictorial story had been inscribed of a rocket leaving a little planet with trees growing out of it, flying to a different planet with swirly patterns, and then to another with mountain peaks sticking out of it, and finally, at the end of the corridor, the rocket faced a five-pointed star. On the other wall were carved an array of creatures, some realistic, like lions and tigers, and others fantastic, like sphinxes and centaurs. A sense of wonder tickled her and she smiled to herself.

The end of the tunnel had no door, just an arched opening. The glowtern revealed a circular room with a domed top. Navis and Taola could comfortably kneel in the center of the room.

"It's like a playroom or a secret clubhouse," Taola said as she picked up a large rolled-up piece of parchment that turned out to be a whimsically illustrated pirate's map. She also found toys in wooden boxes like blocks, chalk, stuffed animals, and marbles. There were cushions of different shapes and sizes, as well as blankets. It was also surprisingly pleasant in temperature, almost breezy. She could feel where the air from outside was ventilated in through little tubular openings along the circumference of the ceiling. *This is a space made for a child,* Taola thought to herself. She was about to share her insight aloud to Navis, but something stopped her. She looked at Navis for a moment while he quietly studied the pirate map. She cleared her throat. "This is a perfect place to plant the seed. Thanks for sharing this treasure, Navis."

"We're sneaking right now. You shouldn't be thanking me. It's not mine to share, Taola. Let's just get it over with." He rolled up the map quickly and put it aside. "So, you're going to place the box with the seed right here somewhere?"

"Well, this is not quite what I expected. I was simply thinking there would be a loose floorboard that I could wedge this into."

Navis seemed to remember something. He crawled to the center of the circular room. In the middle was another, albeit much smaller trap door, two hand lengths in diameter.

"There's a little storage space here that would be perfect," he said.

"Let's see it then."

He lifted it up and then paused for a moment.

"Is there no space?" Taola asked, but he didn't reply. He reached down into the space and lifted out a sealed copper urn. On it was written *Herein are contained the ashes of Ryan Aldarwin: craftsman, sailor, and loving husband.*

Taola couldn't see Navis's face well in the dim lighting of the glow-tern on its lowest setting, but she could tell his mouth was pursed up tight and his brow was furrowed. He quietly passed the urn to her.

After a few moments, she handed the urn back to him. "C'mon, Navis, let's go back up. I can't plant the seed here without Niniola's consent . . . and anyway, we won't need to inoculate this boat if we catch up to the Oaql boat today."

Arionella at Sea
IV. The Fruit of the Tree

Over the hours of the day, as she drifted on the open ocean, Arionella experienced feelings of awe interspersed with moments of sheer panic. Around sunset, two significant things happened: Arionella had a particularly acute episode of fear, and she discovered the fruit of the tree.

It began with a lightning storm so intense that, though taking place far from the treeboat, it could clearly be seen, heard, and felt for miles. The claps of thunder caught her unawares while she dozed under the tree. She was startled awake by a horrendous boom that shook the boat and made the tree leaves rustle. Still half sleep, Arionella pressed herself up against the tree instead of running into the cabin. The barrage of explosive sounds continued, and she held her hands over her ears, shrinking into the moss. Dark clouds covered the sky, but even darker ones with bolts of lightning raining down upon the ocean filled the horizon. The treeboat seemed to be treading water, not moving toward or away from the storm.

Arionella's eyes were tightly shut when something bopped her on the head. With a scream, she opened her eyes and saw a large roundish thing lying on the moss that had not been lying there before. She reached out for it, realizing it must be fruit from the tree. Its fragrance reminded her of honeysuckle, its appearance was as simple as a regular coconut—though with a smooth, softer shell and a cool moist quality to it. Just the smell of the fruit calmed her in the face of the approaching storm. This gave her the presence of mind to slowly stand and make her way over to the cabin on the other side of the tree.

Inside the cabin, things were quieter. Muffled growls of thunder coming through the corky wood—though unsettling—were nothing like the ear-splitting crashes outside. Arionella sat on a little couch and sniffed at the fruit. The honeysuckle aroma invoked nostalgia for the people and places she missed deeply. As tears welled up, she tried to distract herself by fiddling with the shell. She removed the thick stem and found that there was an opening. To her surprise, she was able to use the opening to pry the shell apart with ease. Liquid from inside the fruit spilled all over her—it was slightly viscous and sticky. She nibbled at the white meat of the fruit curiously, the texture reminiscent of the stringy flesh of figs. The taste was bitter and sweet at the same time, leaving her tongue tingling with similar electricity that she had felt when she touched the tree for the first time. Soon, she had eaten the whole thing and was left with only the stem and the husks of the two halves of the shell. There was no seed. Within moments, her chest swelled with energy, and she forgot her worries. Her whole body pulsed with the strange electricity she was now getting more familiar with. She got up, picked up the music making device, and took it outside onto the deck. She fixed the black disk onto it, repositioned the needle and turned up the volume to full blast, and began dancing to a cheery waltz in defiance of the storm. Every so often, she would stop to look at the tree whose bushy leaves danced and made a *shhh* sound as the winds swept through them. Her eyes traced how its branches grew outward before decisively growing in a skyward angle, as well as how its viney tassles hung down, flailing in the wind like charmed serpants. All this caused her stomach to churn with fascination, as well as with a hint of unease. Finally, something she hadn't noticed before came into focus. Appearing in irregular instants above the tree, amongst its leaves, and at its roots were the golden clouds made up of tiny specks she would often see in the forests around Lindum. Here, too, they appeared and disappeared like shimmering vapor blown out from an invisible mouth. For some reason the sight of—what she grew up calling—sprites comforted her, and she turned back toward the dark sky, the claps of thunder, and zigzags of lightning that didn't bother her any longer. Somehow, she felt she was a part of it all.

One thing she didn't notice, however, was that it was only then that the treeboat began moving away from the storm.

Chapter 5

THE DANGERS
OF THE TREEBOAT

"We're getting close; I can feel it" Taola said, eyes closed, and chin held high as the wind swept her hair all about. It had worked. Although as yet unplanted, the seed was already resonating with the Haelin Islands, and its connection grew stronger with each passing hour. They were making great time on Niniola's boat as it sped over the ocean. Taola knew that her Oaql boat did not rely on speed to get around, but all the same, she was hoping to catch up to it on Cedql, the nearest of the Haelin Islands.

Finally, around sunset, they came to a region where the compasses failed and it got foggy all around. It had been just under six hours since they had set out from Miner's Bay. It would have taken the treeboat about seven or eight hours to reach Cedql, and though Arionella had a couple of hours of a head start, Taola was hoping to find the Oaql boat docked at the Haelan Island to rest, as she had kept it on the open sea for days prior. Niniola grudgingly let Taola take over the wheel and controls in this instrument-defying region. With the seed resonating with the island, Taola said she was able to tap into the resonance and use herself as a compass. Everyone else gathered at the front of the Maradona to catch the first sight of the island. Navis, Lemay, Myli, and Tumi were hopeful, expecting to reunite with Arionella. A huge mound of a silhouette loomed in the distance, only to vanish again in the fog. Then, silhouettes of dense brush and trees appeared close to the boat.

"We're moving through the avenues now," Taola said as she slowed the induction motors of the Maradona down to a crawl and navigated her between the pathways of vegetation that were growing out of the sandy tendrils of the island. There was a gentle thud, and the boat stopped. They were in shallow water.

Myli's voice rose up in the silence. "Owla found Ari?"

"Taola's is going to check if she's here," Navis replied and lifted Myli onto his shoulders. "Let me know if you see her first."

"I wanna see. I wanna see," Tumi complained.

"You two are getting big!" Navis laughed. "I don't know if I have enough shoulder for both of you."

Still standing by the controls, Taola hadn't moved an inch, nor did she speak. She squinted her eyes as little blue lights appeared in the fog. A line of them trailed after one another, up and down, winding in an *S* pattern.

"They're the Haelin Keepers, the Reteti of Cedql Island," Taola explained to the others, who were watching the approaching lights with some apprehension. "They're unfamiliar with this boat." She pulled her lower lip forward with her thumb and pointer finger and gave three short and sharp whistles. The march of the lights paused all at once. After what seemed like a few moments of deliberation, three sharp whistles came in response. Then Taola whistled one long note that cut off with a higher pitch. The response came quickly in two whistles of lower pitch.

"The Oaql boat isn't here," Taola said. She looked a little flustered but continued, "We'll wait and see if I sense it. This would be around the time it would arrive from Lindum."

"Let's go!" Tumi was tugging at Navis's pants. "Let's go, Navi!"

"Hold on, Tumi. Ari isn't here yet," Navis said, taking his hand.

"I wanna go see! Please . . . please!" Tumi insisted. Then Myli began to chime in, tugging at Navis's ears while on his shoulders.

"Taola, you think we can get off the boat for a bit?" he asked.

"Yes, but stay close. We may have to play a little cat and mouse when the treeboat shows up, so I want to be ready by the controls for that."

Navis turned to Niniola. "Can we take a canoe, Ms. Niniola? The water still seems deep here."

Niniola's reaction to Navis's question was a tensing of her body and a furrowed brow that revealed she was rapidly considering all the reasons she might say no—but couldn't find a good one. At last, she gave a reluctant nod. She even gave them a basket of food and helped them aboard and then with Taola's assistance, lowered the canoe down on a pulley mechanism attached to the side of the boat.

The kids happily set off with Navis, Myli on his lap on the back seat of the canoe and Tumi on Lemay's lap at the front. The water was crystal clear, with a true seagreen tint, and because of the calm and steady current they could see the seaweed, coral, and sand just below. They made it to shore and pulled the boat onto the sand, letting their clothes get wet in the comfortably cool water. Myli and Tumi seemed to be having trouble finding a firm footing on land and kept tripping over nothing in the sand, which only made them giggle more than ever. Soon, they were running around on the beach, swimming in the water, and climbing all over Navis and Lemay. Later, as the twins busily buried themselves in the sand, Lemay asked Navis about the seed as they strolled along the shore. He told him that Taola decided to keep it portable in her box of soil, instead of inoculating the Maradona.

Back on the boat, Niniola and Taola never took their eyes off of Navis and the kids. Taola was smiling, whereas Niniola had her arms crossed with a stern expression on her face.

"Oy, Captain!" Taola called out from her post on the upper floor. "Sweet bunch, aren't they?" Niniola cocked her head in Taola's direction and unfolding her arms, she tapped her ear with one finger.

"I said, they're sweet, aren't they?" Taola repeated.

"Yes, quite, quite sweet." Niniola folded her arms again and looked around, walked over to one side of the boat as if checking on something and then started toward the back of the boat.

"How old do you think Navis is?" Taola asked Niniola as she strolled nearer.

"Hmm, he must be about twenty-two or so now," she replied.

"Twenty-two! I would never have thought so young!"

"Yes, in many ways he matured quickly. Though raising children like that by himself is not something I would've recommended. He took on the task based on the recommendation of fools, really."

"Kids come from passion sometimes," Taola replied, picking up on Niniola's harsh tone. "They aren't always planned."

Niniola realized that Taola didn't know that the children weren't actually Navis's flesh and blood. "Taola, think for a minute. Lemay is nine, and the girl, Arionella, is twelve, I think. Do you really think Navis had a child at the age of ten? They are all his adopted children. He and the children share the reality of orphanhood. It is only the twins, Myli and Tumi, who are actually related by blood."

"Right! I see!" Taola said, smacking her forehead. "I just didn't connect the dots. And I didn't think Lemay was his kid because he calls Navis uncle while the twins call him Navi."

Niniola paused and then asked, "Anyway, what about you? Do you have children?"

"Well, I was adopted myself. I'm thirty-two years young and have no kids."

"Older than I thought."

"And do you have any children?" Taola asked, ignoring Niniola's comment.

"No, my husband and I were content with each other, and with our work."

"Ah, I see, and when did your husband pass away?"

"Almost ten years ago now."

"That must've been hard for you."

"Yes, it was then, especially because he had so much of life left to live, and we had not completed this boat—the Maradona—when he fell ill."

"But you completed this masterpiece! And by yourself?"

"Thank you. Yes, I had to carry on. That is what Aldarwin would have wanted."

Taola had half expected Niniola to mention Navis's contributions to building the boat, but it didn't seem that she felt the matter important enough to mention. Taola felt the window for conversation slowly closing, but she still wanted to bring up planting the seed, so she said, "Do you think Mr. Aldarwin would have been excited by the thought of transforming the Maradona into a treeboat?" Even before she finished her question, she immediately realized she had made a mistake.

All Niniola said in response was, "Innocent though you may seem, you are a woman of the world, Captain," and she walked away without another word.

———◆———

The sun had set and the children had gotten all their energy out. Navis brought the sleepy bunch back to the boat and found Taola laying down in the bunk room with her eyes closed, the box with the Oaql seed resting on her chest, lightly covered by her hands. Navis was carrying Myli and Tumi, with Lemay dragging his feet behind them. Taola opened her eyes as they entered, slid the box back under the bed, and silently walked out. As Navis put the children to bed, he could feel the Maradona begin to move and turn away from the island.

Back on the open ocean, it was the first time Navis had seen Taola out of sorts, and she actually looked worried. Navis realized that as time had passed cruising on the Maradona, Taola's carefree presence had made him feel confident and relaxed that they would find Arionella soon. In fact, he'd been feeling like they were on a trip of leisure. But now the sinking feeling in his gut had returned. Adding to the tension, a lightning storm was playing out in the distance; rumbles of thunder could be heard in low and ominous registers. Navis thought of talking to Taola, but she was too preoccupied with maps and compasses to speak to anyone. Though they had set out about thirteen hours behind Arionella, their boat was motorized, and Taola had been confident that they would catch the treeboat within a few hours, especially with the expectation that the treeboat would need to stop at the one of the Haelin Islands.

In the dead of the night, Niniola and Navis finally got Taola to speak in the captain's chamber.

"It's changed course," Taola said, leaning over a table with both hands planted firmly on the surface. "I think it knows I'm coming after it, and it doesn't want me to find it. It's staying out at sea instead of visiting the Haelan Islands . . . ."

"Why?" Niniola asked.

"To keep the girl onboard is the only thing I can think of," Taola replied slowly, arriving at new realizations at that very moment.

"Why would it do that?" Navis asked, his nostrils flaring and eyes wide.

"It's found the perfect opportunity to conform a new host," said Taola; then she paused and swallowed. "Arionella is young and impressionable."

Niniola took out a large leather-bound journal and started writing down everything that Taola had said. Navis looked appalled and was trying to find words. Seeing this, Taola continued hurriedly, "To understand the full extent of the Oaql boat's power, it's important to know that it's not just a plant—it is a hybrid organism as much fungus as tree. Its very seeds contain the mycelial component. This plant and fungus made symbiotic bond eons ago and now are one hybrid organism—I mean, it would be just as appropriate to call it a fungus-boat. When you are on that boat, you are in its world. It is a floating biome. One is under its influence just by being in its presence."

"How have you lived on it for so long?" Niniola asked, never looking up from her journal.

"I'd say I've been permanently changed by the Oaql boat's influences, even though I had training from Captain Rainer, the previous captain of the boat. One has to know how to maintain a sense of self. For example, nutritionally, it is important that individuals aboard a treeboat consume salt every now and then. Salt solidifies the self. You can engage in periods of fasting, during which you allow yourself to merge with the consciousness of the treeboat, but pulling oneself out again is key."

"It is true then that there are some humans who are completely . . . ?" Niniola asked as she continued to write furiously.

"Yes, there have been individuals—some by their own choice and some in ignorance—who have become an extension of the fungus and the tree, a thing of nature themselves, without human awareness. Evolutionarily it makes sense. Just as the fungus and the tree became symbiotic, thriving in ways neither could alone, so too there is a great advantage in adding a bipedal organism to the mix."

"How quickly can the erasing of human awareness happen?"

"It depends on the person. Children are more vulnerable, as they have not developed a complete sense of self. They can be converted very quickly. And anyway, it can be a rapid conversion for anyone, child or adult, who consumes the fruit and other parts of the tree."

Niniola put her pen down. Her hands were clasped and resting against her lips. She looked pensive and, one could even say, concerned.

Navis was sitting on a bench, hunched over, gripping his head with his hands. "I told them I wasn't cut out for this. I told them I don't know how to care for children. I knew something would happen someday . . . ," he kept repeating quietly as he swayed back and forth, his hair in disarray.

Taola walked over to him and rubbed his back. "Things happen, Navis. We can't control everything."

Navis didn't reply.

"It's time I visited home," Taola said after a moment. "We will have to get help from Rainer Yansa, the previous captain of the Oaql boat." Then, as if it had just occurred to her, she added, "I just hope Arionella has thought to dip her hand in the ocean and take a taste, because I only got off the boat in the first place to collect some mountain salt from the foot of Mount Lindarious in Lindum."

Arionella at Sea
V. The First Climb

Arionella slowly opened her eyes, emerging from a world of dreams to the sound of birds chirping. Her sight was blurred, and her body ached from the cold. Dew-covered and shivering, she sat up on the mossy bed where she had fallen asleep during the night. She rubbed her eyes. As her vision cleared, the still surface of the ocean came into focus, shimmering with golden strings of light. She sat transfixed, watching the splendor of the dawn swallow the world in an all-encompassing embrace. Soon, the light spread over the boat, and Arionella's cold body began to thaw.

It had been a full twenty-four hours. Now another day of solitude wore on for Arionella. She ate some more nuts and seeds, sharing them with the birds again, which brought her joy, and she walked around the perimeter of the boat a few times. Inside the cabin, she twirled the mobiles, rummaged through the shelves, and sniffed at mostly empty perfume bottles. Finally, while drawing on a sheet of large parchment with some color pastels, she got curious about the fruit of the tree she had tried the night before. This curiosity began with pangs of hunger. It started with Arionella daydreaming about the fried fritters Navis made from corn flour a few times a month. The aromas of spices would quickly be followed by the sizzling and crackling of oil heated over a fire on a large iron skillet. Arionella's mouth began watering when she thought about all this. She grew restless. She was already sick of what she had begun to think of as bird feed stocked in the pantry. Remembering the fruit, so unlike anything she had ever tasted, she ventured out onto the deck and went directly to the tree. She pulled off her dress, feeling much more agile and comfortable in her tank top and shorts. The first climbable branches were just out of reach, but she jumped and caught hold of one. It was almost as if the branch had lowered itself just enough to help her. She barely noticed the electrifying current of the Oaql tree this time. With some effort, she swung her legs up until she was hanging from the branch, perpendicular to the ground. She was surprised at how winded she was. However, she kept at it and soon was standing amidst the network of branches higher up in the central part of the tree. She saw bird nests tucked into crevices and holes, while some larger ones were out in the open, resting upon the branches.

Arionella began to climb about, reminded every so often by an angry squawk to steer clear of any nests. It was a few degrees cooler in the shade of the tree. The ocean breeze would come through and fan the leaves, creating a hypnotic effect of light rays beaming through the large oval leaves of the Oaql tree. The fruit Arionella was hunting for hung plentifully all around her. She went up close to one and—gripping the rough bark of the tree with her toes—tugged at it. With some twisting and pulling, it came off. It was a large one, the size of both of Arionella's hands put together. She wondered why she didn't see more fallen fruits around the boat, like the one that bonked her on the head the night before. She got her answer when she saw shriveled-up versions of the plump fruit she had picked. Their stems were conical like straws. After the fruit ripened, it began to be sucked back into the tree, until there was no trace, save for a flaky husk that would dissipate with a breeze.

Arionella slowly made her way down to the lowest branches and dropped the fruit onto the moss carpet before dangling from the lowest branch and letting herself drop to the soft ground. She sat on the moss with her prize as the Oaql boat kept traversing the ocean at its steady pace. She pried apart the shell, this time careful to not spill its nectar. The tangy liquid left her tongue numb, tingling as it went down her esophagus, giving her the feeling of butterflies in her stomach.

Chapter 6

ABDUCTED

The course was set toward the Haelin Island, where Taola's mentor, Captain Rainer Yansa, lived. He was an old man who had finally left his days of wandering the sea behind and settled on Oaql Island, where the seed of the rogue Oaql boat originally came from. This was because each tree on a treeboat had its origin tree on a Haelin Island; each tree with its own name and, as their keepers would say, each with its own temperament. These origin trees were the only ones to bear fruit with seeds in them, and only very rarely.

To call a Haelin Island home was a privilege reserved for those who commandeered treeboats for most of their lives and, sometimes, for their families. For the indigenous Haelin Keepers, who called themselves *Reteti*, these islands were both origin and end. They were a pygmy people who maintained their tribal lifestyle and their millennia-long relationship to the Haelin Islands and treeboats. They were originally the only ones to serve as captains of treeboats and still constituted the majority of captains, though over the course of prehistory and history a handful of outsiders had risen to that rank. In this century, the only outsiders to become captains were Rainer Yansa and Taola Lonwë.

The Haelin Islands were uncharted on maps and were very difficult to find even when in proximity. It was said that only someone who intimately understood the energy of a treeboat—having lived on one and partaken of its fruit—could sense a Haelin Island when not aboard a treeboat. The treeboats themselves sensed their island of origin and were strongly drawn to it when near, as well as to other islands of the different treeboat species. Over time, a few of the captains of the treeboats, like Rainer Yansa, came to double as taxonomists and scientists, deciphering the makeup of these strange multitiered organisms. They found that the treeboats communicated using chemical signals in the water and powerful pheromonal language through the air, and, much like birds, they were able to tune into the Earth's magnetic field for navigation. Rainer Yansa was the first captain to put into scientific terms what the *Reteti* knew as the "the trees' sorcery"—their ability to essentially conform human consciousness into their own.

———◆———

Niniola had been writing early in the morning when she saw Lemay sitting at the far end of the Maradona with his arms wrapped around his legs and his head bowed. Putting the journal down on her desk, she wrapped herself in a woolen shawl and stepped out of her cabin. The glow of dawn had begun to gently light up the edge of the sky. She strolled over to where Lemay was seated. He lifted his head, revealing sad and sleepy eyes. Sitting beside him, Niniola opened her shawl, reached over him with her right hand, and covered his back with half of it. Her warmth spread over to him. They sat still and silent for a time under the warmth of the shawl as the sun continued to rise and the dark sky above gradually turned to lighter shades of blue.

"Worried?" she asked, breaking the silence. Lemay just nodded in response. "You know, worrying won't help you solve the problem. Think it through and then let it go, until you have to take the next course of action." They were silent again for a time. Then Niniola asked, "How did you two come upon that treeboat?"

Lemay thought for a moment and then looked up as if he remembered something and said in a whisper, "She knew where it would be . . . Arionella knew."

"Really? But how?"

"I don't know. She said she had a dream."

They sat in silence for a long time until Niniola felt Lemay's body slump. She slowly lifted him onto her lap, carried him over to the seating area at the front of the boat, and laid him down on the large cushions. He slept deeply, covered by her warm shawl.

It was midafternoon when they approached the next Haelin Island. Taola emerged from the bunk room, and she didn't look too happy. "Something's not right," she kept saying. Already fine roots and mycelium webbing had spread all around the box that contained the seed, and the fibrous tendrils poked through and delicately gripped whatever surface they came into contact with. Taola stroked the little container of new life and closed her eyes. She realized the frustration she had been feeling was not only her own; the Oaql boat with Arionella on it was in a kind of nervous paralysis as well, and the nearest Haelin Islands were sending out shockwaves of stress as well.

As the Maradona came closer to Oaql Island through the usual gray fog surrounding the Haelin Islands, visibility got even worse and the smell of burning vegetation came with whipping gusts of wind. Then, finally catching a clear glimpse of the island, Taola gasped and covered her mouth with her hands. Rising columns of smoke from the wreckage of felled trees marred a patch of the otherwise dense green cover that wrapped the edges of the island. Navis, who had been dressing the children to venture off the boat, heard Taola's gasp. He ran to the steps that led up to where the controls of the boat were and called out to Taola.

"Is everything alright?" All he could hear were more gasps bordering on sobs from above. He climbed up the steps, saw Taola staring inland with tears streaking her face, and followed her gaze. Even Navis, who had never seen the island in its unspoiled glory, was taken aback at the damage. "What the hell happened here?"

"It's fresh," replied Niniola, stepping out from her cabin that stood adjacent to the controls.

"What do you think happened?" Navis asked again.

"It doesn't seem like a natural occurrence," Niniola responded gravely. "Look at the sawdust and the trees cut down on strange angles . . . . This was a calculated attack of saw and fire."

As if jolted from a trance by these words, Taola took the wheel of the boat and flared the acceleration. "We must hurry! Hopefully the people of the island are safe!"

As they approached the foggy shore, Taola set sharp whistles loose as loudly as she could. There was no response. She pulled the Maradona up to the dock and set down the anchor. Everyone gathered on deck by the docked side of the boat. "Someone should stay on the boat with the children in case it isn't safe," Taola said.

"I'll stay back," said Niniola.

Lemay heard this and ran over to Navis. "No, I want to come with you!"

"Listen, Lemay, you have to stay here and take care of Myli and Tumi," Navis replied firmly as he kneeled down and brought the three children into a group hug. "I love you guys."

Lemay pursed his lips and furrowed his brows. He was about to argue, but the twins leaned into him and took his hands in theirs as Navis stood back up. Upon feeling their touch, Lemay realized Navis was right.

Taola had already climbed down over the side of the boat and was trying to communicate through whistles again as she walked off the dock and onto the sandy shore.

"Still no reply," Taola said to herself, and then broke into a jog toward a trail between the palm trees.

"Wait up!" said Navis who had just begun to climb off the boat, but Taola didn't slow down.

"Hold on, boy," Niniola held something out to Navis in the fog that was sweeping around the boat again. He reached out, and Niniola handed him a small, high-charge electric-prong blaster wrapped in a leather holster. "Be careful with that. You unlock it there and the trigger is just along the hilt."

Navis looked at it for a second, lowered himself awkwardly down onto the dock, and then secured the weapon onto his waist belt before he ran off toward the trail.

The trail started off as soft sand, but soon Navis could feel the harder earth under his sandals through the sandy layer as he approached the dense foliage of the island. Just ahead, a natural arbor of vines framed the end of the trail that stood at the top of a hill, below and beyond which wiry but thick brownish-green grass stretched as far as the eye could see. Palms sprinkled throughout the fields were very tall, towering above the ground well over nine meters high casting shade over thin dusty pathways that looked well-trodden leading toward what seemed like huge multi-colored tents. Suddenly Navis heard shouts. From amongst the trees, small people ran out. They were dressed in well-cut-and-fitted white and beige linens that were dark with soot and mud. Navis instinctively put up his hands in a surrendering motion. This slowed their initial charge, but as they had gotten closer Navis noticed a few of the people wielding staves, spears, and other objects held like weapons. Then he noted that though the people had slowed to a walk, many were pointing their weapons straight ahead, not at Navis's face but at his waist. Glancing down, he saw the blaster conspicuously fixed to his hip.

Navis wasn't sure who these people were. Should he take off the weapon and gesture for peace, or was this the moment that he should make a stand? As they continued to move forward, Navis's trepidations got more acute, and he realized all at once that his right hand, which had been up in the air, was now hovering near the holster. The moment he became aware of this, it didn't feel right in his gut. He raised his hands again. Almost instantaneously, he saw a change in the previously tense body languages of the group of twenty or so individuals, now only a few yards away. He realized the group was mainly composed of small, but fierce looking women. Generally, the people were sturdy and fit, their skin deeply browned by the island sun. Just as Navis was about to venture a hello, a sharp whistle rose from further inland. One of the little people at the front whistled in return, and the last of the pointy weapons were raised.

"Are you here with our lady Taolanta?" the woman who'd whistled asked Navis.

Navis didn't quite catch what she had said, but he replied, "I'm here with Captain Taola. You are the Reteti?"

"Yes, yes. Taolanta has just whistled . . . and you won't be needing the blaster," she added, pointing to his waist. Another sharp whistle came from inland. "Let's go, let's go!" the small woman exclaimed.

Navis hastened forward behind the group of warriors, and soon Taola came into sight under the shade of a large tree just in front of a ravaged garden and house. A beautiful ornamental wooden fence had been toppled in many spots, and fruits and vegetables were strewn all around the dark topsoil of the garden. A little blue cabin with yellow shutters stood at the center of the garden. Its door was wide open, and all of the four glass windows were shattered. Taola and a few of the Reteti were gathered around a larger man who was lying down on a patch of grass. Many people were briskly moving about, obviously tending to more wounded individuals and other damages.

Finally, Navis was close enough to Taola to be able to speak to her. "What's going on?" he managed to say, though he was panting quite a bit.

"Sir Charles is wounded," Taola said, holding back tears. "He and Captain Rainer are the only two residents on this island besides the Reteti. Now it's just them and Sir Charles, because Captain Rainer has been abducted. In the struggle, Sir Charles was wounded by a blaster."

Navis became uncomfortably aware of the sensation of the blaster at his hip.

Meanwhile, Taola continued speaking as she assessed the large graying man who seemed to be unconscious. "It's a bad wound on his upper thigh, but he's stable."

"Are there proper supplies available for his care?" Navis asked.

"Yes, they are fully self-sufficient here and are stocked with materials from the outlands."

A Reteti lady walked over to Taola, bowed slightly, and said, "Ana'ntay."

Taola bowed her head and returned the greeting respectfully, "Ana'ntay Dr. Nstasia."

Then Dr. Nstasia bent over using a hand to hold her long dreadlocks in place and whispered something in Taola's ear. She stood up straight again and signaled to the other Reteti standing near. "We'll move him now all together."

Taola placed a hand on Sir Charles's shoulder. "Sir Charles, Sir Charles . . . it's me, Taola. We're all going to lift you onto a stretcher and carry you indoors. Sir Charles . . ."

Slowly he came to and peered through squinted eyes and bushy white eyebrows. "Ahh, young Captain, it's been some time hasn't it?" Sir Charles said softly.

"Yes, it has," she replied with tenderness in her voice. "And here I thought I'd be sitting down to a great welcome-back feast, with rum coconuts and Haelin chips for snacking after."

Sir Charles chuckled, and then winced from the pain. "Sorry, dear, not today . . . . Agh! And I had just harvested some plump kohlrabi. See if you can collect them—they're strewn about. Those barbarians have no respect for good produce!"

"Well, first we've got to get you to where better care can be given to you," she said. "You know, you've had Dr. Nstasia and her team running around like hens escaping roosters after dawn."

This made Sir Charles heave with laughter, as well as with pain.

Dr. Nstasia cleared her throat and said, "Taolanta, dear, curb your humor for a few minutes, please."

Sir Charles waved a hand dismissively. "Oh, Nstasia, if I'm going to die, let me die laughing."

"No one's died or is going to today . . . thankfully. We did a good job in driving them off."

"Thank gawd!" Turning back to Taola with a smile, Sir Charles continued, "You'll never forget those chickens and their morning madness, huh? Good news though! We've separated those rascal roosters from the hens. Well, for the most part."

"That *is* good news," Taola replied. "Now up you go. Navis, if you could support his lower back . . . ."

Two of the Reteti women lifted Sir Charles by the shoulders while Taola and a Reteti man each held a leg. Navis got on his knees and lifted as well. Then they slipped a stretcher made of flexible bamboo and hemp cloth under the patient and just as quickly had him over their shoulders. Sir Charles was raised only about a yard and a half off the ground as the tallest Reteti was only about that tall. They carried him away from the blue cabin toward colorful circular tent structures to the east amidst many coconut palms and bright green island shrubs.

Taola stood for a moment and looked upon the wreckage of the home she had known for so long now. It was the place where she'd eaten formative meals, played many imaginative games, and impishly defied the countless disciplinary actions that her guardians—Captain Rainer and Sir Charles—tried to implement for her own good.

"Damn." Taola shook her head slowly. "What a mess."

"Truly must have been an irreverent bunch," Navis said. "They couldn't stop at the windowpanes but had to mess with the garden too."

"The bigger mess is what this entails."

"What do you mean?"

"Nobody just sails to a Haelin Island for a visit, much less an attack. Someone has either stolen a treeboat or a treeboat seed . . . or . . . I don't even know." Taola became silent and stared into space. Her eyes had a glossed-over look, as if she were recalling something terrible.

"What about Reteti from another Haelin island?"

Navis's voice startled her out of her reverie, and it took her a moment to reply. "Impossible."

"Shouldn't we take all possibilities into account?"

"You don't understand," she said. "*All* Haelin islands are home for the Reteti. They move about freely between them."

They stood for a few moments in silence. Then it looked as if Taola was bothered by something else. She realized that she had possibly misjudged her treeboat. It was staying away from the islands not necessarily—or only—because it wanted to conform Arionella, but because of the danger afoot. She thought how even now, after so many months of commanding the boat, she still didn't fully understand it, and probably never would. She shared this thought with Navis, then said, "Navis, we must stop here for the night and seek council."

Arionella at Sea
VI. True Imaginings

After eating the fruit of the tree for the second time, Arionella lay back on the moss, tired from the exertion of climbing, and began to daydream. Very quickly, her daydream became a series of visions of great clarity. First, she began visualizing the teeming life in the ocean below and islands she had never seen before, as she had no memories of being anywhere else but Lindum. Then she imagined the underside of the Oaql boat. Long roots stretching deep into the water moved about like giant versions of the legs of the little octopuses she and Lemay would catch now and then around Miner's Bay. The roots of the Oaql tree were covered in barnacles, sea plants, and all sorts of organisms of the ocean, including varieties of fish that sought protection amongst its roots but also ended up as the Oaql tree's meal by way of its electrical charges that would zap them to their death before thin tendrils would reel them into a digestive organ of the tree located near the hull.

Arionella's heart was racing at these amazing and yet, in some ways, alarming insights. Lastly, she visualized herself from an omnipresent viewpoint, pacing around the boat. She could sense that the birds of the tree were aware of her, and furthermore that the tree itself was aware of her every move, as the deck of the boat wasn't hard and hollow but soft and very dense. The boat was like a shell impregnated by a fine mycelial webbing that grew out of the Oaql tree.

Arionella opened her eyes, finding that she couldn't rest after all. With her heart still racing, she went into the cabin and found ways to keep herself busy.

Chapter 7

THE STORY OF MADAM RED AND MISTER SNOW

Back at the Maradona, a few of the Reteti went to receive Niniola and the children. Niniola was greeted by a youthful and lithe woman named Lana-Baboye who led a group of young women like herself called the *Ndi'Kari Reteti*, the Reteti Warriors. Each had hair shaved short, sported sinewy bodies, traveled on bare feet and had penetrating eyes. They looked like soldiers and it was for this reason that Niniola refused them outright, and even kept a hand on a blaster at her hip the whole time they spoke. It wasn't until Lana-Baboye returned with Navis that Niniola relented—she had even moved the Maradona away from the shore in the time they had been away.

Later that night, Navis lay on a bed in one of the grand tents of the Reteti, tossing and turning in a fruitless attempt to escape terrible visions of Arionella alone on a vast ocean with the figure of a clawed and warped-looking tree looming over her. The fires of his anxiety had been stoked even higher at a tense dinner some hours earlier, at which the Reteti recounted the attack on the island and Captain Rainer's abduction. They said they had begun preparations for evacuating the young and elderly, as well as sending communication to the other Haelin Islands about how they had been invaded by a small group of men armed with prong-blasters.

"The group and their leader seemed to be enjoying themselves, like they were out on a field trip," said one Reteti named Loyiso with disgust. "It was clear that they were on a mission to collect Captain Rainer, and they made it known that this was their island now and that they would return soon, even as we drove them out."

Taola sat silent and pensive during the exchange of accounts. Navis noticed that at times she looked distant and tormented.

After dinner, when most of the others were in their beds, Niniola went out for a walk with her journal in hand. Every so often, by the light of wax torches along the paths leading around the settlement, she would jot notes down and stroll casually on. The large red tents were circular and had many pointed spires. They were arranged in concentric circles and most of them were connected to one another by way of veranda extensions.

She looked up at the tall coconut trees and saw that most had been freshly harvested. All around there were little herb gardens—some patches only a meter by a meter in dimension—tucked into corners, just next to tent entrances, and alongside low wooden fences. With a passing breeze, Niniola would catch some combination of the aromas of thyme, basil, rosemary, and anise. When she got off the beaten paths, she noticed that the last waning sliver of the moon was out; she could see silhouettes of the people of the island under its dim silver light, no doubt making preparations against the threat of the attackers. Just as she completed a full circle around the settlement, she came to a white tent with a gold caduceus affixed to the point of its spire. As she got closer, it was apparent that there were others that had been wounded and were receiving medical attention. She went inside and was impressed by the state-of-the-art technology set up throughout the tent. Immediately apparent to Niniola were the holographic devices that the Reteti nurses and doctors were able to interact with by touch and voice. Most places Niniola had been—including Lindum—were living in what, she considered, a stone age. Though the technology existed, it wasn't as accessible as it was in the cityforts scattered around the world. When they were younger, she and Aldarwin had traveled across the Cyan Sea, and even settled at the outskirts of Atlantia, a prominent cityfort. They lived with the poor workers and collected data on the goings-on of the cityfort to add to the encyclopedia they began writing together, both sharing the sentiment that it would be their contribution to recivilize their world. They went to Atlantia for inspiration, as cityforts were considered exemplifications of "the Great Ages" of human civilization. Three months into their stay, instead of finding answers as to how to manifest their vision of a better world, they felt they had visited a cheap anachronism and slowly their will to complete their great endeavor waned. After some more months of travel, they finally settled in Lindum, where their draft for "the Ency-clopedia Cyanica" became dusty and moldy at the back of their humble cabin that they had not yet turned into an antiques store.

These thoughts ran through Niniola's mind as she held—what she would tell people was her journal—close to her chest, but in fact she had taken up the responsibility of writing the encyclopedia again after Aldarwin's passing, finding a fresh surge of willpower to draw its dispa-rate pieces together into one coherent whole.

She walked along the edges of the tent, trying to stay out of the way of busy nurses. She came across a portable X-ray scanner sitting on a wooden shelf—the contrast of the shiny device and the raw, but beautiful wood irked her somehow. She picked up the scanner and held it over her right arm and on its screen saw an image of what seemed to be the bones of her arm with great clarity. A young Reteti man saw her and came over.

"Amazing right?" he said.

"Yes, very," Niniola replied.

"Ana'ntay. I'm Bunda."

"Niniola."

"These are some of the reasons I am training to be a nurse," Bunda said as he passed his hand over a collection of gadgets. "We get to use many devices from the Old World."

"How do you all get these things? Isn't there a limited supply all around the world? I mean, they aren't made anymore, are they?"

"No, we've had these things for ages. They were collected by our ancestors who lived in those times."

"An unbroken thread in your ancestry and material culture . . . amazing. The world is so splintered now it is rare that there are steady family units, let alone steady generations of ancestry," said Niniola and took out her journal to jot down these insights.

"Yes," Bunda agreed. "It is strange to say, but we were lucky that the attackers today were only interested in Captain Rainer. Our technology and our literature could've been plundered, but they did not seem to know about such things. I just wish our elders weren't such pacifists—what I mean is that blasters would've come in handy today."

"Yes, I think we must be ready for anything, and if that means keeping violence in the cards as an option, then so be it. Anyway, those invaders must have known something about your people because from what I heard at dinner, they are planning to return."

"Well, they won't find much if they do, because we've begun the process of hiding and transporting things, as well as evacuating our people."

Doctor Nstasia overheard their conversation and walked over. "Still, Bunda, you must remember that this island itself is what they want. It is more valuable than our tech and our literature." Dr. Nstasia tied her long dreadlocks up in a tall bun and put on a white hair wrap that up till then was being used as a scarf. She looked at the wounded around the tent. "After we evacuate those who cannot fight, we must return with reinforcements to reclaim this land. Now come—I need your help at bed fifteen." She gave a nod to Niniola and walked away briskly.

Bunda looked pensive for a moment, smiled up at Niniola and shrugged in a way that said *Seems like things are going to change around here* before jogging off to assist Dr. Nstasia.

Niniola set the portable X-ray down and turned to leave the tent, but just then someone called to her, "Captain!" Sir Charles, propped up in a bed, was waving at her.

"Captain Niniola of the Maradona, right?" Sir Charles asked cordially.

"Sir Charles," she replied as she walked over to his bedside.

"Just Charles is fine. I attached the 'Sir' for aesthetic purposes to go along with the fuzz on my face when it began to turn white. Please have a seat—I'm starving for fresh company. Since age crept up on me, I've become sedentary on this island. Taola doesn't visit us much anymore either."

Niniola sat down in a sturdy but light chair made of interwoven rattan-style bamboo that seemed to be a staple on the island. "Are you Taola's father?" she asked.

"Adoptive father. Rainer and I raised her like our own child. I've never taken the trouble to procreate. Know what mean?" He chuckled. "And how about you, dear?"

"No. I neither raised children nor had any of my own."

"I see, I see. Would you want to though?"

"I'm not as young as you seem to think, Charles. When my husband was alive, I thought I might, but it was always more his wish than mine.

I personally think that we live in a time where art and invention is more important than procreation and the limitations that come with it."

At this, Charles raised his brow with interest and he pointed to the journal in Niniola's hand. "Is that your labor of love there?" Niniola nodded, and Sir Charles continued speaking. "You know, I'm an artist too—a painter actually. Well, I've been many things, a man of many trades—could you believe I even worked as a research translator for the cityfort Atlantia? Glad that's over. Most of all I was blessed to be a parent later in life. Over the years, I have come to believe that, in our time, a proper foundation of love is the most important thing to be established, especially after the turmoil of the previous eras."

Niniola seemed agitated and said argumentatively, "Love is intangible—it comes and it goes. You never know when someone you love might die. An individual, a culture, is immortalized by what they create—just like the literature and technology preserved on this island. *That* is how we will rebuild. If we didn't have the legacy of the previous age, we'd be nothing better than savages. I assure you that lives would've been lost today if you didn't have this tech available."

Sir Charles looked pensive for a moment and replied, "You know, the Reteti here believe that the spirits of their ancestors persist on these islands. And not only the islands but also the treeboats are imbued with the spirits of Reteti ancestors. Talk about immortalized, and all without tech!"

"And you believe that?" Niniola asked quizzically.

"Well, I've experienced some peculiar things living here, and once on that treeboat of Rainer and Taola's too." Sir Charles seemed to be trying to connect all the dots in his mind.

"Well? What was the experience?" Niniola asked impatiently.

"Hold on! I don't think as quickly as I used to, and I have to give you background first." Sir Charles stroked his beard and then continued.

"This happened when Rainer was still captain of the Oaql boat—which was not too long ago, mind you, maybe six months ago now—and there was a particular couple we often had dealings with. Maya and Jöshi, 'The Wandering Lovers,' but we knew them as Madam Red and Mr. Snow. They were very special, known on the Haelin Islands as well as amongst many of the other tribes, like the Enané, Kompa, and Nawa who live in the forests, deserts, and mountains on the mainland.

"Well, Rainer's final mission on that Oaql boat—before it was to be passed on to Taola—was to transport Madam Red and Mr. Snow to a secret location, one that he hasn't even told me, but one he did say was dangerous. Very dangerous. It is still a wonder why they wanted to go there because Red and Snow were already quite old, and Red was ill with some disease that worsened on the voyage there. She passed away on the Oaql boat just as they arrived at the shores of their destination. I'd say this was, oh, about a year ago now."

Niniola was sitting at the edge of her chair, frozen in attention, for she had made Jöshi and Maya's acquaintance when they had lived in Lindum for a time until they abruptly left two years ago, and also they were intimately tied to Arionella their granddaughter, and Navis and Lemay, their adoptive sons. The movements of the busy nurses, doctors, and volunteers around had her became a blur until a nurse came by to check on Sir Charles and told him that he should rest soon.

"Very soon, my boy, very soon! I am almost done with my story. Yes, that's fine you can leave that there." Sir Charles adjusted himself in his bed, and scratched his head.

Niniola urged him on impatiently. "So, Madam Red passed away on the voyage . . . ."

"Oh yes, of course. However, before she passed away, Red insisted that if anything were to happen to her, she must somehow become part of the Oaql boat. Earlier during the voyage, either when she was deep in slumber or when she was very weak physically, Rainer says he could actually sense her interacting with the boat, sometimes slowing it down, making it turn or shudder. You see, Rainer is connected to the Oaql boat *telempathically*; he went through pains to understand its temperament—partaking of its fruit during long fasts and engaging in fierce struggles against the Oaql tree's consciousness. It's akin to taming a Lypir—those fanged menaces are relentless in their attacks! Well, uh, so . . . What was I getting at?"

"Rainer realized she was controlling the Oaql boat," Niniola reminded him.

"Ah yes. That is why, among other reasons, Red was such an enigma. She never had any training or much exposure to the treeboats, but she was connecting with it like a fully realized captain!

"She knew of the death ritual, the Ritual of Merger, of captains and her last wish was to become one with the Oaql boat. When she died, Rainer and Snow cremated her together on the shore of whatever dreadful land they were on. Rainer said Snow was heartbroken, saying that he was on his knees, and that he cried so much that his tears soaked the sand beneath him." Sir Charles paused, sighed, and wiped his eyes. Then, he continued, "Rainer stayed with Snow for a few days. They made the ashes into a solution and injected it into one of the fruits that was still growing from the tree."

Sir Charles paused for a second, realizing that Niniola might not follow what he was describing so he took the time to explain further. "You see, the Oaql tree only rarely sheds its ripe fruit. Instead, when it's mature, the fruit is retracted into the tree via the stem. You understand?

"Anyway, this was a very difficult decision for Rainer. He had a deep connection to the Oaql boat that he had earned over many years. If anyone was to become one with that little floating world—a world he'd propagated on a boat he made himself—he'd thought it would be him. Since then, he's felt that something's different about the Oaql boat and that this change might have hurt Taola's chances to connect with it on a deeper level.

"So to end the story about Mr. Snow and Madam Red, Mr. Snow insisted he must go on, and though Rainer thought it was a suicide mission, he also knew of Snow's legendary pursuits and let him go—I mean Snow visited City Gardens like they were his mother's house and grappled with some of the most dangerous pirates, who all eventually accepted him as one of their own!

"So uh . . . Upon returning here, Rainer retired, and when Taola completed her initiations here on the island with the elders, she took over full command of the Oaql boat. And that's that!" Sir Charles stretched and yawned.

"All very interesting; however, you never shared your experience of the Oaql boat?" Niniola asked.

Her mind was racing with thoughts making connections to possibilities that made her heart thump heavily, though she found it hard to believe; Sir Charles's words on death, consciousness, and his recounting of Madam Red's ashes ritualistically made one with the tree was compelling enough to keep her from brushing him off as a crazy old man.

"Oh yes! That was how we started the story, wasn't it? Well, when Rainer returned, he told me this story and told me to go on the Oaql boat and see if I felt something different. Now let me tell you; my antenna is dull to this kind of thing. I mean, compared to Taola and Rainer, whose interactions with the treeboat and Islands are palpable. It's amazing, really.

"Uh . . . anyway, I spent some time on the Oaql boat alone and sat by the tree. I'm never able to access the inner dimensions of the tree that Rainer and Taola describe, but I do fall into a bit of a trance now and then. I must say, as I leaned on that tree and meditated, there was an unmistakable sense of nostalgia and an unmistakable feeling that I was in Madam Red's presence, just like how it was in person the few times I met her."

"That's it? Nothing else?" Niniola seemed discouraged.

"Well, yes. You have to understand, dear, that is a lot for me! I mean, in Rainer's case he would actually see her, and I'm sure it's the same or similar for our Taola."

"Very interesting story, Charles. Thanks for sharing it with me." Niniola was trying to come off as calm and collected, but her whole body was tense with ideas bubbling in her head.

"Very good, very good!" Sir Charles clapped his hands together endearingly. "But I forget what we were talking about that led us to this story . . . ."

"Oh, that's okay. It's getting late, and I think the nurses want you to rest."

"No, no! I'm just fine!" Sir Charles said enthusiastically albeit through a hearty yawn.

"Really, Charles, I should rest too. Good night." Niniola stood and tried to contain herself from breaking into a sprint out of the medical tent.

"Alright then. Good night, dear. I've been very grateful for the company."

"Yes, good night." Niniola walked briskly away. When she got out under the open sky, she broke into a jog, making her way straight to the tent where Taola was lodging for the night. She stood outside the long flap. "Taola. Taola!" she called. "Are you there?"

"Niniola? Yes, come inside."

Inside the tent, many orange and yellow drapes hung all around; their colors glowed with the light of dimmed glowterns hanging high on the ceiling behind them. Some young Reteti girls were playing games or getting their hair combed by older teenage girls. Taola sat up in a hammock. "Come sit, Niniola."

"No, actually, I wanted to speak to you in private."

"Okay, sure." Taola stood, wrapping herself in a blanket as a draft had followed Niniola when she'd entered.

"You may want to dress up. I'd like to speak to you on the Maradona."

"Oof. Niniola, is everything okay? I'm so cozy."

"Yes, everything is fine, but this is important."

"Alright . . . ." Taola dragged her feet over to a clothe hamper filled with sarongs and long shawls.

"Do you have the seed with you?" Niniola asked in a low voice.

At that, still bent over her clothes, Taola's whole body language shifted. "Y-e-s?" she said in a slow, questioning manner.

"Well, bring it with you."

Taola turned to the others in the yurt, "I'll be back, ladies."

The responses came from around the yurt, "My lady," and "Go well."

Then, both women were out of the tent and walking briskly in shared silence, their hearts beating rapidly at the thought of the possibilities ahead.

Arionella at Sea
VII. A Cautionary Dream

Later that evening, Arionella was starting to get sleepy, but she decided to have another fruit from the tree before going to bed. A few hours after consuming the fruit, she had a dream.

In the dream, seafoam was gathering all around the treeboat, to the point where it rose up a good meter and a half high, until it was pouring over the sides and onto the boat. The ocean was still, and mist drifted over the surface under the silver light of a bright moon. Arionella first saw everything from her own perspective, leaning against the tree and curiously assessing the gentle march of the foam, wondering if too much of it could sink the boat. Just as she started to make a plan to go fetch a bucket to clear off the foam, the foam began to take on a distinct shape. Arionella watched in terror as it became obvious that the foam was moving with purpose now. She thought of climbing up the tree, which felt like her only source of warmth and safety. Then, as she looked more closely, Arionella recognized something familiar in the form that the foam was taking. Within moments, a humanoid shape draped in a dress of foam stood a few yards away. A shimmering face was visible, and though the figure was in muted transparent blue colors of varying shades, its features were quite distinct. Arionella's eyes widened and then filled with tears. The figure seemed to be looking around, as if curious about the boat, and then turned toward Arionella.

"Mima," Arionella said breathlessly. "Is that you?"

The figure leaned forward and squatted down a little, opening its arms just as Arionella's grandmother Maya used to do. Arionella felt a sense of great joy and tried to step forward, but nothing happened. Suddenly, the perspective switched, and Arionella was outside her body, looking back at the treeboat from a few yards above it. Her body was fused with the trunk of the tree—her face melded with the bark, and her limbs were no longer visible. As if she were in two places at once, the Arionella watching this scene and the one fused with the tree were both filled with a sense of searing terror. She felt desperately claustrophobic because try as she might, she could not move an inch. As if responding to her fear, the figure of foam straightened itself and began moving toward her. Maya's face became clearer and clearer to Arionella in the shimmer of sea foam. However, the more joy Arionella felt at this unexpected reunion with her beloved grandmother, the tighter the grip of the tree became, and soon it was hard for her to breathe. Arionella's terrified green eyes gazed directly into the foamy eyes that still somehow radiated love and serenity. Her grandmother's form lowered itself again and leaned toward where Arionella was fused with the tree. They gazed into each other's eyes for a moment. Then, with a smile, the foam figure kissed Arionella on the forehead. All at once, there was a rush of oxygen and movement. It felt to Arionella like diving into a cold pool of water, but it was the foam that rushed forward into Arionella and the tree.

Arionella awoke under a clear, starry sky. The ocean was still and covered in fog, but the Oaql boat swayed as if it had just been pushed by choppy waters. Arionella looked at the silhouette of the tree in the darkness and considered it in a new way. She got up and walked toward the cabin, eyes narrowed, and lips pursed.

Chapter 8

MAMA GOGO AND NAVIS

The next morning, Sir Charles took it upon himself to commandeer a wheelchair to the dining tent, where breakfast was being served, and requested that Taola, Navis, and Niniola—along with a few Reteti officials—sit aside privately with him.

"Try the papaya and coconut purée; it is unlike any you've ever had. If you're constipated . . . well, consider yourself cured!" Sir Charles patted Navis's arm and laughed at his own words with abandon. Though he was still in pain and wheelchair bound, he was as cheery as ever.

"Just as we are about to eat?" Dr. Nstasia asked sternly, though holding back a smile. Taola sat down on Sir Charles's left side and hugged his arm, leaning into him as he cleared his throat to speak again.

"Real talk for a few moments, if you all don't mind. Yesterday was a terrible day." It was a rare occurrence, but now was one of those times where Sir Charles let his smile fade. "Those men came with a purpose—their leader's purpose. The man who came to our house and demanded our subservience was a dangerous man, not because of his weapons but because of his knowledge and abilities. I am sure he is familiar with the ancient arts. He allies with nature, and in a very particular, sinister way."

Taola let go of Sir Charles's arm and turned toward him with all her attention.

He continued, "I still don't know how he got to this island, but I am convinced it has something to do with his skills with the natural world for, as we know, the Reteti Islands are protected by barriers that only allow treeboats to cross their threshold. Loyiso here noted that the speedboat they arrived on was dragging what seemed to be a treeboat behind it, which he must have been using as a compass to find our island—and that can only mean that he is able to tap into the Resonance of the trees."

Those hearing this for the first time looked startled and deeply stricken by Sir Charles's speculation. With a sigh, Sir Charles added, "And he seemed to sense immediately that Rainer was the one connected to the Oaql boat.

"While his men kicked around in our garden, he came inside our house, sat at our dining table, and asked us to sit as well. He then nonchalantly proposed that either we cooperate with him or that more people on the island would suffer."

"What did he say he wanted?" asked an elderly Reteti woman whom everyone called Mama Gogo.

"He wanted to know where the Oaql boat was. When Rainer and I told him we didn't know, he was unfazed and simply stated that Rainer was to come with him then. Well, you know my temper. I stood and told him to get out of the house, and without warning one of his cronies shot my leg—just like that! Rainer scuffled with them, but it didn't last long. They subdued him, tied him up, and carried him out." Sir Charles became silent, and they all sat still for a few moments.

Navis spoke up, breaking the silence. "That's horrible, sir; I'm very sorry."

Sir Charles knodded in acknowledgement of Navis's empathy and sighed.

"Why do you think they took Captain Rainer?" asked Taola. There was something in her voice that suggested she already knew the answer.

"Well, I think they want to coax information out of him. He isn't one to divulge anything, as we know, but that worries me more. They were nasty people, Taola. They are going to get what they want from him one way or the other." Sir Charles's white beard and stache twitched as he ground his teeth and sank into his wheelchair, looking old and worn in that moment.

Taola put her elbows on the table and held her head in her hands. Then she asked slowly, even as she was dreading the answer, "Was this leader of theirs a short man?"

Sir Charles looked up at her with surprise, and replied, "Yes."

"With brown-olive skin and long, jet-black hair?"

Mama Gogo, who was sitting next to Taola, put her hand on Taola's back and began rubbing it in a circular motion, looking pensive herself.

"Yes . . . ," Sir Charles said slowly, a realization dawning upon him as well, "Don't tell me this is the same bunch that—" he lowered his voice, "—kidnapped you."

Taola only stared into space.

Sir Charles continued, "Then, these are the men that also attacked the Akninka people and others for their fossils decades ago—." And his voice trailed off as he fell into troubled thoughts.

Mama Gogo spoke up in a blend of her native tongue and the common language. Her voice was soft, and yet clear and decisive. "I do not doubt that we have been ambushed by none other than Revalo Otrebor, and that, just as he has been collecting items of power over the years. I believe he is after our eleven remaining *Pashaduma* of each of the

Agwae of *Reteti*—and the seventh that has long been missing, *Pashaduma Sycql of Agwae Sycql*, I now believe must be in his possession and is how he penetrated our barrier yesterday."

A deeper silence spread across the tent as Mama Gogo let her statements sink in. Then she continued, "Charles'sa, we must send out a rescue team to recover Rainer'sa—or they will use him to capture our dear *Pashaduma Oaql*. As for the safety of our people and the evacuation of our *Agwae*, communications with the other *Reteti* have begun.

"Now, as for the *Nafseen*—" a term that loosely translated to the common language as some combination of "the predators" and "the self-possessed, "—their leader, Revalo, is indeed familiar with the ancient ways, as he was once a fledgling of the *Obipisha*, a *Yokati-orina* tribe like our own. However, that tribe is hostile to all outsiders, and though our diplomats are courting their emissaries, we cannot approach them yet. Here on *Agwae Oaql* we have taken more liberal steps to accept those called to be stewards of the Earth, but we understand the *Obipisha's* caution—based on lessons learned from a bloodstained history of our Earth.

"So, Taolanta, I recommend that you and your band of travelers visit one of the *Yokati-kiza* tribes—in this case, the Enané who have long worked with us, and house one of our own in their forest—" Mama Gogo turned to Sir Charles, "—I have always said it would be good for Taolanta to receive training from one of the *Yokati-kiza*. The Enané are a good starting thread for un-stitching this quilt because they have confronted Revalo before and are currently investigating him."

"If you don't mind," interjected Niniola—her pen at the ready. "What are these 'Yoka-' tribes'?"

"*Yokati-orina* the original tribes, and *Yokati-kiza* the blended tribes that have mixed blood. The blended tribes formed over the centuries when individuals left cityforts and sought the wisdom of the indigenous. Those who were able to shed the layers of their conditioning found solace in the indigenous ways and never returned to their old lives. Others tried balancing both worlds. They dreamed of a united world where indigenous wisdom could be brought to the cityforts." The wrinkles along Mama Gogo's eyes deepened and her bright eyes shone through thin slits. "And for an epoch there was fellowship, an exchange of knowledge and culture. It was in this time that progeny was brought into this world that did not belong exclusively to the tall walls and technology of cityforts, or to the boundaries of river and wood utilized by many tribes. They knew both worlds and represented a new hope for unity."

"And now—," Niniola said, putting her pen down. "Those are the very people who are wanderers and have no belonging to any tribe or city. Due to the wars that broke out, barbarism became the norm and now most children end up as orphans."

Niniola's words casted a chill through the tent and people shifted uncomfortably in their chairs.

Navis, on the other hand, felt a mix of shame and a touch of anger—his face flushed, and his ears grew hot.

"And the Reteti?" Niniola continued, not picking up on the atmosphere of disquiet around her. "Your people did not take in those that sought indigenous wisdom?"

"Some things have changed." Mama Gogo smiled and touched Taola's chin. "Our Taolanta is a testimony to that. However, there are still many Reteti that adhere to ancient codes of *weka hakima*, or wisdom keeping, and that entails a secretive preservation of our knowledge and no mixing of blood. The Reteti are one of the few remaining uncontacted tribes, though some of our brothers and sisters argue that our decision to welcome outsiders here on *Agwae Oaql* has changed that status, but it still holds that the majority of Reteti have not revealed themselves to the outside world.

"Those of our people who we disseminate out into the world—the *Ndi'Kari Reteti*, our warriors—do not reveal their origin."

Mama Gogo then turned to face Taola and again took her by the chin with a thin hand, "Face your fears my dear. This *Nafseen*, Revalo Otrebor, does not understand that strength is not power over, but power with. He seeks to dominate us all and take control of our young Earth. Take your comrades and go to the Enané. Wisdom awaits you and your friends, who themselves seek answers to questions that they have not even asked yet—and you all may find that you play a pivotal, codifying role in all this chaos."

This time, even Niniola picked up on the change in the atmosphere when Mama Gogo finished her sentence; the time for speaking had ended. When she stood, the other Reteti rose with her and did not disperse until she slowly made her way out of the tent flaps.

———•———

Navis was anxiously pacing along the island's east shore, blind to the shimmering aqua-green water, bright sand, and the large fleshy leaves of the palms swaying in the breeze. Some time had passed after the briefing at breakfast and Navis had followed the Reteti to where they had tugged the Maradona and other vessels into a secret cove at the far east end of the island sometime in the night. Many thoughts were running through his mind. He felt that with each passing minute, Arionella was drifting farther and farther away, that he was failing her, one of the children he loved and was supposed to protect. He also felt that finding Arionella was becoming less and less of a priority to Taola, who was upset about Captain Rainer's abduction and the attack on the island. And now Mama Gogo had advised Taola to visit some tribe that seemed far away. Navis thought to himself, *Of course, I have compassion for these poor people, but I can't lose sight of what I left Lindum to do. There is a child out at sea, on some damn boat that is trying to consume her mind!*

With that thought, Navis convinced himself that he must confront Taola and anyone else who stood in his way. Chest swelled, jaw clenched, and breathing shallow, he briskly marched back toward the trail connecting to the village. Just as he stepped out into the clearing, he heard a shout.

"Navis!" It was Taola, bounding up a grassy hill. "Where were you?" She grabbed his arm and started dragging him along with her. "I've been looking for you everywhere! I told Mama Gogo and the others about Arionella, and Mama Gogo wants to see you in private." It was as if Taola had awakened Navis from a state of delirium.

"I was just coming to see you," he said. "I was nervous that you had forgotten about Arionella in all the commotion."

Taola stopped to stare at him. "How could you say that?"

He felt heat rising in his cheeks but did not look away. "Well, terrible things have happened here, and that elderly lady told you to visit some tribe, and—"

"She also said that as captain I must find my treeboat before those thugs do." Taola took a deep breath. "Finding Arionella is still at the top of the list, Navis. Just think about it, some Reteti warriors here are being sent off to track Captain Rainer, who Revalo is possibly using to track the Oaql boat—" Taola paused to see if Navis was catching her drift. "That means we're not the only ones looking for Arionella anymore!"

Navis nodded in understanding.

Taola continued, "And visiting the Enané is part of that. I need to learn how to track the moving treeboat, just as I used the Oaql Seed on the Maradona to find the Haelin Islands, but it's a difficult skill to learn. I can imagine what Captain Rainer would say right now. 'I told you not to skip out on your lessons, Taola Lonwë.' He was right. Anyway, I could train on one of the Haelin Islands with the Reteti, but the Enané may be able to give us more leads on this group and their leader who has long been causing trouble around the world for decades apparently."

"But how long will it take to get there? And how long do you need once we're there?"

"It should take us about three or four days to reach there. First, we must make our way southwest along the Cyan to the port at Pansmont and then we'll be going by foot to a settlement where we'll find a guide to the Enané. As for how long it will take once we get there, I'm not sure." Taola noticed the look of concern on Navis's face and added, "But I will be making it very clear that we don't have much time and that I plan to move on if it seems like we're not getting anywhere." They began ascending another knoll, taking giant strides past an organized line of Haelin ants marching diligently from one anthill to the next. "This way," said Taola as she led Navis in a different direction from which they had yet gone. "This is where I grew up, you know." She spread her arms out wide when they got to a better vantage point.

"I'd begun to gather that. But who are your parents?"

"Captain Rainer and Sir Charles are my parents now, but I was actually born in a cityfort—the waterside fort called Atlantia."

"Wow, no way! I've always wondered what they must be like."

"I remember a bit. I was nine or ten years old when Captain Rainer adopted me. When I picture Atlantia today I see shiny things, bright lights, and yet a grayness that I can't really explain. Everyone lives very close together in apartment buildings within the walls of the city."

"Is it true they make their own day and night?" Navis asked.

Taola laughed. "Yes, but it's not as glamorous as you may think. The cityforts have domes that create artificial projections of night and day."

They continued walking along in silence for a while until Navis asked, "You were young when Captain Rainer found you . . . do you remember your real parents?"

"I remember my mother . . . . She actually asked the Captain to take me into his care. He'd come to the outskirts of the cityfort and he'd give treatments to the poor. You see, our treeboats are medicinal when used properly, and they are also used to treat sick water, and therefore, the whole Earth, if you think about it. Anyway, he would bring people aboard the Oaql boat and help them heal from various illnesses, but it had to be done in secret. You heard a little bit about the wars of the past and how, even now, most of the Reteti of other Haelan islands do not want to be revealed to the rest of the world. Well, if they knew about what Captain Rainer did—and what I do now—they'd . . . Well they'd have something to say for sure. They would not want us taking the treeboat anywhere near a cityfort."

"So you treat sick people too?"

"I do, and I visit places that have sick water."

"Wow, that's amazing. I . . . uh, feel bad I was so rude to you when we met. I thought treeboats were just legends and I didn't know what to think of you . . . but here we are on this island and—"

"I accept your apology. By the way, the other Reteti would be very unhappy if they heard that treeboats have become a part of legends and tales. If we end up on any other Haelin Islands, just don't mention that or anything else I've said today."

"Of course, I understand. And what about your mother? She let you go just like that?"

"Well, she was one of the people Captain Rainer tried healing, but she was already very sick—her treatment was ongoing for weeks. We lived on the treeboat with Captain Rainer during this period and I became his helper as he treated people with all kinds of illnesses. Some would come with a nebulous malaise and would simply spend a night under the shade of the Oaql tree and leave the next morning feeling rejuvenated. Others would have issues with inflammation, arthritis, or a viral infection and would require extensive treatment by ingesting parts of the tree. This also for those with *panema* or mental fog.

"Anyway, as time passed it became clear my mother wasn't healing from her condition, but at the same time she was having profound experiences of foresight through her dreams. Finally, one day, she knew death was coming and, at the same time she knew one other thing—I was meant to learn the ways of the Reteti. As it was just me and my mom, poor and usually cleaning the streets of the city to make a living, Captain Rainer agreed to take me in. I didn't know that would lead me to be a captain myself one day, but I know my mom would've been proud of this work I do now."

"I'm sorry about your mother," Navis said. "But I'm glad you remember so much about her."

Taola just smiled, taking his hand she led him around another green knoll to a tree whose trunk for a moment seemed like the face of a brown mountain. The massive being was shaped like a broccoli with meaty vines dangling down from its branches, standing like a monument at the center of a field of flowers. She explained that this was the origin tree of the Oaql boat. It was *the* single Oaql tree of Oaql Island.

"A smaller, younger version of this tree is with Arionella right now," Taola said. "Now come and touch it."

Navis put his hand on the tree's trunk and felt something like static electricity shoot through his body. He looked at Taola, startled.

"That is some of what Arionella is feeling," she told him. "At this moment, you are close to her in a way."

Then Taola led him away from the tree. Navis kept looking over his shoulder at it. It was looking bigger and bigger, towering high in the distance above the other trees of the island, so much so that Navis began wondering if it would be visible far out on the ocean if there wasn't so much fog surrounding the edges of the island. Here there were no signs of human influence, just a pristine island and its animal inhabitants: monkeys crashed through the trees, birds flitted about and the music of insects filled the air. Soon a cove came into sight, where the clear sea water poured into an inlet. There on another high knoll close to the water stood a tent.

Navis noted it indeed was smaller than the ones he had been seeing, which were a good six meters high at their apex with huge diameters. This one was about two meters high, and as they got closer, he saw the tiny figure of Mama Gogo sitting outside it looking even smaller than usual. She sat swaying on a rattan rocking chair, her hands folded on her lap, her lower lip pushing on her upper lip, and her feet crossed just above the ground. When she caught sight of them, she raised her hand and gestured for them to come close.

"Go-go," Taola sweetly greeted her. "Ana'ntay."

"Sit, sit-nah," she said, pointing to a thatched mat laid out in front of her chair. Taola and Navis sat, and Mama Gogo simply looked at them for a while without speaking, as if saving the moment in her memory. Navis looked around casually, though he was aware of her gaze the whole time. Nearby, attached to short wooden sticks were clotheslines covered with multicolored shawls drying under the hot sun. A little farther away, under the shade of leafy palms, was a girthy tree stump with a little hand axe sticking out of it, and piled neatly beside it were split coconut shells.

"How are you, my boy?" she asked finally, as she gazed upon the sunlit island herself.

Navis's first reaction to the question was the automatic "I'm well, and you?" But then he realized she was speaking more seriously than that, and he felt compelled to answer with an equal seriousness. "Well, actually, I've been a little stressed, Mama Gogo, but I'm getting along."

The elderly Reteti nodded, and then turned to Taola. "Taolanta, my dear, retrieve my mirror from inside, please."

"Sure, I'll be right back." Taola sprang up and went inside the tent.

"And you, my boy, I want you to look at your fingers for a moment."

Navis held his hands out, gazing down at them. "Alright, here they are. What am I looking for?"

"Just look closely."

This time, Navis focused his attention, and what he saw was that his fingernails were chewed down into stumps, and his cuticles were red and cut up.

Taola returned, pushing a large oval mirror attached to a beautiful wooden frame on large imperfectly carven wheels.

"Put that in front of Navis'sa, my dear," said Mama Gogo.

Taola did as she was told, parking it just between Mama Gogo and Navis. Navis looked at the mirror and saw the reflection of a gaunt young man, with curly brown hair in disarray and eyes swollen with exhaustion. He was frowning and looking a little disturbed too.

Mama Gogo's voice came from behind the mirror, but it sounded to Navis as if it came from afar, at least farther than it should have. "Our world is much like this mirror, child. It reflects things to us . . . . We go through difficult times, and yes, we must feel the emotions as they come in the moment, but what makes us suffer is when we take pain and worry about it, think about it too much, and force the passing emotion to linger beyond its time."

Navis was still gazing into the mirror and looking at himself with great scrutiny. He did not look well, and thus worrisome thoughts started to arise in his mind. He started thinking he might be sick with some disease, and a familiar voice in his head started insisting that he needed to take better care of himself.

As if right on cue, Mama Gogo's voice came in again. "Now, in frustration or even concern, if you tell this reflection to change or you go up to it and try to physically force it to change, what happens? It just goes on reflecting, doesn't it? Count your blessings now, instead of what you have lost or what you hope to gain. See what fruits life has lavished upon you in this very moment. And, my dear, if you find that the man in the mirror still cannot appreciate the good fruit in life, you must let that *mango*."

Navis was staring at his reflection, listening to Mama Gogo's words intently, but the intonation of last thing she said made him blink repeatedly—almost as if he were waking up out of a trance—because it did not make any sense to him. He furrowed his brow for a moment, and then it clicked. All at once a tickle arose in his belly and rushed up his chest, and out through his mouth came laughter.

Then the joke hit Taola, and she began laughing, and Mama Gogo started snickering too, which made the other two start laughing even more. Mama Gogo stood and pushed the mirror out of the way and started clapping her hands, hooting with laughter and leaning over toward Navis—who was still sitting on the thatched mat—in a motion that said, "I got you!"

This made Navis and Taola lose control. Taola sank back down next to him and they leaned into each other, their laughter melding together and echoing over the knolls and the bay until, at last, laughter turned into giggles and sighs, and finally into full warm smiles.

"Now stand up, my child, and look at that mirror again," Mama Gogo said as she sat down in her chair. Navis stood this time and aligned himself with the mirror. As before, the reflection showed a thin young man with curly unkempt hair. But this man was beaming, handsome, and had softness to his features that revealed a capacity for compassion and love toward other human beings. Tears began to come to his eyes when he saw this about himself. It was as if that voice of concern within him realized that Navis was healthier and more beautiful than it had ever thought he could be. He turned away from the mirror and wiped his tears and then went over and knelt by Mama Gogo in her chair.

"Thank you, Mama Gogo," he said through the balls of emotion welling up in his throat. "I think I understand now."

She leaned forward and hugged him with great warmth. Navis appreciated it but naturally began to straighten up after just a couple of seconds, so as to not overstay the welcome of contact. However, Mama Gogo did not release him. With one hand, she gestured Taola over and then wrapped them both in a long and encompassing embrace within the tiny reach of her arms.

—End of Part I—

PART II

The heavens descend and the hells arise, bubbling like oil and water in the cauldron of the mind

—Encyclopedia Cyanica

Arionella at Sea
VIII. Tug-of-War

Something strange was happening between the Oaql boat and Arionella since she had become more in tune with the microenvironment of the boat. In one way, she was more under the influence of the living aspect of the boat, but her cantankerous nature swelled up in her chest against the feeling of the unseen stifling force—and the tree of the boat itself would shudder. It was as if their wills were engaging in a subtle tug-of-war.

Arionella noticed that they weren't traveling much anymore. The boat was even slower, or now mostly still, and stayed on open waters. She sensed something akin to frustration all around her, like a palpable pressure in the air, and this caused her to feel frustrated as well. She scolded herself out loud a few times about how she should have listened to Lemay and how she would never wish for an adventure ever again. She thought about Myli and Tumi, how they would sleep at her sides during midafternoon naps, and how she liked to comb their wispy blond hair. *Uncle Navis must be going mad looking for me*, she thought. *I've given him so much trouble over the years. Why did Mima and Pa have to leave?*

Arionella wasn't aware of what was happening, but in fact, during these moments of perseveration and reminiscence she was unconsciously moving the Oaql boat back toward Lindum, the only home she knew. However, after a short while of this, she would fall asleep, utterly exhausted, and while she slept, the boat would move in the opposite direction. She didn't understand why she was so tired all the time. Even though the fruit of the tree gave her bursts of energy, she had stopped eating it, because it made her dizzy and feel strange, as if her mind was growing unfastened from her body. So, she grudgingly returned to the bland birdfeed, which didn't seem so bad anymore. Since her strange dream with the foam and the tree's suffocating embrace, she had kept her distance from it, only going near it now and then to feed the birds, and to watch for an appearance of the golden sprites, which brought her comfort.

Chapter 9

TRAVERSING THE PANS

Navis, Myli, Tumi, and Lemay stood at the stern of the Maradona, looking at the bright horizon that seemed to be moving ever away even as the boat sped toward it over the ocean. This endlessness had bothered Navis when he first set out on this journey three days ago, but now he thought of Mama Gogo's words as she saw them off earlier that day. "We are part of something larger, Navis'sa," she said, taking his hand as he leaned over to give her a hug goodbye. "This chain of events is simply part of that something. You are in a story of greater meaning that cannot be completely understood as you are a character within it. All you can do is move forward and see what it has to offer you, my dear." And with a pat on his cheek, she'd sent him off.

Now night was drawing on. Taola looked skyward to get a sense of the constellations. She stood at the controls, filled with fresh vitality and spark, steering the boat tirelessly. Navis noticed this and thought to himself that the visit to the Haelin Island must have done them all some good. Even Niniola seemed less rigid.

"My lady, I've brought you something to eat," said the newest member of the voyage of the Maradona, Lana-Baboye. She stood, always barefoot, at one hundred and forty centimeters tall—taller than most Reteti. She had shaved her black hair down to her scalp and wore an expression that emanated ferocity yet at the same time radiated stillness and understanding. She was a warrior, trained not for aggression but to defend. A mission of initiation was always given to the young warriors of the Reteti upon the completion of their training, and this mission to accompany Taola, Navis, Niniola, and the children was Lana-Baboye's. She was nineteen years old and had graduated at the top of her class.

"My lady? Oof, please don't call me that," Taola replied. She knew that Lana-Baboye's cultural upbringing had included etiquette of hierarchies, an oral tradition that dictated the relative social positions among the Reteti. It was one of the few elements of Reteti culture she strongly disagreed with. "Call me sis or, if you want to use my rank, Captain."

"Captain it is then," Lana-Baboye said with a bow.

Niniola had come out of the cabin and overheard the exchange. Now, clearing her throat, she said, "Excuse me, but I am the captain with a capital *C* on this ship."

"Really, ladies? Are these titles that important?" Taola said, taking the platter of fruit, cheese, and bread from Lana-Baboye's hands. "Well then, it'll just have to be sis, Lana."

"But I couldn't poss—"

"Of course, you can! Let it be with a capital 'S' if you like."

"As you wish," Lana-Baboye accepted with a sigh.

At around eight o'clock, Navis and the kids were sitting on the cushions at the front of the boat and starting to drift off to sleep. Niniola was writing in her cabin, while Taola and Lana-Baboye were up by the controls of the boat. It was dark because the moon was new, the stars shined brilliantly, and there was calm in the water and the wind.

"Look there," Taola said, pointing toward the west where the dark waters were sparkling with light.

"You think it's the reflection of the stars?" Lana-Baboye asked.

"No, we're passing Luminous Reef! This was one of the remediation spots Captain Rainer took me to years ago. I'll get us a little closer. Get the others, will you?" Taola started steering the Maradona to port. As the boat got closer and closer to the sparkle, it became apparent that just beyond the drop-off was a glimmering coral reef spanning miles and miles of ocean.

First Lana-Baboye knocked on Niniola's door, as it was also on the second level, and then she climbed down the steps to get Navis and the kids.

Niniola stepped out to see Taola steering with fervor and wearing a big smile on her face. Niniola rolled her eyes and thought *What now?*

Below, Navis was sitting upright but with his head drooped, a twin on both sides of his chest, each fast asleep. Lemay was stretched out on a bed of cushions he'd made for himself.

Lana-Baboye thought she might start with Lemay first, but as she approached him, Navis awoke with a snort. Lana-Baboye spun to face him, but he didn't see who it was at first—only a blurred silhouette. He inhaled sharply with surprise and his voice got tangled with his breath, creating a strange shriek—*Eeah!*

"It's me Lana!" Lana-Baboye cried out.

Everyone was awake now, and they had a good laugh about it—at least, once the twins stopped crying. Then they all made their way up onto the second level of the boat to join Taola and Niniola. Looking upon the brilliance of the glowing reef, its crystalline water and the blue and yellow-green specks of light twinkling like clustered galaxies, each person onboard was transfixed.

"Captain Rainer told me that Luminous Reef is lit by bioluminescent organisms—microscopic bacteria that are a part of the coral's diet. Then the corals end up with their own internal lights, see?" Taola pointed at particularly bright clusters of bedazzled coral. "These large and densely lit sections have been around since even before the Old Times. Millennia upon millennia!"

"Owla, can I get some shiny ones?" Myli asked Taola, reaching out to the water.

"Ahh, could you imagine snorkeling on this night?" Taola said with a dreamy expression.

"That would be something extraordinary," Lana-Baboye said. "You must have done a lot of diving, my la—I mean Sis, during your remediation mission here?"

"Yes, to take samples and do any cleaning that the Oaql boat couldn't—you know how that adamantine goes deep and clings. Don't get me wrong though, that Oaql boat is a heavy lifter for sure. Because of this luminescence, I was able to see how the polluted water around the hull of the boat began clearing in real-time. It was spectacular." Taola's eyes widened again. "You know what I never thought of? I wonder how long it would take the Oaql tree to become luminescent if we had it live over this reef for a while! It would go about its business filtering and whatnot, but in the process, it would absorb glowing bacterioplankton."

"Maybe it already glows a bit, but you just didn't notice," Navis chimed in.

Taola looked at Navis with deeply furrowed brows and her mouth hanging open—she was really thinking his idea through.

Niniola in the meantime had gone back inside her cabin and reemerged with her journal. "What were you saying before about the treeboat, Taola?"

Taola's mind was racing as she pondered the possibility that her treeboat might be able to glow in the dark, so she didn't even hear the question.

"What were you thinking of in particular, Captain?" Lana-Baboye replied instead.

"The treeboat cleaning and Taola having a mission here."

"I can speak to that," Lana-Baboye replied. "Our tribal name *Reteti* translates to 'remediators' in your language. The treeboats and their captains go around the world remediating damaged, delicate zones of the sea that subtly impact us all because of the food chain and the currents of the ocean. I don't know if Taola mentioned the fungal aspect of the treeboats to you?"

"Yes, she did."

"Ah, good! Well, what we have learnt is that a component of its fungal properties has a powerful digestive—and therefore filtration—system that renders oil, most chemicals, and other toxins into bioavailable nutrients. There is much damage to be slowly undone from the old times, when there were unbridled polluting practices in effect.

"Anyway, there are many other things we Reteti do. For example, my fellow students and I are also trained in deep diving, particularly for the sake of tending to the complex ecosystems and nurseries that lay beneath our Haelin Islands. The Reteti also have purposes outside the water. For example, because treeboat fruit is medicinal when used appropriately, we have used them to treat whole villages overcome with contagious diseases in some cases."

"Can we, can we?" Myli started up her demands for some "shiny ones" again.

"They are alive, sweety," Navis explained gently. "If you take them out of their home, they will soon not glow anymore."

"They would die?" she said, looking sad now, twiddling Navis's earlobe unconsciously with her fingers.

"Yes, they would get very sick and then . . . ."

"They would die?"

"Mmm-hmm." Navis nodded.

Taola finally surfaced out of her reverie. "But we can visit them anytime and get close to them by swimming, Myli."

"Yes, after we complete our missions, we must return here together!" Lana-Baboye said.

"Good! It's a promise, then, everyone?" Taola asked and looked around.

"What do you think, kids? Want to go swimming in the glowing water someday?" Navis asked.

It was a unanimous decision all around, even Niniola grunted in an affirming way when they turned toward her.

After gazing upon the Luminous Reef for a good thirty minutes more, the yawns began, and so the Maradona was moved away from the reef and its anchor lowered. Everyone went to their quarters with the luster of the reef remaining behind closed eyes.

Good night, good night! Dream of glowing waters tonight!

———•———

It had been just under twenty-four hours since the little crew of the Maradona left Oaql Island and finally made it to Pans Harbor—the port of Pansmont—which stood at the tip of the western continent, Citatia. Hidden somewhere on this land lived the Enané people. In fact, Taola had never visited them and didn't actually know where they lived, but she was once told where she might start—Halla Manor, a place she had been to before. Halla Manor had once been a grand and private estate of none other than Jöshi Halla's family, now a community-run place for travelers. It was a hub for trade of goods, services, and information. Over the years, it had gained a reputation as an important stop if anyone found themselves on the east end of the continent Citatia.

While still on the Maradona, Taola was running through her plan of travel with Niniola about getting through some woods and following a dirt path, but then she uttered the words "Halla Manor" and Navis looked up shocked from his travel pack that he had been busily organizing.

"Wait, excuse me, Taola, but where exactly are we going?" he asked incredulously.

"Halla Manor?" she replied in a questioning tone.

Niniola also looked up and glanced at Navis, for in her recent conversation with Sir Charles in the medical tent, the Hallas had come up, but she hadn't found an opportunity to tell Navis yet, mostly because they never spoke to each other much.

"Halla Manor," he said. "The place associated with Jöshi and Maya Halla?"

"Yes, actually. You've heard of them too? I guess the Wandering Lovers are even more famous than I thought!"

"I don't know about Wandering Lovers but—" Navis stood and pointed toward Lemay, who was playing with the twins amongst the cushions across the boat. "The Hallas are the ones who brought this little family together. They adopted me when I was about twelve years old, and they are Arionella's actual grandparents!"

"ARE YOU SERIOUS?" Taola's mouth hung wide open, her arms flung out wide, her palms up and fingers wide. "Why didn't you tell me before?!"

"It never came up. Did you know them too?"

"Yes! Well, Captain Rainer knew them better, but I met them a few times, and . . . my gawd . . . you know what else?"

"What?"

"This is good news!"

"Well, yes, they used to tell me about Halla Manor. I always wanted to see it. However, I don't think any of Jöshi's family actually runs it anymore."

"No, no! I mean, yes, that too, but what is even more important is that when I took over captaincy of the Oaql boat, Captain Rainer told me that Maya Airgialla Halla had passed away on the boat, and furthermore, that it became the final resting place of her ashes."

Taola was brimming with excitement and didn't notice Navis suddenly looking upset. He glanced down at the deck and then slowly sat on a wooden crate. Niniola, who had been standing aside and listening the whole time, looked like she was about to move toward him or say something, but she seemed to reconsider and bit her lip.

Taola continued, "Navis, this is unbelievable! It's such a small world. Who knew we'd have so many connections?" Then Taola finally noticed the change in Navis's demeanor. "Navis, what is it?" She went over to him and sat down next to him.

"I . . . I just didn't know she had passed away," Navis said quietly.

It was almost visible how Taola's internal momentum came to a halt, and with inertia. She hung her head and put her arm over his shoulders. "I'm so sorry."

They sat in silence for a time.

Then Navis said, "I just don't know why Jöshi didn't send me a message—what does our time together back then mean to him? And—"

"Listen, Navis," Taola interrupted. "We don't know what kind of situation they were in. Captain Rainer told me Jöshi's destination was someplace, let's say, uncommon. Better to give Jöshi the benefit of the doubt." Then, Taola's enthusiasm started returning, but this time she tried her best to contain it. "But, Navis, let me tell you why I'm so hopeful."

Navis could sense the place of deep and sheer effervescence Taola was coming from, and this caused him to look up into her eyes.

She held his gaze, gray eyes wide and smiling. Then, she said slowly, "I think there may be a connection between Arionella knowing the Oaql Boat was arriving near Lindum and her grandmother passing away on the boat. I don't want to jump to conclusions, but maybe, maybe this is somehow part of the message you've been waiting for. Maybe Maya's consciousness found Arionella through the Oaql boat!" Taola's face was filled with hope, and Navis didn't want to turn away from it, but he did, shaking his head.

"I'm sorry, Taola, that is too much of a stretch for me," he said. "Anyway, it's amazing enough already that there are these unexpected connections between them, you, me, and Ari. Let's stick to the facts."

Meanwhile, Niniola's internal conflict seemed to be growing more acute. Her face was flushed and every time it looked like she was about to speak she would reconsider and jerk her head away from where Navis and Taola were sitting.

Taola reached out and grabbed Navis's chin and made him look at her again. "I took captaincy of the Oaql boat after Maya's death, but before that, for years, I had been training on it, learning about it, and taking trips with Captain Rainer across the ocean, eventually learning to tune into its energy signal. However, since Maya's passing, something has been distinctly different with the Oaql boat. Captain Rainer and I both noticed it.

"We began to sense Maya very distinctly—the same feeling I got in her presence when she was alive. You see, the Reteti consider the tree-boats—and the Haelin Islands, for that matter—caches of souls. Beyond that, they believe there is a resonance, or residue, of consciousness in anything that has been interacted with by a sentient organism, including inanimate objects."

Navis gave her another look of skepticism.

"You have to understand that in their lexicon, the terms "soul," "spirit," or even "ghost" don't mean the same thing as the generic definitions of the words in the common language. Over the course of eons, meaning was lost in translation, and I was taught that putting experience and knowledge into words in the first place is only an indicator of the truth, not the truth itself."

This time, Navis held her gaze.

Then, Taola added, "In our language, it may be more sophisticated to say the treeboats and Haelin Islands are caches of consciousness."

"Why didn't you tell me all this before?" Navis asked.

"Really?" Taola put her hands on her hips and cocked her head to the side. "I was 'Miss Loopy' when I mentioned treeboats and Haelin Islands a few days ago, and you're saying that I should've been sharing my animistic views about nature, souls, and spirits with you?"

Blinking with surprise at first, Navis sat frozen until a smile appeared on his face. The he said, "You've got me there. Well, I should say that this all gives me some hope, and I want to say that my doubts—including, you know, considering you loopy—from the first time we met, have obviously been put aside for trust." Navis ventured a glance at Taola's eyes to search for signs of forgiveness. "So even though I don't understand many of the things you're talking about yet, all I can say is, lead on, Captain Lonwë." Navis gave her a little salute and a warm smile.

Taola was so happy at this that she leaned forward and gave him a back-cracking hug and a kiss on the cheek. Then they helped each other up and returned their attention to the approaching land just ahead of them.

———— ◆ ————

Niniola was having a difficult time leaving the Maradona behind. She wanted to find a trustworthy dock and keeper but had no luck so far. Though a major port, Pansmont was dirty and rundown. The smell of caught fish was strong and the attempts at making paved walkways were abandoned under mud and weeds. It was midafternoon and the town was bustling with people selling their wares, while boats arrived and departed at the decaying wooden docks overrun with moss and fungus.

Niniola—taking Pansmont's tenor into account—had been considering staying with the Maradona when Taola showed up leading a man with a pep in his steps and a big smile on his bearded face.

"Captain Adeebee, right?" Navis was the first to call out, recognizing the sailor he'd met—and argued with—in Lindum five days ago.

"Abdenbi, Captain Abdenbi, my friend," Captain Abdenbi corrected him. He looked overjoyed to see them all. He leaned over and swept Tumi up off his feet like he had been reunited with his own nephew. "My, have you grown! Wao, Wao! Oh, and the little girl too—come here, precious!" The twins were right at home with him and began laughing and playing with his thick salt and pepper beard. "Ah, and the little messenger. How are you, my boy?"

"Uh, I'm fine," Lemay replied a little less warmly than the twins, who by now had managed to crawl up Captain Abdendi's shoulders and pull his hat off revealing a bald patch skirted by salt and pepper hair.

Smiling, the captain turned to Niniola. "Captain Taola Lonwë tells me you are looking for someone to watch over the Maradona. Look no farther—I'm your man! She'll be happy alongside my ship, *Bartholomew the Unsinkable*!"

Niniola looked distrusting. She excused herself and Taola.

"What is it?" Taola asked when they were out of earshot.

"Why are we trusting this man?"

"I feel people out. I have a good feeling about him."

"Feeling? You're handing over my ship and *everything in it* based on a feeling?"

"Well, yes. How else were you going to find someone? Unless we run into someone from home that you happen to already know and trust?"

"I thought there might be a shipyard run by some organization . . . something official to this town."

"Niniola, you should know better. These days, other than in the cityforts, you're rarely going to find something like that."

Lana-Baboye walked over carrying two empty burlap sacks. "You can trust him," she said.

"See? There you go! Two to one." Taola threw her hands up in the air and then began pulling her long black hair into a tight ponytail. She seemed agitated.

"Do you have a *feeling* too?" Niniola asked Lana-Baboye facetiously.

"Well, I've been trained to read people, and I can say this man has a temper, but he is honest and will go to great lengths to help people"— Lana-Baboye glanced at Abdenbi and added—"especially after he's had a good meal."

Niniola admired the warrior's discipline, solidness, and especially her respectfulness over the time they had gotten to know each other on the boat—as compared to Taola's free-spirited raps against Niniola's attempts to establish authority. After a few moments of silent reflection, she agreed. The three women walked back over to Navis and Captain Abdenbi.

Before they could say anything, Captain Abdenbi held his hands out apologetically and said, "Look, I understand you think the price is too steep, but let me tell you, we would keep your ship in mint condition. Mint!" He kissed his fingers. Before they could respond, he spoke again. "Okay, okay, just treat me and the boys to a meal, and I'll take a whole crown off the price."

Niniola glanced at Lana-Baboye with an amused frown that said, *Damn, you were right.*

"Alright, Captain Abdenbi," she said. "I, Captain Niniola Maradona of the Maradona, will do business with you." She held out her hand, her chin held high.

Captain Abdenbi swelled up his chest and took her had. "Captain Abdenbi Marsi of *Bartholomew the Unsinkable* accepts your business with pleasure." They shook, and then Captain Abdenbi put his hands in his pockets, looked around, and shrugged. "How hungry are you all feeling?"

True to its name, Captain Abdendi's favorite tavern, The Smoky Sailor, was filled with seafaring people, their pipes, and billows of smoke. However, the captain was very clear as to why he had brought the crew of the Maradona to this particular tavern—the food portions were large, and dessert was included in the meal.

A dozen people in total, including Captain Abdenbi's crew of four, were served at once at a long table by tough-looking waiters who each carried a different kind of weapon tucked into a special holster on the side of their apron. Lemay's eye level was low, so he was looking directly at hunting knives, metal batons, and the manager of the tavern was even packing a little electric-prong blaster. Lemay tugged at Navis's sleeve and pointed at the array of things he could only assume were used for inflicting bodily harm.

Navis leaned over and asked Captain Abdenbi if it was safe for the children to be there—he was hoping for an exchange in whispers but that is not what he got.

"Lad!" Captain Abdenbi hooted. "You all are in one of the safest places on the planet! These ruff looking bammerweeds—" he pointed at the waiters serving them, "—could nurse your babies; they're so nice."

Navis turned bright red, put his arm over Lemay, sank low into his chair, and smiled uncomfortably at the men who were now taking special interest in him. He swore to himself that he would only speak to Captain *Adeebee* when necessary.

Taola, on the other hand, was caught up in the atmosphere, laughing and banging the table with her palm at a joke she herself had made. She drew agitated glances from Niniola who had the twins on either side of her along the bench seating against the wall.

Meanwhile, Lana-Baboye seemed distant as she fiddled with a knife and the burlap sacks she'd collected earlier.

The meal they were served was a hearty one of butter melted on freshly baked bread, salted meats, aged cheeses, fluffy eggs, sweet porridge, freshly squeezed juices, aromatic teas, and coffee. Then the dessert came, with a house-special rum cake, blueberry pie, banana bread, oatmeal cookies, and pistachio ice cream.

Everyone was in a jolly frenzy of eating and being entertained by Captain Abdenbi's stories or his philosophies on life: "You know what I say?" said Captain Abdenbi rapping on the table with his hand after one of his crew members made a comment, "Obaidullah here doesn't understand that life doesn't get better just because of your location. I mean wherever you go—there you are!" And so on.

After nearly two hours of eating and chatting, the crew of the Maradona started saying their goodbyes to the jolly crew of the *Bartholomew*. Captain Abdenbi walked them to the door of the tavern, where he addressed them with great tenderness. "As I'm sure you know most people don't know how to make an honest living anymore. Sad to say, it's not safe out there on the trails and in the forests. If you must take the children, you all must be vigilant."

Lana-Baboye put her hands on Myli and Tumi's heads and said, "I'm here to protect them at all costs Captain, don't you worry." Captain Abdenbi blinked, seeming to take her into account for the first time, realizing that she wasn't just a thin girl accompanying them but a bruiser that could challenge even the most stalwart men of his crew. He seemed contented and shook each person's hand, even the children's, and, standing at the door of the tavern, watched them depart as if they had just left the safety of his own home.

The crew of the Maradona gathered by a large fountain in the town center of Pansmont to regroup before they set out.

"What's that you've been making, Lana?" Lemay asked.

Navis, Taola, and Niniola turned at the question because everyone had noticed at some point that Lana-Baboye was rapidly stitching, binding, and twisting something on her lap through the whole meal and had least participated in the merrymaking. She held up the burlap sacks she was carrying before, but now they were lined with scrap sheets of wool and cotton, and sported jute straps and, at the base, a long and wide piece of stretchy cloth.

"Carrier-packs to carry the twins when they get tired."

"I was wondering," Navis said. "If Abdenbi considered it safe in the tavern with all those . . . ruffians, and he considers it dangerous out there, then it may not be a good idea to take the children at all. I've already exposed them to too much since we left Lindum."

Lemay curled his fists—he knew where this was going.

"I agree, that is an important consideration you must take into account Navis'sa," Lana-Baboye replied with a slight bow.

"I think we should, at the very least, stay back on the Maradona and wait for your return."

"No, we have to keep moving!" Lemay cut in.

"Listen Lemay, they're not going to even be directly looking for Arionella out there." Navis retorted. "They're moving inland, while the Oaql boat is out there." He pointed back toward the Cyan Sea.

"But Taola is the one connected to the Oaql boat—without her we won't know anything!" Lemay's point did seem to make Navis think for a spell, but he shook his head.

"I know it doesn't seem right. I want to keep moving too, but there are times when adults have to make decisions that seem unfair but are for the best."

"You're barely an adult yourself!"

"I'm more of an adult than you are and that's what matters." Lemay glared at Navis until tears came into his eyes. Then he turned and ran away blindly. "Where are you going? Stop!"

"Leave me alone!" Lemay shouted back.

"Watch the twins please," Navis said to Lana-Baboye as he broke into a jog behind Lemay.

"They're out of control." Niniola said coldly. "He doesn't know how to discipline them; that's why that girl is out there somewhere—I would see them around town arguing all the time—an accident was bound to happen someday."

"He has a difficult role," Taola cut in. "It's easy to see the solution, but it's harder to implement it."

"A tight smack isn't hard to implement, I assure you." At this, Myli and Tumi both glanced nervously at Niniola. Lana-Baboye crouched down, held them close in an embrace, and smiled warmly. They felt a little better, but Myli said to Tumi, "Nanuna is scary." Tumi nodded in reply.

Lemay didn't think about where he was running; he only began to take in his surroundings as his breaths become labored and his legs heavy.

He was going up a slanted dirt road toward a cliff behind the shops of the town. Here, old trees stood in patches of wiry grass, and a spread of bluebell flowers lined the cliff edge. The Cyan Sea was visible to the east beyond them. Feeling the cool wind against his tear-stained face, Lemay took a deep breath and slowed to a stop on a dense patch of grass and flowers near the cliff's edge where a bench made of cracked gray stone overlooked the ocean. He slumped onto it and gazed out over the endless blue-green water. He began conjuring up an apparition of the Oaql boat through his tear-filled vision where a cluster of clouds had created a shadowy region in the distance. He sprang up and called out as loud as he could, "ARIONELLA!" Realizing his folly as he rubbed his eyes clear, he sank down onto all fours and clenched the grass angrily.

Navis stood watching from the dirt road giving Lemay a few moments to himself. Looking around he saw no one in sight, surprised that the noise and bustle of the town did not make its way up here. The trees rustled and the sun's rays danced through the leaves onto Lemay below. Navis awkwardly made his way over and sat down on the grass next to him. A tense reticence emerged between them as Lemay didn't acknowledge Navis's presence. So Navis plucked a few strands of the grass and began braiding it like Maya had taught him to do with Arionella's hair. He recalled breezy afternoons like this one. Jöshi would be working in the garden, tilling the loamy soil with a hoe—his long white beard getting brown and dusty. Navis would be sitting on a bail of straw holding the round-faced baby Lemay in his arms, watching as Maya crouched comfortably in a low squat, her feet bare, weaving strands of white and purple morning glories through Arionella's red locks in the grass fields adjacent to their cabin.

Navis glanced over at Lemay now and noted his jaw line and the little defining ridge along his brows—he was not the little baby he used to hold anymore—and though he was a quiet child compared to Arionella, he was just as—if not more—passionate then her. Navis looked down at the little green braid he had made and then out over the horizon, and without thinking he began to hum. The slightest movement came from Lemay who immediately recognized the tune. Navis then began to whisper the lyrics:

A star fell into our arms

From the heavens above

Child of the Sun

Child of the Moon

Lemay found that his eyes, that had begun to dry, began pouring out tears again.

Make a wish and be heard

The force of your thoughts

Sing, sing a prayer

The force of your heart

Navis continued singing, but a lump began to form in his throat and his voice trembled to the beats of his heart.

Children of the stars

You were grown in the earth

It is time to shine

To shine with humility

Now, Lemay began to sing in a whisper through skipping breaths too:

Remember to give to all who seek

Know the signs and whispers

And be prepared to receive

You are not alone

Tears appeared in Navis's eyes as well, though he was smiling and holding his head high.

A star fell into our arms

From the heavens above

Child of the Sun

Child of the Moon

Then they were quiet and the sound of the ocean wind rustling the trees took over again. Navis put an arm over Lemay and pulled him close.

After a few moments Lemay said, "I miss Mima and Pa."

"I do too," Navis replied.

"And I miss Ari."

Navis leaned into Lemay and ruffled his hair with a gentle hand. "Me too."

"Do you think she's okay?"

"I—" Navis didn't know what to say, so he took a deep breath and tried picturing Arionella in his mind. He recalled a memory of her shouting down a whole gaggle of boys who had been throwing stones at a wild piglet along the edge of the forest just outside of Lindum. He smiled and said, "All I know is that your sister is one of the toughest people I've ever met. Don't you agree?" Lemay nodded in affirmation. "Well, then we should trust that she's keeping well."

They were silent again for a time. Then, Lemay said, "You know something? Taola reminds me of Ari."

Navis laughed. "Yes, at times. I agree."

"You know something else?"

"What?"

"When I'm with her, Ari doesn't seem so far away." Their eyes met for a moment and then they turned their gazes back to the ocean and sat in silence again.

————◆————

"Navis'sa, please bring Tumi over. There." Lana-Baboye helped lower Tumi into the sack. His little legs and arms popped out in the little openings she had made for them. "Now you can wear this on your chest or your back." Navis turned, and Lana-Baboye helped him put the straps over his shoulders and then tied the straps around him, but what made the greatest difference in support was the large cloth that she wound around his waist like a belt. Navis bounced a couple of times, moved side to side, and then took a jog around the fountain with Tumi happily squealing on his back.

"Well done, Lana!" Navis said, panting. "You've made these kids' dream of having me as their horse a reality!" Everyone laughed at this, except Myli, who was already crying because she "wanted a turn."

"Don't worry, sweetie, you each have one," Lana said. "How about you get in this carrier, and I'll carry you?" Lana-Baboye helped Myli get into the other carrier and then strapped it up to her own back.

Then, they all made their final preparations aboard the Maradona, packing only what they needed.

"Well, now that both children are strapped in and we're all packed, we might as well get going," Taola said. "The rest of us can carry the supply packs. Lemay, you take this one; it's the lightest.

"Okay, loose overview. We're heading through Pans Forest on a winding dirt road that is pretty well established. We should get to the Charred Borders clearing just before sunset. Then we can decide what to do next, based on how we are feeling." Taola then paused and deliberated for a moment. Then she said, "And Captain Abdenbi was right. We need to be careful on these roads. On the sea, we must keep watch for pirates, but on land, there is an even higher risk of running into thugs. During breaks, and when we stop at night, we'll have to take sentry shifts."

Niniola glanced around before repositioning her blaster on her hip. "So, this is your decision Navis? It seems incredibly negligent to take the children on this trip."

It was Taola who responded. "I spoke to Navis about this. Mama Gogo intended for him and the children to visit the Enané as well."

"Yes, Niniola," Navis added. "Lemay and I spoke, and we feel we should stick together at this point."

Niniola only shook her head and shrugged in reply.

The group set out toward the west wall that was made of old red bricks, and then they stepped through its rusted metal gates. They set out alone; no one else was entering or exiting Pansmont at that time. They followed a dirt road that wound itself through Pans Forest. It was cool under the canopy of the maple, oak, beech, and birch trees. Navis, Niniola, and the kids felt at home amongst these hardwoods as the township of Lindum was at the foot of the Lindarious Mountains, which was also home to these trees, as well as pine and cedar at higher elevations. The pleasant weather and the shade made for quick progress. Though the adults had made an unspoken agreement not to walk at full stride for the sake of Lemay, Lemay himself showed no sign of slowing down.

Time and time again, Navis drew strength from the nine-year-old who always wore an expression of determination. It was as if Arionella were visible to Lemay, and for him, all that was left was to walk to her and give her a big hug.

Compared to the usually monotone atmosphere of the ocean, everyone was drinking in the various hues of green set aglow by the sun above the canopy. The *o-ka-lee!* of red-winged blackbirds and the rising and falling pitch of a *cuk-cuk-cuk-cuk-cuk* from a pileated woodpecker rang out among the myriad chirps across the columns of trees. Every so often, with a breeze, the scent of the earthy detritus of the forest bed would rise where their steps sank delicately into fallen leaves and layers of moss—a welcome change from the fishy reek of the docks of Pansmont and the salty nothingness of the sea.

With a contented smile, Navis watched as Myli sat comfortably in her carrier on Lana-Baboye's back, engrossed in her vantage point of a day in Lana-Baboye's life: stones were overturned, trees were climbed, nuts and fruits were tasted; plants and mushrooms were scrutinized, litter discarded by travelers was collected in a long durable sac hung at her waist, and the creek that ran adjacent—and often through the trail—was visited periodically for rinsing any foraged items worth keeping in an oblong, rattan-bamboo container fastened across her chest. And yet somehow, she would always catch up with the rest of the group, never slowing them down.

At one-point Navis, Tumy and Lemay grew curious about what Lana-Baboye was doing and gathered around her. She was crouching over an arched rootbark that had a distinctly smooth and almost fashioned appearance of a miniature cave leading into the ground.

"What'cha doin?" Tumy asked when Navis brought him close enough to Lana-Baboye to see that she was choosing the smoothest and prettiest stones she could find to stack them carefully upon one another just beside the rootbark.

"Come, look closer at how only this root has a little bed of moss growing around it," she replied. "And see how little clovers grow at its doorstep in such an organized manner—and this hole here, what a perfect little window for a little being to gaze out at the golden mystery that gathers here!"

"Golden mystery?" Lemay asked, unintentionally sardonic. "Those are just forest sprites."

As soon as Lemay had said this, Navis blinked as golden specks appeared in and out of sight just above the little rootbark Lana-Baboye was crouched over. He recalled seeing them all the time when he was only a bit younger, and now marveled at how he had ceased to see them at all, and so had forgotten all about them.

"*Just?*" Lana-Baboye asked, an amused expression upon her face as she peered deep into Lemay's eyes.

"Well, I just meant that this stuff is everywhere, just like gnats and mosquitos. They're probably just insects too."

"You must think about your use of the word 'just.'"

"What do you mean?"

"You assume that there is nothing deeper behind any of these beings. Can you tell me what insects are in actuality?"

Lemay thought for a second. "They are little animals, I think."

"And what are animals?"

"Um, creatures, I guess."

"And what are creatures?"

"Things that are alive?"

"And what does it mean to be alive?"

Lemay curled his nose and puckered his lips, thinking hard. Then he said, "To breathe and move around makes you alive."

Lana-Baboye nodded to acknowledge his effort, but then she said, "That's somewhat true except plants are very much alive but do not all move. Anyway, we will explore the definition of life another time. For now, I will tell you what my people think insects and the golden mystery are.

"Starting with the insects, these are the myriad beings that keep life in motion. They are energy weavers, though their duties might be considered 'dirty work' by some, they are vital to our survival." As she spoke, Lana-Baboye set another flat gray-blue stone with rounded edges on her little stack of, what were now, five stones.

Navis had let Tumy down out of the carrier. Tumy went over and stood by Myli, who was still comfortably in her carrier on Lana-Baboye's back, listening to and feeling the vibrations of Lana-Baboye's smooth and gentle voice.

"That's interesting," Lemay replied, and then turned to Navis. "Doesn't this remind you of things Pa and Mima used to tell us, Uncle Navis?"

"Yes, it does," Navis said with a smile.

Lana-Baboye smiled and continued, "And now, about what you call sprites—in our language we call the *edo omimi*, the golden mystery— for as you can see, the nature of their duties is hidden in plain sight. By observation, we cannot perceive any action or duty they take part in, and the way they flicker in and out of existence is even more intriguing.

"Now, what I'm about to share may be hard to understand, but that is because of the mysterious nature of what we speak of. From the oldest traditions, and I mean not only of the Reteti but of the ancients of the Old World and the worlds before it, the seers and shaman who peered into the beyond passed down the wisdom that the sprites appear at different times on the Earth when the other planes of existence—what some call dimensions—are closer to each other than usual. When I say 'closer', it doesn't really mean in distance; it's more about resonance and frequency, but anyway, I digress.

"Our lives are short, so we don't realize how fortunate we are to perceive such things regularly, for there are whole epochs in Earth's history where these sprites were so rare, or so completely invisible, that they would be essentially non-existent to the humans living in that era.

"Hence, they are the golden mystery, hints of planes beyond our own. Some tribes like the Nowwa say that these sprites are residual energies of the spiritual homes of species we see in this world. They believe that the original forms of the creatures on this Earth are determined in the beyond, and when they are born into Earth they all manifest as individuals with slight deviations but are imbued with the original spirit of their ethereal prototypical form—just think of the different birds we see, the insects, the tigers, squirrels, and even humans.

"And yet, other tribes like the Wetobii have disseminated legends that the sprites could be the seams of another forest made up of plants whose colors we could not even begin to imagine. Or, as other tribes have described in their cosmology, the sprites may be the signal of energy given off from invisible beings that are tending to our world, helping things grow and encouraging the formation of little shrines like this here rootbark." Lana-Baboye set yet another gray-blue stone on her set of, now, six stones—and to everyone looking down at the little arched root, her stack seemed like a chimney poking out of a little earthen house for tiny people.

Where Lemay and Navis looked pensive, the twins began to grow antsy, Tumy tried to knock over Lana-Baboye's stones, and Myli began squirming in her carrier.

"Alright, alright. Let's get going," Navis picked up Tumy. "Taola and Niniola are waiting up ahead."

They set out again. The ruminative silence of the little band of travelers was augmented by the sounds of the forest that now, suddenly, seemed so magical and so full of mystery.

———•———

As the trail went deeper into Pans Forest, it became less linear, so the crew of the Maradona helped each other get over and under fallen trees, and across creeks cutting through the trail in some spots. Though it felt good to be able to really use and exert their bodies in a variety of positions and see the occasional black squirrel or badger scurry across their path, after a few hours everyone—except maybe Lana-Baboye—started feeling the blood throb in their legs. Taola kept pressing on, however, making sure that any snacking was done while still in motion, until finally they came to a clearing late in the afternoon after about four hours of hiking. They stood facing an open filed sandwiched in between Pans Forest. Both edges of the forest surrounding the grassy expanse were made up of disfigured trees that were also charred black. It was apparent that a fire had cleaved down a whole section of the forest, which now was a fertile plain, and the trees that withstood the flames had grown warped over a period of recovery. And yet, amazingly, higher up, the same maimed trees sported robust, brown-barked branches and green leaves.

"We've made it to the Charred Borders," Taola said to Lana-Baboye. "I think it's a good place to stop for the night."

"Are you sure you don't just want to stop for food and try to cover more distance?" Lana-Baboye asked.

"Thinking of the kids and taking into account the time we would need to set up the tents and all, I wouldn't want to end up having to camp out in the dark forest," said Taola and pointed across the clearing of grass to where the dirt trail continued into the next patch of forest. "You see there? We'll continue through there in the morning, and by the time the sun is at its zenith we'll have made it to Halla Manor, if we leave early."

"Okay, sounds good Sis," Lana-Baboye replied. She had been happily employing the pet name Taola insisted she use. It brought her a sense of warmth and joy that she could call Taola with familiarity—someone she had admired since she was a young girl. Taola had been the older exotic outsider, but she had quickly gained respect and become an integral part of the Reteti community as an apprentice to the ways of the treeboats. With Niniola and Navis, however, Lana-Baboye maintained her formalities: Niniola was Captain and Navis was Navis'sa. The "-sa" was added in the Reteti language to the end of names of people who were older, and in general to show deference. Navis didn't really notice the difference either way and never asked her about it.

Everyone lent a hand in making a fire in a dusty pit that they only had to reshape into a neater circle with some charred stones, which seemed to have been used by travelers for ages. Bread was cut up and toasted over the flames, cheese was melted, leather satchels of dehydrated vegetables and spices were poured into a pot of boiling water collected from a nearby stream for some instant soup. Then they sat in a ring around the low, smoldering fire, feasting happily and chatting about the little creatures they had seen scurrying by in the forest earlier that day. After a bit of bitter chocolate for dessert, they began setting up the little fold-up tents that the Reteti had provided them. Sunset seemed to have come rapidly, and by now a few other travelers were sprinkled across the grassy plain, setting up their own shelters for the night.

At one-point, Navis lifted Taola's bag to move it out of the way of where he was driving a stake into the earth with a large stone for his tent.

"Be careful!" Taola exclaimed when Navis tossed the bag negligently to one side.

"Oh, my goodness!" he exclaimed. "I'm sorry. I completely forgot about the seed!"

At this, Taola walked over to him and whispered, "Well, actually the seed isn't in there, just some of my navigation instruments and stuff."

"You left it under the bunk on the boat? Isn't that risky?"

"Listen, you can't tell anyone, or Niniola will kill me."

"Nooo, Taola, don't tell me you—"

"Hold on, hold on! Listen to me." Taola grew frustrated and held up a hand, fiercely gesturing for complete silence on Navis's part. "That night on Oaql Island, after everyone went to bed, Niniola showed up at my tent and took me to the Maradona. She—" Taola glanced around quickly, "—she let me plant it."

"In the chamber?" Navis asked a little too loudly.

"Shh, yes!" Taola hissed. "Listen, she has her reasons, and I promised her I would keep them private. Anyway, this is not the time to talk."

"But who's tending to it? Doesn't it need to be watered or something?"

"By now, it's living off the moisture that comes through the vents. It helps that it's predominantly a fungus at this stage of its life." Taola turned at the sound of footsteps and smiled as she saw Myli, Tumi, and Lemay coming over, dragging their feet. "Aww, children, you seem tired. Come here to Aunty Owla." Taola kneeled and pulled them all into a group hug and squeezed them tight. "Time to sleep now. Look, Uncle Navi has your tent all set up." The kids crawled into the tent silently, and Navis threw in blankets after them.

When Taola and Navis were alone again, she put her finger on her lips and widened her eyes at Navis, signaling that he should keep their exchange about the planting of the seed a secret. Then, she said in a normal voice, "Alright. So, you want to take the first watch? Look over there—." Taola used her nose to point at a rainbow-colored tent, with a group of people in rainbow colored clothing, hooting and laughing as they unpacked and passed around musical instruments to one another. "That bunch looks like they'll be up late drinking and playing music late into the night. At least you'll have some entertainment."

Navis shrugged. "Sure."

"Okay, good, I'll work out the last three shifts with the ladies." She spun on her heel, and walked over to the tent she would be sharing with Lana-Baboye and Niniola.

Very soon, all was still at their camp. The gentle evening breeze carried the sounds of merriment from other camps and made the taller spots of grass dance.

Arionella at Sea
IX. The Transition

Arionella had begun to feel a perpetual sense of heaviness in her body and sluggishness of mind. It was as if gravity had a greater pull on the Oaql boat, and her heart had to push against some invisible force just to beat. Instead of playing with the little trinkets in the cabin, she spent most of her time lying down in the loft, exhausted. There was definitely an unseen struggle in and around her, but she could not figure out exactly what it was. Arionella thought, *I'm not having the normal foods I used to have. I miss people; maybe this is what seasickness is, and there is something about this boat and that tree that is definitely odd.*

She found some solace when she would close her eyes and dive into her memories of Navis, Lemay, Myli, Tumi, and her grandparents, Maya and Jöshi. Navis and her grandparents had filled her earliest memories with joy. Whether it was making watermelon gazpacho with her grandmother, woodworking with her grandfather, or climbing trees with Navis, she never really felt the absence of her birth parents—whom she didn't remember or even wonder about. Lemay joined the family when he was only two years old and Arionella was approaching her fifth birthday. He was her early birthday gift, her grandparents had said.

It had been two years since her beloved grandparents had said their goodbyes to her, Lemay, and Navis as if they were leaving for good. Arionella and Maya, her grandmother, were both sitting in the field of flowers outside the cabin as Maya stroked her hair and braided it with white and purple morning glories. Arionella lifted her head out of an embrace and quietly began fiddling with the black hemp necklace Maya always wore. It had a single raw green, garnet gemstone attached to it, one that she would stare at, imagining she could see stone faces in its blocky, multifaceted sides.

"But why can't we go with you, Mima?" Arionella finally asked with tears in her eyes.

"I wish that were possible, my dear," Maya said with great sadness. Save for the creases of wisdom alongside her eyes, and slight indents framing her lips, Maya's red hair and lean frame revealed nothing of the sixty-two years of a full and adventurous life she had led thus far. For Arionella she was truly "mom," and though they had long talked about how this day of parting might come, Arionella felt as if it was the cruelest surprise sprung on her that day. Such were the memories that swirled round her awareness until she fell asleep again.

After some unknown span of time, Arionella forced herself up because she had awoken in a dark cabin with her stomach aching with hunger, realizing that another day had gone by in bed. She went over to the pantry and stuffed herself with seeds, nuts, and dried fruits. Though she felt full now, she still wasn't satiated, and the strong feeling of lethargy began coming over her again. Standing there in the candlelight amidst the dimly lit artifacts in the cabin, she began thinking of the fruit of the tree and found that her mouth began watering. The next thing she knew, she was outside, the door of the cabin closing behind her.

It was a blustery night. The tree's branches swayed and danced in the wind. Arionella thought that if she didn't know what wind was, she would think that trees moved a lot. She approached the tree apprehensively, the candlelight from the cabin only deepening its shadows. When she reached its trunk, she huffed out some of her trepidation and started climbing. The sudden sound of startled birds made Arionella slip and nearly fall, but she caught herself.

"It's okay, birdies, I'm just getting some fruit," she whispered. It was dark under the tree, the network of branches looked like giant webs, and the fruits themselves hung like big round spiders with their legs tucked in. Arionella shook her head hard to thwart her grim fantasy and grabbed a fruit. She tossed it to the ground, climbed down, and took her dinner to the cabin. She drank the nectar of the fruit, which tasted dreadfully sweet, ate the soft meat, which was terribly filling, and soon with her eyes dilated and heart pounding, she started looking around the shadowy cabin with suspicion at the straight edges, angles, and boxy frame of what began to feel like a cage.

She went back outside and ran over to the tree that suddenly seemed so beautiful and uncluttered under the starlight. She nestled at the roots of the tree and picked at the green moss, finally feeling the comfort of tranquility after what seemed like ages but had only been six days.

Chapter 10

THE PIRANHAS

Just past dawn, angry voices were heard from inside a pretty yellow tent. Moments later, hunched over, with her long black hair in disarray, Taola stamped out of the entrance flaps of the tent.

Lemay and Navis had also begun to awaken in their tent and so stuck their heads out of their tent to take a peek at what the commotion might be. First, they saw Taola walking off across the grass farther and farther away, and then they heard the muffled tones of Lana-Baboye and Niniola's voices from inside the tent.

Then, Niniola emerged from the tent, straightened herself up, and planted her hands firmly on her hips.

Lastly, Lana-Baboye's head emerged from the tent. She was the only one that didn't look angry, just sleepy and a bit exasperated.

"I knew I should have packed an extra tent," Niniola said to Lana-Baboye.

"Yes, Captain, so you've been saying, but we wanted to travel as light as possible, didn't we?"

"Well, if we can't get the proper rest, our travels are compromised anyway." Niniola paced around the fire pit. "Even the actual children must be quieter than that snoring and singing overgrown child. Can you believe it, singing in tight quarters like that?"

"She said she thought it would be a nice way to wake us. We are to set out early anyway. We all agreed upon that."

Niniola was still unhappy, and the explanation seemed to bother her more. She threw up her hands in the air, and then got to organize her things.

The day brightened, and though there was unspoken tension between Niniola and Taola, everyone ate and packed up their things diligently. Sprinkled across the field were the other travelers, who seemed to be sleeping in, tucked in their tents oblivious to the morning chill.

Taola was over the argument very quickly and feeling confident that they would get to Halla Manor a little past noon. They formed their line again and marched back into the cool canopy of Pans Forest. As they walked, everyone enjoyed the feeling of being on the move again.

The kids were having fun pointing out the flashes of color or sudden movement of birds and squirrels. Lemay was the one who caught sight of a pair of foxes to the right of the trail, peeking at the que of travelers from behind a tree stump. When everyone stopped and turned to look at them, they bounded gracefully off in airy skips across the forest floor.

This excited the twins, and for the rest of the hike they would point at anything remotely colored red and shout, "Foss! Foss!"

Along the way, other travelers quietly went on their way, sometimes overtaking them from behind, and sometimes passing by from the opposite direction. The children would get really excited when they saw a donkey, horse, or dog traveling alongside the humans, but there was an air of distrust between the strangers, so everyone kept to themselves, much to the children's disappointment. Time wore on, and the rays of the sun that poured through gaps in the trees shifted until streams of light were coming directly down from the canopy above.

Taola indicated that this must mean they were getting close to the next clearing and that from there Halla Manor would only be a short walk away.

As they approached the last leg of the trail, a group of people became visible farther ahead along the trail. It was a cluster of twenty or so individuals walking close together. Taola glanced behind her to check on her group and noticed that Lana-Baboye and Myli, who were all the way at the back of the line, were nowhere to be seen. Nobody else seemed to notice that Lana-Baboye was missing.

Taola cleared her throat and spoke in a low voice. "Alright, everyone, this may be trouble. Look straight ahead." The group had no travel packs and there was something suspicious about the way they walked, clustered together.

Everyone came to attention out of their reveries. Navis took his carrier with Tumi in it off his back and put it around his chest instead, and then turned to check on Myli, who was traveling with Lana-Baboye, but didn't see them.

Before he could panic, Taola said, "Navis, don't worry about Myli. If she's with Lana, then she's as safe as she ever could be."

Lemay moved close to Navis and took hold of his hand. Navis looked down, smiled, and gave Lemay's hand a squeeze.

At the back of the line, Niniola was looking fierce, with narrowed eyes and a frown. She readjusted her backpack and let her hand come to rest on the holster of her blaster.

As the group got closer, Taola saw that it was composed of young children about Lemay's height and age, as well as older kids but no adults. Most of them had their hands in their pockets and wore tattered hooded garments. Besides a few quick glances at their surroundings, they looked down at the ground as they walked.

Finally, the crew of the Maradona and the motley pack of children were pretty much face to face. The group of children moved to their right, seemingly making way, though there was plenty of space to pass by without having to step off the trail and into the woods.

Taola and Navis nodded and smiled at the group, but still no one made eye contact. The tension increased as if there were an invisible rubber band getting stretched around the two groups as they passed by each other. Then, just as Taola and the others reached the middle point of the line of children, the tension snapped. The kids suddenly swarmed the crew of the Maradona, shoving, pushing, pulling, shouting, and even swinging their arms and landing a few hits on Niniola and Taola. Within seconds, the swarm dispersed, the children running wildly in all directions. The goal of the attack was accomplished. Taola, Lemay, and Niniola lost the backpacks they were carrying.

Lemay's shirt was torn, and he was sitting on the ground covered in dust, holding tightly to Navis's leg. Navis had one hand resting on Lemay's head while his other arm clutched Tumi, who was safe on his chest.

Niniola was furious. Drawing her blaster, she ran off into the forest after a group of kids.

Then, from a different direction came a single echoing shriek, followed by angry shouts. Taola, Navis, and Lemay turned toward the noise. Farther up the trail, from where the group of attackers came, was Lana-Baboye. She had pinned down two of the attackers along the edge of the forest just off the trail.

Taola ran toward her while Navis moved more slowly with Tumi and Lemay in his care. When they got close, they saw that Lana-Baboye had everything under control and that Myli was on her back, comfortable in her carrier, clapping and every so often saying "Bad, bad!" to the captives grunting and panting under Lana-Baboye's grasp.

Lana-Baboye was kneeling between two teenagers who were lying flat in the dirt. They were in this position because in her left-hand Lana-Baboye had the left arm of the boy twisted behind his back, and in her right hand she had the right arm of the girl twisted behind her back. Each of these apprehended culprits was only a couple of years younger than Lana-Baboye and more than a foot taller than her but could not so much as move an inch under her grasp.

Lana-Baboye said, "Sis, you can collect your and Lemay's backpacks just over there." Their bags were a few yards away in the foliage off the trail. Then, she looked down at the attackers again and asked in a stoic voice, "Are you two done struggling?"

"WE DON'T ANSWER TO NO ONE!" shrieked the girl, blowing up dirt with her mouth.

"Yeh! The Piranhas ain't afraid of no one," chimed in the boy.

"Ah, the Piranhas. That's what that swarming action was all about?" Lana-Baboye asked derisively.

"Let us go, you bitch!" the boy said with impetuosity, which he immediately regretted because Lana-Baboye tightened her grip on his wrist, twisting it deeply. The boy screamed, "Ahhh! Ahhh! Ahhh!" But despite his cries, she kept his arm in its new painfully contorted position.

Through the boy's shouts, Lana-Baboye asked Taola, "Can you lift Myli off my back? I don't want her to witness what will happen in case these crooks heedlessly continue to invite pain into their short lives." Lana-Baboye, besides being formidable, now sounded the part too in a low and cold register.

Taola came over and slowly lifted Myli out of the harness. Lana-Baboye was steady as ever, as if Myli was no weight for her at all.

"What do you want?" asked the girl through clenched teeth.

Just then, Niniola came crashing through the forest and stumbled back onto the trail. She was hunched over, her face contorted with rage. "Those bastards have my pack with my book in it!" she shouted to everyone and no one.

The pinned teenagers tried to crane their heads in the direction of the livid presence getting closer and closer. Niniola had her blaster drawn but didn't seem to notice that Lana-Baboye had two of the attackers in custody.

"Well, there's your answer, young lady," Taola said to the teenager as she pulled a rope out of her recovered pack and began to tie up her arms and legs.

By the time Lana-Baboye and Taola had the teenagers sitting upright Niniola was close enough to finally understand the situation. Her eyes widened and she froze in place, like a cat fixated on her prey.

"You stray weasels! You motherless animals!" Niniola spat her words out, pounced forward, threw her blaster to the ground, bent over and grabbed them by their ragged shirts. "Where's your band of weasels taking my things? Tell me now!"

The two Piranhas did not look ferocious at all now. They were frightened and kept glancing from Niniola down to her blaster, which was still within her reach.

Niniola shook them again and repeated, "Where did they go?"

Still the teenagers didn't reply. It wasn't clear whether they were too shaken up to speak, or if they were being loyal to their gang. Niniola didn't care either way, she was livid about her book—"her labor of love," as Sir Charles had put it—being stolen. Taola, Navis, Lana-Baboye, Lemay, Myli, and Tumi watched tensely as the scene played out, unsure of what Niniola might do next.

Niniola shouted, "You're going to take me to where they've gone!"

Still no reply.

Niniola suddenly released the girl from her grasp and slapped her hard across the face. The girl fell over, unable to brace herself because she was tied up. Then, Niniola let go of the boy and reached for her blaster.

"NO!" Lemay screamed and ran forward, throwing himself in front of the two teenagers with his arms out wide. "Stop this!"

Everyone became dead silent. Niniola looked straight into Lemay's brown eyes and began blinking rapidly as if she had just awoken from a trance. Breaking the silence, Lemay said, his voice shaking, "We can't treat them this way. If they're motherless . . . they're just like me and . . ." Lemay's chest heaved as he gasped through emotional breaths. "—Myli . . . . Tumi . . . Arionella, and Uncle Navis!" Tears poured from Lemay's eyes, but he didn't budge. The teenagers on the ground behind him looked up at him in awe.

Niniola lowered her gaze from Lemay's stern, wet face. She was already bent over close to the ground, but she let herself sink to her knees, dropping the blaster onto the ground again. "I'm sorry; I'm sorry," she said in a whisper holding her hands over her face.

Without a word, Lemay turned around and started trying to untie the boy and girl. The two Piranhas continued to stare at him in wonder. But try as he might, Lemay couldn't undo the knots with his hands, so he began biting at the rope.

At that, Lana-Baboye stepped forward and placed her hand on Lemay's shoulder. Taola passed Myli to Navis, and then made her way over to help Lana-Baboye undo the knots. Within seconds, the captured boy and girl were sitting free on the dirt road. Taola put her arm around Lemay and led him back toward the trail.

Navis went over to Niniola, helped her up, and slowly began walking away with her, Myli, and Tumi. The twins were shaken up by the energy of the moment and had become morose.

"Navi, what happened?" Myli ventured to ask after a few steps, but Navis just shook his head. She then ran ahead to catch up to Taola and Lemay. Taking hold of Lemay's hand, she walked along in silence, glancing up at Lemay's face every so often.

As the others went on slowly ahead, Lana-Baboye remained with the two teenagers, still on her knees just in front of them.

"I understand things must be hard for you all," Lana-Baboye said softly, "but this is not the way to treat people. There are other ways to get by, and even thrive, in this world." She opened her satchel and took out all the dried fruit, meat, and wafers she had, giving it all to the boy and girl. They looked at her straight in her eyes and she met their gaze, seeing that there was gratitude, confusion, fear, and even innocence in them. "Choose kindness, so that you harmonize with the creative, loving force of the universe, which is ultimately the real you.

"We will meet again, and I will teach you what I know, not so that you can harm people, but so that you can help people." She smiled at them, gave them a pat on their shoulders, and stood. She went over to the blaster Niniola had left behind, packed it away in her satchel, and followed the others toward the exit of the forest.

Arionella at Sea
X. Denizens of the Treeboat

The sun shone upon a fluffy green tree growing out of a worn-looking boat made of white timber. It was moving steadily across the open ocean, seemingly of its own accord for there were no sail and no helm. There was a cabin made for human shelter, but there was no one in it. There were indeed denizens of this treeboat however, including insects, plants, mosses, birds, and a twelve-year-old human girl with red hair and green eyes. She wore a cotton peach-colored tank top that had many little rips in it and shorts of the same color that hung loosely over thin legs. On this day, she was climbing energetically around the wide branches of the tree, scaring the birds as a kind of game. If she got hungry, she would stop to pluck a large coconut-like fruit that was filled with nutritious nectar and meat that kept her healthy.

Though solitary, she seemed happy in her own little world, almost like a feral cat that takes pleasure in the slightest movement of a blade of grass.

Chapter 11

HALLA MANOR

The Manor stood tall beyond its stone border and high metal gates. A triangular roof with dark gray shingles and a sturdy red brick foundation gave the huge mansion a rustic charm, but the Manor was one of many structures spread throughout some five-hundred acres of land devoted to communal living. Aromas of barbecue, sawdust, and honeysuckle mingled with sounds of merry shouting, the buzzing of saws, and echoing knocks of hammers. The crew of the Maradona was greeted by friendly but capable-looking guards dressed in matching uniforms that they were wearing casually; one had his red vest unbuttoned and the other wore his cap backwards.

Please turn in any weapons you might be carrying," the guard with the unbuttoned vest said as if it were no big deal. Lana-Baboye walked up and handed him the blaster. "Thank you, Miss. Just ask for it on your way out." With a bow he pushed the gate open, and the travelers passed through, following the gravel path leading up to the front entrance of the house.

All around the acreage of grass and interspersed trees were people keeping busy with something or other. There were kids playing at an extensively constructed jungle gym, patches of produce were being tended to, sculptures were being erected, freshly carved gazebos were being assessed and put onto wagons seemingly to be delivered elsewhere, as well as a dozen other projects in the midst of coming to fruition were spread out across the property.

The weary crew of the Maradona was lifted out of their melancholy with each step they took. Myli and Tumi's eyes sparkled as they looked up at the colorful paper lamps hanging above the gravel path on strands of thread. Soon they were kicking and struggling to get out of their harnesses, and off their human transports, so they could go play with the other children running about.

"I'll meet you all inside after they get their energy out," Navis said as he followed Myli and Tumi, who were running toward a sandbox filled with other children their age.

The doors of the manor were wide open, revealing hardwood floors and high ceilings with large wooden beams. Under a beautiful chandelier made of bronze and a medley of crystal stones was a high counter with a plump blonde woman behind it sifting through stacks of parchment.

"Oh, hello!" she said with a bright smile, through rouge-painted lips, upon catching sight of the new arrivals. "I'm assuming you're not residents?"

"No, but I've been here before," Taola said, raising her hand. "I'm probably still in your registry—Taola Lonwë—it was only about three years ago that I stayed here." The receptionist quickly tied up her hair in a tall bun, passed a long-feathered pen through it, hopped off her chair, and walked over to a big leather-bound guest registry set on a podium at the mouth of a long corridor leading into the manor.

"Taola Lonwë? Taola Lonwë . . . three years—" she said, biting her lip and pursing her lips tight with concentration she whipped the large heavy pages with her whole hand. "Ah yes! Welcome back, Miss Lonwë! Will you set up camp outdoors, rent one of the cabins around the property, or would you like to stay in our rooms? We have some available at the moment."

"Let's stay in the rooms, huh?" Taola looked at Lana-Baboye, Lemay, and Niniola, seeking affirmation. Everyone nodded or shrugged. "Okay, so how much would two rooms be?"

"Either twenty roials or eight cityfort credits each, or six hours of community service each night you stay. What is best for you all?"

"Well, as we were recently robbed, with only two of us retaining our belongings, maybe we should save our currencies and lend some energy here," Lana-Baboye said.

"Oh no!" the woman exclaimed. "I'm sorry to hear that! This happened along the forest trail?"

"Yes."

"It's a problem that needs taking care of. Fortunately, we are well guarded here and have some tech to keep watch over things. Anyway, doing the community-service option is recommended, as it would be a great way to get to know the place—not to mention we're getting ready to harvest a huge crop of grapes. My name is Meireia, by the way."

"This is Lemay, Lana-Baboye, and Niniola," Taola replied. "Navis and the twins—Myli and Tumi—will be in shortly."

"Nice to meet you all!" Meireia filled in their names in the registry and then let it clap shut. "I imagine you are tired, so let's have you settle in—and did you want two or three rooms?"

"I think two rooms will be sufficient," Taola replied. "From what I remember, you have rooms with multiple cots, right?"

"Yes, indeed. Follow me—I'll have you cozy, clean, and fed before nightfall!"

Their rooms were right across the hall from each other: Navis and the children had one, and the women shared the other. The rooms were decorated with beautiful stretches of cloth hung on the ceiling and on the walls. Each room also had a big fluffy rug that covered most of the floor, and the cots were handmade beds of sturdy wood and fitted with plush mattresses, that were made to be light and easily movable. Warm, scented bubble baths in a bathhouse section of the manor were a welcome extravagance for the crew of the Maradona, who had been taking cool sponge baths since leaving the Haelin Islands nearly three days ago. Then everyone went downstairs to eat, except Niniola, who had been quiet and keeping to herself even more than usual since the events on the Pans Forest trail.

Through the upper halls, which had cathedral ceilings, they walked over the creaky floorboards and past multitudes of framed pictures hanging on the walls, mostly displaying the faces of people—the diversity of appearances created a beautiful gradient of color across the wall.

"We should take a picture while we are all here together!" Taola said as if she had been stuck by an epiphany. "This is one of the few places where they still make and repair camera tech!"

They went down some steps, turned a corner, and found the common hall with tables, chairs, chandeliers, a large fireplace, tall windows, and a layout of food on the far end of the expanse. The hall was filled with the chattering of people speaking various languages, sporting different attires from stuffy looking suits and gowns, to multi-colored patterned-wool ponchos that looked comfortable and yet regal at the same time. Many women and men wore makeup that was representative of their cultures: fine differences in the thickness and length of eyeliner, shade and color of blush, and some had even pasted little rhinestones on their face that flickered in the orange light of the hearth and the hundreds of candles spread throughout the hall in chandeliers, on windowsills, and tables.

As it was time for dinner, residents and guests bartering their services were helping people get into queues at different serving tables. A line was formed by the bread and grains section, another by the meats and cheeses; vegetables, fruits, and nuts; teas, juices, and fresh filtered water from a nearby spring. The food here was fresh from the land, as most of the acreage of land was put to use for complete self-sufficiency in food, fresh water, energy, and medical care. This settlement was one of a kind, as far as anyone knew, in that it wasn't associated with a particular tribe and had been founded by Jöshi Halla's intrepid great-grandmother, Annya Halla. Halla Manor remained open to wayfarers and independents who chose not to take citizenship in any particular cityfort, which had strict laws in place for those who chose to partake in the privilege of a protected and luxurious, technologically advanced lifestyle. Most people who managed to leave the cityfort for good considered themselves "freed" of an oppressive regime, and in stark contrast, those who appreciated the cityforts considered the "outlands" dangerous and barbaric. When in earnest, both sides had their valid points, though if a cityfort citizen had the opportunity to take a peek at the festive dinner at the Halla Manor—technically situated in what was considered the dreaded "outlands"— they might at the very least agree that, though it was not fort life, it was far from barbarism.

Taola was quick to fill her plate, and then she was off mingling, swallowed by a crowd of a hundred or so people. The others found a circular table amidst porcelain sculptures of important-looking heads that were in fact renditions of the Halla family, as Meireia told them when she was passing by with her own plate of food.

Lana-Baboye, Navis, Myli, Tumi, and Lemay ate heartily and reveled in the atmosphere of relaxed human company. They were quiet around the table but listening with pleasure as the individual conversations all around compounded upon one another into a symphony of sounds.

After dinner, a group of kids and a few adults began playing music with bongos, djembe, guitars, and musical pans out on the veranda that connected to an exit at the south end of the common hall. Others joined in with their own instruments, adding flutes, jaw harps, and harmonicas to the whimsical jam. Navis, Lana-Baboye, and the kids walked out onto the porch as well, watching with contentment as the music became the perfect soundtrack to a quiet show of fireflies blinking their little lights in a darkening world. Soon Myli, Tumi, and Lemay were fast asleep, cuddled together on a big plush couch. Lana-Baboye lifted Myli and Tumi one at a time, transferring them to Navis. Then she scooped Lemay up and carried him out of the common hall, around the corridor, and up the stairs to the shared rooms, where she tucked him into his cot and stroked his curly brown hair until he stopped stirring in his sleep. Navis set the twins down on a mattress placed on the ground for them and then sat down on his own cot.

"Special kids," Lana-Baboye said, leaning by the door and watching the sleeping youngsters with a warm smile upon her face.

"Yeah, and they're so cute too," Navis said through a big yawn.

Lana-Baboye chuckled. "Well, goodnight, Navis'sa."

"G'night."

Lana-Baboye went across the hall to her own room and found that Niniola was on her cot, wrapped up in a blanket at the side of the room farthest from the door. She looked cozy under the colorful wispy veils that hung over her from the ceiling. However, when Lana-Baboye started setting up her own cot, she noticed that Niniola was quivering a bit. In the dim light of a single melting candle she slowly made her way over and asked in a soft voice, "Captain? Are you feeling alright?"

Niniola didn't move or respond. She was facing the wall, lying on her side in the fetal position.

Lana-Baboye moved even closer and sat down on the ground next to the cot, leaning her forearms on it. Every so often Lana-Baboye felt Niniola shivering, and so she spoke up again, "Captain, did you get to eat anything? Would you like me to bring you something?"

Niniola's voice came from under the blanket. "Ah, no, that's alright—," she paused as a tremor seized her, and then continued, "I'm not hungry."

"Are you well though?"

"I think I may have a fever, and I'm a little tired."

Lana-Baboye reached over and found her mark—Niniola's forehead was indeed hot. "Yes, you have a bit of a fever." She stood and looked around. "Here, they have given us plenty of water. Careful, the jug and the cups are made of heavy onyx. I'll pour you a cup now but let me know throughout the night if you need more."

"Thank you," Niniola replied.

"I'm moving my cot right here so you can ride out the fever tonight knowing you have support."

"Thank you."

Time passed, and Lana-Baboye only had to get up once to pour a fresh cup of water for Niniola.

When Taola got back to the room, both women were fast asleep, so she quietly settled in and immediately fell asleep herself.

———•———

The next morning, Niniola was the first one to get up. Much of her night had been spent in a twilight state of thought and dreams. However, though she hadn't had a deep sleep, she felt refreshed, nonetheless. Her stomach on the other hand was groaning with hunger. She went downstairs and came upon the hard-to-miss common hall, where breakfast had just begun to be laid out, as it was still only an hour past dawn. She joined in laying out the food and was happy to find that snacking was encouraged.

After that chore was done, she took some food and tea outside. In the distance, she caught sight of shepherd dogs corralling goats and sheep out of their pens and into their pastures for the day. Then she walked down the porch steps and followed a gravel path until she came to a beautifully carved wooden bench. The bright tan-brown bench was specifically made to have no edges. Instead, what might have been corners—of the backrest, seating, and even the armrests—were smoothed out into curves, carved out of a single tree trunk. A carpenter herself, Niniola took pleasure in its craftsmanship. She sat down at one end, leaning against the bubbly armrest, and placed her breakfast next to her. She sipped at her tea while looking out at the grounds still glistening from the morning dew. As if she had set an internal timer, every minute and a half she reached over to pick out a piece of bread and cheese, followed by a slice of apple soaked in honey. Then her cycle of eating ended with sips of tea to wash it all down. Satiated, she sat quiet and reflective as the sun steadily rose higher in the sky.

Back inside the manor, Lana-Baboye was making her bed. Taola was still in bed but was beginning to move about, trying to get comfortable for a few more minutes of dozing. After some more rustling, she finally sat up, frustrated because she couldn't ignore her bladder any longer. She leapt out of bed and stamped off toward the bathroom without a word. Lana-Baboye shook her head and chuckled. After a few minutes, there was a knock at the door.

"Yes, who is it?" Lana-Baboye asked.

"It's Meireia from the front desk."

"Come in!" Taola was the one to reply enthusiastically. She had exited the bathroom and was in the midst of combing her hair by a large mirror, but now she scurried over to the door. "Any news?" she asked as soon as she opened the door.

"Yes, actually!" Meireia said. "Though it took longer than expected because of the confidential nature of your request."

"Still, first thing in the morning is quite good. So, what's the news?"

"Well—as you know—an urgent message was sent out last night. A few hours later, we got a response saying that the message was received. After about an hour we received another message that someone was on their way, and he's just arrived! In fact, even I didn't know he was of the Enané, but I see him often, as he's a regular here. Obviously, some of the older Halla management knew this. Anyway, now I know too, and I'm sworn to secrecy."

"Wait, one of the Enané is here now?" was Taola's only reply to Meireia's monologue.

"Yes, like I said, he's just arrived."

Taola didn't wait another moment. "Let's go to him then! C'mon, Lana!"

Meanwhile, in the room across the hall Navis was getting the kids freshened up and ready for the day ahead. He was expecting to help out around the property. He knew that Myli and Tumi would want to play with the other children and was hoping that Lemay also might get swept up with some kids his age. Navis still had spells of concern about Arionella, especially when he was tired and trying to go to sleep, but lately he had been concerned about Lemay too. Lemay always had an inclination toward being reserved and was always mature for his age, but since Arionella was out of the picture, he mostly seemed solemn. There were times when Lemay would join in the merrymaking, but it was never long before he seemed to get lost in his thoughts again. Also, Navis hadn't spoken to Lemay about the attack of the group of bandits—the Piranhas—or Lemay's reaction to Niniola's treatment of the captured teens in Pans Forest. While he dressed Myli and Tumi in matching overalls, put their shoes on, and had them brush their knotted blond hair, in his mind he was weighing the ways in which he might share his concerns with Lemay. Lost in his thoughts, Navis didn't notice that Lemay was also looking pensive as he got ready. When they were dressed, Navis let Myli and Tumi run out across the hall, but they found the room vacant.

"Nobody home!" Myli's squeaky voice echoed through the hall.

"Nobody home!" Tumi repeated after her.

"Ok, wait for me, I'll be right there," Navis said as he got his boots on, but then he heard the patter of feet. He and Lemay ran out into the hall, for at three years old, the twins still had short legs and therefore had trouble going down stairways. The twins saw Lemay and Navis coming. Joyful yelps and shrieks filled the corridor as they ran from their pursuers. Luckily, Navis and Lemay caught up to them well before the stairs were a threat. They descended safely together, but as soon as they reached the ground floor the twins whined and tried to pull their hands free of Navis's grasp. "Alright, go ahead then. Stay aware of your surroundings, please!"

Navis and the children turned left toward the common hall, while just a few yards to the right, in the foyer, were Taola and Lana-Baboye greeting a tall, dark-skinned man with a salt-and-pepper fro, wearing a handmade crimson sweater.

"You?" Taola was staring at the man with her jaw hanging low. "Danuba! How are you?"

"Ah! Taola Lonwë, I am well! I knew we would meet again, y'know." He reached out and shook her hand with both of his vigorously.

"This is Lana-Baboye," Taola said.

"Hi; nice to meet you, Danuba'sa," Lana-Baboye said, dipping her head slightly in a bow.

"Lana-Baboyanta, it's a pleasure." Danuba dipped his head in the same way, with a knowing smile.

Lana-Baboye looked up in surprise, appreciating his nuanced way of sharing that he knew she was a Haelin Islander.

Then Taola seemed to recall something. She suddenly seemed serious and concerned. "Do you mind if we chat somewhere private?" she asked.

"Of course not. I'll show you one of my favorite spots."

Lana-Baboye and Taola had to walk quickly to keep up with Danuba's long strides. They went outdoors and walked a few meters to a gray stone gazebo that was covered in thin green lianas and moss. Inside were stone benches, and on one side there was a stone wall with a grand mural standing at least seven meters high. It was a painting of a woman with an inscrutable expression, wearing a shawl and a large feather in her hair, looking down, straight into the eyes of her beholders from atop a barren hill.

When they had seated themselves, Taola asked softly, "How is Iloy?"

"He is well, my dear. Very well, in fact. It has been a tough few years for him in many ways, y'know. He's been training, learning, and *unlearning* many things, but he is well."

"So that's what you meant when you said you'd take him into your care. He's been with the Enané all along." Taola smiled as she imagined Mama Gogo humbly weaving webs of contact, foreseeing much but telling little.

"Yes."

"That makes sense." Taola seemed relieved, about the person named Iloy at least. "Well, Danuba, the reason we've come here and reached out to you is because we seek the guidance of the Enané." Danuba leaned forward with his hands clasped, attentive and receptive. "Mama Gogo from Oaql Island recommended this. As you know from our previous meeting, I have had difficulties in connecting with the treeboat I became captain of about six months ago. Well, recently it escaped from me with a young girl named Arionella onboard. She's twelve years old. To complicate matters further, four days ago our Oaql Island was attacked by a small group of armed men whose leader is familiar with the ancient arts of plant medicines and *telempathy*—the one Iloy—" Taola's voice choked off for a moment before she continued. "We think it is Revalo Otrebor, the man Iloy and I escaped from when you picked us up in your plane. He has abducted Captain Rainer Yansa, the previous captain of the treeboat." Taola shook her head after recounting all the issues. "Seems like we are just rife with problems, doesn't it?" Lana-Baboye, who was sitting next to Taola, reached over and rubbed her back.

"Y'know, I understand you're asking that rhetorically, but merely to remind you—and maybe lift your spirits in a way—" Danuba sat up straight and crossed his arms in the warmth of his sweater "—these are not your problems alone, y'know. The Haelin Islands impact us all, humans, plants, and creatures alike. The fact that they are the sanctuaries for various kinds of wildlife, the heritage of the Reteti, and energetic meridians of the planet, affects us all—even those completely ignorant of them, y'know. In short, it would be an honor to help you and in doing so possibly shine more light onto the mystery of the foreboding climate we Enané have been feeling for quite a while now."

"We have been having this discussion for a few months as well," Lana-Baboye said. "Have you come to any conclusions?"

"Not yet. In fact, your friend Iloy is part of Delamina and Jiji's small team that has gone to seek aid from the original tribes in this investigation, much like you have come to us, y'know. Iloy revealed some startling information about Revalo's intentions that we Enané do not have the wisdom to comprehend. I will not speak of it here—we need more time and ceremony to address it.

"Anyway, we have been reflecting on humanity's history, and we do know that ours is a time of fragility. Y'know, things are new again in many ways—the might and global connectivity of old that blessed . . . and cursed the human race is no more, and there are many who seek to determine civilization's fate. Those vying for power—whether with good intentions or bad—will impact the rest of us with unintended consequences . . . y'know, as always has been the case."

The three sat silent for a time, looking out of the gazebo at the little world of Halla Manor coming to life with children starting to run about, people tending to the gardens, and craftspeople picking up their tools for another day of creativity.

Then, Danuba clapped his hands and stood. "So, when would you two like to leave? Taola, y'know I told you back then that you'd have to visit Meisha Forest someday!"

"Actually, we have—" Taola counted on her fingers "—five other people with us."

"Hmm, might be a problem, y'know, because I take a small plane to get to our lands."

"Well, three of the five are children, one nine years old and the others just three. Would that make a difference?"

"Maybe. Let's get everyone together and see." Danuba flared his broad chest in an audible chest-cracking-stretch. "Actually, y'know, something to eat might be good before anything else."

Taola turned to Lana-Baboye and said, "It may be best to simply pay them in roials for the stay if we're going to leave soon."

"Yes, we have more than enough if we pool together what we recovered from the salvaged packs," Lana-Baboye replied.

———•———

The children and Navis had eaten their fill at breakfast. They were outside now, with Navis assigned to the picket ball game as a chaperone for his first community-service job. The Halla management had chosen this particularly for him, considering his children. There was still time before the game, so a tall burly man—no doubt one of Halla Manor's permanent residents and the sports facilitator—explained the rules. It was essentially a large game of keep away or monkey in the middle, except there were several people in the middle, which were one team. The other team surrounded the monkeys and had to pass a small ball to each other within ten seconds of it landing in a team member's hands. They could roll the ball on the ground, or throw it, trying to avoid the players of the team in the center from getting it. If one of the "monkeys" got it, then their team would become the surrounding team trying to keep the ball away from the new set of monkeys. Points were gained for each successful pass and each successful recovery from the opposing team. Groups formed, some composed of only adults and teens, another with older children, and a group with only young children.

The refereeing of the last of these groups was Navis's community-service task. Every now and then he would glance over at Lemay's group and see Lemay laughing or leaping for the ball. Navis smiled and felt greatly relieved, but his task was more difficult than he expected. The children ran about like chickens and would suddenly begin crying, or begin to shout at one another, and there was constant breaking of the rules—to Navis's dismay, Myli and Tumi were often the culprits. However, it was a great way to pass the time. The twins had fun, and Navis and Lemay were so absorbed in the activities that they forgot their troubles for a time.

Niniola had been watching the games too. Her eyes followed Lemay, who seemed transformed amidst others his age. Though he wasn't one of the shouters, he got rough and dirty when he needed to. When Lemay caught the ball, Niniola felt a sense of pride and excitement. When he fell or missed a catch, she had a gut reaction of concern, and when his team won, she cheered and clapped in a reserved manner that didn't reveal the extent of her delight.

Navis, Myli, Tumi, and Lemay regrouped after the games ended. All three of the children were animatedly recounting their favorite moments of picket ball. Niniola waved to them from alongside the playing fields. Navis caught sight of her first, so while the kids spoke over each other in their enthusiasm, he steered them in her direction. When they were only a few yards away, Lemay finally caught sight of Niniola. The change in his disposition was immediate—he stopped smiling, and his body stiffened. Niniola saw this, and her heart sank.

"Hi, Niniola, did you get to catch any of the games?" Navis said while trying to keep Tumi and Myli within arm's reach.

"Yes, I did. Looked like a good time," Niniola replied and tried to share a smile with Lemay, but it ended up being a little awkward for her because Lemay wasn't looking at her at that moment. "Anyway, I've been wanting to talk to you two briefly—."

"I wanna go there, let's go there!" Myli was pulling at Navis's arm, pointing toward the jungle gym and sand boxes.

"Hold on, Myli. Sorry, Niniola. You were saying?"

"Actually, let's go over there. Myli and Tumi can play while we talk."

Niniola, Navis, and Lemay walked along, following the twins. "I wanted to address what happened on the forest trail," Niniola said. Lemay kept his eyes glued to the ground, and Navis unconsciously took a deep breath. She continued, "First of all, I want to apologize for my behavior. I said and did things that I'm ashamed of—"

Here Niniola choked off. Navis cleared his throat, thinking he should offer some words of comfort. "It's okay, Niniola, really."

"No, this is important," she insisted. They stopped walking and stood facing each other. Niniola was visibly emotional—her eyes had hints of tears, and her face was flushed. "I've learned something very important from that encounter. Pushing away love doesn't simply leave a person in a neutral state. It is harmful. All these years I've been turning away from love, even when it has come calling. For nearly fifteen years now I thought I was preserving myself from pain, but I now realize that I've been subjecting myself to hidden anguish."

Niniola's voice cracked, and she looked away for a few seconds. Then she continued. "Well, all I can say after yesterday is my ugliness manifested in a way that even I couldn't ignore, and that was when I treated those children that way. The person Aldarwin loved has become deeply buried away inside me, and I want to dig her out." She looked up at Navis with tears coming to her eyes. "Aldarwin loved you."

Navis stood frozen. He had never expected her to so suddenly acknowledge their past history.

"I'm sorry I didn't listen to my heart and give you a home when you needed it most," Niniola continued. "It . . . it is my greatest regret in life." She began to cry, and she covered her face with her hands.

Navis stood shocked for a few moments before moving forward and gently embracing Niniola. Tears came to his eyes as she rested her head on his chest and put her arms around him. Lemay stood by them a little awkwardly, not because he was apathetic to their exchange but because he was deeply moved. His ears felt hot, and his heart was thumping in his chest.

Niniola and Navis slowly let each other go. Then Niniola turned to Lemay and got on her knees so they could face each other at eye level. Lemay quickly planted his eyes to the ground again, and his hands fidgeted with the loose threads of the cloth in his pants pocket.

"Lemay, please forgive me for what I said and did in Pans Forest. Also, I wanted to say that you are a beautiful boy inside and out. Standing up for those people the way you did was very brave and important. I pray you always keep that sense of justice and the courage to act on it."

Lemay still hadn't looked up from the ground, but through his body language and the pursing of his lips he tried to indicate that he was acknowledging her. Niniola got the message, leaned forward, and gave him a hug. Then she stood up and wiped away her tears. The three of them watched as Myli, Tumi, and the other children played with abandon on the jungle gym. The children's antics brought smiles to their faces, then chuckles, and soon after, Niniola, Navis, and Lemay went over and joined in the fun.

Chapter 12

DEPARTURE: ONWARD TO THE ENANÉ

It was about midday when the whole group reconvened. After Taola introduced Danuba to Navis and the others, he explained how they would be flying in a propeller seaplane, using bodies of water as their runways. This news was a little disquieting, for air travel was extremely uncommon and, therefore, seemed dangerous to most people. The unanimous reaction of anxiety made Danuba laugh, but he assured them he was a great pilot and that he had made this particular trip hundreds of times without a problem.

They were to leave later that afternoon, so Taola paid Meireia in roials—which were silver coins of different sizes to delineate amount—and Meireia discounted the price, saying that Niniola's help in setting up breakfast that morning and Navis's in refereeing picket ball was greatly appreciated. This meant that there was more to spend on new backpacks, clothes, tents, and other traveling utensils, as only Taola, Navis and Lana-Baboye had retained their things during the Piranha attack in Pans Forest.

They laid out their new things in one of the bedrooms. When they started packing, the twins got antsy and, much to everyone's surprise, it was Niniola who got up to humor them most often. At times she would pretend to be a bear, let them ride on her as if she were a horse, or toss them high through the air onto the beds—while still finding time to organize her new travel pack.

After about an hour, the twins ran out of energy, falling asleep on a pile of cushions that they were using to make huts with. Lemay, Taola, Lana-Baboye, and Niniola sat in a circle as they finished packing and took a moment to breathe together.

"So, I was thinking," Niniola said eventually, "that I might return to Pansmont and wait for you." Everyone looked up in surprise. "Of course, if it's alright with you all. It's just that I've never been away from the Maradona for so long. Also, Taola and I didn't tell the rest of you, but while we were docked at Oaql Island, we planted the Oaql seed on it."

Taola glanced over at Navis, but he didn't seem to think it important to share that he knew.

Navis purposely didn't look at Taola, pretending not to remember that she told him anything—he didn't want to invite Taola's anger just when things were pretty good between them all.

Niniola continued, "Besides feeling a calling to be near the boat, I'm probably slowing you young people down anyway."

"Are you kidding, Captain? You're one of the toughest sixty-four-year-olds I've ever met," Lana-Baboye said, and everyone unanimously agreed.

"Thank you, dear. That means a lot coming from a Reteti Warrior."

"She's right, Niniola," Taola said. "You leaving would only be a loss for us, but at this leg of the journey we're being escorted and are going to a settlement where we should be taken care of, so if you really don't want to see and take notes on the Enané settlement for your book, then it's fine with us."

"I'm not going to write that book anyway," Niniola said with a laugh. "I was so obsessed with it, for so long, that since it has been taken away, I feel a sense of freedom, really."

"And what about traveling back to Pansmont? We know from direct experience that it's unsafe!" Navis chimed in.

"I heard a large group of travelers talking about making the trip early tomorrow morning, so I'm going to tag along."

So, it was decided that Niniola would wait for everyone in Pansmont, and the rest of them would continue to the forest of the Enané with Danuba. In fact, Danuba was the one most disappointed that Niniola wouldn't be joining them. Not only was she around his age, but he found Niniola very attractive, and he told her so later that day before he and the others left Halla Manor.

"Y'know, it's a shame you're not coming with us, and I hope you don't mind me saying so, ma'am, but you are one of the most beautiful women I have ever seen."

Niniola didn't know how to react to this, so she just cleared her throat, nodded, and smiled as she felt warmth spread to her ears. Taola, with her mouth wide open, winked and gave the thumbs up to Niniola from behind Danuba. Niniola did her best to ignore her.

"Here, take this." Danuba held up two shiny obsidian-colored palm-sized gadgets and gave one to Niniola. "It is a transmitter and receiver, linked only to its sister transceiver that I have. "This way you can keep in touch with your crew, y'know, and me too, y'know, if you want." Danuba smiled and shrugged, then walked off toward the gates of Halla Manor. Everyone else came over to Niniola and gave her a group hug.

"Where's Nanuna going? Are we saying bye?" Tumi asked, a little confused, and Myli looked confused too.

"Only for a little while," Niniola said and gave them another hug. "I'm going to go take care of our boat, so everything will be shipshape when you get back!"

"Okay, and we'll play horsey and Oogachuka monster?" Tumi said, still clinging to Niniola.

"Yes, of course!" Then, with a final squeeze, she let them go and stood to exchange smiles with Navis and Lemay.

The crew of the Maradona started walking toward the gate. Then all of a sudden, Taola shouted.

"Gawd, I almost forgot! Wait here everyone!" She took off her pack, set it on the ground, and ran back into the Manor. In about a minute, she came running out, Meireia following her with a handheld device in hand. "This is a camera—a moment freezer—and we're going to take a picture with it," Taola said. She gathered everyone around her, including Danuba. She swept up Myli in her arms, and Navis put Tumi on his shoulders, while Lemay stood just in front of them. Niniola put her arm around Lana-Baboye, and Danuba stood behind everyone, being the tallest. Meireia had to squat down because Taola insisted that she get the complete height of the manor in the background.

"Are you all going to smile for this one?" Meireia asked.

"Let this one be a serious one. Nobody smiles!" Taola ordered.

"One . . . two . . . three!" Meireia took the first shot. "Okay, are we smiling for this next one?"

"Yes, anyone know a good joke?" Taola asked.

"I have one!" Navis said slyly. "What do I use when I need to get dry?"

"What?" Lemay asked.

"A Taola!" Navis replied in a comical tone and everyone started laughing except for Taola. Though she made Meireia take another picture after, everyone agreed that the second one—with Taola frowning—was the best. Then they all hugged Niniola again, and Taola told Meireia that they would return for copies of the photos someday.

As they approached the gate, the guard with the unbuttoned vest, who had first welcomed them in, wore no vest at all on this day. He recognized Lana-Baboye as she and others exited.

"Miss! Would you like your blaster?"

"Oh, I forgot about that. No, that's actually hers," said Lana-Baboye and pointed at Niniola, who was still standing by the manor watching them leave. "She'll be leaving tomorrow morning for Pansmont."

"Noted. We will pass it on to her."

"Thank you, sir. Take care."

That blaster, however, became part of the Halla Manor collection, for the next morning Niniola also refused to take it.

———•———

Danuba led everyone to the nearby Pachanai River, where his sea plane was anchored to a dock alongside many boats. There was a little cabin nearby at the edge of the forest that stretched around the Halla

Manor borders, and as they approached, a guard emerged from inside and saluted Danuba informally.

"Welcome back, Mr. Dan. I have your keys right here." He tossed them over to Danuba.

"Thank you, Mikal. How much longer are you stationed here?"

"Just till tonight. Then I'll head back over to the Manor for a few days."

"Sounds good! The peppers have just been harvested, y'know, the sweet ones too. You've got to have some."

"I heard. I'm looking forward to stuffed peppers tonight. My mom's made them especially for me."

Danuba pulled at some ropes, drawing the plane close to the dock, and then hopped onto one of the floats. The plane was colored in patches of different shades of brown. There was a single propeller engine at the nose that Danuba checked briefly before returning to the cockpit door.

"Wow, this thing is still just as I remember it!" Taola said, tiptoeing to touch the wing just out of her reach.

"Yes, she is! I take good care of her," Danuba replied. "Alright every-one, whenever you're ready, this is the only entrance, y'know." He reached his hand out to Lana-Baboye, who was nearest. She clasped his hand and nimbly leapt up onto the plane. "Welcome aboard the *Rusty Otter*, Miss! Oh, and don't forget to kiss her before you climb on."

"Why the *Rusty Otter*?" Lana-Baboye emphasized the word "rusty."

"Well, it used to be just the *Otter*, y'know, named by whoever made it long ago—written here on the body of the craft—but when me and my buddies salvaged it and put it together into working order again, we renamed it the *Rusty Otter* for fun."

"For fun? Why not something for luck instead?" asked Navis, pulling Lemay's arm back, just as Lemay had reached out to Danuba to board the plane.

"Oh, don't worry, my boy, don't let names scare you. I do something else for luck." Danuba seemed to be thoroughly enjoying the trepidation of his passengers. He reached out for Lemay and pulled him up. "Remember to kiss the plane on the way in, like this," Danuba said and demonstrated by kissing his hand and then tapping the plane. Lemay did the same. "There you go! So anyway, kiddo, y'know you're in the cockpit right now. When you walk back into the main body of the plane, you'll be inside the fuselage. Go ahead." Danuba helped the rest on board, making sure everyone gave the plane a kiss.

There were four passenger seats, so Lemay and Lana-Baboye got their own. Tumi sat on Navis's lap, and Myli sat with Taola. When everyone was strapped in, Danuba and Mikal untied the plane from the dock. While Mikal pushed the plane away from the shore, Danuba stood on the left float of the plane and used a paddle to guide it in the direction he wanted for an easy takeoff. Nearby, a few boatmen fishing just off shore craned their necks to watch as the metal bird turned toward the body of the great Pachanai River.

Danuba got into the cockpit and said, "It's going to be hella loud, y'know, so maybe you kids want to plug your ears until you get used to it." The sound of switches being flipped came first, then the plane started rumbling, and finally with a roar the engine came into full power. This startled Myli terribly, who took her hands off her ears at that very moment. She turned and clutched at Taola's shirt, stuffing her face into it while screaming and crying.

"Aww, everything's okay, sweety!" Taola patted her back and tried covering her ears with her hand. The plane gained speed as it glided along the surface of the water—it was a bumpy takeoff for the passengers. Danuba later explained that this was to be expected and was the case for seaplanes more than land planes. Very quickly, however, they were up in the air, and everything stabilized. Though it was still loud on the plane, everyone eventually got used to it, including Myli, who stopped crying because she caught sight of the bird's-eye-view of the river and forest below. Save for Danuba and Taola, it was everyone's first time high up in the air. It was a mind-bending experience that gave them perspective on their otherwise terrestrial lives.

"How are the trees so small?" Tumi asked Navis.

"Because we are high above them in this plane, so they seem that way," Navis replied.

"And that's the river?" Tumi traced the winding line cutting between the trees with his finger on the window.

"Yup, that's a big river, but it also looks small from up here."

After some time Danuba's voice came through the intercom system, "This is Captain Danny speaking. Hope you are enjoying your aerial experience aboard the trusty Rusty Otter! As we fly toward Meisha forest, the eastern region of the rainforest, it is worth taking note of the rest of the jungle which has no name. Y'know, much of it is uninhabitable for us humans, though we do go on expeditions to collect medicine or hold initiation ceremonies. The best way to navigate the rainforest is to understand its . . . let's say, neighborhoods. For example, if you all look out the windows and notice the shores of the Pachanai below, you'll notice violet and pink colors peppering the thick green bushes—those are the *Bobinzana*, making up the *Koprupi Gates*. That is a special plant, y'know; it teaches us to be strong and yet flexible. You see how it grows near the water? Through flood and dry season it endures; its feathery violet flowers are often used to make feathery crowns by various tribes.

"Now, it does not exist in a bubble—y'know, all too often, we humans forget that. The rest of the *Koprupi* neighborhood is made up of dozens of other symbiotic plants and organisms. For example, you may have noticed those tall trees growing out of the violet Bobinzana bushes. Y'know if we were closer to the ground, you would notice their bodies are very spiky and that the main trunk branches off into six or more pillars that bore deep into the ground and carry on as roots—those are the great *Yacusisa* trees, the river patrol. They teach us to be steadfast custodians. These spiky, gray-brown trees are loyal protectors of the pretty *Bobinzana*, living in harmony with them.

"Y'know, this is how the rainforest governs itself, a series of inter-relationships. Just look—this is the perfect vantage point to see the patterns—the subtle changes in greenery and the shift of colors across the canopy is indicative of other neighborhoods, communities . . . nations, y'know the plant nations.

"Though we Enané—and other tribes—call the rainforests 'home,' they are also our pharmacy, our university, and our womb."

The trip only took a little over an hour of actually being in the air, but Danuba's wonderfully detailed descriptions and exposition of the philosophy of his people made his guests feel swept away in a world outside of time, up in the air, above the Earth at a height most of them had never been. It was landing in the craft on the river and then securing it to a dock that added time. This floating dock was anchored out quite far away from the shore, which was densely tucked in and surrounded by foliage.

"See! We made it without a hitch on the trusty *Rusty Otter*." Danuba laughed as he jumped out of the cockpit onto the float of the seaplane. "Now it is my pleasure to welcome you to Meisha, the forest of dreams." He swept his arm across the view of the edge of the rainforest. The forest radiated a warm humidity that the river's breeze circulated, making it feel like a warm breath pungent with the scent of muddy earth, floral perfume, and the occasional rising odor of the very same, once perfumed, beings that were now decomposing on the cadaverous beds of the rainforest.

There was a bunch of simple, hollowed-trunk canoes strung along the side of the floating dock, which they used to get to shore. Danuba, Myli, Tumi, and Navis got into one, while Lemay, Taola, and Lana-Baboye climbed into the other. The river's current was strong, heading south, but they were able to slowly paddle their way west toward the green kingdom where the squawking, hooting, and supersonic chimes both beckoned and discouraged the newcomers at the same time.

"Y'know, the Pachanai is also called the River of Mirrors, as you can see," Danuba called out so that everyone could hear. He was right, the blue sky and puffy white clouds above were consummately reflected in the water below. Only where their paddles stirred up the water was the image of the sky distorted by ripples.

The water level of the river was very high at this time. The vegetation sticking out of the water was so dense that the trunks of trees or stalks of plants were rarely seen. It was their branches and leaves poking out over the surface of the water that defined the avenues of the river's tributaries. As they approached the shore through a particularly narrow avenue of water, branches and logs scraped the bottoms of the canoes.

It was here that Lemay noticed their canoe rocking. He turned around to find that Lana-Baboye was reaching her oar out toward something parting the surface of the water.

"What is it Lana?" Lemay asked. Taola, who was at the front, turned to look too.

At this point, Danuba noticed the commotion and brought his canoe close. "Is it a river dolphin?" he asked. "Y'know . . . , that would be a mighty rare sight!" This caused a whole lot of commotion from Myli and Tumi who began to flail in Navis's grasp trying to get a better look.

"It's something else," Lana-Baboye replied. They paddled forward tender and slow so as not to spook whatever it was.

"Oh! It's a sloth!" Danuba shouted with excitement. "That's pretty rare too, y'know. They don't need to come down from their trees that often."

Sure enough, a little sloth, with gray and brown fur, was intrepidly swimming its way across the tributary. Its flat head poked out of the water, dark bands of fur framing its eyes. It was aiming for a large tree that grew straight up out of the water.

"That's a *setico* tree," Danuba said. "Y'know, these little guys love their leaves. We burn the *setico* leaves for their ashes and use it as an antacid for the stomach."

Meanwhile, the sloth had made it to the trunk of the tree poking out of the water. Though it was relatively fast swimmer, once the sloth started climbing it was like looking at it through a portal in which time was delayed because each of its movements were so lethargic—and yet so fluid.

Once its whole body was out of the water, Lana-Baboye, who was closest to it, again reached out to it with her oar. She was trying to poke at something unnaturally white around its neck and trailing down its back like a cape. She paddled the canoe even closer and saw that besides the green algae growing out of its fur, there was some kind of synthetic netting wrapped around it.

"What's that?" Lemay asked.

"There's *adamantine* stuck to it," Lana-Baboye replied. "I'm going to try and get it off before it's out of reach."

"That stuff never goes away," Taola added. She was leaning forward stabilizing the canoe as best she could with her arms splayed out. "I guess you could call it tech from the Old World."

"Lana-Baboyanta!" Danuba called out when he saw that she reached out even farther. "Y'know, these are not our fishing boats; they are quick transports that love to tip over!" She nodded and gave him a thumbs-up.

The narrow handle of the oar finally reached her target. She was trying to slip it through gaps in the netting that was on the sloth, but it was stuck pretty tight. At one point, the sloth slightly turned its head toward her, the only indication it was even mildly interested before it continued to climb up the tree. Little by little, she loosened the netting, which was not only tangled in the animal's fur but slippery with algae. She had to scrub off the algae and pull at the stuff she'd called adamantine, making it tug on the sloth's neck.

By now, nearly half her body stretched out over the canoe's edge— she had wedged her calves under the seat-planks. She must've been lighter than Taola and Lemay's combined weight, for though the canoe rocked a good deal, it did not flip over.

With a final flick and tug, her attempt at freeing the sloth from its shackle was successful. Everyone cheered and applauded as she carefully settled herself back into the canoe and held the oar high with the netting at the far end shining in the sunlight like a trophy. Now lowering the oar, she asked Lemay to pluck the rubbish off. He took it into his hands and found it was slippery, flexible, stretchy and yet very tough.

"It's so strange," he said.

"Is this your first time touching adamantine?" Taola asked.

Navis overheard them and replied, "Lemay, that's the same stuff that makes up some of the boats that pull into our harbor in Lindum."

"Really?" Lemay looked perplexed. "This?" He looked at it closely and wiped away the loose bits of algae clinging to it. In the light it was somewhat transparent. He then shrugged, reached back and handed it to Lana-Baboye, who folded it and packed it away in her satchel.

Then, they all said goodbye to the seemingly indifferent sloth, who slowly kept making its way up the Setico tree where a cloud of golden sprites had appeared, unbeknownst to the travelers.

Chapter 13

ARRIVAL

Another five minutes of paddling and they reached the muddy shore of the rainforest. Sharp whistles, incessant chiming, hoots, and high-pitched pops filled the air—not uncommon for a mid-afternoon jungle symphony. Danuba recommended they take off their shoes, the rain and humidity rendered the soil was perpetually muddy—footwear only made walking more difficult. Everyone rolled up their pants and took off their shoes, tying them to their packs, except Lana-Baboye, who went everywhere barefoot.

The shore consisted of extremely soft silt. Standing in one place for one too many seconds meant you would sink down knee deep in clay. Danuba led them to firmer ground, though even that was quite slippery.

"Oyyyyyyy!" A lengthy call came from high up a tree.

"The kids have seen us," Danuba said and chuckled. "They are the grapevine of the village, y'know."

They continued up the path of light brown mud that had strong roots of plants and trees crisscrossing through it. The roots made good footholds. The first structure of the village seemed to come into sight suddenly for the newcomers, but in fact it had been within sight right from the shore. It blended into the environment incredibly well because its roof was made of layers of long bushy leaves, and the rest of the multi-tiered hut was made of unfinished, thin-cut wood that formed the boxy frame. People could be seen standing inside, for there were no walls, just transparent screening meant to keep out animals and insects. The sound of thumping baseboards came from inside, and a rush of figures passed behind the screening. Then, a gaggle of children excitedly emerged and came running over the mud like it was a trail of dry grass. Being swarmed by a bunch of children brought back uncomfortable memories for the crew of the Maradona. However, the smiling faces and jolly chatter quickly warmed their hearts.

"Toong-Kaixo, I'm Mossy. What's your name?" A little girl with chubby cheeks, frizzy brown hair and bright almond-shaped eyes stood smiling just in front of Lemay. She held out her hand with her palm facing up.

"Hi, I'm Lemay," he replied.

She was still holding out her hand, like she expected something from him. With a nervous smile, he began to walk past her, not really understanding what she wanted from him—at which the smile dropped from her face. She retracted her hand, turned, and stomped back into the throng of children. Lemay stood confused for a moment but then shrugged and moved forward through the onslaught of greetings.

Lana-Baboye and Taola already had their own fan club of young boys and girls who were introducing themselves and vying for their attention. A couple of boys waved and shouted out to them, "Look, look!" When Taola or Lana-Baboye glanced over, they did handstands, cartwheels, and rolling summersaults that covered their backs in mud.

"Yes, yes, kids. It's all very exciting, y'know, but let them through!" Danuba shouted.

The welcome party cleared the way a little and everyone moved forward slowly but surely.

"I'm going to take you all straight to your yurt," Danuba said to Navis, who was trying to keep hold of Myli and Tumi while their cheeks were being pinched lovingly and lines were being formed to give them hugs. "Otherwise, y'know, it's going to be a whole lot more of this."

Meanwhile, the adults had appeared outside the large hut. Spurred by Danuba's signals, they began calling out to their kids to give space to the newcomers. Finally, the throng had thinned enough for Danuba to lead the thoroughly welcomed crew of the Maradona farther down the jungle path.

"Look above," Danuba said, pointing up.

They all gazed in wonder at a network of rope bridges strung from tree to tree. Again, it was as if the human made structures grew out of the forest itself, melding with the foliage so well that the unwary could very well miss the structures above.

On the ground, there were villagers talking and laughing, working on chores or playing games: some were stirring huge pots of steaming liquid under little thatched shelters, in a clearing some fifteen meters away a group of children were using long curved sticks to whack a ball into netted goals. Nearby the path they were walking on, a pair of elderly men was hunched over the ground, playing a game with seedpods that they rolled like dice into a small pit in the ground. Other villagers were reclining against a set of large rounded boulders on a patch of wiry grass in a sunny glade, smoking out of long wooden pipes.

One thing that seemed peculiar to Lana-Baboye, who came from a homogenous culture, was the blend of ethnicities. Differences of hair and skin color, facial features, and body types were more common than similarities. It was quite a change from her own tribe. Lana-Baboye began to understand why Mama Gogo had called the Enané one of the *Yoka-ti-kiza,* or "hybrid tribes."

Danuba kept leading the way past yurts whose roofs had grass growing out the top of them. Every yurt had an elevated garden bed, each one meticulously tended to with its own variety of vegetables and flowers. It was evident that the Enané were passionate about their gardens, each one was a living work of art.

Seeing Navis admiring them, Danuba said, "Gardening, y'know, it's one of our most difficult undertakings here in this wet desert called Meisha. We have to make our garden soil by mixing our mud with fertilizer from the animal keepers on the leveled borders of the jungle. Then there's the onslaught of insects and animals that attack the produce. So, it's an esteemed art among us. We discover, research, and share ideas of efficient design, combinations of floral and fungal allies to deter pests, and methods of tending y'know."

"That's amazing," Navis said.

"And exhausting," Danuba added without skipping a beat.

"I have my own garden back home in Lindum," Navis said, "though it's probably overrun by now."

"We often have to make fresh starts too, y'know. It'll work out," Danuba said and stopped at a particularly large yurt. "This is Jupiter, our largest guest home."

Jupiter was a pentagonal structure, a wooden cabin that, unlike the first structure they had seen, possessed walls but still included the airy transparent screening all around the top of the walls, where they met the roof, for the sake of ventilation and light.

"Y'know, before you go in you can use this to wash your feet," Danuba said.

On the platform deck leading up to the front door of Jupiter was a spigot that Danuba turned on and washed his feet under. Everyone followed suit and found that the mud came off easily enough.

Once inside, Danuba warned everyone that they should keep their clothes and other items in the sealable clay containers lined up along the walls covered in peppermint, citronella, and tobacco oil infused cork. "Y'know, you will find a tarantula in your pants if you're not careful, and that's the least of your worries." Everyone began scanning the floors with each step they took now—Danuba smiled as he watched them cross another threshold in the process of adapting to jungle life. Inside was one big open space with no partitions, in which were beds covered in mosquito nets, a network of crisscrossing beams that stretched across the ceiling with hammocks hanging down from them, and a rear extension that led to four outhouses. Danuba began to walk toward the rear extension, but then paused and added as an afterthought, "And make sure to keep your mosquito nets tucked under your mattresses."

Out back, after checking out the surprisingly odorless outhouses, Danuba led them along a path that got steamier and steamier the farther they went, until visibility was blurred. They came upon a boardwalk that led to wooden stalls.

"Are there hot springs here?" Taola asked.

"Actually, y'know, you are all at the edge of one of the world's wonders, I'd say," Danuba replied. "The Shanay-Timpishka is a boiling river that stretches for about seventeen kilometers through the jungle. We are close to its origin here, where there are underground hot springs."

"Wow. It is actually boiling hot?" Lana-Baboye asked.

"Y'know, you could stick an egg in there and hard-boil it," Danuba proudly stated. "It is actually because of the boiling river that this part of the jungle has fewer insects and animals than the rest of it. Anyway, in each stall we have showers that take water from drums that hold the water from the river, cooling it a bit. Also, now and then you'll find buckets full of floral water that we make from jungle plants. Y'know, words can't explain the value of aromatherapy first thing in the morning or after a long day."

"Speaking of which, is it already getting dark?" Navis asked, noticing the creeping shadows along the bases of the tall trees towering all around them.

"Yeah, twelve hours of day and twelve hours of night out here—means dinner's nearly ready. Let's head back."

Back in the Accomodor—the giant hut that they had first seen upon arrival—roasted plantains, fish and yuca grilled in banana leaves, vegetable stew, and fruits were being laid out on a long dinner table. The Accomodor was surprisingly vacant except for the cooks dressed in colorful aprons and a few people lying in hammocks or sitting high up on open lofts that overlooked the ground floor.

"Goonja! Goonja!" came the greetings from the lofts above when they stepped in through the door.

"Oh yes, words to learn, y'know," Danuba said. "Toong-Kaixo means good morning or afternoon, and Goonj-Kaixo means good evening or night. Toonga or goonja for short. Ah, and it looks like they listened to me and cleared up the crowd so you all can eat in peace."

After introducing the crew of the Maradona to the cooks, he led them to a table, which he took a quick peek under, then said with a wink, "Always good to take a look for critters, y'know."

The food was spread across the center of the table, so everyone began serving themselves. Taola rubbed her hands together and reached for the fish wrapped in banana leaves, but Danuba stopped her.

"Uh, Taola, I'm sorry. If you want to start your training right away, you'll have to do the fast, y'know."

"Oof." Taola sighed with frustration and crossed her arms.

"You must know it's for—"

"I know, I know." Taola cut Danuba off. "I've just never been a lover of the process."

"I mean, no one enjoys it, y'know . . . unless you're a little abnormal like this guy over here," Danuba said, adding the last part as a man walked over carrying a young woman in his arms.

"Not everyone can be normal like little Danny, *y'know*," the man replied sarcastically with special emphasis on the "y'know."

Danuba sneered lightheartedly and made a face to entertain the children as the man set the woman down at one end of the bench and then sat down himself. "Goonja. I'm Danny's younger brother, Dahrius, and this is my beloved Eza."

"Hello, everyone," Eza said. She was a small, pretty woman with brown skin, long jet-black hair parted at the center, and lips that seldom shifted from a little smirk. Her left leg was limp and frail in comparison to her right leg, and apparently gave her much distress—it was for this reason that Dahrius often carried her around.

The resemblance between Danuba and Dahrius was uncanny in the face, but otherwise they were opposites. Danuba was tall while Dahrius was short. Danuba was lean while Dahrius was broad and stout. Danuba had a puffy salt and pepper afro while Dahrius kept his hair buzzed short. Also, it was clear that Danuba was a bit older than Dahrius.

A man in an apron came over carrying a plate. He placed it down in front of Taola. It was full of white rice, boiled green plantains, and oatmeal in a bowl on the side.

"Thanks," Taola said unenthusiastically. The cook shrugged apologetically.

"What's wrong with it?" Lemay asked, leaning over and looking at her meal.

"It has no flavoring," Taola replied. "There's only exactly what you see in it."

"It doesn't look so bad," Lemay said.

"Here, try some," Taola took a scoop of oatmeal and fed it to Lemay. He scrunched his nose a little and nodded.

"I see what you mean."

"No salt, no sugar, no nothing," Taola said under her breath as she cut the plantain into slivers.

"Why can she eat only that?" Navis asked, genuinely curious.

Lana-Baboye was sitting next to Navis and so replied first. "Well, it's a complex traditional science, but it can be summarized somewhat by the saying 'you are what you eat.' Different foods each affect the way your body functions—consider all your organs, including your brain. Thus, your mental and emotional states are also affected by your intake. The idea behind the bland food for Sis here is that it'll help her body and mind settle into a more neutral state, which is important for her training and when connecting to the more subtle energies of the plant medicines."

"Easy for you to say," Taola said. "I'm mad, not neutral. Mad."

This made everyone smile or laugh, especially Lemay, who ended up choking a little on some rice.

Eza turned to Taola again. "It's okay, dear," Eza said in an uppish way. "It's hard for first-timers."

"Actually, I've done this dozens of times, and it doesn't get any easier for me," Taola replied, picking at her food.

Eza seemed to be a little taken aback that this wasn't Taola's first time doing a traditional diet. She began looking at her and everyone else more carefully, freshly interested in who they were.

While chewing on some sweet plantain, Dahrius said, "Here we also say that fasts help set your intentions by tethering them to a physical process." He stopped talking long enough to swallow then continued. "By bringing your natural bodily abilities, processes, and senses out of overstimulation, you are more prepared to . . . say, learn something new or benefit from a medical treatment, or a medicine, especially some of our natural medicines that wouldn't work at all in the presence of caffeine, for example."

"So why are you fasting? Taola, was it?" Eza asked.

"If you don't mind sharing," Dahrius added quickly, which made Eza's nostrils flare, but she tried to smile over her displeasure.

"That's alright," Taola said. "Taola Lonwë's the name, and I'm fasting because I have some unfinished training to complete." She popped another piece of plantain into her mouth, the only food on her plate she had touched so far.

"Could you pass the fish, Navis?" Danuba asked. He already had two unwrapped banana leaves at the side of his plate, and a stack of fish bones.

Meanwhile, Eza leaned over and whispered to Dahrius, "Hmph, that wasn't really an answer."

Dahrius's only reply was a hushing action with his lips as he continued to dig into his dinner. Ignoring her own food, Eza seemed to be gaining nourishment instead from enacting an inquisition of Taola. "So, where are you from, Taola?"

"Originally from the cityfort Atlantia, but I did most of my growing up on Oaql Island."

"Oaql Island? Where's that?"

"It's a Haelin Island, kind of hard to explain where exactly. Lana is also from there."

Eza's eyes widened. She shifted in her seat and, in a deemphasized manner, said, "Oh, that's nice." Then she turned to Lana-Baboye and continued, "That's how you knew about the traditional diet."

"Yes, it's a part of our culture," Lana-Baboye answered. "We utilize various types of fasts during our training."

"You're one of the Reteti," Eza stated for confirmation.

"Yes, the Reteti," Lana-Baboye replied.

Eza became silent for the rest of the night, not feeling self-assured in the company of Lana-Baboye and Taola. Everyone else continued to converse about nothing in particular, like how the saltiness of the *boki-chiko* fish was balanced by the sweetness of the yuca and how the soup got much of its flavor from an herb called *sacha-culantro*, which most people considered a useless weed.

Soon, villagers kept coming over to greet the newcomers, until the twins began to get chuffy due to exhaustion. This made the crew of the Maradona realize that they too were ready to sleep. Danuba noticed this.

He stood, stretched, and said aloud, "Time for bed! We have a busy day tomorrow. Taola, someone will come early tomorrow to escort you to Sun, our ceremonial house." He started clearing the table. Dahrius and Lana-Baboye started to help, but the brothers took the dirty cups and utensils out of her hands, insisting that she take it easy. So she, Taola, and the others said their "Goonj-Kaixos" and "goonjas" as they made their way out of the Accomodor.

Outside, they became aware of the night song of the jungle, swelling with ultrasonic insect sounds, peeping frogs, and seemingly hundreds of other hooting, braying, and baying creatures. They noticed that the muddy path was delineated on its edges by trailing large white, night-blooming flowers that they hadn't noticed in the daylight, leading all the way back to their lodging.

Chapter 14

AMA-RONOKI

It was a rainy morning in Meisha Forest. High above its mud-sand earth the sound of rainwater falling on the dense canopy was a constant dull tone, except for the occasional patter of rain drops that found their way through the leaves of the trees and fell upon the roof of the yurt called Jupiter. About an hour or so after dawn, the rain became sparse, and thin rays of sunlight shone through the large screened windows of the yurt. Taola and Lana-Baboye had already been awake for a while, each sitting in meditation in their hammock. Taola was taking deep breaths, trying to sense the young Oaql sprout on the Maradona, which she found difficult enough like trying to delicately take hold of loose strands of spider silk in a poorly lit room. Impossible for her, however, was connecting to the rogue Oaql boat with Arionella on it, though that did not stop her from trying. After a time, she grew discouraged and opened her eyes. She lay down in the hammock, letting it sway from side to side.

The sound of footsteps came from the porch, and then the water spigot turned on—someone was washing their feet. Taola sprang out of the hammock, went to the door, and opened it. First, she saw a baby—

who couldn't have been older than a year—on all fours watching as a girl about Lemay's age rubbed away mud from in between her toes.

"Goo . . . ja!" Taola called out, startling both the girl and the baby. The baby fell over and began to cry. "Ohh, it's okay; it's okay." Taola stepped forward and crouched over the baby. The baby paused for a second as he took a moment to look at her, and then began crying even more.

"Oh lala-foo-tha, ooh baybee," the girl said as her long, straight black hair swept forward and her sinewy body tensed as she swept the baby off the ground and set him on her boney hip. The baby almost immediately stopped crying. Then, the baby and the girl looked at Taola, who was still crouching a little below their eye level. "Toonka, Miss," said the girl.

"Toonka!" said Taola and laughed. "Right, it's Toonka for good morning. I messed that one up. Toonka, sweety. Sorry I scared you."

"It's okay. Um, they said to tell you to meet Mr. Dan in Sun," the girl said and then smiled sweetly. With her task complete, she began to walk toward the steps of the platform.

"Wait," Taola said, standing up straight. "What's your name?"

The girl stopped and turned. "Fio."

"Nice to meet you, Fio," she said. "I'm Taola Lonwë. Can you show me the way? I don't know where Sun is, actually."

"Sure."

"Okay, great! Just a moment," Taola said and went back inside the yurt. She was about to tell Lana-Baboye that she was going to head out, but Lana-Baboye had already heard everything. The yurts were remarkably waterproof but not soundproof at all. The baby's cries had awoken everyone inside, so Taola was able to say goodbye to the whole crew. "Well, I'm off. Wish me luck!"

Taola and Fio walked along the muddy trail, turning right at a strange tree that looked like it was pregnant. Its high branches stretched in all directions at the top of its narrow trunk, but nearer to the ground the trunk expanded into a girthy form before thinning out again and disappearing into the soil amongst bulbous roots.

"Interesting tree," Taola remarked.

"It's a *Lopuna*," Fio replied as she adjusted the baby on her hip. "They say it is one of the master plants here." As they walked on Taola thought she could almost feel the presence of it sensing their steps.

"So, what's the little one's name?" Taola asked, noticing that the baby kept looking over Fio's shoulder at her.

"Mendelson."

"That's an interesting choice for name."

"My sister and Mr. Dahrius chose the name," Fio shrugged.

"This is your sister's baby? I met her last night. I can't remember her name."

"Eza."

"Ah yes. Eza."

"Okay; here we are. Sun," Fio said.

Again, an obviously human-made structure came into focus for Taola, which initially she had not noticed at all. This structure did not look like it had tiers but instead was huge in diameter, with a conical roof of made of rows and layers of long, dry, gray leaves that hung off the sides like teeth.

"Excellent. Thank you, Fio."

"You're welcome, Miss. *Toong-Kaixo.*"

"See you later, Mendelson," said Taola and waved at the baby as Fio walked away.

"Taola, is that you?" came a familiar voice from inside the shaggy hut.

"Yes, it's me," Taola replied. "I'll be right in."

Inside Sun, the giant ceremonial hut, it was quite dark. What little light that came through the canopy outside illuminated the interior gently through transparent screens that were higher up on the structure and much smaller than most of the other yurts she had yet seen. The shadiness and high ceiling made for a cool sanctuary from the heat and humidity of the rainforest. The planks that made up the floor consisted of hard rosewood cut and positioned into concentric, ever shortening, dodecagons that began at each of the twelve walls of Sun and met at its center.

"Toonka, young lady," Danuba said as she entered. He was squatting at the center of the yurt near a tree-stump that had been made into a polished table of sorts; otherwise the yurt was mostly empty, save for some clay urns along its shadowy walls and the silhouettes of hammocks strung throughout from the beams above.

As Taola approached, she noticed he was wearing a long rainbow-colored cotton poncho that was cut high at the arms so that it revealed his lean but muscular arms and his bare oblique's. She noted the similarity of his garb to the ceremonial garments of the Reteti.

"Ama-Ronoki is lying on the cushions on the other side, y'know. She is one of our elders and will oversee your training."

"Is she still sleeping?" Taola asked in a whisper. "I don't want to disturb her."

"Well, she often has long nights in here, y'know, but she's expecting you," said Danuba as he stood up from the tree-stump table he had been arranging with many little crystals, glazed pottery containers, fossils, and many other trinkets.

Taola realized that this, in fact, was a ceremonial alter.

Danuba started to lead the way for Taola but then stopped for a moment and added, "Don't be disheartened or daunted if at first Ama seems a little . . . unwelcoming, y'know."

"Don't worry," she said. "I've grown up around Haelin elders. I'm used to it."

Danuba nodded and started walking again. They got close to a little lump of a figure under a colorful sheet with intricately threaded designs all over it.

"Ama? Are you awake?" Danuba said softly, though his deep voice resonated in the expanse of the hut, making it louder than he intended.

First came a muffled snort from under the sheet, and then a quivering voice that shook with passion said, "Impertinent sapling! Waking people when the sun is low in the sky!"

"Taola Lonwë, the young lady of the Oaql boat, is here. She started her fast last night and hasn't eaten yet today, as I instructed her," Danuba said with a hint of a nervous quake in his voice.

Ama-Ronoki swept the sheet off herself in a single motion. A small woman, the size of a Reteti islander, was revealed with her wiry hair standing in disarray, round eyes blinking in the light, and lips frowning deeply. Danuba took a step back, dipping his head slightly into his shoulders. Taola was controlling her laughter because the juxtaposition of Danuba's gentle-giant demeanor and Ama-Ronoki's honey-badger ferocity was wildly entertaining to her in the otherwise tense situation. Ama-Ronoki fixed her eyes on Danuba and started glaring at him. Danuba looked at the floor uncomfortably.

"WELL?" Ama-Ronoki bounced a little in her seated position as she shouted. Danuba stood mute, looking thoroughly flustered. "You going to keep standing there like a tall, dumb pole, or are you going to collect fresh water for us?"

"Oh! Of course!" Danuba stumbled toward the exit, glancing briefly at Taola with embarrassment, while Taola stood wide-eyed with an amused frown upon her face.

"Now that he's out of the way, it's time to get to work," Ama-Ronoki said, suddenly seeming perfectly tranquil. "Come sit here." Taola went over and sat on the planks in front of Ama-Ronoki. "Take these." She gave Taola a thin needle and yellow thread. "Watch." She picked up her own needle and thread and passed the thread through the needle loop with a single swipe. She then picked up a soft fabric of an earthy brown color and weaved a curvy line across the fabric, as quick as if she was using a pen to scribble it on. "It's your turn."

"I've never been good at this sort of thing," Taola said suddenly self-conscious. Ama-Ronoki sat motionless, waiting.

"Okay, let me just . . . ," said Taola as she raised the needle and thread up close to her eyes "get this thread through." The thread kept fraying, so she licked it to straighten it, but it still kept bending over. Ama-Ronoki stood and stretched, scratched her behind and walked sleepily out of the yurt. A few minutes passed. Ama-Ronoki returned and raised a long wooden pipe to her lips, settled into a comfortable position near Taola, and intently watched Taola continue to struggle. A minute passed. "Do you have a larger needle I could use? I think this one is too small," Taola asked as politely as she could. She already knew very well that Ama-Ronoki was unpredictable.

"No. That needle and thread are perfect for each other. It is you who doesn't fit," she said blatantly.

Taola's ears flushed with heat. Apparently, for all the practice she had butting heads with Haelin elders, she wasn't ready for Ama-Ronoki's special form of hectoring. Taola tried again, but she felt the old lady's judgmental eyes on her, and the gloom of the shady hut didn't help either. Hunger was also making it hard to concentrate.

Why on earth was Ama-Ronoki asking me to sew anyway?

Then, it occurred to her that maybe Ama-Ronoki wasn't fully aware of the rush she was in and had enlisted her in a task that she needed assistance with before beginning the training.

"Ama, I would love to help you, but I'm here for urgent training. I'm supposed to figure out how to sense the Oaql boat and rescue a young girl that has been swept away on it."

"You are not *supposed* to do anything," Ama-Ronoki answered. "Remember, this is all your choice—you don't have to save anyone, you don't have to do this *nidaamsan* from foods, and you surely do not have to sew anything here with me." Ignoring Taola's confused expression, Ama-Ronoki paused to relight her pipe. She lowered a lit match over it until the leafy material in the bowl started to glow, then continued, "Now, about your issues with sensing the boat. You, who are in a rush all the time, easily get lost in your own head. You cannot live in a dream world in your head and ignore your waking dream here. They are intertwined. You must ground yourself with skills to help master yourself. What you understand here and now, you translate into your intentions and manifestations for the future. Lastly, about sewing. Sewing will teach you to focus—your concentration on the patterns and the techniques will start to discipline your mind. If I needed help, I would ask one of the roaming chickens here to help before asking you—most of them are more capable and disciplined than you are. Now let's eat and return to your task, if you so choose."

Danuba had just walked in with a large jug full of water and two covered plates stacked on one another. Still reeling from the multi-layered lasagna of information and insults that Ama-Ronoki had offered her, Taola now felt compassion for Danuba, whereas earlier she was entertained more than anything else.

Danuba set down the plates before them and drew off the covers, revealing bland boiled potatoes. Normally, Taola would have made some kind of show of displeasure at such fare, but she wasn't about to provoke Ama-Ronoki. Her spirits elevated a bit when she noticed that Ama-Ronoki too had been served only the unseasoned potatoes. Danuba took his leave while the two women ate in silence.

After only a couple of bites, Ama-Ronoki got up and went outside into the daylight again. She was a very tiny old lady. In fact, she was shorter than Lana-Baboye, which led Taola to wonder if she might be Reteti—she had the complexion and the features for it too.

Taola got through one whole potato before putting her plate aside. She picked up the needle and thread and tried again. Very aware of her choice in the matter this time, she began to reflect on the many important decisions she had made throughout her life so far that had brought her to this moment. After two more failed attempts, the thread finally passed through. Taola thought it was much easier without Ama-Ronoki watching her every movement.

While waiting for Ama-Ronoki to return, Taola took a closer look at the fabrics laid out nearby. She chose one with yellow and green stitch patterns of what looked like leaves growing out of stems. She then picked up a small scrap of torn fabric and started sewing, trying to copy what she saw, making slow progress. Ama-Ronoki returned just as Taola got to one end of the fabric and showed her how to continue the pattern. She then started a new course with a neon green thread that wrapped in crisscrosses around the yellow-leaf pattern Taola had started. Taola could see designs starting to take shape as the thread lines met and dispersed.

"See how form emerges once the digressions of the mind are stilled?" Ama-Ronoki asked. "The spots where you forgot a curve or a cross are representative of where your mind digressed. When you are fully present, your patterns reflect that as well, until that pattern becomes second nature." Ama-Ronoki passed one end of a larger and longer brown tinted fabric to Taola, and without another word she began sewing on the same piece of cloth, but at the other end.

A deep orange glow filled the ceremonial yurt by the time that Taola and Ama-Ronoki stopped sewing. Taola found that she had really enjoyed herself for the most part. There were times when she had completely zoned in, as if the thread, needle, and pattern were all that existed for her. Other times, she had grown anxious about Oaql Island, Arionella, and all the things she still had to do, and that was when she messed up a stitch and had to undo it. Still, the tapestry that had begun to form over the course of the afternoon was now filled with bright colors leaf shapes, circles, and squiggly patterns all came together into one voluminous design of intertwining stems and leaves that connected stitched concentric circles of different sizes and colors of deep navy blue and salmon pink. The two women sat and wordlessly admired their work. Finally, after a few bites of the cold potatoes, they fell asleep in the hammocks hanging off the beams of the hut.

———◦———

Somewhere in the rainforest not too far away, Navis, Lemay, Myli, Tumi, and Lana-Baboye were heading to the Accomodor among a throng of Enané children and adults with whom they had spent the day playing games and making deep crimson-red body paint from *pashako* seeds, which they then painted onto one another.

Lemay's hand was held by Mossy, the girl who had introduced herself the night before. She had gone up to Lemay again that morning when they were collecting the *pashako* seed pods, but this time instead of waiting for him to understand that she was offering her hand, she decisively took his and had seldom let it go ever since. At first, Lemay was uncomfortable, but Mossy didn't make anything else out of the hand holding. In fact, she did it in a businesslike manner, like it was her personal duty to show him around.

Navis would have delighted in Lemay's newfound friendship more if he hadn't been preoccupied by his own social challenges. After having spent most of his childhood as an orphan living in a monastery and now at twenty-two, devoted to raising kids, Navis had no practice with having downtime with people his own age. However, his awkwardness brought him more attention than he had hoped for. A clique of about six extroverted girls in their late teens and early twenties first thought it may be fun to flirt with "the new guy." They were charmed by his soft demeanor, and then as time passed and they learned more about him, they became smitten by the fact that he was a single adoptive father of four children.

Even more difficult for him, however, were the interactions with young men his age. They had their own way of getting close to each other, which came off to Navis as nervous tension a step away from full-blown conflict, so he stayed quiet and distant whenever they approached, which in turn made them feel distrustful of him.

Myli and Tumi, on the other hand, were in heaven. They were showered in affection by Navis's female admirers and were nearly drowning in peers that were just as relentless in play as they were.

Lana-Baboye quickly became a star for everyone, young and old. Daring and experienced climbers would venture high into the treetops to recover the *pashako* seed pods and other treasures from the canopy like the tangy violet *keero* berries that the Enané and spider monkeys would fiercely compete for. Lana-Baboye quickly caught everyone's attention as she nimbly raced up the trees with the best climbers in the tribe. In team games, the winners were the ones who gathered most of the freshest coveted fruits, so fierce arguments erupted as to who would have Lana-Baboye on their team. It was decided that Lana-Baboye would team-hop as a special player, gracing each team with her skills at least once during the multiple runs up to the canopy.

Back in the Accomodor at sunset, things were winding down. Navis asked Lana-Baboye if they should check on how Taola was doing. They went over to a woman with a large inflated stomach who was sitting on a chair, shouting orders out to people working in the kitchen.

"No! I told you to put it there. All you have to do is lift it and put it through the hook!"

"Sorry to disturb you, miss," Navis said. "I just wanted to know how to get to Sun, the ceremonial yurt?"

The woman looked relieved that she had found a reason not to get up out of her chair to enforce her verbal orders.

She slumped back and replied, "That's alright. I'll have you escorted there immediately." With barely a pause to take a breath, she hollered, "Fio!"

From across the Accomodor came a thin girl with dark black hair tied up loosely at the back of her head, carrying a baby at her hip. It was the girl who came to wake up Taola that morning, and was the only child in sight that did not have any face paint on. She saw Navis and tried to fix her hair with her one free hand, blushing a little.

"What is it, Ma?" she asked.

"Take these people to Sun and get back here quick."

"Okay, take Mendelson for a second." Fio quickly leaned forward and passed the baby to her mom before he or she could complain, and then she ran off toward the exit, followed by Lana-Baboye.

"Oof! How much can a pregnant woman be expected to do!" The lady grumbled with distaste as Mendelson began to flail about and cry in her arms.

Navis glanced over at Lemay and the twins, who had been put to work, along with all the other children, by the kitchen staff. They were washing the piles of fresh fruits that had been picked earlier that the day in buckets full of sudsy water. Seeing that they were occupied, Navis took off after Lana-Baboye and Fio.

When they got to Sun, Fio went inside with them. Without the baby attached to her hip she looked and moved like the kid that she in fact was—one that was possibly rambunctious and definitely witty. It was pitch black inside, but Fio knew that there were candles and matches right by the entrance on a little shelf. She lit three candles and held each sideways so that their wax would drip onto little wooden plaques, which she then fixed the candles onto.

Two of the hammocks were lower than the rest and had taken on the forms of their inhabitants, so they moved forward to see which one was Taola's. Taola was asleep in the rainbow-colored one, her arms stretched over her head and both her knees sprawled out with the palms of her feet pressed together.

"Sis. Sis," Lana-Baboye whispered.

Taola awoke, blinking slowly and putting her hands up against the light of the candles.

"Hey, sis," she replied through a yawn. "Navis and Fio too. Wow, I didn't realize how young you are Fio."

"I'm eleven! My mom even says I can have a boyfriend now—" but Fio paused as something dawned upon her. "You remembered my name?" Fio asked with her hands over her heart.

"Yes, of course!" Taola replied.

"But you didn't remember my sister's name before."

"That's true." Taola folded her arms and nodded. "I guess you were more memorable to me."

Taola's words took a moment to sink in. Then, Fio blushed and smiled a big toothy smile. "You want to see something cool?" she asked as she skipped over to the nearest unoccupied hammock.

"Sure, but quietly please." Taola pointed her nose toward the hammock which still contained the sleeping Ama-Ronoki.

Fio faced away from her audience at first, with the hammock in hand. Then she turned around with it so that the hammock cloth crossed around her waist. "Okay, ready?" she asked.

"Ready," said Taola.

Fio dipped her head forward and did a front flip, using the hammock as a brace.

"Wow, very cool, Fio!" Taola gently clapped her hands.

"Yes, well done!" Navis said.

"Now, watch this!" Fio threw her head back, doing a backflip this time. "And you can keep going." Fio executed another front flip, except this time she let herself keep tumbling, legs tucked in. After a dozen dizzying spins she finally came to a halt and let the hammock unwind from around her. She lay flat on the ground until her eyes uncrossed themselves.

"I'm going to try it," Taola said, getting out of her hammock.

Fio quickly sat up, still a little wobbly. "No, you won't," she said and laughed.

"And why not?" Taola asked with her hands on her hips.

Fio thought for a few seconds and said "I dunno" with a shrug.

"Well then; here it goes." Taola took her hammock and wrapped it around her waist in the same way Fio had done—one 360 degree turn that crossed the cloth around her. "Now, I just roll forward?" Fio nodded, and Taola went for it. She spun in a flip and popped up headfirst again. Fio bounced up and down, a big smile on her face, then went over to Taola and gave her a big hug.

"What about me? Don't I get a hug?" Lana-Baboye asked as she flipped herself on a hammock too. Fio skipped over to her and gave her a hug too. Then, Fio, Lana-Baboye, and Taola turned to look at Navis with smirks on their faces. It was his turn.

"I don't think I can do it," he said. "If anything, my legs are too long. I need to tie the hammocks up higher."

"Scaredy cat, scaredy cat!" Fio said loudly, trying to goad Navis.

"Shh, Ama-Ronoki is still sleeping," Taola reminded everyone, but then she added in a whisper, "Scaredy cat."

Navis rolled his eyes, went over to a hammock, swung forward and ... BOOM! He fell hard, right on his behind.

"WUH!" Ama-Ronoki awoke shouting. "What's going on?" Her hair was in disarray, standing up in all directions, and her teeth were bared, making her look positively feral.

Fio didn't waste a second. While Ama-Ronoki's eyes were adjusting to the light, she fled straight to the exit without looking back and was gone like a wisp into the darkness of the jungle.

Ama-Ronoki first laid eyes on Navis, still sitting on the ground. The hammock above was swinging wildly. "No hanky-panky on my watch, Taola!" she shouted.

"Ama! I'm here behind you," Taola called out.

"Where? What? You know as well as I do that the fast includes controlling your base desires!" Ama-Ronoki continued to shout as she turned to face Taola.

Taola walked over to her and made confused face. "What are you talking about?"

"No sex!"

"What in the world? No, no, I just have some visitors. Fio brought them." Taola waved Lana-Baboye over.

Ama-Ronoki glared at Taola and then became pensive. "Fio. She's an interesting one. Don't get me started on her mother and sister though. That family just arrived here recently—" Ama-Ronoki was going off on a tangent, but lost her train of thought when she saw Lana-Baboye. "Now there's a countenance I haven't seen in a long time."

"Goonj-kaixo, Ronoki'sa," Lana-Baboye said with a bow. Ama-Ronoki drank in the greeting with great pleasure. "My name is Lana-Baboye. I have come from Oaql Island."

"I don't know why we ever leave," Ama-Ronoki said. "Well, I can tell you've already found your mission here in the outlands."

"Yes, I have. I will attend to it after this initiatory mission succeeds," Lana-Baboye asserted confidently.

Ama-Ronoki looked at Lana-Baboye closely. "You remind me of myself when I left Maql Island. I found my mission, and it has been the greatest achievement of my life. My skills were meant to be shared. The blessings given to me had to be redistributed in some way, just as yours must be, but I warn you, being away from the ocean for too long takes its toll on you. The sea is our origin—I mean all of humanity, not just us Reteti. Now here I am—the crabby village elder. These younger generations have no appreciation for all the sacrifices I made for their forebears.

"Do what you must do, Lana-Baboyanta, but don't make my mistake. Return now and then, go swimming with the turtles, let the rays nibble at your feet, surf with the dolphins, and dive deep below your island to the aquatic nurseries where you are reminded of how life endures." Ama-Ronoki's eyes filled up with tears as she gazed past the faces in front of her into a portal of memories.

Lana-Baboye kneeled by the old Reteti and held her hands. "I promise I will."

Ama-Ronoki returned from her inner flight and looked down at Lana-Baboye with smiling eyes. Then, she stretched and cleared her throat. "Okay then; enough with the mush. Get out, both of you!" Ama-Ronoki urged Lana-Baboye up by her shoulders and pointed at Navis. "No visitors for Taolanta during her fast unless I say so. Out, out!"

Chapter 15

THE CEREMONY

Navis awoke at dawn. It was misty and drizzling ever so slightly. Back home, he would take early morning walks while the children slept in during weather like this. His cabin was situated on a hillside outside of Lindum, close to the mountains. A large sturdy pine cast a cooling shade over his garden. Surrounding them was a field of tall grass that was crowned with white and purple morning glories. Beyond this was an old-growth forest of evergreens that stood at the feet of the Lindarous Mountains.

With this memory in mind, Navis got up out of bed quietly and tucked his mosquito net back into place. After a quick visit to the outhouses, he took the path down to the boiling river that Danuba had shown them. The rising sun made the mist and the steam glow golden in clusters of bejeweled specks of moisture, Navis looked upon this sight with excitement, thinking it might be golden sprites en masse, but he soon realized it wasn't so. As he continued walking a fantastical bird call echoed across the forest. Its call sounded like something small but heavy was being dropped into the water of a still pool but somehow amplified with a reverberating effect. This plunking sound was followed by high-pitched electrified gargles that gradually faded away. This happened a dozen times while Navis stood looking up at the glistening emerald tree-tops, trying to find whatever was making the sound, but soon he gave up and started walking again, left only with a sense of wonderment.

When Navis got a few meters away from the river, he saw Fio dunking clothes in a bucket full of water and scrubbing others with a sudsy hand brush. Mendelson, the baby, was sitting on the platform where she was working, vying for her attention by crawling over to the little soap bucket she was using to dip the brush in. She moved him away from it a few times a little roughly, clearly frustrated, and tried to give him a yellow bottle to play with. But Mendelson wasn't interested in the toy and threw it away. He returned to the soap bucket repeatedly until he finally tipped it over. Fio grunted with frustration, carried him over to a log, stood him against it, and with a hard smack on his rear left him there to cry at the top of his lungs.

Navis cringed at the sight. He was disturbed by the infant being treated that way but also personally understood the difficulties of raising children. *An eleven-year-old like Fio can't be expected to understand all the nuances that go into infant care, let alone a twenty-two-year-old in most cases*, he thought to himself. Navis also recalled that Fio hadn't been among them yesterday during the fruit-retrieval games and the face-painting festivities. He remembered seeing her helping in the kitchen of the Accomodor when they had returned that evening. Then there was her mother, who had called her over so harshly and was remiss in taking Mendelson when she ordered Fio to escort Navis and Lana-Baboye to the ceremonial hut.

He waited quietly for a couple of minutes until he couldn't take Mendelson's wailing any longer. Then he approached the two children casually, glancing idly about, stopping to look at a large, serrated leaf growing out of a stalk heavy shrub.

Fio saw him coming and dried her hands on her apron before quickly tying up loose strands of her hair that had fallen over her face.

"Toonka," she called out sweetly, blushing when Navis smiled and waved. It was like she had completely forgotten about Mendelson for the moment.

"Hi, how's it going? Fio, right?"

"Yes. And you're Navis," she replied.

"You escaped the wrath of Ama-Ronoki last night. I wish I had followed your lead!" Navis laughed, but Fio only grew silent and wary of Navis, thinking he have been chiding her in some way.

Navis noticed this and cleared his throat. "Anyway, what're you doing out here so early in the morning?" Navis asked.

"Washing clothes."

"But why so early?"

"To quickly get it out of the way, so that I can get my other chores done before the Enané girls wake up. I want to join them in Venus today, where they are going to do their hair care and nail painting."

"In Venus?"

"It's a yurt. You know, like Sun and Jupiter. Venus."

"Ah, I see. The huts here are named after the planets."

"Many of them, yes."

Mendelson's cried got loud again. Navis had been itching to console the baby. He walked over to him. "Why's this little guy crying so much?"

"Oh, he's fine," Fio said. "He's just being a brat."

Navis picked up Mendelson and patted his back. "Hey, little buddy, what's the matter?" Mendelson kept crying but less and less vigorously. "There you go, you're a happy baby, aren't you?" Navis lifted Mendelson and blew into his tummy. Mendelson squeaked with amusement. Navis did it again, and Mendelson started laughing. Then, he walked back over to where Fio was working and sat on the platform next to her, the baby on his knee. "How about I take care of him while you finish this up?"

"Thank you so much! I'm almost done!"

"So, what kind of animal makes that amazing echoey sound?" Navis asked her.

"Maybe you heard the *bocho locho*. It's a kind of bird that makes dangling teardrop shaped nests high up on *kymito* trees. I'll show you a rope-bridge platform from where you can see some." Fio was elated. She was happy for the help but even more grateful for the company.

———•———

Back in Sun, Taola and Ama-Ronoki were also awake. Taola had finally been able to talk sincerely to Ama-Ronoki the night before, while she was a little more receptive after meeting Lana-Baboye. Taola talked in detail about the attack on Oaql Island and the strange man who abducted Captain Rainer. She also told her about Arionella, Maya Airgialla Halla, and the Oaql boat. After hearing all this, Ama-Ronoki admitted that she was expecting Taola to apprentice under her for at least a month. "We will have to expedite things, but it will be more painful for you Taola," she had said.

"I can take it," Taola replied.

So now, bright and early, Ama-Ronoki moved with a sense of urgency. She had gone to her own little hut to get dressed in long pants, a long-sleeve shirt, and tall boots. She tied her hair up tight and buckled a small machete in a sheath to her back. For Taola's jungle-trekking clothing, Ama-Ronoki sent her to get fitted by a middle-aged Enané woman named Nadine.

Nadine was a tall blond woman with perpetually flushed cheeks that she blamed on the jungle heat. She was diligent in fitting Taola with clothes that not only would keep insects out but also made her look sporty and beautiful. Ama-Ronoki appeared at the fitting hut and lost her temper when she saw that Nadine was trying to find a hat that matched Taola's light brown cargo pants.

Taola and Ama-Ronoki had oatmeal in water for breakfast, making faces as they swallowed the stuff down. They were almost ready, but first Ama-Ronoki gave a little pouch to Taola. It was a cute thing with a flower pattern sewed into the hardy material made from amadou mushroom leather. Taola looked inside and saw that there were five cylinders of leaves wrapped in paper. "What's in these, Ama?"

"Tobacco, baku-baku root, and a blend of gray salvias. Don't inhale them, and only use them when I tell you."

Taola was somewhat familiar with the ceremonial and directed use of plants in the form of smoking, teas, tinctures, powders, and topical wraps from her time around Reteti botanists. Though she wasn't trained in their arts, she was reminded of one thing each time she was in their company, that there were important distinctions between the hedonism of casual usage versus the longstanding traditions of intentional usage.

They set out, crossing over thin planks that spanned the rocks jutting out of the boiling river, and entered into the jungle where there were no trails. Ama-Ronoki was quite agile for her age and moved at a fast pace. Following close behind, Taola would catch a glimpse of Ama-Ronoki's profile as she scanned the forest with her sharp eyes. Taola noticed she had a resemblance to Lana-Baboye that went beyond skin color or features. It was in her disposition and eyes—the mannerisms and grace of a Reteti warrior.

Now and then, squawks and hoots pierced through the monotony of the insects chirping as the duo snaked through the jungle around massive trees, sprang over running brooks, swatted at hungry mosquitos, and hacked through the tangled embraces of lianas that blocked their way. There were subtle changes as they walked through the thick vegetation, as if the plants had settled into different neighborhoods just as Danuba had said during his monologue on the Rusty Otter. For example, in some areas there were predominantly sinewy plants with thin vines, sprinkled with many tiny leaves; in other areas, there were mostly plants with great fleshy stems that would sway, perpetually dancing, with large elephant-ear leaves flapping in the breeze; in open glades grew colorful patches of flowers, as well as hardy plants that have a particular thirst for the sun's rays; and so on.

Finally, after about an hour of trekking, Taola and Ama-Ronoki came to a tunnel formed by tall, bristly shrubs leaning into one another, with wide, spade-shaped leaves growing along their tops like a green mohawk. When Taola looked closely, she noticed that there were bees holding little bits of tan-colored clay and flying in and out of ball-shaped nests of the same color. The nests hung like ornaments around the tunnel of vegetation, shaking with the constant motion of the bees entering and exiting through small holes built into their surface.

"Wow, do you see this Ama?"

"Yes, they are the first of our four tasks today. One: Observe beespas and spinner widow spiders. Two: avoid getting stung or bit by beespas or spinner widow spiders. Three: observe the *Pipi-Laris* tailorbird. Four: harvest, consume, and then weather the effects of the *hoa suna* plant." Ama-Ronoki laid out this somewhat informally, but then she continued in a more serious tone. "This passageway is called a *weaver's tunnel*. The major plants, insects, spiders, and animals that form and inhabit this tunnel all, in some way, skillfully craft their shelters—each in their own way and each with their own materials.

"The *hoa suna* plant that we are here to collect is right in front of us. These brown brambles forming the tunnel are it. However, what we need is the fresh emerald green sapling that can be made into a medicine."

An unnerving realization dawned upon Taola. "Don't tell me we need to retrieve this sapling from inside the tunnel."

"Yes, indeed, where they grow well-protected," Ama-Ronoki confirmed. "Not yet though. Come around this way. Let's sit a little farther off, take a break, and wait for the Pipi-Laris to return."

She found a relatively dry and somewhat intact log a good six meters away from the weaver's tunnel. She sat and took a simple tube-shaped bronze spyglass out of her satchel, followed by a water pouch that she drank deeply from and then passed over to Taola.

After ten minutes or so, they saw movement along the top of the tunnel. "Here, take a look through this." Ama-Ronoki handed Taola the spyglass. Taola looked through it. At first, she saw the cream underbelly of a small, plain-looking bird. Then, as it moved around a bit, orange toned feathers were revealed, shimmering in the rays of light from the canopy.

"Beautiful," Taola said.

"Just watch," Ama-Ronoki replied impatiently.

In the bird's thin beak were tufts of stringy, cotton-like material that it set down on the roof of the tunnel. Then, it began poking tiny holes around the edges of the large spade leaves that were pointing skyward. It hopped back over to the tuft of cotton material. Using its feet and beak, it pulled out threads that it began weaving through the little holes in the leaves.

"It's . . . it's sewing!" Taola exclaimed.

"Yes, it will take the Pipi-Laris about five days to construct a fresh new nest for its eggs. You see those shaggy brown tufts sticking out of the top of the tunnel? Those are dried-up nests that it has abandoned."

"Unbelievable," Taola said.

"Okay; now we stir things up." Ama-Ronoki took her pipe and a pouch of dried herbs from her satchel. With her teeth biting down on the stem of the pipe, she managed to tell Toala to take out her cigars. "Start puffing, girl. This herbal mixture repels and has an anesthetizing effect on these beespas and spiders."

Ama-Ronoki then got to her feet. Standing, she was only half a head taller than Taola, who was still seated. Taking a deep drag from her pipe, she pressed her lips against Taola's hair, which was tied up in a bun, and blew the smoke into it. She repeated this a few times.

Taola found she really liked the smell of the smoke. Though she wouldn't wear it to a dinner party as a perfume, out here in the open air of the jungle, the peppery aroma was an invigorating change from the perpetual scent of moist earth. Its dark brown color indicated it to be a different strain of tobacco from the lighter maroons of the Reteti strain. It was very nostalgic to her, as the Reteti had similar rituals. She recalled the time Mama Gogo had told her that if she had to choose one master plant to preserve if the forests were burning, she would choose tobacco.

Ama-Ronoki had moved on to blowing the smoke down the front and back of Taola's shirt. Finally, she squatted down and blew the smoke into Taola's boots. Then Ama-Ronoki handed Taola her own cigar of pure tobacco, which Taola lit and did the same smoke-blowing ritual for Ama-Ronoki.

When Taola was finished, Ama-Ronoki returned to the opening of the tunnel and began blowing smoke from her pipe into it. The smoke wafted in and lingered visibly at the center until slowly it started rising through the narrow crevices of the network of stems. A hum of angry buzzing filled the air, but it slowly subsided into silence. Then Ama-Ronoki motioned Taola to add smoke from her cigars to the mix. Soon, there was a thick cloud of smoke circulating inside the tunnel and rising out of it, which made it look like it was on fire. Ama-Ronoki picked up a thin stick, held it up straight at arm's length, and walked forward without hesitation. "For the webs," she added as an afterthought. Taola picked up one too, took a deep breath, gritted her teeth, and followed the old woman inside, having to stoop low, for the arch of the tunnel was sure to have cobwebs and her head was much closer to the top than Ama-Ronoki's.

"You see the webbing?" Ama-Ronoki's voice drifted back from farther ahead.

"I'm trying not to," was Taola's reply.

"Hahaha! You must at least take a peek, Taolanta," said Ama-Ronoki, amused. She pulled at something tucked away in her shirt: a glowtern around her neck that she activated at its lowest setting, revealing that what looked like gray wisps of smoke lingering along the tangled walls of the tunnel were actually sacks of webbing. "Just under the webs are the spinner widows."

Taola tilted her head to the side to look under a particularly opaque and ovular sack of webbing. At first, she saw nothing. Then, her eye caught the slight movements of something glistening black. It was a spider the width and length of an average human thumb, tucking itself out of sight under its web. Taola choked on her own yelp. Her skin was crawling as she hunched over a little and tucked her arms in close to her body.

"Ama, I can't do this. I have to go outside," Taola said anxiously.

"It is your decision. This is the path I'm laying out for you," Ama-Ronoki replied sternly.

"Ama, that spider had a spiky club growing out of its back . . . and it's huge."

"And dangerous," Ama-Ronoki added. "But they stick to their own business."

Taola whimpered but moved forward in tiny steps.

"I know how you are feeling," Ama-Ronoki said. "Don't forget that I was an ocean girl too. It took me a long time to adjust to the jungle."

After walking a few more meters, Ama-Ronoki stopped, squatted down, and blew smoke over some thin grassy stalks that had tiny spade-shaped leaves poking out in all directions. "This is harvestable *hoa suna.*

We will do this the traditional way, so first I will acknowledge the plants by speaking about them, though you are already familiar with much of what I'm about to say from your years among the Reteti."

Ama-Ronoki reached into her satchel and extracted a single large cigar. "This is pure jungle tobacco. Now, tobacco has a long history of being misunderstood, but there have been unbroken traditions that preserved the integrity of its ceremonial usage. The Reteti consider such plants *Malik Nawasi*, a phrase the Enané translate to "the silent masters." While most people think of plants as ornamental backdrops in the world, others realized that they are sentient organisms that are masterful at the art of survival.

"Just as it is foolhardy to get careless with the spinner widow spiders, so too can tobacco or the *hoa suna* or the myriads of other silent masters be dangerous. They redirect the course of humanity's fate like the turn of a tide can change the course of a boat. Why, just think of how the sugar-cane plant or the rice seed has transformed our world, time and time again. In this way, in this moment, we acknowledge the power of tobacco and *hoa suna*."

Ama-Ronoki lit and then passed the tobacco cigar to Taola and then continued speaking, this time in a tone that sounded like an appeal. It was plain that she was no longer addressing Taola. "We honor your intelligence and interact with you with the awareness and humility that we may not be one of the fortunate ones who are spared from the dangers of your usage. However, we seek your medicinal benefits for the sake of young Taolanta here, who represents a life force in human form that works toward the healthy proliferation of life. Therefore, we speak not so that you understand our crude human tongue but so that we ourselves align our intentions as you enter into our chemistry and amplify only those good intentions in us that are life giving."

Ama-Ronoki lit a match and instructed Taola to inhale the tobacco slowly as she lit the cigar. Taola did so and immediately felt a palpable shift in the air, as if she was suddenly more aware of the livingness of her surroundings, and of how special the weaver's tunnel was as an ecosystem. Taola coughed hard, her eyes tearing and her head spinning, but at the same time it was as if Ama-Ronoki's monologue from a moment ago was forming into a bright path in her mind that brought her stillness against the effects of the jungle tobacco.

Then Taola came back to herself, swaying a little where she sat. She opened her eyes and realized that she didn't remember sitting down in the first place. She looked at Ama-Ronoki, who was now using a tiny mortar and pestle to crush the leaves and roots of the emerald *hoa suna* into a paste.

"How are you?" Ama-Ronoki asked without looking up from her task.

"I'm alright, I think," Taola said, taking in her surroundings with a new level of awareness. She noticed now that the rays of sun from outside made the whole tunnel glow in a deep crimson color, which was enchanting to her. Through the pungent smell of tobacco, she began to pick up garlicky and cinnamon aromas that she hadn't noticed before.

"Done," said Ama-Ronoki in satisfaction. "Your medicine is ready. It is most potent when harvested and consumed within ten minutes. You won't feel anything for at least an hour, but then it will be intense, and you will need your skills as a captain to weather the storm."

"Are we going to stay here?" Taola asked a little nervously.

"No. Its full effects will begin in about an hour and a half. We are using this plant because I have sensed that your inability to track the treeboat has to do with a blockage you have—one that we could have treated with good training and lower doses of this plant, if only we had more time. But since we don't, in this case, we're ripping off the wax, so to speak."

"A blockage?" Taola asked.

"Something that could have been a traumatic event is blocking a particular energetic channel within you. I'm not sure, but we will find out." Ama-Ronoki poured a little water from her pouch into the mortar. "Cheers," she said, and instead of passing the bowl to Taola raised it to her own lips. Taola sat astonished as the old woman took two gulps before lowering the bowl. "Now it's your turn."

"You're taking it too?"

"I've already taken it! I'm your guide in this process, so I'm going with you." She passed the bowl to Taola, who raised it to her own lips and finished the rest.

The garlic and cinnamon aroma Taola noticed before filled her nostrils unbearably now. The drink stung her mouth, and it stung her esophagus as it went down to her stomach, where it burned as if it were boring through her stomach lining. Taola doubled over in pain, her arms around her stomach.

Ama-Ronoki, meanwhile, quickly packed her things away and then rubbed Taola's back.

"It's not hurting you?" Taola asked through a groan.

"It is, but I've spent much time with this plant over the years. We are old friends now."

"You really are a warrior, Ama." Taola drew strength from Ama-Ronoki and stood slowly so as not to hit her head on the roof of the tunnel. They carefully made their way out of the weaver's tunnel.

Once outside, Ama-Ronoki gave her a stern look. "Now, we must hurry, Taola. Follow me." She started off at a quick pace before Taola could answer.

Taola pursed her lips in determination and hurried after her mentor, ignoring the burning sensation in her stomach.

Chapter 16

HISTORY

Back at the settlement, Fio had finished up her chores thanks to Navis's help. Navis returned to Jupiter just as Lemay and the twins were waking up, now that the sun's rays were starting to sneak through the windows and onto their faces. Lana-Baboye's bed was empty and neatly made. Navis went over to his bed, where he had laid out a fresh set of clothes, and right on top of them he found a letter. It was from Lana-Baboye.

Dear Navis'sa,

I have taken the Enané hunters, tree climbers, and swimmers for diving lessons at a location they call the Forest Lakes. Their elders have requested this, based on their experience with Ama-Ronoki, who directly instructed them herself years ago. Now that she doesn't teach anymore, they want to take this opportunity to learn while I'm here. Pray that I don't disappoint.

See you all tonight, or tomorrow morning,

Lana-Baboye

"What're we doing today?" Myli asked as she pulled at the mosquito net, trying to exit the bed.

"Well, Owla is going through some training, so we're waiting for her to finish, and Lana has gone to give some swimming training to the Enané."

"So, we're not leaving yet?" Tumi asked happily as he slipped off the bed after Myli.

"No, we're not leaving just yet. And remember to tuck in your mosquito net—you don't want any bugs in your bed, do you?" Myli and Tumi tucked the net under their mattress. Then, they ran over to Lemay's bed and started shaking it.

"What are you guys doing?" he asked sleepily.

It's time to get up, Lemmy!" Myli said. The twins untucked the netting from under the mattress and crawled into Lemay's bed.

"Uncle Navis, help—bugs have gotten into my bed!" Lemay exclaimed. This made Tumi and Myli laugh. They started making buzzing noises and poking at Lemay. "A Tumi-pillar and Myli-mantis are biting me!" Navis was laughing heartily at their antics. Finally, Lemay shouted, "Okay, guys, stop. I have to pee." He pushed the twins off and escaped out of the bed, running straight for the outhouses.

Navis took the kids to the riverside showers, where buckets of floral water had been prepared the night before. After taking their showers, they bathed in the cool floral water that had a pink color to it and smelled of anise and licorice. Navis had to keep close watch on Myli, who kept trying to drink it.

When they arrived at the Accomodor for breakfast, Danuba and the other Enané were happy to see that little pieces of leaves and flowers were still in their hair from the floral baths.

"The floral bath is lovely, isn't it?" asked a lady who brought out some breakfast for them. She laid out fresh eggs that had been gathered from the known hiding spots of the freely roaming chickens that lived around the settlement and cooked into thick flavorful omelets. Fresh bread and sweet porridge were served along with an array of fruits—mangos, pineapple, passionfruit, and papaya—some of which were mashed and mixed with goat milk and coconut water to make smoothies.

The friends that Lemay, Myli, and Tumi had made the day before had been waiting for them to arrive and joined them for breakfast. Navis met their parents, who were delighted by him and were sympathetic to the fact that Navis was a single parent because they said that they understood the trials of parenthood. Mossy's parents even offered to introduce him to one of Mossy's older cousins who they said was about his age and was looking for "a good man." Navis chuckled nervously and took the first chance to walk off with Danuba, who passed by snickering at the awkward conversation.

"Having a good time, my *good man*?" Danuba asked.

"Yeah, it's been fun. If I'm not careful, I might end up leaving here with a wife!" Navis said, looking over his shoulder at Mossy's parents, who had walked over to a young woman and were directing her attention toward Navis.

"Or staying here with one!" Danuba laughed heartily at his own comment. "Come, follow me; let's go somewhere where you'll be less at risk for catching a wife." At this point, Danuba was just torturing himself with laughter. He barely made it out the screen door without tripping over himself.

He led Navis to a rope ladder that went up a huge tree. They climbed up to a platform that overlooked much of the settlement. It was a beautiful sight to see. The circular roofs of the yurts were sprinkled throughout the forest with the paths linking them like circuitry. Other platforms and rope bridges linked the tallest and stoutest trees, and the Accomodor's triangular roof stood out over a few trees that grew around it. It was covered in large dark blue plates, which Danuba explained were solar panels that drew energy from the sunlight and could power the whole settlement.

"Y'know, here we say, 'Tell us about your travels, recount your story and if you don't have one, make one up!' So, tell me about yourself, kid. You're from Lindum and you have a bunch of adopted kids—that's all I know about you." Danuba sat with his legs hanging off the platform, swinging a good nine meters high in the air.

"Well, let's see," said Navis. "I don't think I've ever gone through the whole thing in one sitting before."

"Here's your chance," Danuba invited.

"Alright. Where should I begin?"

"At the beginning, y'know. Who are your parents?"

"Well, my parents died in an avalanche during the melting period in Lindum over two decades ago. The warm weather had weakened the icecaps of the Lindarious Mountains. I have no memories of them because I was an infant. I'm told I was passed onto different families that had mothers who were nursing children, until finally, from two years old till I was about twelve, I moved into a monastery just outside of Lindum where the monks raised me. It was a good life. I was well-fed, clothed, and generally cared for by many kind hands. I started going to Lindum when I got older, and I picked up odd jobs around the town.

"During that time, when I was about nine years old, I became an apprentice to a very kind man, Ryan Aldarwin, who had moved into Lindum with his wife, Niniola, whom you met at Halla Manor a couple of days ago."

"Ah yes, I will never forget," Danuba said dreamily.

"Oddly enough, Niniola and I talked about Aldarwin for the first time in years at Halla Manor. I still can't believe it.

"Anyway, I became a kind of apprentice to Aldarwin. He was skilled at everything he did. Soon, I spent more and more time in Lindum with him and Niniola than I did at the monastery. The monks were never possessive of me and never tried to force me to adhere to their religious values and rules because to this day it remains an open, volunteer-based place for research and spiritual inquiry. I would fall asleep on the, then incomplete, Maradona they were building, and soon they made me my own loft in their cabin. For a little over two years, the three of us worked on the Maradona, and as we approached my twelfth birthday, it was just about complete. However, Aldarwin was rapidly getting more ill. Something had been ailing him for many years, but it progressively got more severe. Suddenly, he was bedridden, and with our limited resources in Lindum, medical care was no good for anything other than trauma care and treating common diseases. He passed away just after I turned twelve. The Maradona was complete and Aldarwin was gone. Niniola fell into depression, and I was spending more time at the monastery and doing odd jobs around Lindum again."

"Whew, that's tough, kid. How come you didn't stay with Niniola?"

"I don't know. It's hard to explain. She didn't really know how to interact with me, and we never knew each other's feelings. We just drifted apart after Aldarwin died."

"I see. So how did you end up with three kids?" Danuba asked.

"Four, actually, including the one on the Oaql boat. She— Arionella—was the first one I met, but she was still just a baby then. She was brought to Lindum by the Hallas, Maya and Jöshi. They're her grandparents."

"By gawd! So that's the connection. How fascinating!" Danuba had his hands on his puffy hair, and the indents on the sides of his eyes deepened as he smiled.

"You knew them?"

"Great people, Navis, great people! Y'know, it was Maya's family that made the Enané what they are today—though she didn't spend much time here, she's an honorary Enané herself y'know! But I digress, continue your story."

"It's turning out to be a smaller world than I thought. Lindum always felt so isolated." Navis scratched the scruff growing under his chin and then continued. "I met the Hallas at the docks when they first arrived. I was working as a boat hand. I would run in when a boat arrived, tie it to the dock, help people unload their things, and I kept the dock clean. I even had a little business going where I would do boat cleanings for people.

"Well, one day I helped pull in the ferry the Hallas were on. I saw the three of them right away. Maya with her bright red hair swept up by the breeze, Jöshi with his long white beard, and a little two-year-old with the same hair as Maya's in his arms. I helped them get off, and they were so grateful. We got to talking, and they said they were looking for the very monastery I lived at. So, I became their personal escort. I never thought that that business transaction would become so much more."

"Life is funny like that, y'know," Danuba added with a nod.

"Along the way, they learned that my parents had died in an accident and shared with me that Arionella, their granddaughter, had recently lost her mother—their daughter in-law."

"And what about her father? Y'know, their son."

"All I know is that he distanced himself from them and his wife. I don't think he even knew about Arionella. But I'm not sure because they never spoke of him much.

"Anyway, at first, they lived at the monastery. Then, after a few weeks, they found their own place—a beautiful hillside cabin, where we live now. They didn't really ask me if I wanted them to adopt me; they just moved me and my few things in there and started calling me son, which I was completely onboard with. Though, now that I think about it, I never called them Mother or Father. Three years later, when Arionella was five and I was fifteen, we adopted Lemay, who was turned into the monastery as a two-year-old. Five more years passed of us living as a family. Arionella was ten, Lemay was seven, and I was twenty.

"To this day, I'm not clear about what happened, but months before Maya and Jöshi finally said their goodbyes to us, they were incredibly stressed. When they arrived in Lindum, they'd thought they were settled for good. They had come to Lindum because they considered the Lindarious Mountains sacred and in the eight years they spent there they would often take turns, or go together, high into the mountains. They took us a few times too. We would camp out in a cave that overlooked Miner's Bay. They also spent a lot of time in the libraries of the monastery, where they taught me to read. It was their retirement of sorts, and we were a family, but something came up that they just couldn't ignore. The last few weeks before my twentieth birthday, long discussions into the night took place about whether I would be able to take care of the children while they were away. When I asked how long they would be away, they couldn't tell me because they weren't sure. I think they weren't sure if they would be coming back at all." Tears came to Navis's eyes as he continued. "That was only two years ago, and Maya seemed so healthy. I can't believe she's already passed away."

This was news to Danuba, who sighed as he looked out over the village. They sat in silence for a few moments. They watched as some people walked past below them and let the sounds of the rainforest clear their minds.

"It's always sad when someone leaves us, y'know," Danuba said, breaking the silence. "We don't get to interact with them the same way, and nothing I know of beats the interactions we have with each other here on the physical plane. Still, you want to know something strange?"

"Sure," Navis said.

"I have so many new memories of my wife through dreams. Something as simple as her and I going out for a walk in a place we have never been while she was still alive, but this memory is as real and as perfect as my memories of her when we spent time together when she was alive. Y'know, she passed away from an illness herself some years ago."

"That is something to think about indeed. Such a strange life, and we're all just wondering what it's all about, huh?" Navis leaned back on his arms, letting the sun dry his tears.

"That's right," Danuba said. "By the way, you ever plan to get some help in raising the kids?"

"I've started to. Especially since I adopted Myli and Tumi. They became a part of the family about a year after Maya and Jöshi left. They're three years old now."

"How did you end up adopting them?"

"They arrived at the monastery in a similar way that Lemay and I did. Arionella, Lemay, and I would visit the monastery and they very quickly became attached us. They would weep uncontrollably every time we left for our cabin."

"Y'know, you could live here," Danuba said matter-of-factly. Navis glanced at him questioningly, with his eyes narrowed. Danuba laughed. "I'm not trying to get you married, kid, if that's what you're thinking." Danuba paused for a moment and then asked, "But you're not opposed to being with someone, right?"

"No, of course not. I think about it now and then, but I come from a small township where I don't really interact with people my age, so it just hasn't happened yet."

"Y'know, my wife was ten years older than me. I met her when I was a little older than you, and we were happily together for thirty years after. She passed away nearly six years ago at the age of fifty-eight, still young if you ask me. Anyway, the point is that you never know where love takes you, y'know?"

"That's just it. Love is very important." Navis became silent and tense.

"What is it?" Danuba asked.

"No, nothing, I'm just thinking."

"That's something."

"I was just wondering about someone . . . someone who's older than me. Actually, by ten years or so, I think."

"Ah, someone you like!" Danuba said excitedly, sitting up straight now.

"Yeah, but I don't know if she feels the same way."

"Well, that's the best part, kid! It's part of the joy of when you two share your feelings, y'know. So, tell me about this person. What is she like?"

"How do I put her into words? She's bold and yet kind, knowledge-able and yet innocent at times. She's caring but can also be tough. She's beautiful and tall. Her dark hair and light eyes make a striking contrast. And . . . and she's a good person, trying to do good in the world."

"That sounds like an ideal woman, y'know!" Danuba said, slapping Navis's back.

"She is," Navis replied.

———•———

By the time Taola Lonwë and Ama-Ronoki made it back to Sun, they were feeling the effects of the medicine already. They drank water, and Ama-Ronoki instructed Taola to bathe with the *bufeyowampi* floral water that was set up in a stall just behind the ceremonial yurt—it was the same brew that Navis and the children had bathed with earlier that morning. Then, Taola and Ama-Ronoki settled down on sitting cushions and began to do a deep-breathing exercise. They would breathe in deep and sharply about thirty times, and then at the thirtieth breath, they would release their last breath gently and stop breathing for as long as they could. Finally, when the urge to inhale was overwhelming, they took a single, long and deep breath in—holding that for about fifteen seconds. They repeated this cycle five times. Ama-Ronoki noticed that Taola seemed distracted and unstable where she sat. The old Reteti gave her some bright neon-blue thread already attached to a needle. She sat down across from Taola with her own needle and thread and laid out a large piece of dark maroon cloth in between them.

"Continue what I taught you yesterday," she said as she began sewing a pattern into the cloth.

"I'll try, but I'm feeling really strange," Taola said. "How long will the effects last?"

"The whole day and well into the night."

"Does it hurt?" Taola was recalling how the *hoa suna* had made her stomach hurt.

"Well, it can be extremely uncomfortable. You may feel like vomiting and that the world is spinning, but the most challenging thing you will face is no physical symptom but the recall of repressed memories. Unfortunately, I can't prepare you for that. It is different for everyone."

Taola nodded and turned to her task. She fell into a rhythm as she stitched a spiral, transfixed by how sharply the blue thread stood out against the maroon fabric. For no apparent reason, Captain Rainer surfaced in her thoughts. She wondered where he was and whether he was all right. Distracted, she shook her head, trying to focus back on the fabric, but that sudden movement, though slight, hit her with a feeling of extreme dizziness. She dropped the needle and thread and braced herself on all fours. She felt like a spinning top wobbling as it loses momentum.

A groan escaped her lips. She heard footsteps, felt a hand on her back, and for a moment the dizzy spell lifted.

"How are you doing, dear?" The voice was unfamiliar. Taola's heart raced, but when she focused her vision, she saw the kind face of a beautiful young Reteti woman wearing a colorful headscarf, which comforted her.

"Not good," Taola managed to say before the world began spinning lopsidedly again. She closed her eyes. A memory kept coming to her of the first time she'd sat on a spinning carnival ride when she was still in the cityfort Atlantia—she'd thrown up that day. Then she was transported back to a different memory of being gazed upon by silhouetted shapes of a man and woman. She realized that she was the baby in the crib and was reaching out to them. Taola gasped and opened her eyes. Ama-Ronoki's wrinkled face came into focus. She was wearing the same colorful headscarf Taola had seen on the young woman a few moments before—*or had it been hours?*

"Breathe, Taolanta, breathe. Find a pattern in your breath, just as you did with the thread," Ama-Ronoki said softly.

For the first time since the harsher effects of the medicine kicked in, Taola became aware of her breathing. The life force of it was overwhelming, and she started hyperventilating. "It's . . . I . . . I can't . . . I'm getting lightheaded," she said between gasps.

"Breathe deeply but slowly. Use your breath as a guide."

Taola did as instructed and eventually slowed her breathing down.

"Good, in through the nose," came Ama-Ronoki's voice. "Remember four. Slowly, hold for seven, and out through the mouth. Eight. Well done, well done."

Taola continued to breathe in deeply and out completely. She closed her eyes and saw, as clearly as if she had been transported there, the foamy waves of the ocean on Oaql Island's shore. They lapped in and out perfectly to Ama-Ronoki's counting. The floor started to feel like it was stationary again though she still felt a little wobbly.

Then, the vision shifted. Taola began imagining blue loops, much like the ones she had been stitching. An upward stroke of the loop would form on her in-breath, and her out-breath would complete it with a downward stroke. This sequence seemed to take on a life of its own, as the blue loops carried on autonomously while she focused on breathing.

"Found a pretty pattern?" Ama-Ronoki asked.

Taola nodded. She sat still, following the blue loops or letting them follow her . . . she couldn't tell anymore.

———————◆———————

Danuba stood up and stretched on the platform overlooking the Accomodor. "You want to take a tour of the network of rope bridges?" he asked Navis.

"Sure, let's go, and tell me about the Enané. You said Maya's family was influential in creating the Enané?"

"Yes, they were some of the founders of this tribe," Danuba said as he walked onto ramps that were built around the diameter of the tree trunks. Then he began to cross a rope bridge, but Navis was a little apprehensive about stepping onto it. "It's very sturdy, y'know. Look at me. I'm much bigger than you, and I can bounce on this thing without a problem."

After his demonstration, Navis was somewhat convinced and slowly stepped onto the swaying path, gripping the rope banister so hard his knuckles turned white.

"Anyway, Maya's family, the Airgiallas, was part of the founding members of the Enané. It is said her great-great-great grandmother, Claire Airgialla, was a fireball of an individual. From a young age, she would sneak out of the walls of the city state she was born in, and she spent most her time out in nature. By the time she was a teenager, she would lead her friends out too, and by the time she was twenty, she had led many of those friends, as well as one hundred men, women, and children, out into the 'outlands,' never to return to that city state again. That group became the founding members of the Enané, and the city state they left is now known as the cityfort Citadelia."

"I've been so ignorant of all this in the bubble of Lindum," said Navis. "I wonder why Maya and Jöshi never talked about the history of our world. They taught me so many other things, you'd think—," he said as he followed Danuba up another ladder into an even higher level of the canopy where they found another wide platform to sit on and look out over the seemingly endless canopy of the jungle. He became pensive about time and how deeply it stretched into the past. He thought to himself, *How many other countless individuals have faced their own troubles, lost their own loved ones, and still paved their way forward till their own demise? Maya must have seen and done so much. I wonder if she was in pain at the end. I hope I get to dream up new memories of her . . .*

Just then, a shout from below startled Navis out of his contemplations. Fio and Eza were walking by, Eza using the support of a wooden crutch.

"But I wanted to go to Venus for beauty day!" Fio shouted through tears.

"We don't always get what we want, Fio," Eza shouted back.

"I NEVER get what I want! You should take care of Mendelson—he's your baby!"

"Look at me, Fio. I'm disabled! You should be grateful!"

"How can I ever be grateful with witches like you and mom in my life?" Fio spat out her words passionately.

Eza recoiled, wounded by Fio's remark, but she quickly recovered with the help of a fresh rage coursing through her body. She drew her arm up and smacked Fio hard across the face. The sound of the hit reached high into the canopy.

Fio fell to the ground and started to crawl away from her sister, covering herself in mud in the process. With tears streaming down her face, she stood and went bounding into the forest. Eza stood for a few moments longer, shaking with anger, before she turned and limped away.

Back up on the platform, Danuba sighed and shook his head. "Y'know, they've recently come. They are like the emigrants from city-forts I've been telling you about, except you could consider them refugees really."

"I've met them," Navis said. "The little one, Fio, is a sweetheart. She just needs some kindness."

"Yes, they've had a hard life, y'know. A hard life."

Navis took a deep breath and looked around from the high platform they stood on; they were now about fifteen meters high, and he had thought the original nine meters up the first ladder from the ground was high enough. Even more astonishing was to see that in the distance were trees that towered even higher above the forest canopy, giving him a strange sense of vertigo and smallness that gave him conflicting feelings of insignificance and yet a sense self-worth that came from the awe that was overtaking him. Then his eyes caught sight of things he had only visualized in his imagination. Hanging from the nearest skyscraping tree were the teardrop shaped nests of the *bocho locho* bird Fio had described, and he thought he could also make out shimmering golden clouds around them—but it was too far away for him to be sure of it.

"Danuba, where are Fio and her family from? Why would they be considered refugees?"

Danuba sighed. "Y'know, I must respect their privacy, son, but I'll just say that they were born into a dangerous cult-like group of people who have no qualms in treating their own as they treat their enemies."

Eza's disabled leg flashed into Navis's mind when Danuba said this, and there the conversation ended as they silently made their way back toward the earth below.

Chapter 17

BREAKTHROUGH

Nadine, the woman who had helped Taola get dressed earlier that morning, came to Sun just past noon with two other Enané women to check up on Taola and Ama-Ronoki.

"Thank you, sisters," Ama-Ronoki said in a whisper. "I'm fine. Taola has made it through the first wave. Now she is approaching the second."

"Will you need anything?" Nadine asked.

"Keep our fresh water filled in the jug by the entrance door, and if one of your assistants could stay here with us as a helping-hand, I would be grateful."

"Donya, do you mind staying here with them?" Nadine asked a tough-looking woman wearing a tank top that revealed sinewy muscles and an arm covered in colorful tattoos.

"Not at all, it would be an honor," Donya said, her voice soft. "I'm at your service, Ama," she said with a bow.

"Thank you, Donya." Nadine gave a little bow and left with the other woman that was there with her.

"Alright, Donya," said Ama-Ronoki. "Taola's about to go through another phase. I must ask you not to interact with her unless I say so. No touching—no talking."

"I understand. Where would you like me to be?"

"Find some cushions and make yourself comfortable there," Ama-Ronoki pointed to the other end of the yurt. "We will be here for a while."

Taola's breaths grew erratic. She shifted her legs and clenched her fists. For the past hour or so, she had been cruising through many thoughts in her mind, but somehow, she felt detached from any emotions that arose. But now, as if all the emotions she had bypassed in the last hour had compounded and caught up to her at once; a feeling of great energy and discomfort started at the tips of her toes and moved up through her body. Her head grew heavier and heavier, until it felt like a cinder block resting on her neck.

As if she knew what was going on, Ama-Ronoki came over and began whistling softly, shaking a tightly bunched set of dried leaves rhythmically over her head, chest, and torso. When she got to Taola's legs, she swept the leafy maraca down in one brisk movement out and away from her feet. Then she began again from Taola's head and worked her way down, ending with the swift final stroke. After a few minutes of this, the invisible weight upon Taola's body lifted and she sat upright.

"Take this needle and thread and begin sewing in the pattern you've been working on," Ama-Ronoki said, holding out a prepared needle and fabric.

"I don't think I can," Taola said. The dizziness was returning.

"If you *think* you can't, then you can't." Ama-Ronoki took Taola's hand into her own and helped her to grasp the needle. She guided Taola through the first pattern, beginning with a straight line on the dark piece of cloth. When Taola's hand firmed up and moved with fresh purpose, Ama-Ronoki let it go.

Taola continued, her brow furrowed, and her gray eyes fixed on her task. Nothing existed except for what she was doing. The sharp steel of the needle puncturing the fabric made a popping sound, and the variations in the texture and shade of the brown cloth seemed like rolling hills of bare earth to her.

Soon, however, a thought rose up like incense smoke in Taola's mind. Part of her watched it happening. She was losing grip on her concentration, but it was happening in slow motion. Another plume of thoughts acted as a smokescreen, blinding her clear vision as she moved into the realms of the mind. The internal chatter began. *I'm so hungry. I hope the pattern is coming out correctly. What about Sir Charles—is his leg healing? And Captain Rainer—how is he in the captivity of those madmen?*

With that last thought, Taola plunged into a waking dream. She saw a familiar neon-orange sign blinking the word "OPEN," in the distance. She was on a pathway of tar-like mud. It was dark, and there were tall trees everywhere with a sickly green hue to them. It was eerily silent— no music of birds or the chime of insects. She walked forward toward the neon sign affixed to a window of a dilapidated-looking convenience store like she had often seen in the cityforts she had visited. However, this little building was in the middle of a forest, and though she wanted to turn away from it and go the other way, she was compelled forward by a morbid inquisitiveness.

A short man with long greasy hair and an excess of trinkets hanging off his hair, arms, and clothes stood smiling at the entrance of the shop. Taola froze in place when she saw him. He looked familiar to her. Some of his teeth were gold plated, he had a light mustache, a prickly goatee, and one of his eyes had a glassy look to it. He waved in Taola's direction. She gasped and was about to run away, when from behind her a group of five young men and three young women—who didn't seem to see her at all—walked past. They waved back at the figure by the door. Four of the men hugged the strange man by the entrance and then seemed to be introducing the women and the other man to him. Then they all went inside.

Everything seemed like déjà vu to Taola. Without moving, she found herself inside the store, which had some things in dusty adamantine packages but was mostly set up as a living space with worn couches, clothes strewn about, and uncomfortable fluorescent lighting. The people from outside were in a hallway that led into the back of the store. The women were introducing themselves to the little man with the glassy eye, who seemed to enjoy their attention thoroughly. He wore a smirk and appeared distracted at the same time, as if thinking of multiple things at once. The four men, who seemed to be on familiar terms with him, were handing him money, one stack of coins at a time.

"It's all there; I counted," said one of them.

A short, pretty, fair-skinned woman strolled to a mirror that was hanging on the wall and began fixing her hair. The little man with the glassy eye saw her doing so and in the middle of his transaction with the four men walked off and crept up behind her. She didn't notice him at first. He leaned in, and from Taola's angle it looked like he sniffed her. While Taola recoiled with a grimace, the woman swiftly turned around to face her pursuer. Before she could express surprise, the little man pretended to be surprised himself, which made his crew laugh. Then, he began playing with his hair, bunching it up over his head, mimicking the woman. This made the woman blush and laugh too. Then, she pointed at a boil growing out of the right side of her neck and said that she was looking to get it treated.

"I can fix," the little man said in a raspy voice and a heavy south Cyanian accent. Then he turned and led the men into a room while the three women awkwardly stood in the hallway. Taola anxiously walked forward past the other women. The fact that these people apparently couldn't see or sense her gave her a surreal feeling that resulted in body shivers. She stepped into the room, where a familiar lanky young man with very short, buzzed brown hair and olive-brown skin was trying to introduce himself to the glassy-eyed man, who was busily looking for something, ignoring him. The other men sat on couches smoking cigarettes that had a hint of a chemical reek coming from them, unlike Ama-Ronoki's aromatic cigars.

"My name is Iloy," said the lanky young man. "Thanks to Chibuzo picking me to board your treeboat, I was able to leave Citadelia. I was a member of the Seekers, and now I'm here to learn from you."

Taola gasped. She hadn't recognized Iloy, for she had met him when he had longer, puffy afro hair. The glassy-eyed man was only half listening until he found what he was looking for. He grabbed it with his left hand off a shelf and with that arm hidden behind his back he reached his right hand out as if looking to shake Iloy's hand. Iloy reciprocated, but instead of clasping his hand, the little man slapped a piece of sticky black tape onto Iloy's arm.

"Trap! Trap!" laughed the little man, pointing at Iloy.

All the men in the room began to laugh. Slowly, Iloy joined in after his initial shock wore off. He tried to remove the tape, but it was painfully stuck to his arm hair, which made everyone laugh even more. The glassy-eyed man smirked, glancing now and then at the guys' amused faces, still ignoring Iloy for the most part.

Iloy spoke with fervor as the hysterics of the smoking men wore down. "I need your help. You probably know how it is in cityforts—they put people on all sorts of drugs to 'normalize' them. People considered me crazy my whole life for simply asking questions, let alone when I told my parents I could see things they couldn't."

This seemed to catch the glassy-eyed man's attention, "Like what?" he asked.

"Like shimmering figures made of golden vapor-like stuff in the forests outside Citadelia. But it was also stuff I could *do* when I was a kid, before they put me on meds. Like when I found this hurt chipmunk once. It was still breathing but it couldn't move. I tried giving it water and food, but nothing helped him. Finally, I held my hands over him and I got into this trance of sorts—I don't know how to describe it exactly—but after a few seconds of this, he began to twitch. After a few minutes, the chipmunk opened his eyes and suddenly turned himself upright. Then he bolted away, as if nothing had happened to him. You see? I want to learn to tap into that power. I want to learn how to heal people so that I can free my family from that hellhole, and so that I can finally prove that I'm not insane!" Iloy stopped speaking abruptly, panting a little.

"Revalo Otrebor," the little man said dully, negating Iloy's passion as he offered his hand again. Iloy took it with apprehension as Revalo's prank was still fresh in his mind. Iloy's uncertainty made Revalo beam with satisfaction. "You know about *Iansa*?" he asked with a smirk.

"No, I'm not sure."

"Spirits?"

"Not really. They don't allow that kind of talk in cityforts."

"I know that." The reply from Revalo was sharp, but then he continued asking questions. "What about planes of existence and golden mystery, or spirits of species? Projecting consciousness?"

"How the hell would I know any of that?" Now Iloy grew impatient, noticing that with each question and his confession of ignorance, Revalo and the others snickered. "I just told you—." Suddenly, Iloy's voice choked off and he fell to his knees with Revalo peering down at him through a smirk and flared nostrils. Taola had not seen any action that he may have made as an attack.

"Respect," was the single word he said as though it were a curse. Then, all of a sudden, Revalo looked over Iloy's head directly into Taola's eyes. He gave her a knowing smile, revealing gold-plated teeth. She gasped and stepped backward, but instead of slamming into the wall behind her, she fell into darkness.

The next thing she saw was a bright light passing through gaps in a wall made from poorly aligned planks of wood. It was dark, but still she was able to see the outlines of things. There was a foldable table, an adamantine chair, and a dirty mattress on the floor. She recognized where she was—this cabin had been her prison once. She ran toward the door, but it was clamped shut. *Not again,* Taola thought. *This can't be happening again!*

Everything went dark.

It seemed like ages had passed when out of the void Taola began to hear a muffled voice. After a moment, the voice unexpectedly boomed near her ear, causing her to jump and perceive the world clearly again.

"C'mon, hurry!" The voice was Iloy's and he was reaching down to help Taola stand.

This was the Iloy she remembered, with his soft brown eyes and puffy hair. She took his hand, and he pulled her up. Then, they were running through a dark forest with the sound of dogs barking and men shouting from behind them. Iloy ran with a limp, and he was covered in sweat.

"What's happening?" Taola asked, holding tight to his hand.

"They found out I wasn't drugging you," Iloy said breathlessly. "We're escaping—just keep running!"

Then there was nothing underfoot. They plunged and smacked hard into cold, deep water.

"Y'know, you're crazy, kid!" said a familiar voice. "This is where you wanted me to pick you up?"

Strong hands grabbed Taola's arms and lifted her sputtering and coughing out of the water. It was Danuba, and they were on his seaplane, the *Rusty Otter*.

———◆———

The sound of chirping insects and a loud call that sounded like *Vroh! Vroh!* in the distance gradually became audible to Taola as she grew aware of her surroundings. Her eyes adjusted to the soft orange glow of candles that illuminated a high-pointed ceiling with crisscrossing beams and a giant circular space all around her.

"You hear that? The *pumagarsa* is visiting our part of the woods," said a voice that wasn't too far away. Taola shut her eyes tight again, not moving an inch. She was afraid that even breathing too deeply would give her away.

"I told you no talking," said a woman's voice sternly. Then, Taola heard footsteps coming toward her. She clenched her fists, terrified and fighting back a growing sense of nausea. The footsteps stopped beside her, and the floor creaked as the person crouched down. Everything was still for a moment. Taola held her breath. Suddenly, a gust of air followed by the sound of the flapping and rustling of leaves made Taola flinch, and she took a breath. The crouched person began singing in a high-pitched voice. The melody was eerie, and the language was one that Taola could not understand. Though she lay with her eyes closed, swirls of colors filled the darkness of her vision. She wished she could stop the wailing melody, which seemed to be making the colors, along with the nausea, grow in intensity. The singing got louder and louder until Taola couldn't take it anymore. She shot into an upright position, opened her eyes and the person next to her, without skipping a beat, handed her a pail and continued to sing. Someone blew out all the candles, and it became even darker with her eyes open than it had been when they were shut.

The next thing Taola knew, she was leaning over the bucket as the overpowering urge to vomit overtook her. She gagged and spat, trying to resist, until suddenly a rush of fluids came out like a high-pressure faucet had been unleashed somewhere in her stomach. The sounds of splashing liquid, gagging, coughing, flapping of leaves, and singing filled the space in a clashing crescendo. On a high, screeching note, the woman suddenly stopped singing. The rustling of leaves stopped. Taola stopped purging. The song of the insects was audible again, and in the distance the call of the *pumagarsa* rang out: *Vroh! Vroh!*

Taola sat in the darkness, exhausted but tranquil. Her memory slowly came back to her. A single candle was lit across the room, which made Taola blink repeatedly. A tall lanky figure came toward her.

"Taola, are you okay?" asked a voice suffused with concern.

Taola was about to reply, but the figure crouched next to her spoke first. "My boy, she is fine. Please give her space until I say." The woman's voice trembled with exertion, as if she too had just been through an ordeal.

"I just want to know if she's okay," the concerned voice repeated.

"All that has happened is part of the normal effects of the medicine. Now please go and wait."

The figure started to turn away, but Taola reached out and said, "Wait! Iloy, is that you?"

"No, it's me, Navis."

Upon hearing that, Taola remembered what was going on all at once. Navis knelt before her.

"Navis! And Ama?" Taola reached out to the person squatting next to her.

"Yes, dear, it's me," said Ama-Ronoki and clasped Taola's hand in her own.

"Ama, I saw many things."

"Yes, we will address that in a moment." Then, Ama-Ronoki spoke to Navis again. "Please go sit with Danuba. This is a crucial moment. We cannot lose this opportunity." Danuba came over and helped Navis stand up. "I wish I hadn't let these two relieve Donya." She added just loud enough so they could hear her.

"Danuba! I relived the moment you rescued us! I finally remember all that I couldn't, and I saw when Iloy first went to that man!" Taola was speaking rapidly.

Ama-Ronoki squeezed her hand. "Taolanta, listen to me."

Taola looked toward her in the dim lighting.

"This is the moment we've been waiting for. You are an open channel right now. After reliving your blocked memories, you purged built-up energetic impediments, rendering you highly sensitive. Remember, I took the *hoa suna* too, and through you I sensed the treeboat and two other people who are thinking of you—I'm not sure who they are, and I know you just went through a lot, but you must try to connect with them. You have prepared for years as a Captain of a treeboat—you can do this!" Ama-Ronoki let go of Taola's hand and sat down next to her, panting with exhaustion.

Taola took a deep breath as Danuba led Navis away. Danuba looked back at her for a moment. He noted the striking contrast of Taola's light gray eyes and her dark hair. Danuba looked at Navis and all at once felt a gush of empathy and a hint of sadness. He led the young man over to the corner wall, patting his back reassuringly.

Taola wiped her mouth, tied up her hair into a tight bun, and closed her eyes. After taking another deep breath, she began to breathe rhythmically. At first, she felt scattered and couldn't focus, but then she envisioned herself on the Oaql boat with Captain Rainer standing at the helm. She recalled the sense of admiration she felt looking at him with his dark shoulder-length hair tossing about, as well as the trepidation and mystery she felt when she would look at the Oaql tree's leaves rustling in the winds of the ocean.

A voice spoke clearly in her head. "Taola, they're after the Oaql boat. They're using me to track it. Taola, they're after the Oaql boat. They're using me to track it." The message kept repeating. The voice was Captain Rainer's, and it was heavily strained.

With her heart racing, she replied in her mind, "Captain, I hear you. I'm going to track it myself now."

"Taola? Is that you?" asked the voice of Captain Rainer.

"Yes, Captain, it's me."

"You did it, my dear." Captain Rainer's voice sounded relieved.

"Yes, I'll take care of things from here," Taola replied.

"Listen, my child. I love you."

"I love you too, Father," Taola's voice shook with emotion.

"Tell Charles I love him too."

"You'll tell him yourself," Taola said, but there was no reply.

Then, she heard another voice saying, "He's out, sir. No response."

The reply came in a raspy voice and a heavy south Cyanian accent. "I know where it goes. We don't need him anymore."

The connection cut off.

Taola pushed away feelings of dread and focused on the Oaql boat, but she sensed nothing. Usually, she would get frustrated, but now, in her higher state of awareness and sensitivity, she kept her eyes closed and began sifting through her memories and energetic signatures of other beings and places as if they were a scrambled deck of cards that could be reorganized by color and symbol. Her attention returned to the Mara-dona and to the fledgling Oaql sprout growing steadily in its nursery in the *Heart of the Maradona*. The preciousness of its existence struck Taola anew, it being an offspring of an ancient, but endangered species, grown from such a rare and delicate seed, that *she* had planted. She could sense the same pulsating life force in it that existed in the fully realized tree on the Oaql boat, but where it differed was in its simple directed consciousness of developing itself. Here, in contrast, Taola recalled how at times the Oaql tree felt like being in the presence of a *lypir*, one that was thoroughly aware of all in its vicinity and was poised for death rendering action if threatened.

The effects of the *hoa suna* still strong, Taola found herself plunge into an experience of great insight coupled with mind twisting fear, as a voice—which she couldn't distinguish from her own—began reprimanding her with the added intensity of visions to help the points sink in. *Do you still not understand your role in all this?* Taola's lips moved in silence along with the words that streamed across her consciousness. *You are part of the symbiosis of the fungus and plant that makes up the Oaql boat—you have delved too far into the mind and heart of nature to dance through life without a care in the world.* Instantly, Taola was seeing herself aboard the Oaql boat as it pulled into Sea Willow Isle in Lindum—she was listening to the Blue Moon Waltz that she loved. Two children were peeking over a log watching and giggling as the Taola onboard flourished her arms and tossed her hair in the wind. The Oaql tree knew of the children long before it arrived at the shore and if Taola had been more cautious, through it, she would've sensed them too. Taola clenched her teeth with regret as the vision changed to a feral looking child straddling a branch of the Oaql tree with her red hair in tangles and sharp green eyes fixed on a praying mantis that was scuttling out of her reach. The vision blurred and it was dark behind Taola's eyes again as the voice returned: *You are a butterfly whose wings do not simply ride the wind but can summon squalls.* Taola's head sank down in the darkness of Sun the ceremonial yurt. She held her palms over her eyes as tears began pouring forth. A vision of a disheveled Navis, utterly distraught over Arionella's disappearance, made every muscle in her body writhe with tension. She was stuck again, rocking back and forth, hunched over in the darkness.

After a few minutes, the rhythmic sound of Ama-Ronoki's leafy maraca penetrated through the incessant chime of the creatures of the rainforest, a vision of a great scarlet macaw came to Taola as the air from the shaker upon her skin began to feel like a cleansing gale.

Taola's lips began moving again, as the words—*it's good to have a conscience; that's what makes you human*—formulated upon them. This time a voice with a different tenor than the one before filled her consciousness, and yet, this voice too could not be distinguished from her own. *But you cannot allow it to cripple you. Rise again after your day of judgement. Move forward with renewed intention, and create the goodness you want to see in the world.* Energy bubbled in Taola's core; then it surged upward and out.

"I *will* dance!" Taola shouted aloud into Sun, her voice reverberated along its walls. Ama-Ronoki stopped playing her leafy maraca. Taola continued, her voice raw with emotion, "But I will also learn from my mistakes and grow wiser."

Taola then took a deep breath—a big smile upon her face as she straightened up. She settled into a cross-legged position with the backs of her hands upon her knees, her palms open and facing up. She tuned into the energy signature of the Maradona and the Oaql seedling again, but this time in her mind's eye, she saw Niniola sleeping upon the bed of mycelium that had formed in the Heart of the Maradona, a sacred space Niniola had originally used as a crypt for her husband's ashes. As Taola keyed into Niniola's energy she felt great warmth and a deep unshakable strength emanating from her—a powerful blaze in a stone hearth. Taola recalled the night on Oaql Island when Niniola took her to the Maradona under the light of the moon, asking her about spirits and if she could sense the presence of anyone on the Oaql boat when she had been on it. Taola had replied that she could indeed sense Maya Airgialla Halla upon it at times, as could Captain Rainer, and some nights when she had slept deeply upon it, she dreamt that Maya was strolling upon the deck, a visage of blue-white foam sparkling under a starry sky upon the open ocean. In this moment, an idea occurred to Taola as she thought about how Niniola asked her with profound embarrassment whether inoculating the Maradona with the Oaql Seed would have any chance of her convening with the spirit of Ryan Aldarwin Maradona.

Taola now pictured Maya Airgialla Halla the few times she had met her when she was still alive—the bright red hair, her knowing gaze. Almost immediately and for the first time, the Oaql boat came into focus in what seemed like real-time. Taola was exhilarated. The Oaql boat was out on the far southern reaches of the Cyan Sea where the sea-green waters began to change in tint to ice blue. Only a few kilometers away from the treeboat was a landmass with a huge mountain towering out of it. A presence tugged at Taola. Interestingly, it wasn't the boat or anything on the boat, but it was something near the boat. Thinking it might be Captain Rainer reaching out again, she tuned out the Oaql boat for a moment.

But instead of Captain Rainer, she saw Iloy. Taola's heart thumped heavily in her chest. He was lying on a bunk with his legs crossed and his hands behind his head. She could now see he was nodding off to sleep, and she began to perceive his thoughts of her were turning into dreams. All at once, Taola realized that he was on a boat that was passing close by the Oaql boat, but no one onboard was aware of it. Taola set out to try and communicate with him, as she had with Captain Rainer.

———•———

Iloy was dreaming of the time he and Taola had spent together. They were at Halla Manor, in a flower garden. He was walking behind Taola with his hands in his pockets while she was skipping ahead, stopping now and then to smell the large red roses. She was wearing a navy blue dress and matching flats made of cloth. Her wavy black hair trailed down over her chest whenever she leaned forward to sniff the flowers. It was a beautiful sunny day, and the flowers were dancing in the breeze, but Iloy had eyes only for Taola.

Suddenly, there was a slight stutter in the dream sequence, and Taola straightened up, looking very serious, and marched over to him. She took his hands and said, "Iloy, something very serious is happening right now."

Iloy stood frozen, looking into her gray eyes, his cheeks flushing with heat.

"There is a treeboat very close to you," she said, speaking clearly and forcefully. "When you wake up, have your boat moved starboard. There is a twelve-year-old girl named Arionella on the treeboat; she and the boat are being pursued by dangerous people. They are getting close." Iloy nodded, and she continued. "I'll try to be there soon, but you must do something now! Now wake up, and don't forget what I told you. Wake up!"

Iloy kept looking at her in his dream, still asleep on his bunk.

"Wake up!" Taola repeated, feeling exasperated. "Wake up, Iloy!"

Taola's telepathic message was now the equivalent of a shout. Though Iloy started to stir, he still wouldn't wake up. Taola grew more and more flustered, and then, with her face beet red, she leaned forward and kissed him on the lips.

—End of Part II—

PART III

Giggling, we run from the predator; we love the game
of life too much to let it be over.

—The Encyclopedia Cyanica

Chapter 18

CONTACT

Iloy awoke with a start. He could almost feel Taola's warm breath on his face. He sighed and sat up, bunching his pillows behind his back as the metal bunk squeaked loudly.

"I told you to sleep on the bottom bunk," said Kukine drowsily. He was a burly eighteen-year-old Enané boy with straight black hair that was cut in bangs above his brow, while the rest of his hair fell over his ears like a helmet. "I knew you'd be keeping me awake."

"Gawd, just switch with me," Iloy replied. He scooted forward and climbed down the bunk ladder. Kukine had a pillow over his head and was grumbling. Iloy rolled his eyes and said, "Oh, stop whining, Cookie. It must only be a couple of hours past sundown."

"I'm all warm under the blanket now . . ."

"What's the matter, my boy?" came a voice from across the room.

"Nothing, Jiji. I was just having a dream," Iloy replied, standing on the floor of the rocking boat.

"Well, what was happening in the dream?" Jiji asked, and Iloy began to blush in the dim silver light of the moon pouring through a window.

"Oh, uh, it was nothing . . . j-just a whole bunch of nonsense," Iloy stammered. The dream played over in his head, however—Taola, her navy dress, the flowers, the kiss. Iloy felt all warm inside, and his heart fluttered. However, behind the happy feelings, he also felt jittery and anxious. Maybe the dream wasn't as cheerful as he'd thought. He took a gulp of water from a mushroom-leather pouch that was set on a little wooden table by the exit door and stood silently for a few moments while the others lay quietly in their beds—no doubt sifting through memories of their own dreams to enjoy once they fell asleep. Iloy turned back toward his bunk when he had a flash of recollection, and he mouthed the words, "Wake up, don't forget what I told you."

Iloy gasped loudly as it all came back to him. The noise startled Kukine, who nearly fell out of bed.

"WHOZZAYT?" Kukine shouted unintelligibly, now fully awake and partially off the small bed that he had taken pains to fit his large self into.

"We have to turn the boat starboard!" Iloy shouted, running out of the bunk room.

Jiji sprang up after him without a shirt on, trying to at least tighten the cord that held his loose pajama pants in place around his bony waist. Jiji was an elder of the Enané in his seventies, with a full head of black hair, only a few missing teeth, and bowed legs, but he was spry and hardy.

Iloy ran to the control room and insisted the captain turn the boat.

"But Wetembi Island is just ahead!" the captain said, clearly frustrated. He was tired and already stressed that he had undertaken this charter through rough waters to a place most people avoided.

"Please, I just need you to simply turn and cast a light to check if there is a boat nearby."

The captain grumbled but did as he was told.

"Thank you, sir," Iloy said and flipped on the flood light. "Jiji, Kukine! Keep your eyes peeled for a boat."

Jiji stood by the rails, peering across the dark waters as Iloy moved the flood light slowly back and forth—while Kukine was still emerging out of the bunk room, looking very, very grumpy.

"What's going on out here?" said a tall, fair woman with long white hair. Though a few years younger than Jiji, she was an honorary elder of the Enané herself. She'd come out of a cabin at the far end of the boat wrapped in a long embroidered red and white shawl.

She was followed by a young Enané woman in her mid-twenties with tan-brown skin and light brown shoulder-length hair. Her neck was long and her sharp collar bones poked out from behind a white boat-neck t-shirt that was tucked into wide flaring pajama pants that looked like a skirt in most angles.

"Sorry to wake you, Delamina," Jiji replied. "Iloy thinks there may be a boat out here near us."

"That would be odd, in these parts," Delamina said. She wrapped herself more tightly in her shawl and went to the starboard edge of the boat where Iloy was pointing the light.

The young woman ran the other way, up to where Iloy was with the captain. "What's going on, Iloy?" she asked.

"Hey, Azura. I think there's a boat nearby. I had this strange dream, where that girl I told you about, Taola, came to me and insisted I wake up. She said that there is a boat with a girl on it, who might be in danger."

The captain looked over at Iloy wearing an expression that said, *All this because of a dream? You lot are crazy, like I thought.*

Azura saw the captain and glared at him. His eyes met hers for a moment, and he quickly looked away.

"Wait! I see something! Don't move the light!" Kukine shouted. "Look there—what the hell is it?"

A large tree loomed just a few yards away. It was growing out of a white boat.

"My gawd! It's a treeboat!" Delamina announced.

The captain, Iloy, and Azura leaned forward, trying to get a better view from the captain's control room; below, the others stared at it in awe.

"Slow down and pull up next it," Iloy instructed the captain, who was now looking aghast at the fact that Iloy's dream had come true and that there was actually something out there. A boat, and not just any boat, but a thing of legend.

"It's a demon boat!" the captain cried. "I'm not going that way!" He spun his wheel with quick, thin arms, turning his boat away from the treeboat—which immediately was swallowed by the dark of night again.

"No! There might be someone on it, who needs our help!" Iloy was furious, but the captain kept the wheel of the helm pointed in the opposite direction. Iloy grabbed at the wheel, but the captain shoved him hard. Iloy shoved back and Azura jumped in too, starting a brawl. The captain threw a punch that made contact with Iloy's throat, and though the captain was skinny and usually the weakest in a group of average people, the hit on such a vulnerable spot made Iloy fall onto the floor, gasping for breath. Azura, positioning herself behind the captain, sank her fingers into his hair and yanked with all her might. He shrieked in pain and jabbed an elbow into Azura's ribs.

Just then, Kukine appeared at the door because he, Jiji, and Delamina knew something had gone awry when boat lurched to port and continued off course. Kukine stood shocked for a moment and then lunged forward, hauling the captain away from Azura. Kukine was a big guy, his arms were round and thick, and he used those arms to wrap the captain in a suffocating choke hold. Iloy was still on the ground, gasping for air himself. Azura, hunched over from the captain's blows, staggered to the wheel. She spun it back to starboard until the floodlight fell upon the treeboat again. Kukine dragged the struggling captain out of the control room. Jiji picked up some rope, and he and Kukine lashed the terrified man to a post.

Iloy, who had by now gotten his breath back, made his way to the door and shouted out hoarsely to Delamina, "There may be someone on that boat who needs our help."

Delamina threw off her shawl revealing a lithe frame covered in a sleeveless black nightgown. She made her way to a gangplank to use as a bridge to cross over to the treeboat, which would be tricky because the boat they were on stood a good yard taller at its gunwales. Interestingly, the treeboat started moving and stopping as if it too was experiencing a struggle between two parties with different intentions. Finally, it came to a halt, and Azura was able to pull up next to it and lay anchor.

Kukine and Jiji helped Delamina lay the gangplank, and then Jiji and Delamina crossed over onto the treeboat while Kukine held it in place. As soon as they set foot on the deck of the treeboat, it began to move again as if someone had held it in place just long enough for them to get on. Kukine used all his strength to retract the gangplank and watched as the treeboat drifted on.

"Azura!" Kukine shouted, but she was already on it. She pulled the lever to retract the anchor and started pursuing the treeboat again.

To Jiji and Delamina, two leaders of the Enané people, the life force of the treeboat was palpable. The moistness of the deck, with little roots, plants, and moss growing out of it, felt cool and alive under their feet. The figure of the tree stood tall, and though there was a waxing moon to reveal some details of it, the giant broccoli-shaped form with thin tassel-like vines was shrouded in shadows. There were creaking sounds as the treeboat swayed, moving steadily forward.

"Wow. This is incredible," Jiji said, looking around.

"Yes, but let's be careful. Remember, Iloy said there may be some-one on the boat," Delamina cautioned.

"I just hope it's not *something*, if you know what I mean."

"Honestly, humans worry me more than anything else. Anyway, let's find out."

They moved toward the tree. Other than the fact that it was grow-ing right out of the boat, it looked perfectly normal. There was a thick patch of moss around the base of the tree, forming a circular mat around it, which made Jiji's and Delamina's hair stand on end when they stepped on it.

"Did you feel that?" asked Jiji.

"Yes, it was like an electrical current," Delamina replied. "This tree is like one of the few rare ones in the jungle that we know of."

"I know what you mean, much like the lapunas, but here I feel like I'm on a different planet. It's like gravity is different on this boat."

They took two more steps toward the trunk of the tree when, suddenly, the branch stretching out above them shook, making large fan-shaped leaves rain down on them. Looking up, they caught sight of a crouched figure making its way to the central part of the tree.

"Hello!" Jiji called out. "We come in peace."

In reply came a sound that wasn't quite a hiss but close to it. Jiji and Delamina took a few steps back.

"Did you notice that there is a cabin past the tree on the other side of the boat?" Delamina asked Jiji.

"No, I didn't."

"From my angle, I saw the outline of a rectangular structure with a door, but let's move away from the tree for the moment."

"Good idea; in case whoever is onboard has a guard monkey up there that'll leap down on us if we try to walk across," Jiji said, nervously laughing.

Kukine, Iloy, and Azura had no experience managing a large, motored boat, but they utilized what they learned during the last three days they had spent on the water to catch up to the treeboat and keep close. They saw Jiji waving at them and pointing at the tree. He wanted them to illuminate a certain point of the tree just above Delamina and himself. They directed the flood light as best as they could. The tree was lit up brightly. The leaves shone transparent green, and deep shadows were cast by the branches.

It was a light show on an otherwise dark ocean that caught the attention of people on another boat nineteen kilometers away, who started heading their way.

On the treeboat, Jiji and Delamina saw the figure again.

"It's a child," Jiji said. "A girl!"

The girl was making grunting sounds, hiding on the dark side of the tree trunk.

"It's okay, sweetie, we won't hurt you," Delamina said. "We're here to help." She turned and gestured for Kukine to point the light away from the tree. Once it was gone, Delamina spoke to the child again. "Hello, my dear; it seems like you've been on this boat for a long time. Come down and talk to us. We have food and water."

Jiji decided to move to the farthest end of the boat, away from the tree, so that the child would feel safer with just Delamina. This, in fact, seemed to help because from the shadows a little head poked out. Delamina kneeled and for a moment had an odd feeling that she was trying to call over a child in the same way she would've beckoned a scared cat. However, it seemed to be working, so Delamina kept talking softly, assuring the child more with her gentle tone than her words.

The girl climbed down the tree. She did not have an ounce of body fat on her body. Yet, she did not look malnourished, but sinewy and strong. Her gaze was piercing, her body language feral. A tattered tank top and shorts were her only clothing. The girl stood on the moss and kept leaning to one side to check on Jiji. Then, Delamina noticed something that made her eyes grow wide with interest. Golden particles blinked in and out of sight around the feral child, following her movements with a slight lag in time.

"Maybe you should sit too, so she feels safe," Delamina advised.

Jiji sat down.

As soon as he did, the girl moved forward slowly. Delamina kept still, but she smiled and tried to make eye contact. The girl was examining Delamina thoroughly, making her way over in an indirect way, sidling to the right in an angled approach. Finally, she was only a yard away. Delamina could make out her features. The girl had long red hair, bright green eyes, and light freckles speckled across her nose and cheeks.

She moved closer and reached out to the kneeling Delamina as if unable to contain her curiosity, swiping her hand through Delamina's silky white hair that was so long it nearly touched the deck of the boat. Delamina chuckled, and the girl pulled her hand back and watched warily. Delamina took a bunch of her own hair in hand and held it out to the girl. The girl saw this and moved forward again. Delamina put the hair in the little outstretched hand, and while the girl studied how the hair changed from white under the shade of the tree to silvery under the dim moonlight, Delamina said aloud to Jiji behind her, "She needs salt. We need to have some food tossed over to feed her."

"Understood," Jiji replied. At the sound of his voice, the girl retreated a step back toward the tree.

"Wait," Delamina said. "Wouldn't you like to eat something?" She gestured to her own mouth to indicate she was talking about food.

The girl considered Delamina for a moment and then sprang lightly up the tree. Delamina stood, about to walk toward Jiji, but something fell out of the tree. The girl climbed back down, picked up the spherical object, and carried it over to Delamina.

"Ah, is this the fruit of the tree?" she asked.

"Mmkeh," came the unintelligible response. Raising the fruit to her mouth, the girl pried off the stem with her teeth and then split the shell open with her hands. She laid both halves on the moss and backed away.

Delamina picked up one of the halves. She looked at it and saw that much like coconut there was water inside it. She carefully tasted it and found that it had a tangy flavor that made her tongue tingle. Like coconut, there was also white meat inside the fruit but in more copious amounts. Delamina considered how it had evolved differently from coconuts on land—the fact that it was easier to pry open indicated that in this environment it didn't suffer the onslaught of many hungry animals or humans. On the other hand, Delamina also thought that this kind of fruit may in fact have evolved to make it easy for unwary travelers who were hungry and thirsty to have a taste. She thought to herself, *For someone so young to be isolated and dieting only on what this tree gives, she must be exceedingly purified but also on the verge of losing her human consciousness. And look how the sprites have gathered around her. I'm not sure what this means, but I hope she isn't too far gone.*

"Mmhmm," Delamina licked her lips to indicate that she appreciated the gift.

Meanwhile, Jiji had called out to Kukine to throw over a banana, a loaf of bread, butter, and a sack of salt. The boats were side by side, only about four yards away from one another. When Kukine had thrown down the last of the food, Azura pulled their boat away a few extra yards, for it was difficult to keep it so close in the dark without crashing.

"How do you want to do this, Dela?" Jiji asked, holding the food in his arms.

"I'll come over to you and then bring it over to her," Delamina replied. She set down the fruit the girl had given her and slowly got up. The girl watched carefully, standing by the trunk of the tree. Delamina walked away, gathered the food from Jiji, and made her way back, sitting down on the moss, cross-legged this time. She laid out the food with great care while humming softly. She broke off a few pieces of bread from the loaf, dipping them in a little container of butter before sprinkling dashes of fine-grained salt on each. She held out a piece to the girl, who was watching with rapt attention. After waiting for a good thirty seconds with her arm outstretched, Delamina brought the piece of buttered and salted bread to her own mouth and ate it slowly, flaunting expressions of great pleasure. The girl unconsciously began to make chewing movements with her mouth and licked her lips. Delamina held out another piece. This time, the girl couldn't resist. She walked forward and took it from Delamina, immediately licking it. Her eyes widened, and she stood blinking with surprise before she scarfed down the rest.

For the next ten minutes, Delamina fed the girl piece after piece of bread, adding more salt each time. The girl also tried a bit of the banana, which made her squint her eyes and pucker her lips. In time, the girl's eyes began to droop, but she continued to nibble sleepily on pieces of bread, one in each hand. Finally, she was nodding off, so Delamina slowly moved over to her and carefully put an arm around her, not knowing how she might react. However, as soon as Delamina touched her, she snuggled into the warmth and was fast asleep on Delamina's lap within seconds.

Jiji came over with his hands on his hips. "Seems the salt has finally brought her a restful sleep."

"As well as human contact," Delamina added, gently grasping the girl's red hair that was dusty and tangled. "By the way, that fruit she gave me is psychoactive. She's been a caught fly in this treeboat's web for a little too long, it seems. I think she has amnesia, and unless she's been feral up to this age, she's lost her ability to speak."

"She's a tough one," Jiji said. "While I was waiting on the other end, I tried to tune into the tree, and what I sensed was that she has been wrestling it in some way. It's as if they've been engaged in a tug of war with each other and are both exhausted."

"But she was getting close to losing, wasn't she?"

"I think so, but there is another presence on the boat, one I can't seem to figure out. It may have had a hand in her survival."

"You know, I feel it too. It seems familiar in some way . . . I wonder if it was what Iloy picked up on."

"We'll have to ask him. But you know he's had contact with a tree-boat before, so maybe that was it. Anyway—," Jiji scratched his head as he walked to the other side of the tree, "—I'll go check out the cabin."

The white cabin made from the same wood as the rest of the boat was surprisingly unspoilt by the roots of the tree and the other forms of vegetation that seemed to halt at an invisible barrier around it. It had two windows and a door that opened easily. Inside, Jiji reached for a candle and matches that he could see by the flood light of the other boat reflecting off the water. Lighting the candle revealed a small space that was ingeniously made to fit a lot. Aromas of tinctures and essential oils permeated the space. To the left of the entrance was a workspace with a large table that was fixed to the wall like a counter, framed by shelving that was stuffed with brass drafting instruments, paints, brushes, pencils, and aged stacks of paper. Hung from the ceiling were elaborately carved figurines and mobiles of treeboats, islands, and animals. Across from the entrance, small boxy steps led up to a loft area. Under the spacing of the steps was more storage space, and under a larger gap was a phonograph with a stack of records next to it. Along the walls to the right were more surfaces and shelving that were crammed with glass vials, tools, books, tiny wooden boxes, maps, and many other things. This led to an area where there was a large sink made of clay, filled with broken and dirty dishware. Through a door was a little bathroom, complete with a little tub and wooden toilet that had surprisingly little stench coming out of it.

"It's just the girl onboard," Jiji said when he was back outside. "We can have her safe easily enough, but what about this boat now? We should get it to the Reteti."

"How will we do that?" Delamina asked. "Our mission is the priority, and, from what I understand, the only way to steer a treeboat is by synching with it and maintaining your own will over it. As well as other little details we have no idea about."

"Yes, it would be very difficult, but we shouldn't have it roaming without a guardian, both for its sake and to protect others from it, if you know what I mean," he added, looking down at the sleeping child.

"We should contact Danuba," Delamina said.

"Are you going to ask him to fly that plane of his all the way out here? He only sticks to the river."

"At this point, we may not have a choice. Where we're going we may as well leave this child here rather than take her."

"You're exaggerating, Dela. At least, we'd be there to care for her."

"That's assuming we all make it there and back alive."

"You've always had a propensity for grim prophecies," Jiji said dismissively.

Delamina glanced at him, debating whether she might tell him how he on the other hand had his head in the clouds, but she decided against it. "Let's get her onto our boat before she wakes up."

Delamina got to her feet, cradling Arionella in her arms. Jiji waved to Azura and the others, gesturing for them to come close.

"This is going to be tricky!" Kukine called out from across the gap of water. He and Iloy had the gangplank ready, but back at the controls Azura was having trouble matching the slow speed of the treeboat. At this point, the sound of a loud motor was heard.

Jiji looked to his left but couldn't see anything. "Do you hear that?" he asked. Everybody affirmed that they did.

"This could be trouble," Iloy said. "You three have to get across now!"

He and Kukine laid out the plank, which slid from right to left by the lurches of the vessels skimming over the choppy waters. Jiji took hold of the other end, using all of his body weight to keep it somewhat steady.

"Go, Delamina! Go!" Jiji shouted.

The girl began to stir in Delamina's arms. Then one, two, three flood lights turned on from the approaching speed boat. Delamina had one leg up on the gangplank and she could feel it shuddering through her whole body. The girl in her arms groggily opened her eyes—that was Delamina's cue. She sprang up onto the plank and ran across the gap onto the other boat. They made it safely, but the girl began struggling, so Delamina put her down but still held her wrist tight.

Back on the treeboat, Jiji couldn't hold the plank any longer. He let go. Kukine and Iloy staggered to their right, tripping over one another and losing their grasp on the plank. In an instant it slipped and fell onto the dark water with a splash.

———•———

The speed boat was now on Azura's port side. Its crew shined a light into the control room. She squinted, unable to see, and terrified that she would either crash into the treeboat on the right or into this new boat on her left. The only thing she could think of was to slow her boat down, and that's what she did. She, Delamina, the girl, Kukine, and Iloy fell forward due to the rapid deceleration.

Whoever was driving the speedboat used this moment to swerve across to starboard, pulling up close to the treeboat. Men could be heard shouting, and then grappling hooks with ropes attached were fired, roughly attaching themselves to the white body of the treeboat. Within a minute, they systematically pulled themselves up against the treeboat, and two men leapt over onto it.

Iloy ran up to the control room and pointed the light toward the action. There were three people on the treeboat, Jiji and two strangers. At first, they only seemed to be talking, but then the larger of the two men moved forward aggressively, brandishing a blaster. Jiji put his hands up. But what made Iloy's heart sink into his stomach was the sight of the smaller man, his long black hair whipping in the wind—he knew this person all too well. It was Revalo Otrebor—and though it had only been three years since they last saw each other—he was sporting a bald patch at the center of his head, which wasn't there before. This made Iloy do a double take, but he shook off his puzzlement and sprang into action.

"We have to help Jiji!" Iloy shouted as he turned and began scrambling around the room. "I'm sure there are blasters onboard somewhere."

"I don't know, Iloy," Azura replied. "We don't know what kind of weapons they have, and they definitely have a faster boat than ours. Also, we have a mission to accomplish."

"A mission? Are you kidding me?" Iloy was exasperated, "Jiji's at blaster point, and you're talking about a mission?"

"Iloy, you have to control your impulsiveness! Isn't that what you've been learning day after day from Jiji himself?"

Iloy wasn't listening. He was scouring the control room, looking for weapons. He found a small handblaster in a crate and rushed out onto the deck.

"Shut up for a second!" Iloy shouted back at the despairing captain who had begun to cry out for help. "Where are the other blasters on this boat?" The sound of thumping footsteps made Iloy look away from the captain for a moment.

"Did you see them threatening Jiji?" It was Kukine. "He can't swim, but we have to get him to jump ship and be ready to scoop him out," he said breathlessly.

"I saw. I'm trying to gather the blasters we have on this boat," Iloy replied.

"Blasters?" Kukine looked surprised. "I don't think that's a good idea."

"Karma acts swiftly!" the captain interrupted. "Just you wait till I get free!"

"What is with you people?" Iloy threw his arms up in the air, ignoring the captain's curses. "I know you're all for peace and love, but you have to judge the situation at hand!"

"I'm doing just that!" Kukine replied passionately. "Do you really think that you, Delamina, Azura, I, and a wild child should engage a bunch of dangerous pirates who obviously know what they're doing?"

"We should at least try!" Iloy shouted.

"With the bigger picture in mind," Kukine shouted back.

Meanwhile, the girl they had rescued was pulling Delamina to the bow of the boat, calling out wildly to the treeboat. "Kehhh! Kehhh!" Delamina was silent, analyzing the situation carefully while still holding on to the girl who kept struggling and screaming into the night. Delamina looked at Jiji holding his arms up in the air, the two men on the treeboat, and two other men on the speedboat—also factoring in at least one other person who might be driving it. She took a deep breath and then turned toward the control room and shouted, "Full speed to Wetembi Island! There is nothing stopping them from coming after us next!"

"Did you hear her, Azura?" Kukine shouted over the sound of motors and ocean water slapping their hull.

"Yes!" Azura replied. She turned the boat to port, toward the dark mass of land some eight kilometers away.

Delamina watched as Iloy turned toward her in a hot rage. "We're just abandoning him?" he screamed from across the boat. She could see that he was enraged to tears as he began stomping his way over to her.

"Iloy, we're sitting ducks out here!" Delamina shouted back. "We need the cover of land to escape." Delamina had wrapped the girl's arms behind her back now because she had started trying to bite and kick Delamina.

"We're being cowards! You know who's leading them?" Iloy's voice shook with emotion. "Revalo! It's Revalo Otrebor!"

They were close to each other now and their eyes met like powerful magnets. Delamina's expression was one of deep consternation, her eyes full of tears. "I know," she said.

"They're coming for us!" The sound of Kukine's voice snapped Iloy and Delamina out of their ocular clash. Kukine was abaft on the starboard side of the boat, keeping an eye on Revalo and his henchman. Now, they all watched in horror as the floodlights of the speedboat that had been focused on the treeboat slid away across the ocean and fell upon Kukine's face. "They're sawing the grapples off the treeboat to free themselves!"

Iloy heard this and realized that Azura, Kukine, and Delamina had been right.

"I'm at top speed!" Azura shouted back. "We're close to the island!"

The shore drew closer, and Mount Wetembi towered higher into the sky until its peaks were no longer visible from the low viewpoint of the edge of the island. At the bow, Delamina and Iloy saw the black sands of the shore first—the arid borders of the island approaching dangerously fast.

"Azura! You have to slow us down—we're going to crash!" Delamina shouted.

Azura shut off the engine, but their momentum and the current of the ocean drove them forward at an alarming speed.

"Azura!" Delamina shouted again.

"I'm trying!" Azura replied. "Move away from the front!"

Iloy stuffed the handblaster into his pocket and helped Delamina move the child by picking up her up by her legs while Delamina scooped her up under her armpits. She was hissing, kicking, and snapping at them ferociously.

In the chaos, the captain shouted helplessly at everyone within his sight, "You fools! You fools! Untie me! I can save us from ruin!"

The speedboat was now close enough that the sound of its motor was loud in everyone's ears. Iloy watched tensely as Kukine untied the captain, who, once free, immediately ran to the control room to try and save his boat from the impending collision. Azura ran out and joined the others at the back of the boat, where they hung onto wooden crates strapped to the deck.

Loud scraping and banging sounds came from the hull of the boat. They were now in shallow water, and the boat was dragging itself through sand, coral, and stones. Suddenly, everyone was jerked to the right because the captain lowered his anchor and turned sharply to port to point the boat away from the shore.

Finally, they came to a rough halt. The beach was less than a kilometer away, but the men on the speedboat had caught up to them and by pointing their lights onto the water were slowly guiding their craft toward them through the shallow waters. The only disadvantage the thugs had now was that their speedboat was a great deal shorter and that meant they had to climb vertically aboard if they wanted to.

"We won't make it to the beach by swimming," Azura said. "They'll pick us off easily."

"This is where we make our stand," Delamina said resolutely.

Just then, the captain appeared. He held a large blaster in each of his hands—both were pointing at them. "What the hell is going on?" he demanded.

"We didn't expect all this to happen," Iloy replied. "We're as shocked as you are."

"I should've listened to my wife," the captain moaned. "Bad things happen here beyond the Cyan Sea. Now, for the last time, why are you all going to Wetembi? I have a right to know!"

"We are going to see the Wetobii people," said Delamina.

At this, the captain shrank further into his baggy clothes. "Cursed from the start," he said in a fatalistic tone.

The shouts of the men from the speedboat could be heard clearly now. They were trolling their vessel slowly, positioning it so that they could pull themselves aboard the boat.

"Listen, Roi," Delamina said, using his name for the first time. "If you want to go home to that wife of yours, you're going to have to make a stand with us. These men are the worst kind of people, worse than pirates. We cannot let them board this vessel."

The captain looked into Delamina's sincere hazel eyes. Then, he glanced down at the feral girl panting in Delamina's and Iloy's grasp. There was the sound of a loud thud against his boat—the thugs had parked their speedboat right against it. Roi grinded his teeth as he grappled with an internal conflict. At the sound of another loud thud, he finally made up his mind and tossed Kukine one of his blasters and ran to the port side of the boat.

Letting go of the feral child's ankles, Iloy drew the handblaster out of his pocket and followed.

Kukine passed the blaster to Azura like it was something that sickened him and instead went to assist Delamina in restraining the child.

A minute later, Azura, Iloy, and Roi crouched against the side of the boat, peeking down at the smaller speedboat. Two men—that Iloy recognized immediately—carefully emerged from the control room, which was embedded within the hull, with their blasters drawn. One's name was Blaise. He was holding a loop of rope with a grapple attached to one end. Iloy heard him casually say, "Cover me." He threaded a length of rope out of his hand and began spinning the heavy grapple at an angle, and then he released it, while the other guy—called Chibuzo—scanned the top of Roi's boat, his blaster at the ready. The grapple flew up and clanged onto the deck. Then, with a tug from Blaise below, it scraped across the floor and dug into the wood of the side wall. Blaise and Chibuzo barely had a two-and-a-half-meter climb, so Iloy tensed and prepared to attack, knowing that whatever happened next would happen very quickly.

"Don't do anything yet," Iloy whispered, "Wait for one of them to start climbing."

Roi and Azura nodded.

Iloy took aim and waited until Blaise was halfway up the hull, and then just as he reached out to pull himself up further, Iloy fired a shot. With a shriek, Blaise fell back onto the speedboat, writhing in pain—clutching at his ribs.

Chibuzo started firing wildly, scorching the side of Roi's boat with high-voltage prongs. When he finally stopped shooting, Iloy shouted, "We have the high ground, and we're heavily armed! This is your only chance to surrender!"

There was no response, and as the seconds passed, a silent tension was palpable.

Then suddenly, Chibuzo shouted furiously, "ILOY, is that you?!"

Iloy gasped but didn't reply. He was shaken to his core. *How did he recognize my voice so quickly?*

"You son of a bitch!" Chibuzo shouted. "After all we've done for you! You came to us like a sulking stray. Master gave you a new start and taught you the way of power, only for you to take it all and use it against us?"

Iloy was tempted to reply but shook off his rage and, in a whisper, instructed Roi and Azura to fire a few warning shots onto the speedboat together to reinforce his previous threats. "Ready? One, Two, Three!"

They fired, and the sound of snapping electricity rang out. The fiberglass body of the speedboat turned black in multiple spots. Apparently, there was someone else on board in the control room because the motor of the speedboat turned on again, and then it began moving forward and to the left, away from Roi's boat.

"You're going to regret this!" Chibuzo shouted hatefully. "We have the old man, remember? Too bad he's going to be the one to pay for *all* that you've done!"

Chapter 19

THE MAZES OF
EAST WETEMBII

Besides being underdressed for the night chill, Iloy, Azura, and Delamina were all half soaked from wading through the water. The redheaded girl and Kukine were completely soaked because she had continued to fight in the water while Kukine tried to carry her safely to land.

The black sands of the Wetembii shore were sharp and cold. Having gathered their packs from the boat, everyone quickly changed their clothes, and because they couldn't get the feral child to put on one of Azura's shirts, they swaddled her in a blanket—she passed out with exhaustion soon after. Roi and his boat were already out of sight as he quickly made his way back home, never to return to what—he was now fully convinced—were cursed waters.

The weary travelers were silent and in a somber mood, thinking about Jiji stuck on the treeboat with Revalo and his henchman. Iloy, who had the most extensive contact with Revalo—being his apprentice for a time—was the most anxious and he kept ruminating on what Chibuzo had said to him only a few minutes ago, "We have the old man, remember? Too bad he's going to be the one to pay for *all* that you've done!"

Also, Iloy couldn't get Taola off his mind. He tried to push away dreadful spells of paranoia where he considered whether Revalo had recaptured Taola or not. *Where was she communicating with me from? Was she on the speedboat too?*

The others watched as he paced back and forth, his face contorted with angst. Finally, thinking of the next steps they would have to take, Delamina ventured to speak with him. "Iloy, my dear," she said, "take a deep breath. Remember, Jiji himself advised you that this mission would be fraught with danger."

With tears in his eyes and voice cracking Iloy replied, "But they may have Taola too. I don't know what to do—."

"No, I don't think so." It was Azura who replied to him immediately, with such confidence that it made him blink with surprise. "That guy, who threatened you about Jiji's safety, would've used her as leverage against us as well."

For a moment, Iloy felt relief, but then all his concern returned to Jiji and he found himself spiraling down a pit of despair.

"So that's it? We just leave him to die at the hands of the man who is definitely evil, and based on what he's trying to do, insane too."

"They will not kill Jiji, just as they collected Taola and kept her prisoner," Delamina replied. "Jiji is too valuable; they'd want intel and his abilities—they'd hope to have him join their folly."

"And they'd quickly find he isn't for it—maybe they'll even realize that he was on this mission with us to dismantle Revalo's plans. And if they don't kill him, there are fates worse than death. You know that better than I do."

"Yes, and that is why it was a miracle that we made it here, for imagine that fate upon all humanity if Revalo's intentions are actually possible—which is what we have to confirm with the Wetobii people—and why we must move forward with focus and resilience. Jiji's capture will not be in vain." Delamina stood, riveted by her own words. She pulled a green cloth out of her bag and attached it to a stick, which she surrounded by stones arranged in concentric circles. "This is a marker for Danuba, if we are lucky enough to get in touch with him, this may help him find us.

"I know that each of us is utterly depleted physically and emotionally, but we must put as much distance as we can between ourselves and the threat of Revalo's henchman returning for us—those thugs now know Iloy is with us and will take into account that we may be here to act against them." Delamina fiercely made eye contact with each of her disciples, and then she turned away from the shore and made her way into the darkness of cavernous rock formations that rose like a stone forest under the dark clouds of Wetembii Mountain.

Back on the open sea, Jiji lay fettered by thick and itchy rope at the foot of the Oaql tree as footsteps clomped roughly upon the hull, crushing and disrupting the moss and plants that were growing out of the wooden seams.

"Master, Iloy was with them," Jiji listened as one of the men who had returned on speedboat spoke severely. "They can only be going to Wetembii for one reason. Give the word and I will call in reinforcements to pursue them." There was a pause and Jiji closed his eyes waiting for the fatal order, but instead, the sound of repulsive laughter filled the air. It was Revalo—he turned away from his subordinate and set his glassy eye upon Jiji. Jiji shifted in place as Revalo approached.

Through choking, dry heaves that formed his guffawing, Revalo said, "You are lucky one, Jiji of Enané. You no waste time up there on Wetembii, trying to stop me. You see new dawn of species from up close—" Revalo bared his remaining gold-plated teeth. "I give you time to think, to choose side.

"Take him away to site B!" Revalo's sneering whispers suddenly turned to loud barks as he ordered his men. "And move out; we're leaving!"

At some point in the dead of the night, Iloy and the others stopped on a patch of rough, wiry grass and fell asleep, huddled close together for warmth.

The adults awoke near dawn with their teeth chattering and their bodies aching. The child, however, was still asleep, warmly swaddled in her blanket and sandwiched between Azura and Delamina. They could tell it was daytime because somewhere high above, the sun's rays were refracting through a dense fog that perpetually hung like a skirt around Mount Wetembii, creating a dim gray light to see by. All around them towered great formations of arid stone and bedrock. They sat for a time eating, rehydrating, and taking in all that came to pass only a few hours ago. Delamina reached into Jiji's pack, which Kukine had brought along with his own from their bunk room, extracting a little black device. It was a transceiver much like the one Danuba had given to Niniola at Halla Manor. Delamina brought it close to her mouth and pressed down on it, but all that was heard were crackling sounds of static.

"Same as last night. We've lost all connection here, it seems," Delamina said with a sigh. "I should've expected that and made contact with Danuba at least once last night before we arrived—."

"Last night was out of control, Delamina," Iloy cut in, "There's many things I wish we could have done differently too."

"Well, from here on out, let's take informed steps to tighten any loose knots, so to speak." Delamina looked at the sleeping child noting silently to herself that the golden sprites she had seen while they were still on the treeboat were no longer appearing. "We must continue to feed this child, giving her plenty of salt, as well as plenty of loving human contact. She has had an experience similar to some of your most difficult trainings with plant medicines and dieting. However, because she has had no guidance, she is on the verge of losing her humanity—Azura, you must take charge of this task of rehabilitation; I'm afraid she will no longer trust me."

"She's part of the crew now," Azura said as she looked down at the child's peaceful face that emanated an angelic clarity while she slept. "We might as well give her a name; let's call her Atali, shall we?"

———◆———

Atali awoke from the sensation of something gently being applied to her lips. She licked them and tasted salted butter. She breathed in deeply, her eyelids fluttering—she sat up to see a young woman walking toward a brown backpack that she then crouched in front of. She had light brown hair that was longest at the front by her jaws but cut short on an angle at the back of her head. She turned to smile at Atali briefly. Her eyes were a dark shade of midnight blue that only stood out in the light, and her skin was olive toned. They were alone, and for a moment, Atali tensed up as the woman walked back to her, but the woman leaned forward with a piece of bread and butter and pushed it into Atali's mouth. Atali was surprised but began chewing with her brows intensely furrowed, looking sidelong at her benefactor.

This went on for a couple of minutes until the young woman said, pointing at herself, "I'm Azura." Then she pointed at the little girl. "And you're Atali. I'm adopting you. Here, drink some water." Azura demonstrated how to drink from a mushroom-leather water pouch and then passed it to Atali, who drank from it deeply as soon as she figured it out. Letting Atali hang on to the pouch, Azura stood up, slinging her satchel over her shoulder, and then casually patted the dirt off her pants and the cotton poncho she was now wearing. Atali was watching her every movement. Azura walked a few yards away and beckoned to Atali before continuing to walk along the narrow gaps of the stony avenues.

Atali stood and slowly began following Azura, keeping some distance between them. Azura stopped now and then, holding up a rock or pointing at a gnarled bush or random scurrying insect, creating reasons to interact with Atali. Atali unwittingly drew close to Azura in these moments, and Azura took the opportunity to pat Atali's back or rough up her hair or bump her with her hip. Atali was spooked each time contact was made, but she seemed to appreciate it more than anything else.

During one of their stops, Azura took off her poncho and held it out to Atali, who was still in her ragged clothes. She wouldn't come forward to accept the offer though, so Azura simply set it down on the ground and kept walking ahead. After a minute or two, Atali appeared around a corner with the poncho draped over her, nearly trailing along the ground, the water pouch held close to her chest. She already seemed tamer.

They navigated this way, stopping and going, for a few hours. They had to scramble over heavily bouldered areas and crawl under craggy passages when climbing was precarious. Azura was following a trail of rocks that Iloy was leaving behind for her. They had planned this temporary split of the group because they were concerned that Delamina was now a figure of fear in Atali's mind because she had been the key person in subduing Atali during the chaos of the night. Kukine and Iloy had also played parts in restraining her, while Azura had almost no exchanges with Atali until now. So, she and Atali kept sharing snacks, bonding as the time passed. Soon Atali was letting Azura touch her hair, pinch her cheeks, and feed her without exhibiting much resistance.

Around midafternoon, the time came to regroup. This part they hadn't planned at all, except that Azura and the others had agreed upon the symbol of a circle of rocks to indicate that they would be stopping to eat and presenting a chance to regroup if Azura felt it was going well with Atali. Azura, however, had been brewing a bit of a charade in mind for the reunion. So, when the others came into view, sitting around a fire, Azura crouched down and gestured for Atali to come over from behind a boulder. Azura signaled for silence with a finger on her lips and then pointed at Iloy, Delamina, and Kukine. Crouching next to Azura,

Atali saw them and became tense. She began scowling, so Azura put an arm over Atali and scowled with her. After a few moments, Azura stood and walked out of hiding with a brazen strut. Atali's eyes were wide. She tried to reach out to Azura, but Azura walked over to the camp with her hands on her hips.

"Now, all of you!" she declared in a commanding voice, "Be gone from here and leave us the food!" She pointed past them into the distance. "You may only satiate your hunger if Atali forgives you. Come seek your pardon one by one after she has eaten her fill. Now, be gone!" Azura stomped her foot down and pointed vehemently again.

Iloy and Delamina were quick to understand what she was getting at and began to play along, acting as if they were cowed by the great and powerful Azura. Conversely, Kukine had a bowl of soup in his hand and stared blankly at Azura, not understanding at all.

Iloy gave Kukine a shove, stood, and said, "Well, Cookie, seems like we better go."

Kukine grumbled back argumentatively. "But I just—"

"*Now* would be good," Iloy pressured.

Kukine stood slowly, complaining the whole time, refusing to leave his bowl of soup behind.

When they had gone, Azura ladled some warm soup into a bowl, cut slices of bread and cheese, gathered pieces of dehydrated meat and fruit, and then waved at Atali to come over. Atali peeked out from behind the boulder and made her way to the campfire, drawn by the aroma of heated foods. Azura sat her down and asked, "Would you like some hot soup?"

"Mm-hmm." Atali nodded eagerly. Azura passed her the bowl. Atali raised it to her lips and sipped at it slowly. It was only a simple, salty bone broth with hints of chili spice, but Atali's expression was one of deep satisfaction, as if she had just drunk from a goblet of ambrosia.

She sat in silence, sipping at the soup until it was finished. "Keh?" she questioned, pointing to the other food items.

"All for you," Azura replied.

As Atali ate, Kukine was the first to come back over to the camp—he was hungry and had been arguing with the others that he should return first. Atali watched him lumber over while she nibbled on some bread and cheese. He sat down at the opposite end of the fire and reached for some dried meat.

"Ah, ah!" Azura chided. "No, Cookie, no food for you until you apologize to Atali." Azura was enjoying the game a little too much.

Irked and hungry, Kukine exhaled sharply through his nose. "I'm sorry, Atali," he said without looking at Atali. Then, reached for the meat again.

"Cookie!" Azura said loudly, trying to hide a smirk. "Is that how we apologize?"

"Oh gawd! What do you want, Azura?" Kukine groaned, looking longingly at the food.

"I want Atali here to feel perfectly safe with us, and that means she would like to know she won't be bothered again. Isn't that right, Atali?" Azura looked at Atali, who nodded right on cue and then picked up another piece of bread, sprinkling salt on it herself this time.

"Fine," Kukine said and made eye contact with Atali, folded his hands together, and said, "I'm very, very sorry, Atali." Then, he added under his breath, "I forgive you too for the kicking and scratching."

Both Azura and Atali heard this last part, and they narrowed their eyes, but finally they let Kukine eat. After a few minutes, Iloy came over, sat next to Kukine, and apologized too. Atali didn't seem to pay him much mind. Lastly, it was Delamina's turn.

As soon as Delamina came into sight, Atali became tense and moved closer to Azura. Delamina carefully made her way over to Atali, stopped just over an arm's length away, and gently set down a bouquet of dried twigs and hardy evergreen leaves bound together by a thin vine as an offering.

"I'm sorry I got rough with you, my dear," she said. "We were being attacked, and I had no other choice." Delamina went to sit down next to the guys, where Atali could keep her in sight.

At first, Atali's eyes followed Delamina's every movement, but after a while they settled on the fire. For the rest of lunch, Atali nibbled at a dehydrated piece of fruit, looking pensive.

After they had eaten, they set out again. Delamina was using an old, worn map that itself was a redrawn copy of an ancient map of Mount Wetembii that Jiji had brought and who was the one originally navigating it for them. So far, all they knew was that they were in what was called "Lower Wetembii." The key to navigating the labyrinthine landscape of the base of Wetembii was to dock at the west end of the island using key landmarks as a starting point—including a giant boulder that looked like the head of an elephant, appropriately labeled *Elephant Rock* on the map. The problem was that Delamina and the others had nearly crash-landed on the far eastside of the island. The author had not mapped any other region but the west end that led up to the *Plateau of Kavalos*, which then led to *Spring Passages*, and finally terminated at *Wetobii*.

Due to this handicap, they were making very slow progress, and more than a few times they went in loops, returning to where they had started. When they did make it to a location that seemed somewhat different—for the avenues of stone were hard to distinguish from one another—they weren't sure whether they were going in the right direction. The light of day was quickly fading. Besides the dense fog that cut down the light, the steep stone walls—reaching heights of nine meters or more—began casting deep shadows well before the sun began to set. Not fully rested from the night before, they settled down early to make a fire in a spot where a wall of stone curved in a way that kept in the warmth but redirected the smoke.

———————•———————

The next morning, they set out again, refreshed and resolute on making good progress. They wandered through the maze-like landscape in the dimly lit world for hours. It was sometime in the hazy heat of midday that they felt their spirits getting bogged down again. Atali and Azura were at the back of the line because every so often Atali would tug Azura in a different direction from the one that Delamina was leading. Azura thought Atali was trying to ditch the group, so she and Atali would engage in a physical struggle while Azura tried to explain that it was safer to stick together. It was when they all arrived at a distinct fork in the path that it became clear that Atali was not trying to abandon the others. It happened when Delamina, Iloy, and Kukine were all considering what the best option was when Azura and Atali caught up to them covered in sweat.

"You want me to help you with her?" Iloy asked Azura.

"I'm fine," Azura replied.

Iloy shrugged. "Alright, if you insist."

Meanwhile, Delamina was looking flustered. She walked a few steps along the path to the right, and then turned back to walk along the one at the left, before returning to the crossroads with her hands on her hips. Finally, she said with a huff, "I guess we should keep trying to move inland to the left."

At this, Atali began tugging at Azura's arm again, and this time, instead of resisting, Azura let Atali drag her forward. Atali led her to the path on the right.

"No, Atali, we're trying to go up to find the Wetobii people," Azura said, pointing inland and upward to the mountain. Azura tried moving back toward the path to the left, but Atali pulled hard at her arm to keep her where she was.

Delamina noticed the resolve with which Atali insisted on the other path and began to surmise that Atali somehow knew which way to go.

"Would you like us to follow you, dear?" Delamina asked. Atali blinked a few times—surprised by Delamina's quick insight into what she had been trying to communicate to Azura for hours—then, nodded and began to lead the way down the path that trailed off to the right.

Kukine began expressing his doubts to Delamina, but she held up her hand, admitting that she had been feeling lost since the outset into the labyrinth the day before. "We might as well try something different."

They walked along in a line, following the little girl in the large poncho. She kept making directional decisions that to the others intuitively didn't make sense. The pathways she was choosing seemed to turn them back toward the shore, and they felt themselves descending rather than ascending, seemingly undoing all the progress they had made.

Sunset came quickly, and they stopped to eat. By the time they had finished, it was already dark, so they began setting up camp for the long night ahead—that is, everyone except Atali, who repacked anything that Azura took out of her satchel. Azura was not in the mood to contend with Atali, so she sat down, leaning against a wall of stone with her arms crossed and her eyes closed, pretending to sleep. Atali pursed her lips and furrowed her brows, turning red in the face. Though she was still wary of Delamina, Atali had very quickly adapted to communicating with her in moments like these because Delamina was more responsive to instructions. She walked past where Delamina was settling herself, making sure that Delamina noticed her as she made her way farther and farther from the camp.

What Delamina hadn't mentioned to anyone during the latter part of the day's hike was that she had begun to sense something akin to a magnetizing life force from somewhere on the island. She had long instructed young initiates how to sense energies, so now she realized that Atali must have been sensing this too, only much more acutely. Atali stopped and looked back toward Delamina, who pointed to herself and the others, and then back to Atali. The girl nodded purposefully.

"Well, let's get going everyone," Delamina said as she stood up. "We have a leader that's not done leading us yet."

Chapter 20

THE PLATEAU OF
KAVALOS AND BEYOND

The sun was already hot on the faces of the sleepy travelers when they awoke to the sound of thundering in the distance and the sensation of a dull rumble through the ground they were resting on. They looked up, expecting to see thunder clouds, but instead squinted in the light. Sometime in the dead of the night, following Atali's lead, they had made their way out of the mazes of stone and into a clearing where the dim grayness they had suffered for two days began tapering off into a clearer sky that sported a few bright stars. Atali had essentially been sleepwalking, moving forward in the dark by the tingling in her gut that felt like an invisible thread was tied to her stomach. She had finally let herself collapse on the part of the island that contrasted strongly to the deadlands they had been traversing for nearly two days on its outskirts.

The sound of thunder grew louder, and the earth shook in a way that alarmed the travelers into alertness. "Everyone up!" came Delamina's voice over the increasing noise.

Iloy rubbed his eyes and stood, feeling a little disoriented upon finding that he was standing on a vast open plain of tough straw-colored grasses accented by wild flowers. When his eyes focused on the source of the din, he realized that it wasn't a storm from above, but a storm of wild horses charging straight toward their camp. Iloy's first thought was that they should try to run for their lives, but he staggered at the rapid approach of the horses, just as he had once done when misjudging the speed of a bullet-train careening down a track in the cityfort Citadelia.

"Stand together!" Delamina shouted over the sound of hooves hammering the ground.

Azura wrapped Atali in a bear hug, and Kukine pulled Iloy close, standing back-to-back with him. Then, the horses were upon them. The rush of what felt like a gale whipped their bodies, the earth quaked, and powerful figures swept past the band of the defenseless humans. Iloy and the others ventured to peel their eyes open and were glad they had because all at once they saw that they were plunged in a sea of horses racing at top speed. It was all a blur, but it was apparent that the horses came in a variety of colors. For a few moments of awe, not a single thought passed through anyone's mind but only the sensation of divine terror gripping their bodies. Then, they came back to themselves as they watched the storm of horses drive on, turning ever so slightly at a dip in the land and then rising over minute hills along the landscape—a stream of free, magnificent beasts tossing their heads and whipping their long tails.

Before Iloy had a chance to take in what had happened, breathy snorts from close by startled him out of his skin. He turned around to see that a string of baby horses that must have been following the harras of charging adults had stopped out of curiosity to check on the unusual occurrence of bipedal creatures obstructing their morning run. They sniffed and stamped, seemingly making a game of who was the boldest by coming close to the group of humans before springing away.

Azura was already over her shock of the near-death experience via stampede and lifted Atali onto her shoulders, holding one of her legs to stabilize her while reaching her other hand out to the nearest foal. The young horses stood still and blinked. Two out of the seven of them, who seemed a little older, began to graze on the grass as if they were disinterested, but their ears were intently perked toward the humans. Azura slowly kneeled down, bringing Atali to eye level with a small sandy-colored filly that began walking foward with her head lowered, neck stretched as far as possible, and her nose way out at the tip, twitching with curiosity. Now only a yard away, the filly stopped moving and sniffed the air, trying to get her nose as close to Atali's red tresses as she could without taking another step. Azura reached out toward the filly's hoof. The filly stepped back, so engrossed in the interaction that it unconsciously left one of its legs dangling in the air. Azura made a huffing noise and flubbed her lips, mimicking a horse sound as best as she could. At this, the sandy foal's dark brown hairs bristled along her neck, and she turned her head to look sidelong at Azura and Atali. The other foals' ears also twitched as they cocked their heads toward the sound in surprise, and the two oldest that were grazing stopped midchew with long pieces of grass still dangling out of their mouths. Now, Atali began to flub her lips and huff, reaching her own hand out while Azura inched forward on her knees.

A few yards away, Iloy and Delamina smiled at the human-horse interactions, but Kukine was biting his nails and looking very pale. Having lived in the jungle his whole life, and this being his first expedition out of the Enané village, Kukine had never seen a horse before.

The filly had put its dangling leg down and again stuck its nose out to try and get a proper whiff of Atali. Azura leaned forward, and Atali lowered her hands to brace herself on Azura's shoulders. At this moment, the little horse took the opportunity to get a good whiff of

Atali's head. The puffs of air from its snout lifted a few strands of Atali's hair into the air.

"What a marvelous creature," Delamina whispered to Iloy and Kukine. "Our mission is blessed by a representative of the horse totem."

Out of the corner of his eye, Iloy noticed some tall figures approaching in the distance. "These must be their mothers," Iloy said loudly, calling the large horses to Azura's attention. The sound of powerful neighing emanated from where six adult horses stood. The young horses immediately turned tail and galloped to their mothers, all except the sandy-colored one, which was now allowing Atali to pet its muzzle.

The others reached the mares, which turned and began leading their babies away. Even farther in the distance, another horse came into view. This one was immense in size relative to the other adults, which were huge themselves. It was a male, one that seemed very old. His mane was as white as Delamina's hair, and it hung low over his shoulders. His body was gray-black in shade with a white tail whose hairs swept along the ground. He was truly a sight to behold, and so he was beheld in wonder by the group of humans, dwarfed by his size and presence. The young sandy-colored filly seemed to sense the old sire's gaze, and, with a last nuzzle against Atali's hand it slowly turned and trotted away.

———◆———

The sky was clear—at first glance seeming like it was of a normal blue color, but upon closer scrutiny, a green tint was revealed that seemed to shimmer at times, giving the landscape an otherworldly quality. In the distance loomed the shadowy mass of the endless heights of Mount Wetembii. It was shrouded in fluffy, low-hanging clouds that were often broken off and swept through the grasses by strong gusts of wind, which left the otherwise arid plains instantly soaked in fresh dew. This cool, moisturizing system of the mountain was a relief for the travelers, who would get misted by the passing fog and then quickly dry off again in the sun. Though it had been a tiresome walk for Atali and the others under the blazing sun that shone uninterrupted across the open plains, they made their way across steadily, aided by these unexpected alleviations provided by the environment.

They came to a point where the plains bottlenecked into a great ravine whose steep rocky walls dripped with moisture. At the base, a gushing creek had formed, and an explosion of green foliage thrived all around it. The travelers filled their water pouches with the crystalline water and walked through the passage, listening to the echoes of the bubbling creek, which sounded like whispering voices at times. This gorge ended abruptly, opening into another valley where the creek thinned out but continued to flow, leading straight to another gorge. It became a pattern of valleys connected to other valleys by way of glistening stony passageways, all threaded together by the whispering stream of water. Everyone could now feel the effects of the altitude on their bodies. Though passing feelings of nausea and dizzy spells slowed them down, their hearts fluttered with a newfound vitality that kept them going. Atali was no longer leading the group. They moved forward together in silence, rapt in the beauty and energy of the landscape.

High in the mountain Iloy felt as if he were in an alien world, having spent much of his life in adamantine artificiality of Citadelia, and then years at Revalo's sunless camps in caves and toxic forests, and most recently, the bosky lands of the Enané. The thin ravines allowed only a strip of sky to light their way most of the time, but when the light did shine upon them, most of the stones and cliff faces were revealed to be of a smooth ceramic-like substance of dark brown color—they reminded Iloy of globules of caramel chocolate.

Soon, a golden sunset flooded the mountain's many shelved peaks, valleys, and gorges. The slanted light illuminated the brown crystal stones anew as their moisture-covered surfaces sparkled while the creek shone gold. The cliffs sparkled too, and all-around little waterfalls spilled like torrents of jewels crashing into rainbow pools. Flying insects like drag-onflies, butterflies, and others that seemed to be of strange hybridized species filled the air, flitting around the heads of the travelers, catching golden light on their bejeweled bodies. *I wish I could shine with them . . . with all of this*, thought Iloy to himself. Then, as he looked down upon himself, he found that his skin and the fine brown hairs that grew out of it shone in harmony with the lightshow encompassing him. He pictured himself and his companions from a bird's-eye view, perfectly embedded within nature's canvas, just as mysterious, alive, and illuminated as every-thing around them. He smiled but then frowned again when he thought of how Jiji wasn't there to share in the splendor with them.

The glistening sunset was only a momentary spell of time within the *Spring Passages* of Mount Wetembii before the magic of the night sky took its turn to stun its audience. Atali, Iloy, Azura, Kukine, and Delam-ina lay in the grass, pointing up at shapes they could see in the stars, and made countless wishes at the ceaseless shower of falling stars until they fell asleep without so much as a thought for dinner.

————◆————

The next morning, the travelers awoke brimming with energy. Delamina took care to feed Atali some bread seasoned with salt, but everyone else took only a few sips of mountain water from their pouches before they were off again without breakfast. Aside from the bouts of alti-tude sickness, everyone felt highly invigorated, with a sense that there was something distinctly different about the land they walked upon as compared to everywhere else they had been throughout their lives. Delamina was able to draw a comparison to the difference in gravity and electric atmosphere she had experienced aboard the Oaql boat, but still, it was not exactly the same.

Finally, they came upon the largest ravine they had yet seen. Its smooth, glistening walls of brown-black stone rose high out of sight, into a swirl of clouds, and a chilly breeze brought the first signs of crystals of powdery snow. Everyone moved forward except Atali, who stood staring up at a particular spot of the ravine's shelves of rock.

"What is it, Atali?" Azura asked. Atali pointed, and Azura knelt down to her level to get a better view. Azura's stomach lurched upon seeing a strange pale figure standing on a large overhang of smooth stone nearly twelve meters from ground level. Even from this distance, the individual seemed unusually tall and somehow anatomically disproportionate, standing motionless for a moment longer before slowly turning, bending over slightly, and walking into a dark opening in the stone face that was otherwise hard to see because of its shaded and bubbly contours. "Delamina!" Azura called out. "Did you see that?"

"I saw some movement," Delamina replied. "Did you see what it was?"

"It was a tall human-like being wearing a single dark garment that might have been transparent. He was bald and white skinned."

"Could have been a Wetobii. Let's get into formation then," Delamina said. "Iloy, you stand next to me where Jiji would have been. Azura and Kukine, stand Atali between you." Delamina then reached into her satchel and pulled out a container. She opened it and plucked out a gray fossil with the detailed outline of a small prehistoric creature that rose up out of the frame of stone it was embedded in. Then they waited.

A person wearing an opaque white toga-like garment emerged from an unassuming opening at the base of the gorge. This individual was different from the one Atali and Azura had seen but was also bald and very pale, so much so that blue veins could be seen at his temples and along his bare arms and feet. There was no hair anywhere on his face or body, except for long bushy black eyelashes that were accentuated due to the lack of eyebrows.

"Greetings!" Delamina said. "We come in peace." She held out her hands, presenting the offering to the approaching stranger, who raised a thin hand in acknowledgment. He picked the fossil out of Delamina's hands, not paying it any mind and holding it awkwardly in his open palm. Then, he browsed each individual in the group of travelers with his discerning eyes. His attention kept returning to Atali, who gazed back at him with a curious look in her eyes.

His voice came as if through a hollow tube. "Folloh." He said this slowly and with a heavy accent that deemphasized any hard consonant or vowel sounds. It was clear that the common language was not at all common to him, or at the very least rarely used up on the isolated peaks of Wetembii.

They made their way silently into the gorge that echoed with howls of wind. Soon, everyone except the pale stranger was shivering. Thin bits of ice had formed along the same narrow creek Delamina and the others had long been following, and the moisture along the walls of the ravine formed thin icicles that glittered in the light. However, refuge from the cold came quickly when the gorge opened into a bright canyon where there flurries of snow were still falling, but the warmth of the sun was surprisingly robust at the same time. Long strands of bright green grass with paddle-shaped tips grew for miles, filling in spaces where the same dark crystal stones of the gorges seemed to grow right out of the bedrock of the mountain, forming the massive walls of the canyon. A few more figures in white togas were silently going about their business, entering and exiting openings in the canyon walls as if it were a giant hive of sorts. Delamina did a double take as she saw the similarity of baldness of head and body in all of them, but what was strangest to her was that they were diverse in skin tone, height, and facial features, which for a people who had been isolated for eons and—as far as Delamina knew—unlike her own tribe the Enané, didn't allow mingling with outsiders.

"Is this the land of the Wetobii?" Delamina ventured to ask the guide.

He tilted his head to the side as if trying to recall the term, or exactly how to respond in the common language, but then, he said in his strange resonant voice, "Yehs, Wehsobee, yehs."

Kukine looked at Azura and Iloy with a frown and wide eyes that said, *He's creeping me out, guys.* And they reciprocated the look. Still, there was something tranquil and slow about the pale stranger's movements and his soft face and long eyebrows were somewhat disarming.

Delamina spoke up again, trying to get a sense of the situation. "My name is Delamina. What is yours, friend?"

"Elehsihs," he said, seemingly having difficulty pronouncing his own name.

"Elésix?"

"Yehs," he replied in his breathy manner.

"Nice to meet you. This is Iloy, Azura, Kukine, and Atali."

Elésix nodded in reply and kept walking toward a large cave glowing with muted teal-colored lights. The light came from fluorescent crystals that were mined right out of the walls of the cave but left in place like lamps, which kept extending into a tunnel lined with rooms carved out of the stone.

"You lif heehr," said Elésix, extending his arm out across the many empty rooms.

"Thank you, Elésix. We would be happy to lodge here, but we have limited time." Delamina tried to say this with great care so as not to unwittingly offend their host. "We would like to speak to you and your people about something that has been troubling us for some time now."

It was very difficult to discern what Elésix was thinking, as his face was very unexpressive, especially because he had no eyebrows, and in the dimly glowing cave, details of his features seemed even more ambiguous.

"Spea-hing difficuhl in yoh lan-gu-age," Elésix said slowly. "Connech ah imag-puhl ah undursahn."

Delamina and Azura listened closely to what he was saying and deciphered it, though it was hard to understand. Iloy and Kukine entirely missed what he said, so they nudged Azura, who paraphrased in a whisper, "He says that speaking is difficult in our language and that we'll connect at . . . something called a pool to understand each other."

While Delamina, Kukine, Iloy, and Azura set their things down in a room shaped out of the stone of the mountain, Atali kept hold of Azura's free hand, never taking her eyes off Elésix, who stood waiting silently, his pale skin glowing in the teal light of the crystal tunnel.

Chapter 21

THE MYSTERIES
OF THE WETOBII

Kukine and the others walked back out into the light, which made them squint. The flurries of snow kept falling but disappeared before they made contact with the green grass below. Elésix walked ahead, leading them all toward a ramp of stone that led to another level of pathways cut out of the towering walls of the canyon. Soon, they encountered other individuals like Elésix who took no notice of them, except to let them pass at particularly narrow parts of the stone passage. They had hairless bodies from head to toe, except for their eyelashes, and though some had darker skin tones than others, all shared paleness and a transparency of skin that made them look sickly. Though they were of varying heights, their bodies were similar in their boxiness, which led Delamina to wonder how to distinguish males from females, and if Elésix was in fact a male at all.

They came to another glowing tunnel of teal-colored light, which they entered and walked along for what felt like ten minutes or more. Finally, at the end of the tunnel was a large opening that led into a massive cavern lit by huge luminescent crystals all along the ceiling and edges of the walls. They walked down a ramp that trailed down and around the diameter of the chamber until they came to a large fountain of dark brown crystal that was shaped right out of the dark brown floor in which it was embedded. Elésix set down the fossil Delamina had given him on a stone table nearby, and then motioned toward the fountain and said, "Eahs."

"I think he's telling us to eat," Azura said quickly when Delamina looked like she was about to ask Elésix to repeat himself.

"Oh, I see," Delamina replied, and then turned back to Elésix and said, "That's okay. We are not hungry, and we've collected plenty of water in our pouches already."

"Help you heal and connech to Wehsobee," Elésix replied.

Delamina looked into Azura's eyes and then moved toward the fountain. Iloy moved forward as well, but Azura subtly reached out at her side and blocked his path. Realizing he had made a mistake, and that he needed to be more vigilant, he looked around nonchalantly as he moved back a couple of paces from the fountain again.

Meanwhile, Delamina approached the crystal fountain, where the water bubbled over the smooth surface gently from a thin central point that rose like a stamen with a five-pronged tip shaped much like a hibiscus flower. She took out her water pouch, but as she lowered it toward the fountain, Elésix said, "Noh." He moved close to Delamina—who smelled a musty but sweet pine odor coming from him—and demonstrated how to "eat" the water by cupping his hands together, gathering as much liquid as he could into them, raising it all carefully to his mouth, and drinking it in with motions of puffy lips that reminded Delamina of a baby suckling at its mother's teat. The skin on his scalp moved with each sucking draft he took, until he was done. He took a deep breath and shifted in place slightly, as if regaining balance.

Delamina's plan had been to gather some of the water in her pouch and then feign a swig from it, but now, Elésix was watching her closely with eyes whose pupils appeared freshly dilated. Delamina reached into the water and found it was surprisingly viscous. She gathered a miniscule amount into her hands and drank it. Delamina had long trained in the art of consuming natural medicines, most of which had powerful effects on human beings, and most recently, she had realized that the fruit from the Oaql boat was one such potent medicine that had quickly altered Atali while she was alone on the boat. In this moment, upon drinking the liquid from the crystal fountain, Delamina immediately felt the effects of one of the most powerful substances she had ever consumed. First the nagging nausea from the elevation-induced hypoxia vanished instantly, and then all soreness in her body—from the recent trials they had all faced—vanished too. Her limbs, which had been feeling cold, now flushed with heat, and her awareness grew attuned to the vibrations of the cavern, which she realized was like an organ of Mount Wetembii, and that she had just partaken of its lifeblood. She took a deep breath and opened her eyes.

Elésix turned to the others and waited, expressionless as usual. Azura, Kukine, and Iloy all looked to Delamina, who nodded and mouthed the word *careful* at them. As her students, they understood immediately what she meant, and so they approached the fountain. Atali was still holding Azura's hand tightly and wouldn't let go when Azura tried to use both hands to gather the liquid, so she settled for using just one hand, which Elésix didn't seem to mind. The three young Enané took in the liquid and staggered a bit but then opened their eyes. They glanced at one another with understanding, feeling refreshed, each now savvy to the power, and the potential danger, of the strange environment they found themselves in.

Elésix looked down at Atali, who was the only one who had not partaken in the draught of the mountain, but Azura spoke up quickly, "Thank you, Elésix, that was very refreshing."

Elésix paid Azura no mind. He pointed to Atali and said, "Eahs."

Atali moved behind Azura.

"That's okay; she isn't hungry," Azura said with an edge of rising temper.

Elésix finally looked directly at Azura and considered her for a moment. Then, he said "Folloh" and began walking toward another glowing tunnel at the far end of the cavern. As Delamina, Azura, Iloy, Kukine, and Atali walked through the passage, they felt tremors pass through their bodies, and their hairs stood on end because of what felt like an electrical current permeating the space around them—even the glow of the crystals lighting the passage was an electric yellow. They came to another huge cavern that was lit up from the blue light of many pools of water embedded into the stone foundation. As they descended toward the pools, they could see that each one regularly rippled with a yellow shimmer, as if something was dripping into the pools from above. They walked over to one of the larger pools, about seven meters in diameter, and Elésix knelt down at one end.

"Nawh, whe connech," he said as he dipped his hand into the pool of water. He shuddered, his eyes rolled up in their sockets, and then he fell still, waiting.

Delamina took off her satchel and handed it to Kukine. "This is going to be uncomfortable, I think." She sighed and took a few steps forward then knelt by the shimmering pool. Before she did anything else, she closed her eyes for a time and slowed her breathing. Still feeling the effects of the draught of the fountain, she sensed the livingness of the mountain and the presence of many other nameless beings that inhabited it. At last, she was ready. She opened her eyes and reached toward the water. Just before she breached its surface, she felt something akin to a static shock. She flinched and then plunged a single finger into the water.

She gritted her teeth and panted as the muscles of her body convulsed from the electrical current present in the water. Behind her, the others watched in horror as her beautiful white hairs began to rise into the air. Iloy and Kukine sprang forward to help, but she raised her free hand, motioning for them to stop, obviously aware of their movements without looking at them.

You'll get used to it, said an unfamiliar voice in Delamina's head.

I'm not trying to get electrocuted more than just this once, Delamina replied with her thoughts.

Well, when you put it that way . . . Anyway, what are you seeking here?

The voice was sure of itself and had a sense of witty humor that seemed very different from Elésix's stoic personality.

Are you one of the Wetobii of Mount Wetembii? Delamina asked.

Weto—transparent, *and Wetem*—opaque—*old names in an old language. Yes, we represent, "the transparent-skinned dwellers of the opaque mountains." A derogatory classification, don't you think?*

I apologize, Delamina replied with the psychic equivalent of a bow. *I meant no harm. What shall I call your people instead?*

You are quite good at this, aren't you? What are the chances of another adept visitor within the span of such a short time, after decades of no contact? At this moment, the voice spoke more to itself than to Delamina.

I am one of the elders of the Enané, so I have trained in similar states my whole life, Delamina said, drawing Elésix's attention to herself again. She wondered about what he'd said but did not want to ask questions beyond those that pertained to her mission—not knowing how long this opportunity would last, or rather, how long she would last under the circumstances.

Seems like the young tribes have been doing well for themselves then, said the voice somewhat condescendingly. *Not that it matters, but we are the Eldeshians of Aléon. Aléon is what you call Wetembii, so we guess it would be Mount Aléon for you.*

And what is your name? Delamina asked. There was a pause and a most subtle quiver of frustration from the other side of the pool.

Elésix, as we told you before, the voice calmly replied, revealing nothing of the disturbance a second earlier. *Now, what is it that you are seeking, Delamina of the Enané?*

Your wisdom, came Delamina's simple reply. *The sole reason I am here is because of a man, Revalo Otrebor, of native south Cyanian decent. Do you know of him?*

We are not all seeing from Mount Aléon. Tell us what you know about this man that you have come so far—and through peril—to inquire about, so that we can further understand your intentions for wanting to obtain any wisdom, that we may or may not decide to impart to you.

I understand. Again, Delamina performed the psychic equivalent of a bow. *It may seem strange that instead of all the things we could learn from you, we have a very simplistic sounding intention to inquire about one individual's intentions. I will try and be thorough to convince you otherwise.*

From what I have learned about Revalo Otrebor, he was a gifted child and was raised in the ancient shamanic arts of the Obipisha, his people. As he approached his thirtieth birthday, he abandoned his native roots and training to become a master to seekers from cityforts himself. When the hybrid tribes first learned of his efforts, we thought it noble—though it was a bit strange that he distanced himself from the Obipisha so completely—as we learned from our diplomats who have some contact with their envoys. We reasoned his decision to defect was because the Obipisha are restrictive to outsiders in general.

Over time, Delamina went on, *it became evident, however, that instead of empowering his followers, he became entrenched as the leader of a new cult-like following—usually of young men from cityforts who were especially vulnerable due to lives spent in poverty, or worse, normalization efforts by use of medicalized drugs that the cityfort leaders have long implemented on their citizens.*

Anyway, for years we assumed his goal was to create his own tribe and though we admonished his hierarchal inclination in summits with other hybrid tribes like the Kampa and Nawa, our conversations never grew past gossip really. That is, until two decades later when multiple tribes had to confront him in battle because he openly attacked the Akninka, one of the original hidden tribes like the Reteti Islanders and yourselves the Weto—I apologize, the Eldeshians. He sought all the Akninka's fossils of power for himself, rather than partake in the gift-exchange cycle of tribes to acquire what he needed, or simply wanted. It was clear to many of us now that he was a dangerous figure, one that was actually consequential to the delicate balance of our young world due to the power he had amassed in only part of one human lifespan—I hear that he has even rallied the people of the Moravia Underlands to surface and join him—and not to mention we think he is involved with the cityfort Atlantia somehow, if not others as well. There we thought his devices ended. Yes, he wanted power. Yes, he wanted to create his own tribe and to be supreme leader of dogmatic followers. Yes, that made sense and we thought—what more could there be?

The answer came when one of his own apprentices, the first ever—as far as we know who was able to dissent and escape—found us and divulged a much more disturbing and far-reaching conspiracy Revalo Otrebor has long been weaving and amassing power to accomplish. You may ask, as we did—is it to overthrow all the other tribes, take control of the cityforts and rule the world of humans? Yes, it somehow includes these terrible goals, but it is yet stranger and more heinous . . . something that we do not know is even possible at all. Delamina paused and contained the energy she felt surging through her veins augmented by the subject she was addressing.

He seeks to somehow take control, or possess, the archetype of the human species—our collective mind.

Delamina silenced her thoughts and waited for some kind of reaction from the Eldeshian after divulging this theory, but nothing came from the other side of the pool. So, a bit perturbed, she continued, making up her mind to end with a clearer question as she had first been intending to do.

We, the Enané, loosely understand the concept of the protos, and we even work somewhat blindly with the proto-beings that exist as energy— and are called "spirits" and "sprites" in the common tongue—represented by tobacco, hoa suna, and the lapunas—the plant masters. However, we have never dreamed of shattering the sacred boundaries of our dimension to such an extent as to take control of what shapes existence as we know it.

So, I ask you for guidance. What wisdom can the Eldeshians impart to us younger tribes? Is such a thing that Revalo Otrebor plans possible and where do we go from here if so?

Go from here? came the reply immediately. *You are exactly where you need to be and furthermore, we have deemed it worthwhile to share our wisdom on this matter.*

Human pursuit for power is very real, but you all have been reading too deeply into what may, at most, be a grim fantasy of a power-hungry fool. We have sensed this man's conquest for power—he is the one I mentioned before— another who was able to interact with us so skillfully as you are, Delamina of the Enané. And it makes us wonder how much power is being amassed by yet others, considering your abilities as well as Revalo of the Obipisha. Humans have never done well with abilities beyond a certain scope.

There was a pause and Delamina became increasingly wary of what the Eldeshian had just said. It seemed to sense this and quickly tried comforting her by adding, *We shall equip you with what you need to help resolve this terrible issue of one man's unchecked power once and for all.*

Elésix's eyes rolled back into place, and he withdrew his hand from the shimmering pool and stood. Delamina did likewise but swayed weakly. Iloy and Kukine shot forward, receiving static shocks upon touching Delamina as they steadied her.

"Are you alright, Dela?" Iloy asked anxiously while Kukine felt her pulse and found that it was throbbing vigorously. Delamina hadn't replied, so Kukine took off the satchel she had handed to him and passed it to Iloy. Then, Kukine lifted her into his arms.

"Show us the way out," Kukine said in a severe tone to Elésix, who had walked back over to the group, unfazed by the image pool's effects.

"Neehs wahrah frahm fahownain," Elésix replied in his breathy voice and slow accent.

"No, thank you," Azure cut in curtly. "She's had enough to drink for today."

"Folloh," Elésix said after a moment's pause, turning back toward the ramp that led to the exit.

Kukine followed Elésix, and Azura and Atali followed Kukine. Iloy looked at the pool distrustfully, and then he looked appalled at something that none of them had noticed—fallen clumps of Delamina's white hair brightly contrasted against the dark floor of the cavern.

———◆———

Outside, the snow continued to surreally blow about under the warm sun. Kukine was still holding Delamina in his arms. Every so often, he would look down at her tense face and at the spots of her scalp with missing patches of hair, which made him frown and pant ever more deeply as he marched impatiently behind Elésix's slow, cumbersome strides. Azura and Iloy, behind him, were solemn watching as wisps of

Delamina's tresses drifted by in the air, and Atali too seemed shaken up by the intense exchange of energies.

They were walking down the same pathway cut into the wall of the canyon that they had used to get to the fountain and image pools, and where they had passed other people like Elésix going about their business, when suddenly Atali went ballistic.

First, she broke the tense silence with a shrill wail. Yanking her hand out of Azura's for the first time since they had met Elésix, she ran forward past Kukine, past Elésix, and farther still. Azura and Iloy stood shocked for a moment but quickly recovered. They broke out into a sprint after her.

"Atali! What are you doing?" Azura shouted. Atali had run right up to a toga-clad individual and had grasped his waist with all her might. The individual kept looking straight ahead as best as he could but began dropping large milky-colored crystals that he was carrying as he tried to maintain balance.

"I'm so sorry, Sir," Azura said when she caught up. She pried Atali's hands off of the tall man, who was now grasping his toga in an effort to keep the feral child from stripping him in public.

Iloy began picking up the fallen pieces of crystal, many of which had shattered. "I'm so sorry, sir. Here you are," Iloy said as he straightened up and looked at the disheveled man clearly for the first time.

Like the others, the man was indeed bald, but unlike them he had light fuzz where his brows should have been and, even more notably, the remnants of a long white beard that seemed to either be growing or thinning out in sparse patches over his cheeks and under his chin.

The man met Iloy's eyes but quickly looked away and took the crystals Iloy was offering him.

Azura held Atali in a bear hug as the girl wept, kicked, spat, and screamed. The bearded man quickly walked off as Elésix and Kukine caught up to the scene.

Delamina, still in Kukine's arms with her eyes closed, stirred at the sound of Atali's cries. Azura and Iloy carried the struggling child all the way down the ramp, and when they finally got off the ramp, Iloy let her go while Azura fell onto a clump of grass with Atali tight in her embrace.

"I'm sorry, baby, I'm so sorry . . . I can't let you run off right now," Azura said with a hoarse voice, welling up with tears herself.

Atali continued to moan and weep with utter hopelessness and fury at the betrayal as Azura lay on her, pinning her to the ground.

"I don't know what you want," Azura said half in apology, half in frustration. "I don't understand what's happening to you but, I'm sorry . . . I can't let you go. It's dangerous to let you run off here. Please understand. Please."

Azura broke into sobs, heaped on top of the little weeping girl who couldn't tell her captor that she had just seen and touched Jöshi, her long-lost grandfather.

After a few minutes, Atali fell still, but her tears continued to flow. Elésix stood nearby, his head cocked to the side and the skin where his brows should have been slightly raised. He watched intently as Azura lifted Atali off the ground. She walked forward, carrying the child. Iloy, and Kukine joined her, and Elésix followed.

"We know where to go from here," said Kukine, turning to Elésix, who stared blankly back at him. Kukine turned away and followed his comrades to the crystal cave in which they were expected to lodge. Elésix stood watching them for a while and then turned away, making his way back toward the ramp that led into the caverns of the mountain.

In the dimness of the stone room, lit only by the fluorescent crystals growing out of the walls, Kukine and Iloy did their best to create padding with their clothes and packs, and then laid Delamina gently down. Though she was stirring, she was still unconscious, and her pulse was fast. Azura sat cross-legged, Atali lying exhausted on her lap. Everyone was silent for a time, collecting their thoughts.

Iloy finally grabbed his head and said, "What's going on here? Jiji's gone, now Dela's . . . well, I don't even know what's happened to her. What are we going to do? These people, this mountain—there is something wrong with it all!"

Iloy's words and exasperation only increased the tension in the room. The sound of Kukine swallowing was heard by everyone.

"We better stay armed at the very least," Iloy said, "and maybe forget about playing defense and make the first move."

Kukine turned to him angrily and opened his mouth, but Azura cut in with a steely voice, "She's asleep." She carefully laid Atali down. Then, she stood and made her way to Delamina. "Our teachers may not be able to guide us, but their lessons and training are within us. I want you two to help me, when you're in the right state of mind." Without another word, she placed her hands a few centimeters over Delamina's forehead and chest, closed her eyes, and stilled herself.

Kukine took a deep breath. Then he stood and joined Azura. He placed his hands just above Azura's.

Iloy shook his head, folding his arms tightly across his chest. The sight of Azura and Kukine, stock still and kneeling with their hands extended, reminded him of the Enané settlement and the times Jiji had made him do the same, except over the body of an injured butterfly or bird. The desire to learn the healing arts was one of the main reasons Iloy had left Citadelia in the first place. Jiji's words surfaced in his memory, *Happiness is not a state of mind; it's a way of thinking.* Iloy drooped his head and shook it a few times. Then he straightened his back, took a deep breath, and walked over to his companions. He dropped to his knees, placed his hands above Kukine and Azura's, and closed his eyes.

Azura peeked open an eye and smiled before she closed it again.

After about thirty minutes, Azura reached over to Delamina's wrist and took her pulse. It had slowed, and her breathing was deeper and calmer.

"She's resting," Azura said. "Well done."

Kukine and Iloy opened their eyes and nodded.

Chapter 22

THE WANDERING LOVER

It was growing dark outside, and Iloy was growing antsy again. He insisted that he take the first watch while the others rested. The cave and its passages grew brighter as the last of the sun's light waned. The glow of the crystals made Iloy feel somewhat better, but the whole time he paced back and forth outside of the stone room, he kept his hand clutched around the prong-blaster in his pocket.

Think positive, think positive, Iloy thought insistently, but as his eyes drooped and his legs felt like lead, his anxiety grew too. He tried to divert his attention by running his free hand along the glossy surfaces of the cool, dark stone around him. He stopped at a large crack in the wall where a crystal network of blue and peach colors frosted the innards of the rock like shiny sugar cubes. He felt relaxed, and the crystals' phosphorescence filled his vision as his eyelids began to shut.

Suddenly, the slightest change in the light of the tunnel made Iloy snap awake, spin a hundred and eighty degrees to his left, and draw out his blaster. A small figure was silhouetted at the mouth of the cave, and the next second it vanished out into the night.

Iloy dashed after it and saw that it was Atali running away under the light of the waning moon.

Iloy broke into a sprint. Atali saw him coming over her shoulder and, rather than trying to get away came to a sudden halt. Iloy wasn't expecting this. He had to leap over her to avoid running into her. He fell to the grassy ground.

Before he could stand, Atali appeared over him. Her eyes radiated aggression, and she had her left hand raised with her pointer finger held high, as if to say, *Don't you dare, Iloy. Don't you dare cross me.*

Iloy could only sit still and blink. He had the same anxiety he had felt when he was a child and a goose had suddenly come out from behind a bush while he was playing by the water. It had fiercely advanced toward him, and though he had never thought he'd be scared of a goose, in that moment he had been.

Finally, recovering his wits, he furrowed his brows and opened his mouth to say something, but Atali put a finger to her lips and extended her other hand to Iloy. Again, Iloy was dumbstruck. He considered Atali quite feral, and he realized that he had never looked into her eyes. What he saw now were sharply present green irises that demanded his attention and respect. Large flakes of snow continued to fall on and around them, without sticking for too long, and the sky above was clear and sparkling with stars. He took her hand and stood. She gripped him tight and began pulling him along with her.

"But, Atali," Iloy whispered, "the others won't know where we've gone, and besides, they're unprotected now."

She wheeled toward him and raised her commanding finger again before turning and tugging him harder in the direction of the rocky walls of the Wetembii valley.

After walking for about ten minutes, they came to a small hill of boulders made by a rockslide of the same dark, glossy stone that characterized the peaks of the mountain. Suddenly, Atali let go of Iloy's hand and ran ahead.

"Hey wait!" Iloy ran after her. First, he was only looking at the back of her head, but as he ran, he happened to look up. Along the foot of a cliff, a pile of boulders made their own elevated landscape, on top of one of them sat the ragged-bearded man whom Atali had embraced earlier that day.

The man saw Iloy and Atali approaching. He stood and climbed down to the ground, where he kneeled with his arms spread wide. Atali ran at full speed straight into his arms. The old man and the girl tightly embraced, and Atali began sobbing again. The man too, was visibly emotional as he combed Atali's tangled red hair with one hand and every so often leaned back to look at her face and wipe away her tears.

Iloy walked toward them, both utterly confounded and deeply moved. The display made him think of how his mother, Lina, would have hugged him if he returned to Citadelia after all these years of absence. He folded his hands and waited with his head bowed, giving Atali and the old man the time they needed.

A few minutes later, the old man stood, holding Atali's hand. He beckoned to Iloy and pointed at the boulders.

Iloy followed and scrambled up behind them, surprised at how quickly he was so high off the ground. From this vantage point, it was revealed that the field of boulder stones created deep-gapped passages. The old man stopped here and turned to Iloy.

"What's your name?" he asked in a husky voice that had higher youthful tones in it.

"I'm Iloy. Who are you?"

"Iloy." A look of recognition passed across the old man's face. "My name is Jöshi Halla, I am this child's grandfather." The man narrowed his eyes and raised his chin. To Iloy, this old man suddenly seemed very tall and surprisingly muscular. Jöshi continued, "She does not seem too fond of your company—it seems you are still strangers to each other."

"Well—yes," Iloy stammered. "It's only been two days since we rescued her from a treeboat. That situation got complicated fast. There are attackers that have taken the treeboat, as well as one of our teachers, Jirinjin of the Enané."

At this, Jöshi looked straight into Iloy's eyes with surprise. "That's a name I haven't heard in a long time," he said slowly.

"You know him?"

"Yes, I've spent time with the Enané. Jiji and I, we were much younger then, but we shared a common vision for the world."

"Then you must know Delamina as well."

"Yes. She was a bit younger, and yet even back then she was wise beyond her years."

"She's here with us."

When Iloy said this, Jöshi's energy changed even more. His deep brown eyes seemed to glow with a rush of new ideas. Then he said, "What you have just told me is very good news. And you mentioned the treeboat was taken, I assume you were on another vessel?"

"Let's just say a whole thing broke out—" Iloy scoffed when he thought of Roi, the superstitious captain that they commissioned "—that guy and his boat are looong gone."

"Hmm . . . that complicates things. Does anyone else know you are here?"

"We haven't been able to give more recent updates because our transceiver doesn't work here. However, some of the Enané—like Danuba—know that we were chartering a boat to find the Wetembii. And I think they know of Mount Wetembii."

"Well, I guess it can't *all* be laid out in a platter for us. Anyway, I am familiar with your name too. I am aware of your quest, Delamina contacted me some three years ago now with news of your former master's insidious plans. I wish I could have spared all of you the visit here, but I have been isolated and had no way to contact anyone."

"How long have you been here?"

"Six long months," Jöshi said and stared into the distance, seemingly reliving traumatic events, but he finally cleared his throat and said, "Anyway, now I feel more inclined to believe that Arionella is in good hands, and the blame for any conflict between you lies more with her than with any of you." He gave his granddaughter a stern look, at which she crossed her arms and looked away, pouting.

"Is that . . . is her name Arionella? We have been calling her Atali."

She stuck her tongue out at him, sneering boldly.

"Well, I'm sorry, Arionella, but there was no way we could have known," Iloy said. Then, something occurred to him, and he turned to address Jöshi. "Wait, she spoke to you?"

"Not in words. If Jiji and Delamina are your teachers, then you might understand how I am able to communicate with her."

"Oh, yes, I see." But Iloy still looked confused, and added, "However, I don't understand how Delamina didn't connect with her *telempathically* all this time then."

"The answer is right in the word the Enané must've taught you: tel-*empath*-ically. Telepathy, or tel-*empathy* works best when it is in harmony, in proper vibrational tune with the other—simply, when it is empathetic. That is why couples in love, mothers and their babies, and people and their pets seem to communicate without uttering a word at times . . .

"Anyway, it seems to me that, though Ari knows very well the sacrifices charged her, she's still not aware of the powers she has gained from her time on the treeboat. Seeing me earlier today opened her on many levels. In her desperation, she began calling out to me and seeking me with her consciousness at such a magnitude that I am sure the dweller of the mountain has noticed."

"You mean Elésix? That Elésix guy is creepier than anyone I've ever met," Iloy said with a shiver. "And what's up with the people here anyway? They look and feel like they're not really *here*, like the walking dead or something."

Jöshi's stern face softened a bit, but his tone was solemn. "No, Elésix is just one of the many pawns, and they *are* alive, no doubt about that. You've probably been taught amongst the Enané that too much medicine, or rather, medicine used improperly, can become poison. Well, this whole mountain is medicine in itself. But now, the dweller of the mountain is taking advantage of this and can only be considered a parasite, taking the unsuspecting and recreating them in its image.

"That is what is going on here with these people—Ari must have experienced something similar on the treeboat. The pale figures you see roaming about like ghouls came here individually at different times—some ages ago and some more recently—seeking enlightenment, while others were part of a group of conquerors that attacked the Wetobii long ago. In the case of those seeking enlightenment, they found it in some capacity, though this form of unmitigated oneness with nature leaves nothing of the human experience most souls come to this earth to experience."

Iloy was about to ask for clarification, but Jöshi looked into his eyes and continued, "The medicine I speak of is the elixir of the fountain. I've been able to slow its effects on myself, but it is our main sustenance up here, and without salt, humanizing foods, and rituals, the rest of these humans have become extensions of nature."

"And what about the Wetobii, the uncontacted tribe of Wetembii? We came to seek their aid and their advice. Did any survive?"

"That is deep history that will require much time to elucidate. What I'll say is the Wetobii were, in fact, contacted a century or more ago and not only by wayfarers. Sadly, it led to the Wetobii's ruin—on a physical level. Now their resonance—or the "Iansa," as the Reteti call it, or "ghosts," in the common tongue—influences the ruling being here, the Eldeshian. This being was created thousands of years ago through autonomous computation applied to genetics, another curio of the Old World. The Eldeshian was brought here to aid in the efforts of a hostile takeover, and in the wake of the genocide enacted upon the Wetobii, it is now a full-blown parasite that harbors the spite and odium of centuries ago and has taken control of this sacred land. It seems to have adopted the Wetobii's history, thinking of itself as indigenous to this mountain."

Iloy looked utterly perplexed. Even Arionella looked somewhat disturbed.

"And it never discovered you?"

"I've been painstakingly hiding in plain sight, but still I can't believe it has worked for this long.

"I was fortunate to have sensed the Eldeshian's presence before revealing myself when I first arrived. For a while, I remained on the outskirts of its nest, but caution seemed craven when I thought of the opportunity given me to investigate . . . many things." Jöshi paused upon seeing their focused—albeit confused—expressions and said, "Yes, there is much to talk about, and I have many questions about your journeys as well, but now is not the time. As I said, I am sure Ari here has caught the attention of the Eldeshian by *telempathically* seeking me, and furthermore if Delamina and her students are here, you are all on its radar." Jöshi pointed down. "These stone trenches lead to passages underground and through the walls of the mountain. Tell Delamina that you met me, Jöshi Halla. Bring your crew here, and we can plan our next steps together."

"So, if Elésix is not a Wetobii . . ." Iloy's voice trailed off as he remembered the strange exchange in the cavern with the electric pools.

He shuddered, vividly recalling the clumps of hair that had fallen from Delamina's head. "I think Delamina was attacked by this thing you spoke of," he said.

"Why do you think that?" Jöshi asked.

"Elésix took us to caverns inside the mountain. First, we drank from a fountain, all of us except Arionella—we made sure of that. It was a powerful medicine, for sure. However, to communicate with us, he took us to some kind of electric pool. Delamina was the only one to touch it. She was obviously making contact—even I could sense that. The energy in the room was crazy. And not only that; at first, I didn't notice it, but Dela was losing her hair. By the end, she was left unconscious and nearly bald!"

"What? You should have told me sooner," Jöshi said with a tinge of anger to his voice. "Where is she now? And did any of you aggress against Elésix or anyone else?"

"She's resting in the crystal cave Elésix assigned us, and no, not that I can think of. I mean, I know I didn't have the most positive thoughts, and we were stern with Elésix at times. But—"

"Was there any moment of conflict you can think of?"

"No, I guess not."

Jöshi looked pensive and was quiet for a time. Then, with his voice sinking to a low register, he said, "We must get her the elixir from the fountain. If you're up for it, the three of us can retrieve the water from the fountain right now."

Iloy looked at Jöshi in surprise. "Well, of course I'll go with you, if it'll help. I didn't mention that Elésix offered the water from the fountain after the electric pool incident, but we were against it."

At this, Jöshi seemed relieved. "Interesting. That might put your fears to rest that Delamina was attacked, for the water would have helped her, and Elésix—who is controlled by the Eldeshian—would not have offered it, if the intent was to harm her in the first place. However, you must remember that it *is* the Eldeshian's intention to consume whoever comes here in its own way—by sucking them dry of their own will and converting them into a pale ghoul, like the ones you have seen here.

"I understand why you refused the elixir but remember that nature—its places and its medicines—are not owned by anyone. They work for whomever indiscriminately, when partaken of properly. Remember that about this very mountain. You have been trained by Jiji in the arts of the mind, I take it?"

"Yes, I'd say he's tried. Though I think he made a mistake in choosing me as an apprentice. I have difficulty in clearing my mind and I've . . . I've been tainted. I was too overzealous to learn a few years ago, and I got in with the wrong people."

The lines of Jöshi's scalp deepened as he raised a fuzzy brow. "I see. Well, I guarantee we'll all need each other up here, so have faith in your teacher."

Iloy nodded.

"And how about you, Ari? Are you ready?" Jöshi asked, patting her head with his large hand. She raised her head and gave a single nod. It was the first time Iloy had seen Jöshi smile. "Confidence has always been strong, a strong trait in this one, and it seems her time on a treeboat has only bolstered that."

Then, Jöshi closed his eyes for a spell, his nostrils flared, and he raised his chin. Iloy saw a resemblance between grandfather and granddaughter in that moment.

Finally, Jöshi said, "Alright, we can't waste any more time. Let's move."

The three of them climbed higher, until they reached a ledge that jutted out alongside a stone wall. Here they were able to make quick progress.

At one-point, Iloy slipped a little from the dampness the large flakes of snow created on the stone underfoot. "How is it that it keeps snowing here, though the skies are clear?" he asked.

"It comes from the Storm. Did you see the clouds swirling over the highest peaks?"

"Yes, I remember."

"It's freezing up there, and the moisture that is sustaining it is from the elixir of the mountain that we are about to collect. So, this snow is even more of a miracle than regular snow already is. In fact, if you laid Delamina out under it all night, I'd say she'd be better by the morning. But we don't have that kind of time; as I said, I am convinced the Eldeshian took acute notice of Arionella earlier today and I feel uneasy about keeping her here much longer."

They moved forward again. Intrigued about what Jöshi said about the snow, Iloy stuck his tongue out and realized that what he had been associating with the cold sensation of the snow on his skin was more a lingering tingle that reminded him of the water he had drunk from the fountain.

After a few more minutes, and a few precarious ledges, they came to an opening in the rock wall, leading to a cave and tunnels within.

Before entering, Jöshi turned his head to the side and whispered, "Before we go in, I'd like you both to visualize our safe passage and our task unfolding without any hitches. Three minds are better than one." Arionella and Iloy nodded. "Also, when we pass anyone, don't interact with them; just imagine yourself as invisible or somehow undetectable. Understood?"

Arionella nodded, but Iloy shrugged and said, "Not really, but . . . ."

"Try it right now," Jöshi said and pointed at Iloy's shadow on the ground. "Imagine yourself as but a shadow—when you move you are weightless, silent, and transparent."

Iloy did as he was told. He kept his eyes on his shadow, and when he moved his arm, he imagined that it was his shadow making the first move, as if his body were the projection of the dark figure on the ground.

"Perfect," Jöshi said decisively.

"Shouldn't I practice a little more first?"

"You must apply what you have learned over the years. I'm sure Jiji and Delamina would not have brought you this far if they did not feel you were a capable student." With that, Jöshi walked into the cave, with Arionella following close behind him. Iloy hesitated, looked down at his own shadow, and walked forward.

After walking for about five minutes, the figures of the people of the mountain came into view in the dimly lit corridors of the tunnel. They walked slowly, like specters of the night, steadily going about their business. The trio walked past them, and not so much as a glance came from anyone. They turned a corner and kept going. Jöshi led with long paces that Arionella had to jog a little to keep up with.

Some twenty minutes later, they came to a cavern that looked familiar to Iloy. They were at a different end of the chamber where the fountain stood. They moved forward, and on a stone table sat the fossil that Delamina had given to Elésix when they had first met. Jöshi saw Iloy looking at it as they walked past.

"Is that a helix fossil?" he asked.

"Yes, Delamina brought it. It comes from Fossil Lake in Meisha," Iloy replied.

"I thought as much. You won't find something like that up here. I recommend you take it back—it is a valuable tool that will be wasted here." Jöshi shook his head. "Delamina was truly taken by surprise, wasn't she?"

"What do you mean?"

"These fossils have long been used ceremoniously between tribes, as an offering of peace. It is said to have powers of disclosure, revealing any bad intent held by the receiver when offered to them as a gift." Jöshi pursed his lips. "Delamina was expecting to meet the Wetobii, and for all her precautions, the shell of a human being that Elésix is revealed nothing."

"But I'm telling you, her radar was on," Iloy said. "She was very protective over all of us."

Jöshi nodded and hastened forward again. After a few meters, he came to a halt and stuck out his hand at his side. The pale ghouls of the mountain were gathered around the fountain, cupping their hands into the water and drinking from it heartily.

"You two wait here," Jöshi whispered. "I'll go and retrieve the elixir." He took a step forward and paused again. "Would either of you happen to have a flask on your person?" The silence from Arionella and Iloy was self-explanatory. Jöshi moved on without another word.

Iloy and Arionella watched as Jöshi made his way into the group of a dozen or so individuals. They didn't acknowledge his presence except to make space for him beside the basin. To Iloy, it was strangely like watching animals at a watering hole. Jöshi lowered both hands into the water and raised them to his mouth, and then turned away and walked back toward his two confused companions. However, as he got closer, all was made clear—his cheeks were puffed up, filled with liquid.

They moved quietly through the deep shadows of the cavern. Iloy looked up, taking in more of what he had missed the first time he came here. Close to where the ceiling shrouded in darkness might have been, large yellow crystals glowed. They passed many other tunnels as they made their way back to the tunnel from which they emerged.

As they got close to it, someone's profile was visible at the entrance, and it wasn't moving. Iloy's hair stood on end, then his heart raced as he recognized Elésix.

If Jöshi had any reaction, it was to walk a little slower. Arionella frowned and glared at the strange being blocking their path. As they approached him, they saw that Elésix was looking straight at Jöshi with a blank expression.

Iloy quickly stepped forward. "We were just gathering some of the water from the fountain for Delamina. She still isn't well." However, Elésix did not acknowledge Iloy's presence at all. He pressed on. "I realize you offered it to us before, to help her. I thank you for that. We were alarmed and didn't know better."

Still no reply.

Jöshi lifted his hand toward Iloy and shook his head. It dawned on Iloy that he had forgotten what Jöshi had told them before they entered the tunnels—to not interact with anyone. Iloy cringed and ground his teeth at his own carelessness.

Elésix continued to stare at Jöshi, until finally the sound of his breathy speech traveled through the air like a stale odor. "Who ah yooh?"

Jöshi didn't reply. He and Elésix stood silently staring each other down. Then, Jöshi began to walk forward, his head held high and his shoulders squared. He motioned to Arionella and Iloy to follow, and they did, close behind him.

Elésix's eyes followed Jöshi's movements, until Jöshi was at his side, right at the entrance to the tunnel. There was plenty of space on both sides of Elésix to pass by, but Jöshi had stopped.

"Who ah yooh?" Elésix asked again.

Then a sound, like a snarl, came out of Arionella's mouth. She poked at Iloy and pointed at her grandfather.

"What? What is it?" Iloy asked.

Arionella took a step forward, her fists clenched.

Iloy looked more closely at Jöshi and saw that he was straining. His whole body shook, the muscles of his neck protruding with tension, and his bare feet were pressing hard on the ground. Then, Iloy looked at Elésix, his eyeballs fixed in Jöshi's direction, his body stalk still.

All of a sudden, Elésix's face displayed the most complex expression Iloy had yet seen, though it really was a contortion of pain. Elésix's eyes rolled to the back of his head, until only white showed in his sockets. Then, he fell limply to the stone floor.

Jöshi stumbled forward, released from his invisible bonds. He whipped his head back toward Arionella and Iloy with a look of fury upon his face. Arionella turned to look at him, the same as if he had shouted for her. Then, she ran to him and took his outstretched hand. The three of them ran.

They passed through the tunnels again, and though Iloy kept his eyes fixed on Jöshi's feet ahead of him, in his periphery he noticed that this time the pale ghouls were much more reactive to their presence. Many of them looked up and watched the trio pass; others even took steps in the direction of the fleeing trio. The labyrinthian tunnels felt endless. Iloy's chest was tight, and his stomach squirmed. The lights of the crystals embedded in the walls made his skin crawl, instead of comforting him, as they did before.

Forty-five minutes had passed when Iloy was sure that they were in the tunnels longer than they had been on their way to the fountain. He wanted to ask Jöshi for an update, but he knew he wouldn't be able to reply.

After another five minutes, Iloy felt a cool gust of air from ahead. Then, with a sharp turn to the right, they were suddenly outside.

Jöshi had avoided the path along the cliff and the scramble down the boulders, which could be seen in the distance to their far right. Iloy and Arionella knew what to do. They began leading the way back to the crystal cave where Delamina and the others were waiting.

When the cave was in sight, they saw Azura pacing back and forth outside the entrance. She saw Iloy first and planted her hands firmly on her hips.

"You can scold me later," Iloy said, but Azura had already seen the tall, bearded man. Her mouth hung loose and her hands fell from her hips.

Jöshi hurriedly walked past her, and she made toward him, alarmed, but Iloy took hold of her forearm and patted her shoulder with his other hand reassuringly. "His name is Jöshi. He's Atali's—or I should say, *Arionella's*—grandfather," Iloy whispered.

Azura mouthed the words, "What?! Are you serious?"

Iloy nodded in reply.

Arionella heard their exchange and turned toward Azura with a forbidding look that said, *That's right; he's my grandfather and you better watch out!* Then, she flicked her hair and ran after her grandfather.

Azura exchanged a look with Iloy and was glad to see that he was smiling at her antics.

Inside, Kukine lay sleeping on the stone floor as deeply as if he was happy in his own bed—his arms were sprawled over his head and his mouth hung wide open.

Jöshi went straight to Delamina and sank to his hands and knees beside her. Gently, he opened Delamina's mouth with his hand and lowered his head until his mouth met hers.

Azura cocked her head forward and raised her brow, but Iloy whispered in her ear, "Don't worry, he's giving her water from the fountain."

Still, Azura looked very uncomfortable with the whole situation.

Jöshi sat up and raised Delamina into a sitting position. Then, he waited. Arionella stood beside him, watching with undivided attention. Delamina's eyelids fluttered, and she took a deep breath.

"Iloy, wake your friend," Jöshi said. "We must get out of here."

"Right, I'm on it."

"What's going on?" Azura asked.

"We ran into Elésix on our way back from the fountain," Iloy replied. "He and Jöshi had some kind of invisible clash, and finally Jöshi laid him out cold."

"That I did not do," Jöshi said firmly, and he glanced at Arionella, who lowered her eyes to the ground, not daring to look back at him. "What's done is done. However, how it works with the Eldeshian is, there is calculation based on a given input. The input given tonight was one of aggression, so it will be met with a balancing output."

Again, Iloy and Azura exchanged a look—neither of them was smiling this time. Then, they looked at the little girl standing quietly, her tangled red hair draped over her thin shoulders as she leaned forward to touch Delamina's balding scalp with curiosity.

Chapter 23

REVELATIONS

Ari, I love you very much dear, Jöshi spoke to Arionella *telempathically* as they stood by the exit to the cave, while the others gathered Delamina and their things. *And just as you want to defend me, I would give my life to protect you.*

However, in this situation, none of us know the extent of the Eldeshian's power and what triggers it, so therefore, I need you to control your impulses . . . and that of the treeboat's as well.

At this, Arionella glanced up at him with surprise.

Yes, it is imperative that you be aware of this. I sensed it when you attacked Elésix, the remediative will of the Reteti and their treeboats is acting through you now.

What you did to Elésix could very well be done to you, or to any of us, if we are not careful. Understood?

Arionella nodded, but clenched her fists and let out a quiet growl as if she was frustrated at the leash of restraint she was agreeing upon.

"Alright, we're ready," said Azura walking up behind them with her travel-pack on her back and Delamina's satchel hung over her chest. Kukine came up behind her with Delamina herself on his back, and Iloy exited last, with the remaining gear.

Jöshi turned toward them all, his thinning beard had caught a few crystals of the perpetual snowfall of Wetembii, and his bald scalp revealed fresh grooves of stress as he spoke.

"Now that we are all together, I would like to tell you all something. My name is Jöshi Halla, I am acquainted with Delamina here, and I—"

"You are a legend," said Kukine. "I've only heard stories about you and your wife, Sir. It's an honor to meet you." He scanned Jöshi from head to foot, eyes twinkling with admiration, as if he was trying to reconcile his mental image of the legend with what stood before him.

"Well, thank you, young man. And what is your name?"

"I am Kukine of the Enané. Is it true that you two defeated an army of mercenaries all by yourselves?"

"Cookie, please, control yourself." Azura snapped. "Now isn't the time."

Jöshi just laughed. "That isn't quite correct, son. I will tell you the real story some other time." Jöshi scratched his scalp. "I haven't laughed in six months, so my first here and now is quite unexpected, especially under these circumstances." Then he turned to Azura with a warm smile. "And you, my dear, what is your name?"

"I am Azura of the Enané."

"Pleased to meet you," Jöshi said and bowed his head slightly in acknowledgement of them both and then he continued. "Now, back to business, we don't have much time. Delamina contacted me about three years ago shortly after Iloy told her about Revalo Otrebor's intentions. And so, I am aware of why you are here, and I have the answer you are seeking . . . we lost touch since then and I wish I could've saved you all a trip here . . . but . . . ," Jöshi sighed. "The answer is yes." When he said this, everyone—except Arionella who was busy studying the landscape suspiciously outside—stopped dead in place. "I'm sorry to say, it is possible to take control of the archetypes that influence our world."

"But—" a voice rose in a whisper "—the Eldeshian said it was not possible . . . he said he would help stop Revalo—" the voice touched everyone's ears with great clarity in the silence of the cave. It was Delamina. "I'm sorry to say that *It*, not he, lied to you, my dear."

"How do you know this?"

"Revalo Otrebor was here—"

"Oh gawd," Iloy gasped as something dawned upon him. "When I saw him two nights ago, I noticed he had lost his hair at the center of his head, and I thought—only three years couldn't have changed him that much. But now, seeing what happened to Delamina . . . if he used the electric pools then—"

Jöshi picked up where Iloy left off, "Though I do not know exactly what transpired between him and the Eldeshian, he exited through the Spring Passages from where he entered—and that does not happen, ever. I can only assume they reached some kind of agreement."

Delamina weakly opened her eyes wider and looked into Jöshi's, "But how can you be sure it can be done?"

"Because it has been done before, many times."

"What do you mean?"

"I realized this in meditation here, after I got off Captain Rainer Yansa's Oaql boat about six months ago." Jöshi looked down at his granddaughter through eyes that now seemed baggy with sadness. "You sensed that your grandmother Maya has become one with the treeboat, yes?"

To everyone's surprise, Arionella nodded serenely, and the memory of her desperately crying out to the Oaql boat the night they rescued her, stuck them with new insight and cringe-inducing empathy.

Jöshi continued, "Captain Rainer Yansa performed the Ritual of Merger for Maya when we were on the treeboat, and though that doesn't guarantee anything, Maya found a way to maintain her consciousness through the treeboat. It was risky because the Oaql tree is still very much sentient itself, but I believe she collected Arionella and brought her here to me.

"Before this, Maya and I had been traveling alone for about a year and a half, gathering information from within the City Gardens and city-forts. We visited hybrid tribes as well as the camps of Seekers and mercenaries who have joined the Cult of Knoa. It became clear that Revalo has collected many fossils of power—their amplifying effects strengthening his psychic abilities—and now his sights are set on gathering the twelve treeboats of the twelve Reteti Islands. For the longest time, I could not understand how they fit into his plan."

Iloy clenched his jaw, a grim expression upon his face and his breathing heavy, as word after word, Jöshi confirmed his worst fears. Azura rested her hand on his shoulder and squeezed it to offer him some comfort.

Jöshi continued, "It was after I climbed out of a pit of sorrow upon losing Maya that all the pieces of information in my mind fit began to fit together. By seeing Captain Rainer Yansa enact the ritual on the Oaql boat for Maya and learning the implications from him, I realized that Revalo knows of this practice himself.

"Though the Reteti have enacted this ritual for eons, they never conceived of it the way Revalo Otrebor has come to do so. I believe that he is aiming to gather all the treeboats to perform the ritual with *all* of them—he is on the path to immortalizing his consciousness and no one I know of on this Earth has the capacity to contend with that sort of power."

Kukine cut in, turning toward Iloy, "Do you remember Revalo saying any of this when you were with him, Iloy?"

"No, he never spoke of the *how*—he only spoke of *what* he wanted to do. He would tell us that he wanted to rule humanity—'not in fool-way by blaster and stick'—but by possessing the mind of the species. We were promised everything we wanted in his Kingdom of Knoa. Anyway, though I've been on a treeboat, I never knew of any kind of merging ritual." Iloy looked at Jöshi and asked, "What does the ritual entail?"

"That's what troubles me still," Jöshi replied, looking troubled. "I can't imagine Revalo wants to commit suicide." He gazed off into the glowing crystal cave, lost in his thoughts for a few moments. "Though each tree of the Reteti bears its own kind of fruit, one thing they all share is that they have hollow tubes that retract the fruit sometime after they have ripened—a clever evolutionary technique to reabsorb nutrients on an isolated, moving vessel.

"Since ancient times, the ritual has always entailed cremating the corpse of a treeboat captain and injecting a solution formed with the ashes into fruits of the tree that are in the process of being retracted."

Azura looked confused. "But—" she interjected "—what do the ashes of the material body of a person have to do with their consciousness? We, in the Enané tradition, have always understood that the body only houses our mind temporarily—the brain being a kind of radio receiver for consciousness."

"Yes, I agree; however, there is more to it than that. During our studies in Lindum at the monastery, Maya and I studied ancient holo-texts that confirmed that the brain is an organ like the liver, which—instead of bile—secretes thoughts. It is also a kind of antenna for consciousness, but this quality is not exclusive to the brain; it is our whole body that is the antenna and the medium. Practices for strengthening and keeping the body healthy fine-tune our ability to stream consciousness. In short, we are more aware when we are fit and healthy.

"Now, what I think is significant about the Reteti's Ritual of Merger is their understanding of what they call *Iansa*; it is somewhat related to the word 'ghost' in the common tongue, but actually *Iansa* is better translated to 'residues of consciousness.' The particles that come together to house our mind and awareness are imbued with *Iansa*. So, the ritual is a way to fortify the fusion of human and tree, or *Pashaduma*, as they call the treeboats.

"However, I have reflected about this process, and, in my limited understanding, I have concluded that the ritual does not absolutely have to be performed for the connection between human and *Pashaduma* to be complete. It has more to do with the residues I mentioned, or rather, the resonance of consciousness. I mean, even Ari is so thoroughly connected to the treeboat she was on, I wonder how deep the coupling between them actually goes."

"Still, though there might be a less invasive way, I wouldn't put the extreme way past him either," Iloy said. "He is *insane*, Jöshi—we can't count anything out."

"I understand. But again, I doubt Revalo has so much faith in this ritual that he is willing to end his physical life to perform it. Wisdom across the ages tells us that physical life is something rare in this universe. He must have found another way. Furthermore, by gathering artifacts of power over the course of decades, I surmise that once he gets his plan into motion, he will be able to augment his own power and overwhelm any *Iansa* that inhabit the treeboats—like Maya's or of the Reteti captains of old—or any of us here on the physical plane that stand in his way." Jöshi then became silent and turned back to the mouth of the cave to inspect the landscape.

Meanwhile, Iloy had begun to pace back and forth, shaking his head and gritting his teeth.

"What is it, Iloy?" Azura asked him impatiently.

He paused for a moment and then replied, "It's just that this only gets worse when one thinks it all the way through. The tribes made the mistake of allowing Revalo to create the Cult of Knoa over the years. Hundreds, if not thousands of followers now, already call him master and do his bidding without asking any questions. I know him. I know how this maniac wants to control us. If Jöshi's hunch turns out to be true, once he has merged with the treeboats, he will have his disciples—whom he has already trained—to ritualistically use the fruit of the treeboats as a sacrament for a new religion. He has already been doing experimental versions of this since before I joined them.

"The first damn thing they did after I joined them was to feed me the putrid fruit of that rotting motorized treeboat. Those who already follow him will be more than willing to fall in line, and others—like the Seekers from the cityforts that are on a miserable quest to find greater meaning—will be tempted by promises of healing and enlightenment, only to have Revalo's consciousness—or *Iansa*, or whatever you want to call it—spread like a wildfire through humanity. Can't you see it?" Iloy looked around at the others fiercely.

Bleak silence filled the cave.

Iloy stretched his fingers into his hair, looking more disquieted with each passing second. He was speaking more to himself now, "Dogmatic parents will force sacramental poison down their children's throats—making them adhere to the B.S. Way of Knoa or I should say Way of Otrebor—temples will be erected, organizations and denominations will form, and those who resist, will be crusaded against! It's just another version of what they did to me—what they do to citizens in the name of normalization in cityforts—."

"My boy—," Jöshi interjected, his voice low and steady. "Your passion comes from a good place. Now, you must remember to catch your breath, breathe deeply, for our night has just begun and we will need that passion when confronting the Eldeshian."

Iloy came back to himself, realizing that in a spell of anxiety, he'd been unconsciously pacing back and forth, and digging his fingertips into his temples.

Jöshi walked over to him and placed both of his large, weathered hands on Iloy's shoulders. He said, "Though I ask you to be calm, I do not take your vision of a plundered future lightly. I understand your fears— we must do everything we can to stop Revalo. Otherwise, our world will be ruled by a demigod that poses as the divine, demanding ill worship from the well-meaning and causing atrocity by way of doctrinaires. We will not let this happen in our fragile and beautiful world."

———•———

"There's the first sign," Jöshi said after a few minutes. He had instructed everyone to wait in silence. "I can see a whole troop of the sallow humans in the distance—the Eldeshian is barring the Spring Passages with his subjects. The rest are probably coming for us. Follow me."

Jöshi led the way back into the cave, past the stone room, and into a long tunnel lined with crystals that they had not yet traversed. Jöshi moved quickly holding Arionella's hand, while the others followed close in line. The light of the crystals embedded in the walls was enough to see by.

After about twenty minutes, Jöshi paused and said, "It should be here somewhere."

"What're you looking for?" Kukine asked.

"There's a secret passage, blocked by a boulder."

Jöshi ran his hand along a dark wall of the tunnel, where there were no glowing crystals. A minute passed—Azura activated a glowtern. It wasn't the right spot. So, they advanced further until they came to another darkened wall. Still nothing.

After about ten minutes of stopping and going, Arionella got very anxious. While her grandfather was inspecting another rocky wall, she pulled at his toga, ran a few yards back in the direction they had come from, and stood still with her head craned as if she was listening for something. Then, she ran further into the tunnel where more glowing crystals were embedded along a bend in the tunnel.

"I know Ari, I feel them too," Jöshi muttered as he now ran both hands along a particularly bulbous protrusion of dark caramel colored stone.

"Can we help in any way?" Azura asked. "What should we be looking for?"

"I have not entered the secret passage from this direction. I was on the other end when I found the exit to this primary tunnel. I could see the light of the crystals shining here through cracks on the other side where it is much darker, so I pushed the boulder blocking the opening myself, enough to make the gaps larger to see where it led. I was much stronger a few months ago, by the way; we'll all need to tug at it this time. I left it at that and returned to exploring of the tunnels of Wetembii, making a map in my mind for an emergency like this, but it's harder than I thought to pinpoint the intersection."

"Keh!" Arionella called out.

Everyone turned to look in her direction; she was pointing down in the direction they had not gone yet.

"You all would be better off putting your things down and setting Delamina here. I'm afraid we'll have to have our second scuffle tonight.

Luckily, these poor things aren't too strong, but we'll be overwhelmed in numbers if we don't act quickly."

Kukine laid Delamina against the smoothest portion of wall and floor he could find. Then he stood, stretched, and cracked his knuckles—though he wasn't one for violence, he was a plucky brawler when he was backed into a corner. Iloy and Azura set their packs down. Azura took a hair tie from around her wrist and tied up her hair, while Iloy extracted the blaster he had been carrying.

"That won't work well, son," Jöshi said. "Much like drugged berserkers, these people are moved by the will of the Eldeshian and will keep fighting while their blood still circulates—also, the smell of burning flesh in these tunnels would be terribly unpleasant."

"Then, how are we going to stop them?" Iloy retorted.

"We'll have to overpower them with our minds. The Eldeshian's mind is spread thin across the population of his subjects here—though we should not underestimate It in anyway—I think we can deactivate many of our pursuers."

Iloy recalled how, at Revalo's camp, there would be "pit-fights" where two people in a trench would be pitted against one another, using their minds to see who could render the other unconscious. Iloy was never able to succeed in knocking out his opponents—most times, he would return to consciousness flat in the mud, the sound of hooting and laughter disorienting and cruel.

"I'm out of practice. I don't think I can help in that way," he said.

"Iloy." It was Delamina who spoke "For the past three years, we've been training you to help things grow, to heal yourself and others—"

"That's different, Dela."

"At first glance maybe, but the powers of the mind are two sides of the same coin. You've been strengthening your willpower all along. Close your eyes."

"Now?"

"Yes. I want you to picture your sapling tree, the *shiwawako*. All the energy you spent sitting by it and imagining it grow, blessing it, giving it your life force—all this was an active process of transmitting. Now, you've sensed it could go in the other direction, yes?"

Iloy took a deep breath in affirmation.

"Well, you can retract life force too. Humans do this all too often unconsciously—we often dwell in negativity—a way of thinking that has repeatedly polluted the Earth. This necromancy concentrated and done with intention is devastating, but here, you must bring yourself to do what needs to be done."

The sound of shuffling from farther down the tunnel could be heard now. In response to this, Iloy watched as Azura, Kukine, Jōshi, and even Arionella lined up next to each other with their hands clasped.

The first shadows cast by the dim light of the crystals appeared around the bend and Iloy felt his skin erupt into goose pimples. Then, three pale beings appeared about twenty yards away, two of which were naked, revealing more blue veins all over their bodies that could be seen through their skin. More than ever, they seemed spiritless and heavy, moving forward by no will of their own. Their expressions vacant and their goal myopic. When they saw their targets, they raised their arms hungrily and immediately Iloy felt a tug in his gut—something he had felt before in Revalo's trenches.

Just as quickly, the pull vanished as the three fell limply to the ground. Iloy knew that his companions had discharged their first attack. Iloy ran forward and took Kukine's hand. It was now Iloy at the left end of the line, Kukine beside him, then Azura, Arionella, and Jōshi at the other end, while Delamina was propped up against the stone wall behind them.

Iloy closed his eyes and telepathically searched for the energy signature of the next set of sallow ghouls approaching. When he finally locked-on, he sensed what he had felt in the chamber with the electric pools where Delamina and Elésix had communicated. Just like before, he felt the presence of something akin to a human, but it had been somehow different—cold, technological, and distant.

Now, six figures appeared around the bend, charging forward with ghoulish movements, the pull in Iloy's gut stronger this time, making him feel nauseated. Feeling the tendrils of energy—like puppet strings moving them—Iloy impressed his energy back upon them, trying to push them away. He gasped in surprise when instead of any headway against them, he felt Kukine squeeze his hand, very hard. He glanced at Kukine, who continued to look straight ahead.

Wondering what he was trying to convey, Iloy tried tuning into the energy of his comrades—a great ball of heat and vitality—and realized that he had been approaching the battle incorrectly. He could feel the rest of his group *pull* their wills in conjunction toward themselves, like a boat rowing team in the power phase of a stroke. Delamina's words about his appointed sapling in Meisha came to mind, *All the energy you spent sitting by it and imagining it grow, blessing it, giving it your life force—all this was an active process of transmitting. Now, you've sensed it could go in the other direction, yes?* As the others completed their inward stroke, the six figures fell. However, this bunch of aggressors had made it some ten yards farther than the last bunch did.

It can go in the other direction, the other direction—Iloy thought to himself as the next onslaught of attackers approached. This time, when ten of them appeared—ignoring a strong spell of dizziness—he locked onto to the energetic tendrils moving them, but instead of pushing, he pulled the force away from them toward the gyre of energy his comrades were creating. In this moment, he finally understood what Delamina had meant by necromancy—this was an act of *taking* unsparingly, of being an agent of death. It was parasitic and he didn't like it at all.

The onslaught had suddenly ended, and without a word, Jöshi turned back toward the walls, followed by Arionella, continuing his search for the secret passage.

Iloy hadn't moved. He was still holding Kukine's hand as he stood rapt in the waves of fresh—albeit stolen—energy coursing through his body. He felt like he had awoken from a deep sleep, fully charged and refreshed, much like he had felt when he drank the water from the fountain.

"Ah! This is it!" Jöshi exclaimed after a minute.

"Iloy. Kukine. Let's go," Azura said. They finally broke formation.

Iloy turned to see that even Delamina looked somewhat revitalized, sitting more erect, her usual vigilant expression returning to her face. This was a great relief, but he still felt disquieted at the sight of her round skull clinging to a few patches of straggly silver hairs.

"That recharge should help us move this boulder with more ease now," Jöshi said. He dug his fingers into a crevice that, when illuminated by Azura's glowtern, revealed space and depth beyond it. They all found a spot to pry in their fingers and, with Delamina cheering them on, they pulled with all their might.

Soon, the passage was wide enough for them all to squeeze through. On the other side, Kukine lifted Delamina onto his back again, while the others gathered the backpacks. Even on its dimmest setting, the glowtern seemed bright here. Though there was some light seeping through cracks in the stone walls and ceiling, without any mining, the glowing crystals were mostly covered.

Jöshi moved more quickly now. The tunnels were wide enough for three people to walk beside each other, though the low ceilings had the adults hunching over often, especially making it difficult for Kukine who otherwise barely noticed Delamina's weight. As they moved forward, Jöshi explained that there was a spring within the mountain that led out to another part of Wetembii, and maybe even the sea, but about that he wasn't sure. There was what was left of an ancient mooring in a cavern where the water passed through. All that remained there were a few rafts, one of which Jöshi had reconditioned as best as he could with what tools he had brought in his pack—which they now recovered from a crawl space he had hidden it in—and ancient Wetobii artifacts, like stone and cord hammers and chert knives that were still surprisingly sharp.

There came a point in the snaking tunnels where the brown-caramel stone in the distance had a sheen that, as they got closer, shined more brightly until the glowtern was drowned out completely.

"The inner sanctum of Wetembii," Jöshi said, coming to a stop at the mouth of an opening that led to a vast cavern with cathedral ceilings reaching to unknown heights. When the others gathered around, and when their squinted eyes adjusted to the radiance, they saw what was generating the white light—light that gleamed like it was refracting and reflecting off a million mirrors, which in a sense it was, for at the center stood a delicate and yet towering monument made of crystals.

"What is that?" Iloy asked in awe, marveling at the perfect angles of the edges of the wide base—some three yards across—and the exceedingly fine tapering of the pyramidal body to an assumed, albeit unobservable, apex.

"The Obelisk of Wetobii," Jöshi replied. "This was where the Wetobii tribe once prayed and communed with the spirits of the Earth and the stars."

Though the structure was mostly transparent quartz, there were other smoky hues in places and touches of light blue that seemed to be in swirling motion at times. The individual crystals of varying sizes were somehow delicately fitted together like ideally cut puzzle pieces, and yet much of the outer surfaces were left unpolished and jagged, creating an attractive raw-order juxtaposition.

"It's so strange," Azura said breaking the silence. "There is something about it that makes a part of me want to take a hammer and break it all down, and yet another part of me feels repulsed by that very thought and wants to preserve it forever."

Jöshi let out a breathy chuckle. "Look over there," he said and pointed to a spot in the cavern along the wall to the left. There was a pile of stone and cord sledgehammers, looking primitive and unlit, and though they were about seven yards away from the obelisk, they seemed too close—like rotting limbs of bone and flesh in a bed of fresh flowers. "At one point, I was deciding whether to destroy it or not."

Taken aback, everyone turned to look at him.

"But why?" Kukine asked, as if Jöshi had betrayed him somehow.

"What Azura expressed, summarizes the state of this sacred space. It's all in conflict, and I wondered if the Eldeshian could use this pyramid in some dangerous manner. However, it doesn't seem like it's interested in—or isn't capable of tuning into—the subtle human frequencies this tool was designed for. I spent months meditating here before I could tap into its augury properties. This is where I learned much of what I told you about Revalo and what I told Iloy about the past history of this mountain. Some things came as insight and others I was able to envision; for example, I saw the way the Wetobii met their end—at the hand of Old World opportunists who wanted to bottle the waters of this mountain in adamantine so they could sell it—and how the Eldeshian slowly became imbued with foul *Iansa* in the wake of the genocide, betraying its Old World masters. Now, It is the master, a parasitic spider with many innocents in its web, the sallow humans that pursue us now.

"And so, I reasoned with myself—maybe there was a way to dissemble the Eldeshian instead of this monument. Maybe that would start to clear things up; maybe this could be a place of communion with the benevolent mysteries of the Earth and sky again.

"Anyway, on the other side of this chamber is the mooring and the spring. Time has run out to consider whether I can do something about the Eldeshian and finally give peace to its poor half-dead slaves. We should move forward; there are many connections to these inner chambers, and I don't wish for us to face another onslaught of attackers."

Everyone exchanged apprehensive glances, but they silently moved forward. Halfway through the chamber Iloy found he could not take his eyes off the obelisk. The dark but glistening caramel-brown stone of the cavern he was treading upon seemed liquidy somehow. The others kept walking, but he stood transfixed. In his periphery, he began to see something—he gasped and broke his eyes away from the obelisk for a moment. When he saw nothing around him, his gaze was magnetized to the light source again like a moth to a flame. In an instant, the cavern seemed to expand tenfold, an ocean of ink with a lighthouse at the center beckoning to him, warning him of a storm. Again, images rose in his periphery, but this time, he didn't look away from the beacon at the center. As clear as day, a place he had not seen in seven years came into focus—the cityfort Citadelia, his birthplace.

White buildings, most doubling as huge projection screens for erratic and colorful advertisements, were woven together on the ground by the dark moving sidewalks, all within the confines of curved adamantine walls creating a circle around the city. It had been so long, Iloy didn't know what to think of it all. Then, he heard voices. Briefly, it was Jöshi's voice saying, "The fossil—it must be in his pack—it's reacting to the obelisk!"

Then, a voice, whose very tone made him well up with emotion, was saying, "I told you, Chent! He's out there chasing delusions. He's going to become like those non-citizen vagrants. What are we going to do? What are we going to tell people?"

His mother Lina came into focus; she was holding her head in her thin hands. She was wearing the same black and white pant–suit combination she'd been wearing when he'd left all those years ago. Then, she stood and tied back her fizzy black hair into a bun the same way she always had, and the electric kettle glowed blue as it had every morning, filling itself with water from one of the many little white pipes sticking out of the adamantine walls of the kitchen.

"We did everything we could—every damn step of the normalization process—since he was young, but it is his life now." It was his father who replied in a cold voice without looking up from a glowing holo-tablet, his dark face illuminated in blue light, spotlighting the shadows where his facial hair was again defied in its attempts to grow.

"But I'm sure he stopped taking his medication long ago."

Iloy then noticed another presence there; it was his cousin Ica, the same thirteen-year-old he last saw years ago—brown hair buzzed short, smooth dark skin, a perpetual frown and observant brown eyes. For her, to be at his parent's apartment was unexpected because she lived in the tenements on the outer perimeter of the cityfort with her mom and her uncle—who were Iloy's father's half-siblings. Iloy's father, Chent, only rarely visited them to give them Citadelian credits to get by.

"Um wait," Ica spoke up with some difficulty, which was also strange because she was usually discourteous and combative "—maybe you should read what Iloy wrote . . . ."

"Ica, please," Chent cut her off sharply. "We've dealt with a lot of this since he was young—seeing things, hearing things." His voice trailed off into angry mumbling at the sound of Lina's gasp, which called for privacy of her son's matters. Frustrated, Ica slammed the stack of journals wrapped in adamantine down on the white coffee table and stomped off to the exit door.

Iloy watched from a growing distance as his mother gathered his journals into the waste incinerator chute. He felt a wave of regret, anger, and longing all at once—a longing to prove himself. Then, the scenes

Iloy was seeing began to flip by rapidly: he saw Ica sitting on a fountain in the central plaza drinking a tall kool-shake, glaring at someone across a mob of people. Iloy tried following her gaze and he saw someone, or something, that looked very familiar. This made his stomach lurch. It had gangly arms, a round head, a hairless body, and a vacant but inspecting expression. The scene cut out with Ica falling into the fountain and people helping to fish her out.

Now, it was dark along the perimeter of Citadelia, and Ica was running in the shadows, until she was beyond the walls, alone in the outlands.

"Iloy, we have to move forward now; they're coming. C'mon!" He blinked and for a moment he thought he saw clouds of golden dust all around the cavern. His cheek was sore—Azura came into focus, her hand poised to land another smack.

"Wait, wait! I'm good. I'm good," Iloy stammered raising his hands defensively.

Azura pushed away his hands and took hold of his jaw in her hand, inspecting his pupils, and then when she was content, she said, "It was the fossil in your bag, Jöshi said it connected you to the obelisk—we took it out. He has it now."

"I saw Citadelia . . . and you know what?"

"Yes, I think I know what you're going to tell me. This whole cavern became a theater of images projected along the stone. We were able to see some of what you were seeing."

"Then you saw the—?"

"The sallow humans in Citadelia? Yes, we did."

"I have to go back. I have to help my family—we have to help them all."

"We'll talk about that if we get out of this alive. C'mon!"

Azura pulled Iloy up onto his feet and dragged him toward the exit that led to the mooring. The sound of rushing water became apparent. Then, he saw the rest of his companions standing beside a raft—precarious and smaller than he was expecting—near the edge of a cleft, some seven yards wide in the bedrock, with water swiftly flowing into a shadowy archway. They had formed a line holding hands again and this time Delamina stood with them, resolutely facing a blitz of more pale bodies, descending a steep stone ramp than he could count.

A powerful wave of nausea overtook him. Already reeling from the experience within the cavern, he found his legs could no longer hold his weight. He collapsed, bringing Azura down with him.

"Gawdamit, Iloy!" she shouted, rising as quickly as she could, pulling at his limp body.

"Stand with the others!" shouted Jöshi, as he broke rank and ran over to where Iloy lay on the hard bedrock. Kneeling, he lifted him onto his shoulders and squatted himself up, turning red in the face.

The first line of a dozen sallow humans fell twenty yards away but a dozen more staggered over the bodies.

"They're relentless!" Kukine cried as Jöshi carried Iloy to the raft set at the bank of the river.

"The vile creature has invoked the preserved bodies of the Wetobii and its old masters!" Jöshi replied. After hauling Iloy onto the raft, he called for Arionella.

The second line of sallow humans fell twenty yards away, while two dozen more appeared at the mouth of cavernous tunnels that stood at the top of the stone ramp.

"Arionella!"

Arionella heard the second, more ferocious, call of her grandfather. She let go of Delamina's hand and ran over to him.

"Listen, my dear," Jöshi spoke to Arionella aloud while placing his hands on her cheeks. "Somehow, you must find your father in *Atlantia* and communicate to him all that you've seen and understood about the Eldeshian here."

Arionella gripped his wrists, her mouth falling open.

"Yes, he is alive, and he has been working on tech in the cityforts. He renounced the ways your grandmother and I have followed, but he has a good heart.

"I wish I could've had more time to explain things to you, but now, time has run out. I hope this raft will keep for you and Iloy. Though I don't know where it'll take you—you saw it in the Obelisk's cavern too—Navis is here with someone from the Enané, somewhere on this island. You must find them and escape."

Arionella wildly shook her head in protest, batting Jöshi's arms as he reached around her waist and put her aboard the raft with Iloy. Then, she wrapped her arms around her grandfather's neck, sobbing as he pushed the raft closer and closer to the water, until it only needed a single push more. "I love you, my child," was the last thing he said before unbinding himself from her embrace, throwing her onto Iloy.

With a final push, he released the raft to the will of the mountain's gushing spring.

Chapter 24

EPILOGUE

Niniola set the Maradona at full speed across the ocean with Captain Abdenbi Marsai at her side. During the night, Danuba had called Niniola on the transceiver he had given her at Halla Manor. She was in the heart of the Maradona when she received the call, sitting beside the Oaql seed she and Taola had planted, except that it was now a leafy sapling with a cushion of white mycelium growing all along the floor and the ceiling of the room. Apparently, Taola had somehow found the Oaql boat around the choppy waters of Wetembii, and it and Arionella were in danger.

Meanwhile, within the forested lands of the Enané, Taola and Ama-Ronoki were being nursed back to health after the rigors of the *hoa suna* ceremony. Under the light of flickering candles, Nadine and Donya washed Taola and Ama's heads in buckets of cold and aromatic floral water to bring down their fevers.

Taola had fallen into unconsciousness but kept repeating the name "Iloy" repeatedly, while Navis knelt at her side, holding her hand tightly.

Danuba had run off to prepare the *Rusty Otter* for the longest trip it would yet take under his command.

Lemay, Myli, and Tumi were asleep in hammocks near their new Enané friends in the Accomodor, still unaware of all that was happening.

One other person became aware of the goings-on, unbeknownst to anyone else. She had been standing in the dark outside Sun, leaning on a crutch and listening intently to the interactions that had gone on between Taola, Ama, and the others. Now, as things had settled down, she slowly and quietly moved away from the ceremonial yurt. When she judged herself far enough away, she broke into a painful run down a muddy path toward a small yurt. It was dark inside, but she lit a candle— with difficulty, because her hands were shaking with excitement. She saw that Mendelson and Fio lay sleeping on a mattress in a shadowy part of the yurt.

"Mother, mother, wake up!" the girl hissed as she slumped down onto her mother's bed.

"Wha . . . what is it, Eza?" asked the startled woman.

"You won't believe what I just heard at Sun!"

"What did you hear?" the woman suddenly asked with vigor, as if she had just been given a shot of caffeine.

"The woman Taola, from the Haelin Island, is the captain of a tree-boat!" Eza could barely get the words out in her frenzy.

"Agh, what nonsense! Let me sleep, girl," the woman huffed and turned away, but her eyes darted around the yurt, spurred by a mind suddenly busy in calculation.

"No, no! You don't understand, Ma!" Eza seemed beside herself with impatience. "I heard Ama-Ronoki say to Taola, 'You have prepared for years as a Captain of a treeboat.' And Ma . . . Taola keeps calling 'Iloy,' 'Iloy,' 'Iloy,' over and over again!" Eza said this last bit in a mocking tone that choked off into a strange emotional cracking of her voice. She coughed, swallowed, cleared her throat, and continued. "Do you know what this means? She might be the one father captured a few years ago— the one Iloy ran away with! If we tell father and get everything sorted for him, we could go back home. He'd accept us with open arms!"

"Quiet for a second. I'm thinking," Eza's mother said as she chewed at her fingernails and stared darkly across the yurt.

"C'mon, Ma!" Eza pulled at her mother's sleeping gown. "You want to live this way, at the bottom of the heap here?"

"You calm down and say nothing to anyone, including your sister."

Eza scoffed. "Why should I tell her anything?"

"Alright then. We have to be smart about this."

"I'll get the transceiver," Eza said, positioning herself to stand.

"No, you fool! Not yet," her mother said and yanked her back down. "We have to make sure things are laid out for Revalo on a silver platter before we call him."

"But things *are* on a silver platter now! Danuba has gone running to his rust-bucket plane, their Reteti friend is gone to the Forest Lakes, and Ama-Ronoki and the Taola are incapacitated. I tell you, Ma, now is the time to act!" Eza hissed these words with her eyes bulging out of her head and her beautiful sleek black hair falling over her face in disarray.

"Fine, go get it," came the command in a cold voice from her mother.

Eza smiled thirstily and stood, taking the candle with her as she limped over to a trunk that sat at the end of another bed and began shuffling impatiently through it.

A few yards away in the dark of the cabin, Fio lay wide awake with her heart pounding in her chest. Her pillow was wet with tears, her right cheek was still red and sore from the merciless slap Eza had given her earlier that day.

—End of Book One: *The Oaql Seed*—

Prelude

—Ica's Tale—

Chapter 2

THE GANGLIES

There, in the crowds of people, I figured that the Ganglies would be less likely to notice me noticing them. I was proved wrong. It was June fifteenth, I was observing one of the Ganglies from a good distance, in the middle of the plaza circle. As I mentioned before, these Ganglies were paler than everyone else and this one was a tall one too, so I never lost sight of him. On this day though, the only thing I did different (and I distinctly remember it) was that instead of just thinking that he looked stupid, I said it.

Not out loud, no. He probably wouldn't have heard me amidst the mob anyway. I said it in my mind. I know that sounds crazy, and Mainard would have had the best time of his life roasting me with his "witty" insults if I had told him this then but let me explain.

I remember I was concentrating on the Gangly, but I was relaxed at the same time, sitting on the border of the multi-colored lighted fountain, sipping on a pink kool-shake (gawd I miss those) while watching this creepy, hairless, and vacant looking thing amble through the crowd. He looked so stupid that I just said it in my mind, you look so stupid, right at him. Right then, he moved like I had never seen any Gangly move. He whipped his head around in an instant and his wide, circular blue eyes looked right at me, and I felt something equivalent to an electric shock in my brain. Before I knew it, I fell backwards, and water engulfed me.

Two people pulled me out of the fountain, I was coughing and sputtering like crazy (it was deep, and as many of you know, I can't swim). When I caught my breath and my eyes cleared, I looked around for the Gangly, but he was gone. For a while after that I didn't see any Ganglies, in Central or anywhere around the perimeters, and that's why Shilo, Terence, and I went hunting for them.

Prelude

— Book Two of The Treeboat Series —

Chapter 1

THE PERFUMED SCORPION

7 years before the events of the Oaql Seed

Some leaped for joy when the treeboat came into sight, others just closed their eyes in gratitude and raised their hands in prayer. Much of the crowd had stepped right into the shallow waters along the shore of the murky River Superior, in a hidden location a few kilometers away from the ramparts of the cityfort Citadelia.

"He's come!" shouted a woman at the sight of a tall man who stepped into view at the bow of the treeboat donned in white. He was smiling and had his arms outstretched in a gesture of welcome. Then as the boat pulled up to the shore, he turned his palms down and waved them in a downward motion, gesturing for silence. The throng grew still and quiet.

"Today . . ." the man said with great preeminence. "I shall take four Seekers with me on a journey of awakening!" Murmurs of excitement rose from the crowd and the man in white continued over the noise, "Those seekers who are pure of heart may board this Perennial Ark of Knoa."

At this the crowd went wild. People raised their hands, held up offerings, men leapt where they stood, and women held up their children toward the boat . . .

Coming Soon from the Treeboat World

———•———

Ica's Tale

Book Two of the Treeboat Series

Biyan the Rainbringer

Acknowledgements

I'm blessed with a wife who has taught me to trust in love. She radiates an unshakable knowing of what a gift it is to be alive. Her effervescence when reading drafts of my Treeboat stories helped me rise out of murky pools of doubt, revitalizing my will to return to the manuscript and fill yet another blank page.

Another source of undying support has come in the form of my brother who has fanned my flames whenever he's noticed them dimming and has repeatedly provided editorial insights on a par with what professionals have offered this novel.

Along with these two pillars of support, my parents have always seen my potential, and with their blessings, I've learned how to believe in myself.

Finally, I give my deepest gratitude to the plant masters of the Amazonian Rainforest and the indigenous wisdom keepers, who so graciously provide knowledge and healing to those that seek it.

About the Author

Z.A. Ispharazi's writings spring from a heart deeply moved by indigenous wisdom while doing rogue anthropology in South America. Inspired by the mystique of the Amazon Rainforest, where late-night lore by candlelight is still common, the Treeboat world began to unfold from the pages of his journals. Ispharazi currently lives in New York with his wife, where he finds great joy in tending to his garden, trail running, and facilitating the integration of indigenous wisdom into the global community.

Contact information:

https://www.weavingthevine.com
https://www.facebook.com/weavingthevine/
@weavingthevine on Instagram

About the Illustrator

Visionary artist Ruysen Flores channels an urgent cry from Mother Earth herself, borne of his self-sustaining life in the Amazon Jungle in Peru. His is a life inspired by sacred indigenous knowledge.

Contact information:

@ruvexen on Instagram